& Me

Erika Rummel

DX VAROS PUBLISHING

Published by:
DX Varos Publishing
7665 E. Eastman Ave. #B101
Denver, CO 80231

Book cover design and layout by D. X. Varos
using images from ©Graham Lute

ISBN: 978-1-955065-31-3 (paperback)
ISBN: 978-1-955065-32-0 (ebook)

Mona

1

I knew she was dying, but when I saw the obituary in the *Globe and Mail*, it triggered an inner quake. The print lines wavered so that I had a hard time reading the words. *She made herself one of the most powerful women in the world. She founded charitable institutions. She battled on behalf of workers and women.* The print lines steadied, but I still couldn't make sense of the words. They sounded unfamiliar. I didn't recognize the woman on the page. Of course, that was the official version of Evita, as opposed to my private memories. And I'm no longer sure about them either. If I knew anything about Evita once, I gave it up when we said goodbye in Madrid, five years ago. I could feel her retreating even earlier. During the last days of our togetherness, she took all the necessary steps, preparing to go away and vanish from my life. That's why I stole her necklace. I needed a tangible connection, a solid piece made of precious metal and stone, with its own expensive light, something she had touched and I could touch in turn, something that was forever. It was theft, yes, but was it a crime? It's not as if I had a choice. I didn't weigh the pros and cons. I didn't make a conscious decision to act. It was more like basic instinct, an overwhelming need that could not be denied. I can't be blamed for doing what I had to do.

After I got back to Toronto, I pushed the memory of Evita to the back of my mind, but I couldn't keep it shut up there entirely. It lay in ambush for me, waiting to stab me with the sudden recall of a personal detail - the perfect curve of Evita's lips, for example, or the elegant movement of her hand waving to the people as we drove through the city in an open car, the sudden roughness in her voice when she was angry, the way she kissed Juan, carnal and angelic at once. I had these retro-glimpses of Evita, but I never looked at her life as a whole the way the obituary did. I couldn't come up with a coherent story to explain who she was and how she lived and why I adored her. In fact, you can't compose a person's life story until they are dead and can no longer interfere with your imagination or the memories that have congealed into nostalgia. As long as people are alive, there is always a chance they might disappoint you. I mean, you think of them as young and beautiful, the way they were when you saw them last, and then you run into them again and they have become old and their faces have turned to dust, a sight from which you cannot recover. Or you remember them as brilliant, and the next time you see them, they talk about the weather or their allergies and bore you until you have no goodwill left.

But Evita was dead now. I felt a strange lightheadedness when I thought of her, a centrifugal pull to lose myself in the memory of her beauty and the beauty surrounding her, the presidential palace which must be hollow now without her, but with everything still intact, the white bedroom, the dressers full of lingerie and closets full of haute couture dresses, dozens of furs – an ermine bed jacket and an ostrich feather cloak, rows and rows of delicate high-heeled shoes and designer purses. Only Evita was missing, and I felt a longing for her ardent temper, her vivacious gestures, and electric intensity — a longing beyond adoration. I wanted to be like her.

I turned back to the obituary and the photo spread that went with it. There was a picture of people lining up to see Evita lying in state. They knelt in prayer on the rain-soaked pavement. A field kitchen had been set up for them, the article said. The queue was twenty blocks long, and they were standing four abreast. They were like pilgrims who had come to visit the shrine of a miracle-working saint. There was also a close-up of Evita lying in state in a mahogany coffin with a glass lid, surrounded by mauve and white orchids. She looked tranquil and beautiful. Her hands were folded in prayer, a rosary of silver and mother of pearl wound around them – a gift from the Pope, the article said. On the fingers of her left hand were the three rings she always wore: a large solitaire diamond, an eternity ring set with sapphires, rubies, and emeralds, and a simple band of gold – her wedding ring. But the bulk of her jewels, worth millions, was missing, the article said. Yes, and I wonder how long it will take Peron to catch up with us. I never told anyone about our night journey or the two steel caskets we deposited in the bank vault. Did the others keep their mouths shut as well?

We didn't stay in touch after that escapade. I heard nothing more from them, or from Evita, who arranged the journey — except of course my little detour involving her necklace. Her lawyer wrote to me eventually. At first, I didn't have the courage to open his letter. My fingers lost their dexterity, my brain the ability to command them. She has found out about the missing necklace, I thought. She will come after me, with fury instead of love, with her lips compressed into a hard line instead of a caressing smile, but when my fingers regained their flexibility and I opened the letter, it wasn't what I had feared. There was nothing in it about the necklace. The lawyer merely informed me that Evita was too ill to make decisions. She had given him power of attorney. He was aware that I held one of the keys to the safe but he had no instructions for me at this time. "I ask you to continue keeping the matter confidential until further notice," he wrote. I assume he wrote to the others as well.

I read Evita's obituary, lying on the sofa in our apartment on Brunswick Avenue. It was a brooding, humid day, and I was torpid with heat even though the windows and screen doors were wide open and two whirring fans were blowing air at me. I was in my underwear and the nubby material of the sofa felt itchy on my bare thighs and the furniture seemed to hold and radiate heat, especially the dark walnut bookcases. The weather in Toronto is never right. Too cold in winter, too hot in summer. There was no getting away from the heat in the room. It had seeped into my body, keeping me down and strung out on the sofa. I regretted everything, my whole dull wasted life. I wanted to be like Evita. Why had I not followed her example and run away? She left her hometown as a teenager because, she said, "my mother would have married me to an ordinary man." That's what happened to me. I married a man who turned out to be unbearably ordinary, although I can't blame my mother for that. It was my own fault.

I was eighteen, a freshman at U of T where Phil taught English Lit 101: The Great Books. He charmed me with the way he leaned against the edge of the desk and spoke to the far corner of the ceiling in an accent of his own invention, never lowering his gaze to the keeners in the first row, but I persevered until I caught his eye. I thought he was an intellectual giant, but he just quoted intellectual giants, the same authors, the same words, every semester. It was the only thing he had in his head, other people's words and thoughts, and the knack to spin them into lectures and papers that, he bragged, only a dozen people could "really" understand.

Maybe I expected too much of Philip. Maybe that's what happens when you marry someone after a three-months' "courtship" or whatever you want to call the madness of violent physical attraction, the powerful volatility of lust, the desire for sex. It was good while it lasted. The mistake was to make it permanent, to marry him and fall into the dullness of repetition. I had an imperfect understanding of myself then — who doesn't at eighteen? Now I know; I prefer the new to the old, going forward to treading on the spot. I am done as soon as I discover a pattern. I loathe routine. It digs a rut into the soft parts of your brain and throws up protective mounds on either side of the path, so you can't jump the curb and go off in a new direction. Philip likes routine. Repetition doesn't wear thin on him. On the contrary. Order is his governing principle. It has the force of a God-given law. I mean it's alright to live with order where you find it, but to actually put things in order is a waste of time in my opinion, a waste of your life.

As our marriage deteriorated, I lapsed into angry silence, ate a lot and grew heavy around the waist. The added weight made me more civil, I noticed, more patient, or just more lethargic. But not on that occasion. I showed Phil the obituary of Evita and started crying, not just tears gently rolling down my face, but snotty, face-destroying tears accompanied by wailing.

"Now what?" he said, scanning the obituary. "You are crying over a little whore who made good?"

I ripped the paper out of his hands. All my lethargy fell away. My energies revived in a burst of anger. I don't think I'd ever been this aware of Phil's receding hairline, his limp tawny hair and narrow shoulders. I should have known on our first morning together, when I watched him at breakfast decapitating his soft-boiled egg so cleanly, so neatly. The sight got something roiling in me. I wanted to smash up his egg and smear the yolk all over his plate, mess up his tidy arrangement. But I didn't. I was too much in awe of him. I was still thinking of him as my guru, someone to teach me about life. But the lesson I was after can't be taught. I wanted to be like Evita who rose from illegitimate birth to celebrity, from the unpaved streets of Los Toldos to the 348-room presidential palace in Buenos Aires. Could I too move on from a messy childhood and an alcoholic mother to a life of success? I come to think that you can do that kind of transformation only if the seed is in you - a seed that will grow inexorably and can't be stopped by anyone or anything. If you don't have it in you, the transformation is just a mirage: outward success, inside the old miserable you. Evita remade herself and became beautiful throughout, as if she had captured the sun. The light was in her eyes and surrounded her body like an aura. She was luminous. That's why people called her a saint. They mistook the brightness for a halo.

And Phil, that idiot, had the nerve to call her "a little whore".

I ripped the paper out his hand and screamed: "You don't know what you are talking about!"

"And you do?"

I didn't bother to reply. There was no way I could make him understand. I wasn't only crying for her. I was crying for myself, out of a feeling of being deserted forever, out of a longing to be Evita, to slip out of my dull life with Phil and be glamorous. And let's be honest, because I was afraid when I thought of the stolen necklace wrapped in tissue, which might get me into trouble now. Well, not immediately. It would take Peron and his men some time to figure out the existence of those steel caskets and their location, but once they got hold of them, they would inspect the contents and see the empty tray that once held Evita's necklace. That necklace was sitting at the back of my underwear drawer, where Phil found it one day. I don't know what he was looking for. Presumably he was putting my things in order, folding the panties into triangles and rolling up my socks – something like that.

He came to me with the necklace puddling in the palm of his hand, a pile of precious stones set in platinum.

"I found this in your drawer, what the heck —?"

"Oh that," I said, giving him the slip with a lie. "It's an heirloom, from my grandmother."

"So why don't you wear it?"

"Come on," I said. "When would I wear a thing like that? It's too showy."

"Are those stones real?" he said, fingering the rubies and black pearls.

I shrugged. "For all I know they are cut glass."

"Take the necklace to a jeweler and have it appraised. It may be worth something. In which case you should sell the thing — I mean, if you don't want to wear it, if it's just cluttering up your drawer."

"It's an heirloom," I said. "And it's not cluttering up anything. Put it back where you found it."

"Okay," he said, but I could see the wheels turning in his orderly mind. He wasn't going to let this pass without action. He was already searching for the proper place, where such things belong. No doubt, Peron's lawyers were looking too. I wish I hadn't stolen the necklace and had left it in the place where it belonged. But then again I am glad I took it. It is the only tangible reminder of Evita and of my time with her, when I felt an overwhelming desire to be singled out and be seen, and she answered my prayer.

2

I didn't know my life was about to change when I came downstairs one Saturday morning in the spring of 1947. I found my mother sitting in the living room, which was practically unheard of. She never got up before two in the afternoon at the earliest, and then she never descended to the living room. There was no need to. She had a bar set up in her bedroom, an array of vodka and whiskey bottles and a mini fridge. But on that occasion, she was downstairs, sitting on the sofa, holding a glass of what we both pretended was water.

The house was the only constant in my life and the only thing my mother could show for her two marriages and rotating boyfriends whose generosity kept her afloat, and she was barely hanging on to the house. The roof needed reshingling, the windows repainting, but there was no money to do anything except making the monthly mortgage payments.

The curtains in the living room were usually drawn to keep the daylight out. My mother preferred the dim light of the floor lamp because it camouflaged the puffy skin under her eyes and the sad décor, the sofa — sand-coloured once but now worn to a dirty beige— and the maple coffee table marked by the wet bottoms of glasses. The bookcase held no books, only a stack of magazines and an assortment of knick-knacks. I hated the sight of the room, most of all the bucolic kitsch of the pictures on the walls — mountains and lakes under cobalt blue skies. It was not a place to impress my friends. Just as well that I didn't have any.

My mother was wearing her pink terrycloth robe and looked only slightly disheveled. In fact, she looked pretty good, considering, which made me guess that she was into a promising phase of dating. John, the man who had been showing up regularly for a couple of months now, might remain with us for a while.

She put on a pleated smile and said: "Darling, Liliana wants you to visit her in Buenos Aires."

She picked up a letter from the coffee table and waved it at me.

"Who?" I said. Then I remembered. The peroxide blonde we met last summer when we were in Southampton, sponging off some rich American friends of my mother's. What I best remembered about Liliana was the way she overlooked me. I could have jumped up and down in front of her and waved my arms, and she wouldn't have blinked. People like me and my mother simply didn't exist for her. It's not that she avoided me, but she had a way of looking past me as if searching for something in the distance. She looked distracted. Her eyes focused only when my mother's friends came in sight. They counted. They went to the same parties as Liliana, they got their clothes from the same haute couture places, they ate in the same five-star restaurants. We didn't. We got to see the high-end restaurants and clothing stores only from the outside. Once or twice my mother snagged invitations to the exclusive Meadow Club. She didn't play tennis or croquet, but she held her own with the rich when it came to drinking. The Meadow Club and the equally exclusive Southampton Bathing Corporation were home turf for Liliana Gutierrez. She belonged. She was always impeccably made up, with nails lacquered a bright red, and clothes with designer labels. The Gutierrez were renting the mansion next door to our rich friends. Liliana's husband was a banker somewhere exotic — Buenos Aires, as my mother reminded me. They had three kids, ranging from newborn to ten, always underfoot.

"She wants an au pair, I guess, someone to teach her kids English," I said.

"No, I told her we don't like children. Besides, she has a nanny – that French woman, Nancy, remember?"

"Quebecois. She was from Montreal."

"Whatever. She had some kind of accent. But you are wrong about Liliana. She doesn't need an au pair. She just wants company. She used to complain to me. Her husband was never around. He practically lived on the golf course. She was bored. She was lonely. 'And you two are so amusing,' she used to say, meaning you and me."

"She said that?" I'd never seen Liliana talking to my mother.

"She did. So then she said: 'Why don't you come and visit me in Buenos Aires some time?' I told her I couldn't

11

possibly get away, but you might want to see Argentina and practice your Spanish. So now she's sent you an invitation."

I was sure my mother was lying, but why was she lying?

"Let me see what she writes," I said and held out my hand for the letter, but she hung on to it.

"There are some private things here, which aren't meant for your eyes," she said.

It's a trap, I thought. She wants something from me, but I'm not going to fall for it.

"I don't know about going to South America," I said lightly. "All the guys there are short and hairy."

"That's all you can think about: guys. When I was your age, I was still playing with dolls."

I doubt she was playing with dolls when she was sixteen. I sure as hell was not. On my last birthday I drew up a list of the sexual encounters I'd had so far. Five. I made a cryptic notation in my diary: old man in Odeon, M in park, K at her place, S in car, myself. I counted myself only once, although I'd done it many times, and it was definitely the best sex. The old man sitting beside me in the movie theatre had just stroked my thigh furtively, but I completed the act in my head. With Marco, who was in my class, it was the usual deep kissing in the park and groping in the back of his father's car. We all did that. But the afternoon session I had with Katie in her bedroom was epic. We took turns playing boyfriend on each other, using our fingers. And since my birthday, there had been one more: Mr. Singer, who drove me home one night after I babysat for them. He was half-drunk when he took out his dick and asked me to stroke him. Afterwards he gave me a generous tip, which I thought was pathetic. I would have preferred it if he had done something for me in turn, but he was a bloodless coward, and I never babysat for the Singers again.

"I don't want to go to Buenos Aires," I said, although I badly wanted to go. "I'll miss school." I was trying to throw my mother off whatever game she was playing.

"You'll catch up on your schoolwork. It's only for a few weeks, and it will do you good to travel."

I was in advanced placement and, yes, I was going to graduate whether or not I attended the rest of the term, but the whole thing was fishy.

My mother pressed on. She gave me the usual hackneyed reasons why I should travel – immersion in a foreign culture, becoming independent, broadening my horizons. Gradually it dawned on me what was going on. She was at a crucial phase in the dating game, the end run, when she was going to push John to propose to her and rush him off to Niagara Falls before he could change his mind. I would only be in the way. She must have begged Liliana to take me for a few weeks. A trip to Buenos Aires was expensive of course, but she was prepared to beg and borrow to get me off her back. In the end I shrugged and said okay, as if I was making a concession, but I was secretly thrilled with the idea of a trip to Argentina and, mainly, with the chance to get away from my mother. I certainly didn't want to hang around and watch the spooning that was bound to happen between her and John. It would gross me out.

Of course I had to travel the cheapest possible way. John drove me to the bus depot and put me on the overnight to New York. From there I would travel by ship.

A cousin by the name of Anne had agreed to pick me up in New York and make sure I got on board. I had never heard my mother mention Anne before that trip or after, and it was clear that she was doing us a favour under duress.

The bus pulled into the Greyhound terminal at six in the morning and angle-parked alongside the depot on 33rd Street. My mother had described Anne to me: in her thirties, short blonde hair, wearing glasses. I had no difficulty recognizing her, coming out of the waiting room. She was wearing a beige suit and narrow skirt, smart but a little mannish. She too spotted me at once. I was the only teenager travelling alone on that bus.

"You must be Mona," she said. "Let's go. My car is over there." She pointed to the Chevrolet parked at the curb. She didn't say "How was the trip?" or "I bet you are tired." She wasn't exactly unfriendly to me, but she kept courtesies to a minimum.

"Is that all the luggage you have?" she said, as she opened the trunk of the car and I lifted in my small suitcase and the tote.

"That's all."

She raised her eyebrows but said nothing more. I could see she pitied me.

I got into the passenger seat, and she started driving. She wasn't wearing a wedding ring, I noticed, although she was quite good-looking — apart from the metal-rimmed glasses and a certain sternness about the mouth. That's probably what put men off.

"It was very nice of you to pick me up," I said as she was merging into the traffic.

She nodded curtly. "No problem."

14

I was hoping she'd stop somewhere for breakfast, but she didn't.

"So how exactly are you related to my mother?" I asked.

"I'm not sure," she said.

"I thought she and you were cousins."

"Second or third cousin maybe," she said, and the conversation dried up again.

Nothing further was said until she delivered me to the harbour office, hungry and rumpled as I was from the bus trip, and wished me a good journey.

A cab driver would have made more conversation with me than Anne, but then she probably felt that she was providing exactly that — a taxi service, without the remuneration. I too was tired of depending on favours from my mother's many connections, good for being milked once or twice and forgotten when they lost their usefulness or when they balked at providing services. Some of her connections were more willing to help than others, but it was always a humiliating experience, me ducking down and making myself very small so as not to be a nuisance, and them trying to ignore me and not letting their impatience show. Staying with the Gutierrez family in Buenos Aires would be no different. More ducking and squirming. I was able to cope with the humiliations by day, but by night they energized my anxieties and caused intractable dreams in which I could not find my way to where I was supposed to go or suffered from an undefinable illness and spun into a dizzy blackness. During that cold encounter with Anne when she wouldn't talk or even look at me, when she pretended I wasn't there and concentrated on the traffic as if the line of cars ahead of us was more interesting than her passenger – that's when the fear of humiliation flickered into acuteness, and I made up my mind. From now on things would be different. No more put-downs from my mother's so-called friends and distant relations, who were trying to make me invisible. They had a way of keeping their eyes on a level just above my head to make it easier for them to forget I was there. And when they did look at me, it was with pity, offering me the clothes their teenage daughters had grown out of or had discarded because they were so last year, so not in anymore. And I was expected to smile graciously and thank them for the hand-me-downs. A black cloud of anger was building inside me. I won't play along anymore, I thought, but even that resolve wasn't enough to ease the pressure in my chest because I knew those people didn't care if I sat out the game. I needed to get back at them. At the thought of doing something, I felt the cloud lift a little and thin out. I won't permit Liliana Gutierrez to ignore me when I get to Buenos Aires, I thought. I'll make her uncomfortable in turn. From the relief I felt then, I knew I'd hit on the right way to deal with the bad weather inside: Make those people look at me and take notice!

My mother had made arrangements for me to travel from New York to Buenos Aires on a cargo freighter that took passengers. The ship was called the Anchor Hitch – who comes up with crap names like that, I asked myself, but as the tugboat steered us out of the harbour, I was happy. The skyline of New York was impressive, and I felt like a world traveller. My room was less impressive. It was called a state room but looked more like a storage space with a narrow cot, a small wash basin in one corner, and a porthole that looked out on a portion of the deck. The lack of view didn't matter much for the first three days because I was seasick. When my gut stopped churning and my eyes focused again, I saw only the blur of the marine fog. When it lifted at noon, I could see a sturdy rail and beyond it the choppy grey waters of the Atlantic, a view cut off occasionally by the rubber boots of the men scrubbing the deck.

On day four I ventured on board and watched the loading and unloading when the boat stopped at the port of Concedo. Otherwise nothing much of interest was going on. The most entertaining sight was of a seaman working the ropes and going up and down on a kind of elevator, called a bosun's chair – entertaining if you are bored out of your mind, that is. As soon as I had tottered on deck, the captain offered me a tour of the steamer, but I really didn't care about the gyro compass, or the rotating radar, or the charts he pulled out of drawers to show me the route. I did feel a certain interest in the steersman who looked good in his leather jacket and cap and had a brusque masculinity about him, but like all the other men on board, he kept his eye on the job and didn't say a word more to me than he had to. I don't know if I was more sex-crazed than other teenagers, but I often felt a heat-shivering lust. I kept it hidden because I realized that it was taboo or at any rate frowned upon, unlike love of the romantic kind which was thought to be a nice thing and therefore could be confessed openly. The uneven valuation baffled me. My sexual appetite was as true as romantic love, only riskier, and whose business was it if I wanted to run a risk? In my private thoughts, then, I didn't hold back. I indulged in visions of sex with the more virile crew members. There were about thirty, bluntly handsome men, whose heavy muscles sliding beneath the skin reminded me of tigers and lions, but nothing concrete came of my fantasies. They shot me a few interested glances, but then they had to get on with their work. I never saw any of them at leisure during the whole journey.

The dining room wasn't a mixer either. The passengers shared a table. We were five – two couples and me. They were too old or looked too old to be of interest to me, but I was stuck with them, at least at dinner time. They didn't make any great effort to socialize with me either. The women spent their days reading and playing cards. They were total bores, especially one of them, Mary, who spoke in a gentle, wispy voice, and had a talent for banal sketchy talk. Her movements were always delicate, quite out of sync with the general greasy factory atmosphere of the ship. The two men were into the mechanics of the ship and had no other talk, although I noticed that Mary's husband, Gerald, was ogling me occasionally. We both wandered around deck a lot, I because I had nothing better to do, Gerald with his camera, taking pictures of nothing: the unvarying sea and sky. He was pretty careless with his camera, I noticed, leaving it sitting around on deck chairs when he went off to talk to a crew member or to the women. I was tempted to swipe it, but he would probably have made a big fuss, and I wasn't into cameras, so the risk of being caught wasn't worth it.

For a guy his age, Gerald wasn't bad-looking but his pink hairless arms put me off, and he had a slightly lost bearing, swaying when he talked, shifting his weight from one foot to the other. When I first saw Gerald, he looked as if he hadn't shaved for a couple of days, but as it turned out the stubble was an incipient beard. Some people think they can change their personality by changing their hairdo or by growing a beard. Maybe that's what he was after, changing into someone more virile.

One morning when I was sunning myself on deck, Gerald came by and lingered. He looked around carefully as if to make sure we were out of sight and couldn't be seen by the two reading, card playing women. He had his camera slung around his neck, and I thought he might take a picture of me — a worthwhile subject for a change — but he only leaned against the railing, making small talk and looking down on me with a slack smile, one hand buried in his pant pocket. I was wondering whether he was jerking off. I was wearing a bathing suit but had modestly draped a towel over my thighs. I took it off and moved my legs slightly apart, testing him. The conversation ceased. We just stared at each other. The slow and deliberate movement of his hand was mesmerizing. I felt good in our silence, our mutual knowledge kept in a fine balance, neither concealed nor revealed. Then Gerald sighed deeply, lowered his eyes, took his hand out of his pocket and moved off without another word. After that he avoided me. I think he was afraid of getting caught in another encounter with me and losing control, or maybe I was making the whole thing up. Perhaps I had just picked up Gerald's dirty thoughts. It was as if I had a sensor for prurience, especially when I was at leisure, sunning myself on deck. That's when my thoughts roamed like radar, picking up weird waves.

Gerald and his wispy-voiced wife got off at Rio, the other couple was bound for Buenos Aires like myself. They had been there before, they told me, and were now going on a tour of Patagonia. They treated me to statistics, trivia, and good advice at dinner time when I couldn't escape them. They had population figures at their fingertips. Buenos Aires was the largest city in the world without traffic lights, I learned. Keep to the elegant city centre, they told me, it was safe and very European. Don't stray into the Boca, the harbour area, it was dangerous, full of criminal types. That got my attention. I always come down in favour of excitement over risk. I fear only boredom. The Boca was one area I was definitely going to visit. Then they asked if I spoke Spanish. I told them it was an option at my school. I said I spoke it tolerably well. I didn't tell them that I got extra practice talking with Marco, whose parents were immigrants from Costa Rica. He wasn't popular because he was brown-skinned. Some people called him a nigger. I don't know what they called me behind my back. A nigger lover? In any case, we were a good match because neither of us had friends at school. It made me wonder about popularity. I had a theory that you had to fit in to make friends, and Marco and I didn't. We were the odd ones out. His parents were the wrong colour and didn't have a grip on the language. I lacked a father, and my mother was a lush. It wasn't until I got to know Evita that I realized my theory was wrong. She didn't fit in. She wasn't like everyone else. So how did she become popular? Here is my new theory. First of all, she was a believer. She was convinced she could make things happen. Most of the time she did, by sheer will power. And she looked you directly in the eye and made you feel loved. No one can resist that combination: love and will power. That's my new theory. The question was, could I make it work for myself? Could I be like Evita? I worked on it after I came back from the Argentinian adventure, but it was hard to believe in myself and even harder to love other people. I think I need them to go first, showing me love. Even then I can't reciprocate immediately. They have to keep loving me until I forget that there was a time when I counted for nothing.

3

I arrived in Buenos Aires at the beginning of April — our spring, their fall. Apparently everyone had just come back from their seaside villas in Mar del Plata or Punta del Este, where the oligarchs (Evita's word) spend their summers. I found out that they move to the coast en masse after Christmas to escape the heat and dust of the city and move back again en masse when the school year and the social season starts.

Liliana picked me up at the cargo port of Buenos Aires. If she was surprised that I arrived there rather than at the airport, as did people of her own class, she didn't show it. Between formal embraces and near-kisses so as not to smear her lipstick, she apologized because she was in a rush and hadn't had time yet to make plans for my stay.

"I want you to have a good time here, but I need to sort out a few things first," she said. "There's been a change since I wrote that letter to your mother. I seem to have a job now."

She gave me a slow binding look as if she expected me to understand, but I didn't. *Seem to have a job?* Was that an idiomatic glitch? It couldn't be. Her English was perfect. She had gone to an exclusive boarding school for girls in Boston. She spoke English like a native. So why *seem?* Didn't she know whether or not she had a job? And why did she need a job in the first place? Boredom, as my mother suspected?

"What kind of job?" I said.

"I'll tell you later when we have a minute to sit down and talk in peace."

I had the distinct feeling Liliana hadn't expected me (or rather, my mother) to accept her invitation, or not so soon at any rate. I wondered whether there had been an invitation in the first place. My doubts in my mother's story revived. Perhaps Liliana had made no more than a polite gesture and ended her letter with a vague phrase like "hope to see you sometime in Buenos Aires."

In any case I could tell that I'd arrived at an inconvenient time. The chauffeur took my one piece of luggage, the small suitcase with decals dating back to my mother's travels. He kept a straight face, but with difficulty, I thought. His lips curled, as if he was holding back a laugh, but didn't dare to let go in Liliana's presence. Maybe curling his lip was part of his posture, to go along with the royal blue suit and matching brimmed cap.

We got into the car, elegant with whitewall tires. It was a make I didn't recognize. The interior was gleaming new and the car moved so smoothly that it seemed to glide. We drove a stretch on a highway that circled past the city centre, then exited and glided on into the suburbs along a tree-lined avenue. The Gutierrez house was very grand and a little intimidating, but I held to my decision never to be humble again. I didn't say "wow" and carefully refrained from making any complimentary remarks about the car or the house or Liliana's fabulous outfit, a mauve jacket with leaf-shaped lapels and a pleated skirt. I pretended that I had expected nothing less, and in a way that was true.

Liliana took me to the guestroom upstairs and handed me over to the housekeeper, a heavy-set woman in a bottle-green uniform and white shoes that made her look like a nurse.

"Rosa will show you around," she said airily and rushed off after more embraces and air kisses. "See you in the evening."

Rosa gave me a dull look focused somewhere mid-air between us. She wasn't keen on showing me around, either because she was shy of foreigners or because she had already assessed my tipping capacity as negligible. She only pointed to the house phone on the bedside table, told me to call her if I needed anything, and trundled off.

The guestroom was actually a suite with its own bathroom. The furniture in the bedroom was a little old-fashioned, French-provincial or some Spanish version of it. The windows were draped with pale blue curtains, lined to block out the sun. They matched the satin bedspread. In fact the bed, which could have slept three, was the centre piece of the room, and there was a walk-in closet as big as my bedroom at home. I only wished I had clothes to fill it. My small suitcase looked lost in space there. I could put my clothes on three hangers and pack the rest into one drawer. The bedroom opened up into a sitting room with apricot walls and a chintzy sofa and love chair. A balcony overlooked the grounds, a perfect lawn with perfectly manicured shrubs and a gazebo. The property must have been half an acre and was surrounded by a high wrought-iron fence.

I didn't mind Rosa defying Liliana's instruction to show me around. I preferred to explore the house by myself, although I quickly noticed that I was never by myself. There was always personnel skulking around. You couldn't move anything in that house without someone wiping it off and putting it back. Never mind *re*moving anything for good. I was itching to steal something, to get even with Liliana for handing me off to the housekeeper and shirking her hostess duties. I wasn't going to let her get away with that. No more truckling, I kept reminding myself.

The rooms on the main floor were huge and ornately furnished. You could hold a banquet there or a wedding or a family reunion. The house was a mini palace. After I got out my map of Buenos Aires and oriented myself, I saw that we were in a suburb called Palermo. I decided to go out and do a half-hour walking tour to get a sense of the surroundings, but no one else was out walking, maybe it was the time of the day – siesta. There were no shops or cafés in the vicinity. The area was like a vast landscaped park, dotted with chateaus in various fake styles: Plateresque, Georgian, Creole, Victorian. I retraced my steps, was let in by the stony-faced butler or whatever he was, and sat in the sun on the terrace, bored. After a while I went back in to see if I could find a book to read. There was a "library" with books behind glass, but I had a feeling they were only for decoration. They were all leather-bound and gold-stamped and mostly of a uniform size. I wouldn't have been surprised to find that they were false fronts – or backs, rather – with hollow insides, but when I opened the glass doors and took out a few, they were real. I went along the shelves and read the titles on the spines: the classics in Spanish and a lot of legal volumes and biographies. Maybe it was also the "music room" because there was a Philco phonograph in a polished walnut cabinet and beside it a matching glass-fronted cabinet with records. I wanted to check them out, but the cabinet was locked. I had tried other cabinets and doors earlier and already knew this was a house under lock and key. Then I lifted up the lid of the phonograph and saw that there was a Frankie Laine record on the turntable: *All of me*. Someone in the house was up to date on American hits. Liliana? Maybe I underestimated her and she had some funk in her, hidden under the heavy makeup and the expensive clothes.

I started up the record and just got into the groove, so to speak, dancing by myself, when the nanny appeared at the door, baby in arms – what was her name again? Nancy. She had a narrow chest and a wide bottom, so that the top of her dress sloughed off her body in loose folds while the skirt stretched tightly over her hips. She didn't even say hello. She moved right by me, lifted up the tonearm and shut the music down.

"You aren't supposed to touch that," she said by way of acknowledging my presence. "And definitely not during siesta."

The baby on her arm was looking at me wide-eyed. He was drooling and threatening to break into tears.

"You are Mona, right?" she said. "They told me you were coming, but not when. Liliana was in a tizzy. She's always in a rush now, what with her new job, and when I asked Rosa — well, when I ask her anything, the answer is *no se*, 'I don't know.' She does know of course. She knows everything, but if she says *no se*, it means it's none of my business. So how are you, anyway? I hear they put you into one of the guest suites."

"On the second floor, yes."

"That's a surprise. I thought they'd put you on the third floor, with me and the children."

"Why?"

She shrugged. "They must have something in mind for you. They don't treat you well out of the goodness of their hearts, you know. If you get the special treatment, they expect something in return."

"Like what?"

"No idea. You'll find out."

The baby who had only been fussing so far, broke into a long wail.

"I'd better feed and change him," Nancy said. "And then I have to pick up the other two from school. Liliana could send the chauffeur to pick them up, you know, but she says it's healthier for them to walk. The truth is: she wants to keep me busy, get her money's worth out of me. Want to come along?"

I said yes because I wanted company and I had a few questions for Nancy, like: How do I get downtown from here? Where are the parties? What's the dirt on Liliana? If I tagged along, I might get a few answers.

"So, what's this job Liliana got?" I asked Nancy as she pushed the deluxe baby carriage along the sidewalk. A few other nannies were out now as well, and here and there a gardener was hand-trimming a hedge or a maid polishing the brass lock on a gate.

"She is Evita Peron's assistant," Nancy said. She looked at me sideways to see if I caught the significance. "The president's wife, you know."

"I know. And what exactly does she do as her assistant?"

"That's my question too. Liliana is hard to read. She pretends it's a great honour, but I've heard her complain to her husband." She mimicked Liliana's high-pitched voice. "'Evita is treating me like a servant. She just wants me to stick around and wait for orders.' That's what she said to him."

I absorbed Nancy's information, putting it away for later use.

We were getting closer to the school. I could see a line-up of big cars, black Daimlers mostly, even a Rolls, with the chauffeurs leaning against the cars, smoking and checking out the nanny crowd, which was getting thicker. None of them gave Nancy a second glance. She had a dull face with gray eyes like ice water and cut a poor figure in her ill-fitting clothes. The nannies were coming from all sides now. They waved to Nancy and gave me curious looks.

"Even if it was the best job in the world," Nancy said, "Liliana wouldn't like it. She is lazy, you know. She hates getting up early. She likes taking it easy, primping in front of the mirror or lounging on the sofa and reading magazines or playing bridge with her friends. She only gets energetic when it comes to shopping for clothes. She loves clothes."

Nancy looked a little stale, but her knowledge was fresh and she knew what was what. I realized she could teach me a great deal. When she talked, her mouth took on an almost roguish twist. Things were moving behind her face, as if she was going through a register, picking out the relevant facts from her vast store of knowledge.

"So why did Liliana take the job if she doesn't want it?" I asked.

"You don't say no to Evita, not if you want your husband to have a career. She decides who gets what position and who gets fired. Everyone is afraid of her."

"Why's that?"

But Nancy had no time to give me more explanations. We had arrived at the school gate, and the kids jumped us, Lisa, a pouty-faced girl, overweight, and Carlito, a precocious boy who asked me a lot of questions. Why are you staying with us? When are you going home again? How old are you? I was glad when we arrived back at the house and Nancy took them away, upstairs. I loathe kids.

I just had one more question for Nancy: "What are you doing in the evening?"

"Nothing much," she said. "Reading, usually."

"Why don't we go out?"

She looked at me as if I was a madwoman. "Out, where?" she said.

"We could go to the movies."

"I'm too tired to go anywhere," she said. "Those three kids are a handful."

"So maybe I'll go on my own," I said.

She gave me another sideways glance. "I don't think Liliana would like that. Girls your age don't go out on their own in the evening."

So how old was Nancy? Twenty? Twenty-five? Hard to tell. She looked past her best date at any rate. Not much she could do about that. Or about her flat chest. But she wasn't totally without attractions if you bothered to look more closely. For one thing, she had a mane of thick, glossy-brown hair. And I had seen the liquid patches of mischievousness in her eyes. She was definitely not a truckler. She was ahead of me there. She already had the level of confidence I was determined to achieve.

Liliana came home at seven and gave me an exasperated look, like "you still here?" Maybe she had forgotten about me, or wanted to.

"I should warn you," she said. "We eat dinner late, around 10. I know that's very late for North Americans. If you don't want to wait, you can always take your meals with Nancy and the kids. They eat at 7.30. She wants them in bed by 9. Lisa doesn't like it. Even Carlito balks. None of their friends go to bed that early, but I guess Nancy wants some time to herself, so I allow her to set the bedtime."

I wasn't going to let Liliana get away with that and make me eat with Nancy and the kids, so I said nothing. When she saw that she was stuck with me, she waved me into the library and sank down on one of the hideous sofas covered in moss-green velvet. A maid brought us a platter with little dishes of olives, nuts, and tapas. She poured Liliana a glass of wine.

"And the señorita?" she asked without bothering to look my way.

"Lemonade, I suppose." Liliana said. She didn't look at me either, so I had to speak up.

"I'll have glass of wine with you."

31

Then she did turn to me. "Is that a good idea, *querida*?"

She was determined to treat me like a child, I don't know why. They make a big fuss about *quinceañeras*, the coming-out parties for fifteen-year old girls. In this country I was a debutante. So I wasn't going to let her get away with this nonsense.

"Don't worry," I said. "My mom doesn't mind me drinking wine."

She pressed her lips together. "A glass of wine for the señorita, with Seltzer," she said to the maid.

"You were going to tell me about your job," I said when we had settled in.

She sighed, looking up at the portrait of a forefather above the fireplace, as if to blame him. "My job? Well, maybe that's the wrong word. It's more like helping a friend. Doing Evita a favour. Evita Peron – the president's wife. We are very close. She has just taken over the Department of Social Welfare and is working herself to the bone. I keep saying to her: you must learn to delegate, Evita. But no, she wants to be personally involved in every detail and make all the decisions, so every day there is this long line-up of petitioners, the most awful people you can imagine."

She took a long sip of wine, almost a third of the glass. Perhaps she was in need of something stronger to continue the story.

"I don't know why she wants to deal in person with this scum – stinking old women and men in rags with open sores, syphilis, if you ask me, and pregnant moms with bawling kids in tow. And she exchanges kisses with them, can you imagine? I tell her, no, Evita, don't. You'll get some horrible disease, but she says they are all human beings and if it hadn't been for Juan raising her up and lifting her out of poverty, she'd be like them, too. That's how she talks, but it's nonsense. She would have clawed her way to the top, with or without Juan Peron, because that's how she is. So I don't know why she listens to these petitioners, to their pathetic sob stories. I guess it makes her feel good to solve whatever little problems they have, to arrange for pensions and accommodation and food and the like. Of course, she only has to snap her fingers, and someone takes care of it. Still she's sitting there in her office from nine in the morning till six or seven in the evening, and I can't just look on and let her work herself to death. I thought I should do what a friend can do, be at her side and help when there is so much to do." She sighed again and looked at me beagle-eyed. "But never mind my job. Tell me about your day."

I decided to be honest for a change. The situation called for radical honesty.

"I was bored to death. There is nothing to do here."

She winced. I guess she wasn't used to hearing the truth without prettification and didn't quite know how to handle it. In that respect I had the advantage over her now that I had decided I would no longer try to be nice and make a good impression. So I wasn't too bothered about being impolite to Liliana. It wasn't my preferred mode of operation. I still wanted to get along and keep things pleasant, but I wasn't going to let her ride roughshod over me or ignore my needs.

The resolve I had made in New York after Anne gave me the silent treatment was still fresh in my mind and I stuck to it. I used plain language, and Liliana got the idea.

It was gloves off between us. From now on we merely pretended to be on friendly terms, keeping up a thin veneer.

"I'm so sorry, *querida*. I'm a terrible hostess, but this is the worst time for me to have a guest, what with my new job. Maybe you should come downtown with me tomorrow morning. Antonio — the chauffeur — will drop me off at the ministry and take you to Calle Florida."

"What's on Calle Florida?"

"It's an exclusive shopping district, just around the corner from Evita's office. A very nice area."

"You shop there?"

"It's where everybody gets their clothes. It's like going to Paris. You can do some window-shopping. Or you can sit at one of the sidewalk cafés and watch people."

"Sounds good. What time do you want me downstairs?"

"Between 8.30 and 9."

She made another attempt to get rid of me for the rest of the evening.

"As for dinner," she said, "I'd move it up a bit for you, but Carlos has a meeting and won't be home before 10. Well, as I said, you can always eat with Nancy."

"No, that's fine," I said. "I'll eat with you and Carlos. The tapas will tide me over."

I had scarfed down all the tapas in fact, and Liliana had to call for more. I bet she wanted to have some time to herself, but after that bit of impertinence — about this being the worst time to visit — I wasn't going to let her get away with anything.

We both had a second glass of wine and became a little more sociable.

"Maybe you should take me along to Evita Peron's office one day. I could make myself useful."

She thought about that.

"Tell you what," she said. "Evita and Juan are coming over for dinner on Thursday and you can ask her yourself. She won't have anyone making decisions for her, you know. If she likes you, you get whatever you want. If she doesn't like you—" She trailed off. "Well, I'm sure you will make a good impression."

Then we made small talk until Nancy came in with the kids for what looked like their daily mommy ration. Nancy took in the tableau, Liliana and me lounging on the sofa and drinking wine, and I could see that something in her opinion of me was shifting. I moved up a notch in her estimation. She realized that I wasn't a kid she could talk down to. She and I were at least on a par. In fact, at this point, I was doing better than she.

After the kids had gone off to bed, Liliana said: "Carlos will be home soon. I'd better change for dinner, and you, too."

"Change into what?"

"Oh, it doesn't have to be anything special, just a nice dress."

"I didn't bring any nice dresses."

She raised her eyebrows. "I forget how informal North Americans are," she said. "Well, you'll have to borrow one of mine. It might be a little short on you, though."

And a little wide, too, I thought, because Liliana was on the fleshy side.

I followed her upstairs to her bedroom. She had a closet full of expensive clothes, but what she selected for me was drab and slightly dated, stuff she had probably already marked to give to charity. Or to the maid.

"Let me have a look," I said, moving past her and looking through the row of dresses, choosing a couple of nice ones.

Her face darkened. "Not that one," she said, snatching one of them back. "That's very special to me." But she let me have the other one, with a sigh.

It was pretty funky, although the colour, lime green, didn't do much for me. I tried it on. It was on the short side, as predicted, but otherwise it fit. The material was stretchy. It must be tight as hell on Liliana, I thought.

"Too low-cut for you," she said. "Better put a little jacket on top."

I was going to ask her for some earrings, but that was probably going too far.

"Did you buy that dress on Calle Florida?" I said.

"At Drecoll's, yes. They do have the most gorgeous fashions."

At ten we assembled in what she called the "small" dining room, although the table was still too big for three people. Carlos was a corpulent man with a florid face, a stroke candidate, balding and quite a bit older than Liliana. She was in her thirties, I guessed. He was maybe fifty. Older men can be sexy — I'm thinking Clark Gable — but Carlos looked like a lame duck. I doubt he could get it up. Liliana must be starved for sex. He was heavy-lidded, as if he was going to nod off any time now and fall asleep over his dinner, but he did wake up from his larded stupor for a moment and gave me an appreciative look when I took the jacket off and he saw the mounds of my breasts rising above the square cut. Halfway through dinner, he was called away. There was a phone call for him. He dumped his napkin on the table and left the room. He didn't come back.

"It's always like that," Liliana said. I noted with approval that she was starting to treat me like an adult. In fact, I expected to be upgraded to confidante shortly. There was no danger in telling me anything after all. I didn't know anyone in Buenos Aires and had no opportunity to spread rumors about her. I'd be back in Canada in a few weeks. There was no risk talking to me.

I was right in my assessment of the situation. Pretty soon Liliana relaxed and no longer made a secret out of the fact that she was unhappy. Carlos neglected her. The children were a pain. Life in the suburb of Palermo was boring. Evita was a tyrant and had no class.

By tradition, the wife of the president was also the Chair of the Women's Charitable Society, she told me. Evita might have had the decency to decline the position. How could she preside over a club that prided itself on admitting only the crème de la crème? Evita was an illegitimate child, grew up in a dirty village, and had a Grade Six education. She had been an actress in a provincial theatre, for Heaven's sake, before she made up to a soap manufacturer who had connections and got her into a radio programme.

"She was the voice of Catherine the Great, can you believe it? Ridiculous! I think that's where she got her notion of how to act as the president's wife - like a Russian empress. Anyway, we couldn't possible have her as our chairwoman and we couldn't very well tell her that she didn't belong, so we said she was too young. And you know what she said? Then why don't you elect my mother instead? So now we are stuck with Evita's mother – a fat old domestic with a bunch of illegitimate children, the ex-mistress of a rancher! I mean all men, who can afford it, keep mistresses. Only most have the decency not to compromise their families and father illegitimate children. But what can you do?"

Liliana was very bitter – so much for Evita being her "friend".

The story about the Women's Charitable Society wasn't the end of her complaints. She had a long list of grievances.

"Evita doles out jobs to her family. As they say here, *los palitos empiezan a nadar*, the little twigs begin to float. Her brother is Juan Peron's private secretary. I'm not saying that he shouldn't have the job. In fact, Juancito has the smarts for it and knows how to take charge, if you ask me."

"Juancito – sounds like a little boy."

"Evita's pet name for her brother. We all use it because otherwise you couldn't tell which Juan anyone is talking about. Well, you'll meet the three of them at dinner tomorrow: Juan, Evita, and her brother."

She stopped, exhausted by so much that was wrong with the world. I could see there was an epic list of grievances stored up in Liliana's mind, several evenings' worth of companionable drinking and griping. Plenty of material to work with, I thought. I might even get her to go out with me one evening

4

The next morning, the chauffeur drove us downtown. Liliana was in a stinking mood.

"I don't even know why Evita wants me to be there all day. You know what she said when I asked her 'What exactly am I supposed to do here?' She said 'Oh nothing in particular. It just gives me peace to see you sitting there' – What a thing to say! I wish I hadn't asked in the first place, because now she takes me along on factory visits, which is worse than sitting around in her office. Do I want to see pasta factories or slaughterhouses? No, I don't, but she won't accept a no. She even made me ride in an open truck with her to hand out food parcels to the poor. My dress was ruined from all the dust blowing in the road, and every bone in my body hurt from bouncing over the ruts on the way to that wretched village. I can't take it any longer, you know. I said to her: I must have three days a week to be with my family. Alright, she said, but of course she doesn't keep to the arrangement. She still calls me in every day."

Liliana went on and on, with the chauffeur hearing every word she said, but she didn't care. I could see that he was a non-person to her, a tool who makes the car go from A to B. I had been in that place of non-existence once, but now I had her attention, and I intended to keep it that way.

I looked out at the cars we passed carrying well-dressed men, presumably on their way to the office, at the trams rattling by packed with ordinary folk, the policeman directing traffic who looked like an Arab, with a piece of cloth hanging down the back of his cap to protect his neck from the sun. I recognized the Plaza de Mayo and the presidential palace from the photos in my guidebook. Then we arrived at the Ministry of Labour, where Evita had her office.

The chauffeur stopped in the driveway to drop Liliana off.

She sighed as she got out of the car and said, "Antonio will take you to Calle Florida," but I declined the ride and got out with her.

"I have a map," I said to Liliana. "I'll find my way." I was eager to explore the town on my own.

"Fine. Whatever you want to do," Liliana said and climbed the stairs to the entrance of the Ministry, slump-shouldered and looking defeated.

Antonio drove off and parked the car at the curb opposite the building, at the end of a long queue of chauffeured cars. I said I'd look out for him there when I was done with sightseeing and was ready to go home. I watched him join a group of drivers lounging in the shade of an acacia tree. It occurred to me that a lot of people were stuck like that, condemned to a life of waiting for others. I didn't want to become one of them, ever.

I headed off in the direction of the shopping district, crossing through a park with marble monuments and palm trees. The nannies were starting to take up their stations at the stone benches, giving the little ones their toddling exercise, I suppose. A man dressed like a gaucho, in a loose-fitting white outfit and a red kerchief around his neck, was sitting on the lawn cross-legged, surrounded by pigeons. The kids watched him as the birds tamely landed in his lap and he painted their wings red and blue and yellow, kissed them and let them go again. The children clapped. "Do another one, Benito!" they called, fascinated by the spectacle. I thought it was pretty disgusting seeing the painted birds flutter around Benito and peck at the breadcrumbs he had strewn on the grass.

It was still early when I arrived at the Calle Florida. There were few shoppers. I walked up and down the street, looking into the windows of the glittering shops. I spotted Drecoll's, where Liliana said she bought her clothes, and on impulse went in. A young woman was lingering by the door, a greeter, or maybe a gatekeeper. She eyed me suspiciously and discreetly signaled to an older saleswoman, who came out from behind the counter. She looked matronly in her dark suit and had the stern face of a judge. I guess my plaid skirt and fuzzy sweater weren't the right outfit for an haute couture place. Besides, my olive skin and long dark hair, which was an asset back home because it made me look "exotic", was a drawback in this country, where they worshipped blond and blue-eyed women and equated dark with indigenous trash.

"May I help you?" the matron said coldly, but her expression changed when I answered in English. North Americans were allowed to be olive-skinned and eccentric in dress, as long as they opened their wallets. There is a notion in South America that we are all filthy rich, and perhaps the genuine tourists are. In any case, she switched to English and became civil. I casually told her that Liliana Gutierrez had recommended the store to me, that I was her guest for a few weeks.

"Oh yes," she said. "The Señora buys all her outfits here. May I show you some tailored jackets perhaps? – We just got in a new consignment from Paris."

"No," I said, "what I need is a dress. You see, the President and his wife are coming for dinner tomorrow, and I didn't bring anything suitable for the occasion. I don't want to make a bad impression and embarrass Liliana."

"Absolutely," she said. "You must dress up for La Presidenta. Such a beautiful woman and such exquisite taste." I definitely had her attention now.

"Alicia will model a few dresses for you," she said, beckoning to the greeter. "She is your size, more or less." She took me upstairs into a kind of sitting room with mirrors arranged in a round, so you could get a good look at yourself, front and back.

Alicia paraded three or four cocktail dresses, one of which was stunning: a backless design in white taffeta, but I needed to be practical. That dress required a strapless bra, which I didn't have, and there would never be an occasion to wear such a thing again, back home.

"A little too showy," I said. "I don't want to upstage anyone."

"Upstage?" The matron looked confused.

"Compete," I explained. "I want to stay in the background, so to speak. Mrs. Peron is the guest of honour after all."

"Oh, I see. No, it would not be right to – she hesitated a little – to upstage Mrs. Peron." I could see she was a fast learner.

"Alicia," she said to the girl, "get the dress that came yesterday from Milan. I think that will be the right thing."

It was. Pale yellow, a square neckline with white piping, puff sleeves, and a tight bodice that showed off my waist, or would have if it fitted better.

"A tad too big," I said after I'd tried it on.

"We can take it in," the matron said.

"I need it today, though."

"No problem. It will only take two hours to alter it."

She called the seamstress, an aproned woman wearing slippers as if she lived on the premises. She had a pin-cushion on her arm like a bracelet and started pinning me up and taking measurements. They would keep my measurements on file, the matron said, just in case I wanted to order something else. I submitted. No one mentioned the price of the dress, and I didn't ask. It would not have been in good taste.

"I wonder what Evita will wear," I said to keep up the conversation, "and if she'll like my dress."

"Oh, I'm sure you'll get compliments," the saleswoman said.

"Perhaps I should mention your name to her."

Now I really had her hooked.

"That would be wonderful," she gushed. Her voice was genuinely grateful. "And your name, Miss?"

"Mona — that's short for Monica — Ford."

Back home, people always asked with a wink whether I was related to Henry Ford, and I always said yes, as a joke. Too bad the matron didn't ask. I would have given her a suitably evasive answer. Who knows, she might have swallowed the story.

To pass the time until the seamstress was done with the alterations, I walked around Calle Florida some more and looked into the shop windows stacked with the newest fashions, perfumes, and European antiques. The shoppers were out in droves now as were the flower sellers hawking bouquets of roses and gardenias. Here and there I heard English spoken, and French. At the far end of the street was another park and, on the opposite side, I could see massive baroque mansions with wrought iron gilded gates. I sat down on one of the benches, but that wasn't a good idea because almost immediately a man sat down beside me and maneuvered closer, shifting his elbow and knee until they touched mine. He was a scrawny character with a pronounced Adam's apple and a narrow weaselly face. I shot him a poison look and got up, wandering back in the direction of Drecoll's. I began to see the pattern, noticed the persistent attention of men, their dark eyes following me. Maybe it was my Americanness that attracted them, that pleated skirt and Sloppy Joe sweater, or maybe ogling single women was the custom of the country.

Back at Drecoll's, I tried on the yellow dress again. It fit perfectly, and they wrapped it up for me.

"And how would you like to pay for it?" the matron asked. She presented me with the bill, discreetly folded. I opened it up. I had expected the dress to be expensive, but

44

this was beyond anything I had imagined. Well, it didn't matter because I had no intention of paying.

"Maybe you could put it on Liliana's account for the time being," I said. "I haven't had time to go to the bank yet or set up anything."

There was a slight hesitation and exchange of looks between Alice and the matron, but I had them caught. The dress had been altered to my measurements. And there was my promise to mention the shop to Evita.

"Perhaps we should phone Mrs. Gutierrez and let her know," she said.

"I'm afraid we can't reach her now," I said. "She is with Evita Peron. She is her assistant, you know."

"If you'll permit me, I'll phone and leave a message at the house," the matron said. Oh, she was clever. "Do you have the number?" she asked.

I gave her the number, and she disappeared in the back of the store. After a few minutes she came back, deflated.

"She is out, as you said. I left a message with the housekeeper," she said. "We'll put it on Mrs. Gutierrez' account then, but perhaps I could give you a copy of the receipt. Just send the chauffeur with a cheque whenever convenient."

"That's a good idea," I said lightly.

5

"My mom will pay you back," I told Liliana when I modelled the yellow dress for her.

Rosa had given her the message from Drecoll's, and Liliana had come to my room — to see the dress, she said, although I could see she had come to confront me. She tried to at any rate, but she ended up flustered. In response to the promise that my mother would pay, she got out a strangled, "Oh, that won't be necessary."

I knew she would say that. It was a turn of phrase, a meaningless piece of courtesy, but she was obliged to decline payment by the local code of honour, and I jumped on those words ruthlessly, locking her in. Liliana had made the mistake of thinking that I was bound by the same etiquette and would proudly refuse her insincere offer, but I had no such pride.

I made a big show of gratitude, embraced Liliana, held her tight and gushed: "That's so generous of you! I'll consider it a belated *quinceañera* present."

I had her trapped and I had the added advantage of a witness being present. The maid happened to straighten out the bedroom at the time and overheard our conversation.

Liliana was unprepared for such shamelessness. She looked pinched, but there was nothing she could do about it.

"I hope you'll enjoy the dress," she said.

A stilted silence hung between us. She got up from the window bench, where she had been sitting, and closed the door on the maid.

"Just don't mention it to Carlos because he isn't as generous as I am," she said when we were alone. "He will make a fuss and tell me I'm crazy to buy you a dress at Drecoll's."

We had reached a remarkably honest stage in our relationship, the kind of intimacy, or illusion of intimacy, that develops between people who have to put up with each other only for a short time and know, when that time is over, they will never see each other again.

I triumphantly wore the yellow dress at the dinner with the Perons, the evening that changed my life. When Evita came into the room, it hit me right away, a strange feeling of weakness, a sudden lack of grip on my thoughts. I couldn't identify what it was until half-way through dinner: For the first time in my life, I was truly and helplessly in love. It wasn't just Evita's looks, which were stunning. It was fate.

Evita was a tall woman. At first I thought she only appeared tall because she wore high heels but it wasn't something that could be measured in inches. She looked statuesque in her white satin dress, shirred at the waist and cross-wrapped in the style of an ancient tunic. Her platinum blond hair was pulled back tightly into a knot. She had the aura of a Greek goddess. I didn't know where to look first in my hunger to take in all of her, but it was her mouth that fascinated me most, those smiling, softly curved lips made for speaking words of healing or blessing.

By the time I woke up from my fascination, we were into the main course of the meal. I had missed the taste of the hors d'oeuvres, just staring at Evita. She directed a few questions at me, and I answered her in a stunned, idiot fashion. Sometime later, midway through dinner, I finally registered the other guests, Juan Peron in his white general's uniform, a tall, muscular man with a wide face, his black hair combed back and plastered down. There was something creepy about his movie actor's smile, all gleaming white teeth, and the puckered reptile skin of his cheeks. He looked as if he was wearing makeup, but then I remembered Liliana telling me that he had some sort of skin problem and needed to apply a special cream that stuck to his cheeks like a mask. It was off-putting at first, but you forgot about it after a while because he had a deep, velvety voice and a direct, friendly way of talking that put you at ease, a politician's way, I suppose.

I was seated next to Evita's brother. Under normal circumstances, I would have taken notice of him immediately and sized him up as a potential escort. He was in his twenties or maybe early thirties and radiated heavy masculinity. There was a leer buried in his brown eyes, which he tried hard to suppress, but I could read it clearly. It was in his voice as well, something caressing even though he talked about sports, the races at the Hippodrome and the polo fields. The desire to attract his

49

attention would have been paramount a few hours ago, but that desire lost its potency in the overwhelming presence of Evita. Besides, after a while it dawned on me that his submerged leer and the show of masculinity was aimed at Liliana. He kept talking at her, strafing her with suggestive looks, and she shifted in her seat and lowered her eyes in a corresponding way. There was something going on between the two of them. I looked at Carlos, but he was oblivious to the game they were playing. He was talking business with Juan and Evita, something about financing the "show in Spain", although I may have gotten that wrong. His voice was too soft and he talked too fast. Evita at any rate had caught on to Juancito's moves and disapproved. Under the beam of her eyes, he stopped talking to Liliana and turned to me:

"So, are you enjoying your holiday?"

Liliana came to her senses as well, pried her eyes away from Juancito, and chimed in with an apologetic: "I'm afraid I have been a terrible hostess. I haven't taken Mona anywhere, but it's your sister's fault, Juancito. She is keeping me busy, which reminds me-" She put her hand on Carlo's arm to interrupt the business talk and said to Evita: "Mona is interested in your work, Evita. She wants me to take her along to your office. Would that be okay?"

Evita gave me a loving smile. "And I wanted to ask if you would come and let me practice my English on you." The conversation around the table was in Spanish, but luckily Evita had a habit of saying everything at least three times, just varying the words. It was a trick she worked to make sure everyone got her message. It also made it easier for me to catch up. "I mean, could you listen to me and correct me?" she said. "It would be such good practice to talk to you."

"I'd love to," I said. The words came out in a jumble in my eagerness to oblige, to make an impression, to captivate her all at once. "When do you want me to come?"

"Tomorrow evening? It has to be after hours, I'm afraid. There is no time between nine and six. During the day I am not my own person, you know. I belong to the people, I'm completely theirs. Will you come in the evening?"

It was a question, but she took my answer for granted, and she was right. I could not have said no to Evita. I was mesmerized. It was as if she had cut the tendons of my will.

"I'll send my chauffeur to pick you up, *querida*," she said.

6

The next evening, Evita's chauffeur came and took me to Unzue Palace, the official residence of the Perons. It was both grand and gaudy and all lit up as if there was a fairytale ball going on inside. The architecture was a dizzying mix of styles. It looked like the builder couldn't make up his mind whether to make it an English castle or a French chateau. The walls were brick and gray stone, the entrance flanked with Corinthian pillars, and the windows decorated with stone garlands of fruit or shields crossed with spears. There wasn't a single flat spot to rest your eye on.

The chauffeur turned into the circular driveway and let me off at the pillared entrance. The lobby was gigantic, a cavern of a hall with coffered ceilings and marble floors. The butler handed me off to a maid, who led me up the grand staircase shaped like an inverted Y. I turned to look back at the entrance hall and fought the temptation to slide down the wrought-iron bannister.

Upstairs, Evita received me in her bedroom. It was suitably royal – with gleaming oak floors, white paneled walls with gold trim, frescoes above, a vast chandelier overhead, and alabaster lamps flanking the bed. In the midst of this regal luxury, there was Evita sitting on the bed, stripped of divinity and become human. She was wearing a man's striped pajamas. They were too large for her. She had pulled up the waistband over her small breasts and rolled up the trouser legs. Her hair was twisted into two thick plaits hanging down the back, artlessly. She had turned into a girl my age and behaved like one, bouncing on the bed and inviting me to sit beside her on the silky white duvet.

She is protean, I thought. She can change into anything. It was magic, but the kind of magic that was dangerous work. I too liked trying out different roles, but I noticed it was always difficult to find a way back to my old self, which seemed to have moved in the meantime or weakened. Such mutations thin the substance of your mind and make you vulnerable. I was afraid for Evita but I also saw my chance.

I looked at her with the eyes of an intruder. I wanted to get inside her mind.

She touched my hand lightly and gave me a searching look.

"What's the problem, *querida?*"

"Nothing."

She squeezed my hand. "You look – troubled. An unhappy love affair?"

I looked into her eyes. Surely she could decipher the text in mine. I might as well say the words out loud.

"I'm in love with you, don't you know?" I said boldly.

She laughed pleasantly and kissed my cheek. Because I turned toward her at the same time, her lips touched the corner of my mouth. I wasn't sure what I was feeling, an erotic pull, a limbic desire, the unquenchable hunger of a starveling for love. I grabbed her shoulders. I wanted to hold her close.

She pulled back, still laughing.

"Fierce like a puma," she said. "I like that."

She didn't put her arms around me in turn. She didn't have to. Her words had reach, and I could see that she had accepted my offering.

We sat side by side, leaning back against the padded headboard. I was trying to catch my breath. My heart was racing.

"But now we must work," she said. "I have to improve my English. I am going to Europe on a state visit. I need to practice."

"When are you going?" I asked.

"Soon. The diplomats are still working on the dates. First I will go to Spain, then to Rome for an audience with the Pope. I don't need to worry about that part. My confessor is coming along and will translate for me, and the Holy Father speaks Spanish, I am told. Then I will go to London, to a reception with the King, although that is not completely certain. Still, I must prepare. I will be representing the country after all, and the presidency."

"You are going on your own? Your husband isn't coming along?"

"He has a country to run, and this is not a good time for him to be away."

"I wish I could come with you," I said.

She paused as if she was giving serious consideration to my wish, but then she carried on.

"So you see I have to practice my English, speaking and listening. Tell me about yourself, *querida*. How old are you?"

"Sixteen."

"The beginning of life. So much to do and enjoy. I left my family when I was fourteen and struck out on my own." She spoke in a mixture of English and Spanish, pausing from time to time to check if I understood and to give me a chance to correct her. "I left because I was afraid my mother would marry me to an ordinary man and I would turn into an ordinary housewife and waste my life shopping, doing laundry, and wiping the bottoms and noses of children. I ran away from all that. I wanted to be an actress."

"And you became a politician — which is the same thing, I guess."

"The same thing?"

"I mean it's like being on stage. You speak, people applaud. The papers carry pictures of you. You are a celebrity. Liliana says, people love you."

She frowned. "No, Mona, listen to me." Now she did take me into her arms. She cradled me like a child. "It is the other way round. I love the people. Liliana does not understand that because she is an oligarch."

"What's an oligarch?" I said, looking up into her face, watching her mouth move.

"She and Carlos come from families that own huge tracts of land with thousands of heads of cattle and dozens of oil rigs. They have so much money, they don't know what to do with it, and still they want more."

"Then it was probably okay that I cheated Liliana out of money," I said and told Evita the story of the dress, for a laugh. Only she wasn't amused.

"You should never cheat, Mona," she said, "but this little affair of the dress is of no importance. Never mind petty theft. I am thinking of the large issues: widespread poverty, ill health among the poor, lack of schooling and opportunities to improve their lives. I am trying to educate Liliana, to make her understand. Every day I show her the terrible want of the people, but she is bored or worse, disgusted by what she sees. She is not interested in ideas, only in things, the gifts I receive, for example. She inspects them, but she does not understand their value. She knows the difference between Dresden and Sevres porcelain, yes, and between quality emeralds or just run of the mill, but she turns up her nose at the gifts of love: the flowers, the letters, the kisses, the smiles, the tears of gratitude I receive from the people. Liliana has been a good tutor of manners to me. She tells me how to behave at state dinners and diplomatic functions. She knows all about that, but not how to deal with the people. That cannot be found in the book of etiquette, you see. That is why I asked her to come to my office and watch me. I thought perhaps she would learn, but I am making no progress. The only thing she cares about is appearance – dress, makeup, hairdo."

"But don't you care about appearance? That outfit you wore last night was gorgeous, and you look stunning in all the photos I have seen of you."

"I dress for the people, *querida*, for all the people who come to see me. They want a heroine, someone to admire. They all have their dreams about me, a poor woman, one of them, who made it to the top, and I don't want to disappoint them. Liliana thinks I'm a fanatic. Yes, I am! I surrender myself completely to the people. I live for others, I live for an ideal."

Her voice turned strident, losing all smoothness, but she caught herself and ended up smiling. "Life has no real value when you live it just for yourself."

I didn't know what to do with that lecture. It was out of tune with my mood. It didn't fit. "Your English is very good," I said lamely. "Who taught you?"

"Juan. He reads to me and makes me read to him. His favorite book is Lord Chesterfield's letters to his son."

I had never heard of Lord Chesterfield.

"An English gentleman who admired formality and discipline," Evita explained. "I must get you a copy of the book. Or better—"

She reached over to her bedside table on which there was a pile of books and handed one of them to me, a slim volume bound in red leather, with the title stenciled in gold.

"For you. Read it. I will get another copy for myself."

"For me? Then I want you to sign it. With a dedication."

"*Bueno*," she said and fished for a pen in the drawer of her bedside table. "What do you want me to write?"

"To Mona, with all my love," I said.

To Mona, with all my love, she wrote and signed it. I ran my fingers over her signature and smeared it a little. She had given me her name. It seemed an intimate gift.

"Thanks," I said, and this time she reached for me and kissed me on the mouth. Already the name was working its voodoo magic. We lingered in each other's arms.

"So what does he write about – Lord Chesterfield?" I asked because I didn't want to go too fast with the kisses. I was still confused, in a state of knowing and not knowing, I felt something uncontrollable, something nameless which didn't fit any category, love or sex or admiration or hunger. I was scared of what I was getting myself into.

"He gives advice to his son like 'Often be seen to smile, but never be heard to laugh' – because a loud laugh sounds silly. Or: 'Gain people's love by doing them favours and by complimenting them.' That opens the way to the heart, he says, and he is right. But you must read his words for yourself."

"Okay," I said, "if you say so, but who needs that kind of advice? It's pretty basic stuff, isn't it?"

"To you perhaps, because you are smart. And sometimes Lord Chesterfield's advice is wrong. He doesn't know anything about women. He thinks they have the brains of children and no capacity for reasoning. He tells men not to take women seriously. I laughed when I read that. He also writes that women have a weakness for men as if the opposite weren't true as well, men having a weakness for women."

I was going to ask, do you have a weakness for me? But her eyes warned me off. Instead I asked:

"Like your brother for Liliana?"

She nodded. "You are using your head and your eyes, I notice. That is another reason why it's good to have Liliana with me during the day. It keeps her from seeing Juancito."

So that's why she held Liliana captive, I thought, to keep an eye on her, and all that talk about educating her to love the people was just bull. But maybe I was wrong and it was a combination of things: She loved the people, she wanted to teach Liliana to love them, and she wanted to prevent her seeing Juancito. She did have a didactic streak, I noticed, when she pushed Lord Chesterfield's stuff on me. I didn't want Evita to treat me like a pupil, although I knew that she could teach me a great deal.

Evita leaned back and sighed.

"I am tired," she said. "Unfortunately. Because there is so much to do. Every day, hundreds of people write to me, crying for help. I have my assistants read their letters and arrange for whatever is necessary. I know people expect me to read their complaints myself and answer them, but there isn't enough time. I feel bad about that, so every day I pick a handful of letters from the mailbag and bring them home with me, to read in the evening and to answer in person."

She reached for a small basket sitting on the floor beside the bed. It was full of letters, some neatly addressed, some just pieces of paper folded over and glued shut, with her name written on the outside, others in dirty and torn envelopes that looked like they had travelled a long distance.

"That is my last job before I go to sleep," she said, and sighed. "Thank you so much for visiting, Mona, and for letting me practice my English on you. You must come every evening and you must also tell me what you think of our country, but all that has to wait, and by now you will be starving. I have asked Juancito to take you out for dinner. He will be here at ten. But you cannot go out to dinner like this."

She looked me up and down. I was back to my Canadian school girl look of pleated skirt and sweater. It was what everyone wore back home, but it didn't fit my new life.

"Come," she said. "I'll see what I can find for you." She led me to her dressing room, a two-story affair, with a small wrought iron staircase leading up to a gangway that wound all around.

"We don't need to look up there," she said. "Those drawers are only for gloves and hats. The dresses are right here."

We looked through them, rows and rows arranged by colour, first short, casual dresses, then suits, then cocktail and ballroom dresses, and on the other side fur jackets and coats, some of them floor-length.

She chose a simple shift, teal, not my favourite colour, but so what? It was a gift from Evita. I put it on. It was too long on me, and we improvised with a belt to hitch it up. We looked into her jewelry drawers as well. The stuff there took my breath away. She lifted up a massive piece with diamonds and rubies. It was the first time I laid eyes on that necklace, although I didn't think of theft then. The gems were so large it was hard to believe they were real. They looked like fakes. The thing must have weighed five pounds.

Evita smiled at me.

"I'll leave you something grand like this in my will, *querida*, for the time when you are an old woman and need to dazzle the world with jewels."

The idea struck me as absurd. I couldn't think of a time when Evita was no longer around, and I couldn't picture myself as an old woman. I put my hand on the monster necklace and jingled it. "You are joking," I said, and we laughed together like conspirators, but silently, as recommended by Lord Chesterfield.

"For now you need something simple," Evita said and picked out a small pearl necklace.

I put it on and she showed me into the bathroom, so I could have a look at myself in the mirror there. The bathroom was grand like the rest of the house, clad in regal marble with veins of green, grey, and white spreading like tree limbs, mystical and imperial.

There was a knock. Someone entered the bedroom, and a man's voice called out: "Evita?"

"That's Juancito," she whispered and grabbed my arm. "Do me a favour, *querida*, and keep him safe for me. Take his mind off Liliana."

It was the first of several favours Evita asked of me and I did not have the strength to refuse, although I was hoping for something in return. I wanted her to love me, to draw that warmth out of her and make it part of my bloodstream. That was going to be my reward.

I followed Evita back into the bedroom, where Juancito was waiting.

He took in my dress with his roaming eyes.

"Very nice," he said, meaning me rather than the dress, judging by his leer.

"Turn around," he said.

Like a fool I did, and he patted my behind. I slapped his hand away.

Evita looked annoyed. I had a feeling he was another recalcitrant pupil, like Liliana, unwilling to learn.

"What?" he said to her. There was defiance in his voice. "I am just admiring your protégée."

"Don't talk to me like that, Juancito. You know I don't like it."

He gave her an ironic bow.

"*A sus órdenes, señora.*"

7

Juancito wasn't using a chauffeur. He drove a sleek Packard Clipper, maroon with whitewall tires. I'd seen a picture in *Movie Life*, of Errol Flynn leaning against the long hood of a Clipper. Maybe it was the car of square-jawed men. In any case, it suited Juancito's style, somewhere between gutsy and come-on-baby.

We drove for a long stretch, out of the suburbs and down to the harbor. Juancito played the car radio at a volume that made it hard to carry on a conversation. In any case, we didn't need words. There was a non-committal friendliness between us, which I recognized from my mother's dates. It was the friendliness of men who didn't care what you thought of them, men with money who were used to getting their will and turned ugly fast if you irritated them.

We were driving through a run-down area with odd little houses painted in gaudy colours when Juancito slowed down, threaded through a narrow street and turned into a parking lot beside a bar. The sound of tango music was seeping through the door and seasoned the air.

"What is this place?" I said to Juancito as he opened the car door for me. I looked around. "It doesn't look particularly inviting."

"I am giving you local flavour," he said. "Tourists don't come here."

"I can imagine," I said. "It looks like a place where they'll put a knife in your back."

He grinned. "Don't worry, *chiquita*. I'll watch your back."

"I know you do," I said. His grin broadened.

"But take off that pearl necklace. I don't want it to come loose in the crowd," he said.

I took off Evita's present and put it into the bag with the book she had given me, and with my Canadian school girl outfit.

"You dance the tango?" Juanito asked.

"I've never tried it."

"It's easy," he said. "We'll practice."

He led me to a corner of the parking lot and put his arm around me, pressing me against his body. I could feel the energy and the tension in his body.

"Cheek against cheek," he said and put his face flat against mine. "Now walk outside my legs. It's just walking to the music, you see. Counter-clockwise." He began humming a tango, darum-dee-dumdum, darum darumdum, dum-dee-dumdum, and marched me around the edge of the parking lot. He was right, it wasn't difficult. I managed to navigate around his legs without stepping on his toes.

"You've got it," he said. "You are a natural talent."

We went in. The place was packed. A haze of smoke hung over the bar and dimmed the lights above the dance floor. The tables and chairs along the wall were of dark wood, scuffed and heavy as if they were carrying too much weight.

Juancito took me to a table up front, working the room as he went, shaking hands and patting shoulders. He was a regular, clearly. Our table was the best in the joint: private, tucked into a recess, but with a full view of both the musicians and the dancers. The waiter whisked off the reserved sign and, without being asked, brought a bottle of gin with two glasses, and a bowl of lime wedges.

"You were supposed to take me to dinner," I said.

Juancito called the waiter back. "And a plate of empanadas."

"That's all they have here," he said to me. "Maybe some olives."

The band, which occupied a small platform at one end of the room, consisted of a double bass, a guitar, and an accordion – "a *bandoneón*," Juancito said.

On the dancefloor the pairs moved to the music in smooth, pulsing steps. They seemed to keep to unmarked lanes. Somehow they avoided colliding or crowding each other. No one talked. Their mouths were pressed shut, their faces sallow-eyed and stern, as if they were engaged in serious business or in a competition. The dresses of the women were flimsy, their heels too high, their legs too scrawny, but they danced divinely, caught up in the rhythm, as they crossed and hooked legs, all in a close embrace, and cheeks touching.

Watching them pace the dancefloor, I forgot about Juancito until I heard him curse under his breath.

"*Hijo de puta!*"

I followed his glance. He was looking at someone sitting at the bar, a slim young man with a bland face. In the hazy light, he looked pasty, like someone who didn't spend much time outdoors. I hadn't seen him earlier. He must have just come in. He returned Juancito's look, nodding his head, as if he was acknowledging the curse. There was no surprise in his face. He may have been watching us all along.

"Someone you know?" I said to Juancito.

"Evita's spy."

The man slid off the bar stool and came over to our table.

"May I?" he said and pulled out a chair. "Pierre Adams," he said to me, with a bow before sitting down.

"Mona Ford," I said, since Juancito did not bother to introduce me in turn.

"You are from Canada?" he asked. It wasn't a question, more like a statement confirming what he already knew. He had pale eyes concealed under long, girlish eyelashes. The eyes didn't go with the rest of his face, which was angular, and they were too wise for a man his age. He looked about twenty-five.

"Fancy meeting you at Albano's," Juancito said.

Pierre gave him a mild look. "It's turning into my favourite place. And yours."

"That's why you are here, Pierre. Because of me, right?"

Pierre didn't reply.

"And what would you do without me?" Juancito asked sarcastically. "Get a real job?"

Pierre didn't rise to the bait.

"I quite like my present occupation," he said. "It's real enough to me." He had a gentle voice for a spy, if that's what he was.

Juancito only sneered.

The musicians reached the end of the set, and the dancing came to a halt. Some pairs returned to their tables. A few remained on the dance floor, waiting for the next *tanda* to begin.

"Why don't you give them a demonstration of your famous skills, Pierre?" Juancito said.

Pierre protested politely, but Juancito was already walking up to the small stage and talking to the band leader, the man with the *bandoneón*. He nodded, and Juancito waved to Pierre, shouting "Come on. *Vámonos*."

The pairs on the dance floor looked at Pierre expectantly. He got up and made his way to the stage.

The dancers watched, half curious, half suspicious of the newcomer. The band leader introduced him.

"Ladies and gentlemen, Señor Pierre Adams, all the way from France."

Pierre leaned forward, his lips moving, and the man corrected himself: "From Belgium."

The dancers clapped politely, but I could see that they considered it a bit of an imposition to have to listen to a gringo and wanted to get it over with. The band leader played a few chords, the bass and the guitar fell in with him. Pierre stepped up to the edge of the podium and began to sing with the unerring instinct and the voice of a seasoned performer.

Cuando yo te vuelvo ver, no habra penas ni olvidos, he sang. When I see you again, there will be no tears and no forgetting.

The drinkers at the bar fell silent and the pairs on the dance floor caught the rhythm.

Juancito bent forward and said to me: "Not bad, hey?" *Oigo la queja de un bandeón, dento del pecho pide rienda el corazón.* I hear the complaint of a *bandoneón*, it calls for my heart.

For a moment I, and everyone at the bar, the tables, the dance floor fell in love with Pierre. When he came to the end of the song, there was enthusiastic applause. Even Juancito had a moment of non-levity and clapped. But the magic stopped the moment Pierre closed his mouth and he turned back into a "spy".

When he arrived at our table, Juancito said:

"So, if all fails, you can still get a job as a singer."

"I'd rather keep it a hobby," Pierre said. "More satisfying, you know. Once you do it professionally, the fun is over."

Juancito answered him with a braying laugh and trilled a line from a tango: *Fue el centinela de mis promesas.* He was the guardian of my promises.

The two men locked eyes, as if daring each other to a fist fight. Then the tension broke and Juancito got up.

"Excuse me," he said and headed for the washroom.

"And what *do* you do professionally?" I asked Pierre when we were alone.

"I'm in security," he said.

"What kind of training do you need for that? Is there a degree in security?"

He laughed noiselessly in a series of exhalations, as if I had made a tremendous joke.

"I have a degree in literature and languages," he said. "I used to edit a magazine, but then the war came and made literature redundant."

"Really? What about 'the word is mightier than the sword'?"

"One of the many proverbs that are wrong." He gave me a sober look, assessing my abilities, I think. "Shall we dance?"

"Okay," I said, and we joined the pairs on the dance floor. Although we were cheek to cheek, as required, and our bodies were touching, Pierre kept his cool and never tried to feel me up. I wouldn't have minded if he had made a move on me. The steamy atmosphere of the place had sharpened my appetite, but he made no attempt to take advantage of the closeness of our bodies. It must be his training in security, I thought. They are probably taught to keep their distance and remain watchful at all times.

When he took me back to the table, Juancito still hadn't returned.

"He isn't coming back," Pierre said. "He has skipped out. I'll drive you home."

He waved the waiter over and asked for his bar tab and the bill for the bottle of gin on our table and the plate of empanadas, on which I had nibbled.

"It's paid for," the waiter said. "Compliments of Señor Duarte."

"Ah, very good," Pierre said. "This is for you, then."

He left a large tip. The waiter grinned, I don't know whether he was pleased or just amused.

Pierre's car was a sturdy black Ford, nothing fancy. It came with his job, I assumed. On the way home, he made light conversation and kept it going as if he wanted to prevent me from asking him any questions, such as what did working in "security" really mean? Was he one of the men walking two steps behind the Perons on official visits, the men you saw in the newspapers, wearing dark sunglasses?

I looked at his face in profile. It gave nothing away. I noticed his hands resting on the steering wheel. His long, slim fingers tapered off into buffed nails.

"You play the piano?" I said.

"So-so. Why do you ask?"

"Your hands. They look like the hands of a pianist."

"I play the violin. Used to."

We drove on in silence, but even the silence seemed to have implications. After a while he said:

"And you – what do you like to do?" He sounded as if he was actually interested in an answer, but maybe that was just a confidence trick.

"I don't know," I said. "I don't have any hobbies."

We came to a stop sign, and he looked at me attentively before turning his eyes back to the road and driving on. His attention unleashed something corresponding in me. I took a closer look at him. He had an air of confidence, not the cockiness of Juancito but a quiet assurance that made me feel safe, like nothing bad could happen to me as long as he was around. I kept looking at his profile until he said: "So now that you've looked me over, what's the conclusion?"

"That you are okay?" I said. It came out a question as if I needed his confirmation.

"That's good then," he said.

I followed up. "And what's your conclusion? About me, I mean?"

"I can't tell," he said. "I take a long time to make up my mind," but he smiled at me almost lovingly. It was an odd smile and an odd conversation. I was beginning to like him. Usually men leered at me and followed up with lewd suggestions. He was just friendly – it was a new sensation, and it felt good.

Liliana's house was dark except for a light above the entrance. The gate in the wrought-iron fence was locked. Pierre got out of the car and rang the bell. After a while the butler appeared and let us in. He looked puffy-eyed, like a man awoken from sleep. It occurred to me that it must be past midnight.

"Thanks for taking me home," I said to Pierre.

"My pleasure," he said and took a step back, as if he wanted to avoid too much familiarity when saying good-bye. I found his old-fashioned manner oddly attractive, although I suspected that he was putting it on, or putting me on. I couldn't make him out.

As I followed the butler into the house, I remembered that I had left the bag with my clothes and Evita's presents in Juancito's car. I felt a sharp stab of loss, not about my clothes or even about the string of pearls. I wanted the book with the lines in Evita's hand, to put under my pillow maybe, to go to sleep with. I had a vague plan of cutting out the page with her signature when I got home to Toronto and framing it. I'll get it back from Juancito tomorrow, I thought and felt half-way comforted. I went upstairs and was about to turn into my bedroom, when I saw a movement in the semi-dark of the hall. There was a small, glassed-in terrace at the end of the corridor. The door to the terrace opened noiselessly, and Nancy appeared.

She signaled to me, a silent invitation to join her. What the hell was she doing out there at this time of night? She put a finger to her lips, pulled me over to one side of the terrace and pointed toward the shrubs. After my eyes got used to the dark, I saw that two people were making out on a blanket in the grass, humping vigorously. Liliana and Juancito!

Nancy elbowed me and pressed something into my hand: a pair of binoculars. But I had seen enough of their love-making. I didn't need a closer look and trained the binoculars on the fence and the street beyond. A maroon Clipper was parked at the curb, and behind it a black Ford, an obdurate and silent presence.

8

I woke to the shrilling of the house phone on my nightstand. It was Liliana.

"I hope I didn't wake you up," she said. I could hear her fake smile over the phone.

For a moment I thought it was still night. The heavy drapes kept the room in darkness, but the sun cast a shaft of light through the narrow opening between the two panels. It was eight in the morning.

"I was fast asleep," I said and sat up, swinging my legs over the edge of the bed. "What's the matter?"

"So sorry," she said with a sympathy as stagey as her invisible smile. "Could I ask you to take my place in Evita's office this morning? We have a dinner invitation for tonight, and the only time my hairdresser can take me is 9: 30."

"Does Evita want me to come? Did you check with her?"

"No, I didn't check with her," she said, "but she has taken such a liking to you-"

"She said that?"

"Not in so many words, but I could tell from the way she talked to you at dinner the other day."

I hesitated. I wasn't prepared to do Liliana a favour, but I did want to see Evita.

"Okay," I said. "I'll be downstairs in ten minutes and have a quick breakfast. But you'd better phone Evita and let her know. She likes to make up her own mind – isn't that what you told me?"

I was pleased with the way that came out, putting Liliana in her place using her own words.

"You are probably right. I should call her," Liliana said meekly.

Antonio drove us downtown and dropped me off at the Ministry before taking Liliana to the hairdresser. Or maybe she lied about that appointment and just wanted time out.

"I'll be back by one," she said as I got out of the car. "Let's have a bite to eat then, and you can fill me in on your morning."

I didn't reply. I didn't want to commit myself because I was hoping to have lunch with Evita.

There was a lineup of people all the way from the entrance of the building up the stairs to Evita's office on the first floor. The benches in the hallway outside her office were packed with ragged people, and I had to dodge children playing tag to get to the usher guarding her door. He was already on the lookout for me because he waved as soon as he caught sight of me and motioned me past with an impatient gesture, as if I was late for the job.

I expected Evita's office to be like all government offices, a drab affair matching the bedraggled people in the hall. But it was nothing like that. The walls were covered in red damask. By the door was a large bronze bust of a man — José Martí, *libertador*, according to the inscription on the plaque.

Evita was sitting at a massive rosewood desk. On the wall behind her were three large oil paintings: Christ with a crown of thorns, Juan Peron in his white president's uniform, and a melancholy looking lady with a black mantilla covering her head and shoulders. Evita looked royal. Enthroned. Right away I knew I had made a mistake, taking Liliana's place. I wanted to be with the Evita of last night, the woman with girlish braids and dressed in oversized pajamas — not with the mystical mother of the country, the national treasure, or whatever role she was playing sitting there at her desk under a huge chandelier. Even the way she rose to greet me was theatrical. It wasn't a welcome. It was the opening scene of a play or the overture to an act of state.

It was only when she took both of my hands in hers and pulled me into an embrace that she became human. Her scent mingled with my breath, we were flesh to flesh, and I felt loved once more. She looked glamorous even in her sober blue suit devoid of jewelry except for a brooch in the shape of two clasped hands —the Peronist emblem — pinned to the lapel of her jacket.

She kissed me like a long-lost child.

"*Querida!*" she said. "I'm so glad you could come. What do you think of my *despachito*?"

I laughed at her use of the diminutive for "office".

"Your grand office, you mean."

"I want only the best for my people," she said, releasing me from her arms and taking her seat on stage again, under the floodlights of the chandelier. She turned serious. Her eyes had an official gravity. I could tell she had dismissed me from her mind and was already thinking of the people waiting in the corridor.

"Sit there," she said, pointing to a chair beside her desk. "It will be good to see everything I say and do reflected in your eyes. It will give me courage."

Courage? She didn't need courage. She needed an audience. She wanted applause.

For the next four hours I watched Evita perform. With her secretary on one side and me on the other, she talked to a procession of supplicants, listening to their troubles. The secretary, Michel Costa, was a young man with a haggard brown face matching the misery of the petitioners. He was hollow-chested, painfully thin and permanently bent over like a worshipper, handing Evita a pen when needed, or a pad with clothing tickets and food stamps, or the pink slips on which she wrote out orders — medication for the sick, toys for the children, and housing for the homeless. He seemed to be part of her act, whereas I was only a spectator.

The first petitioner was a young woman in a faded blue dress and espadrilles worn down at the heel. She brought with her a whiff of dried sweat. Her messy tangled hair looked as if she hadn't combed it in days.

She stood slump-shouldered at first, with her eyes lowered, then taking her cue from Evita's soft questions, she started in with her request.

"Respected Lady," she said, using a formal address totally at odds with her sloppy appearance. She went on talking in a monotone, as if she was reading from a prepared speech, a speech someone had written for her. "First of all, please forgive me for daring to trouble you with my difficulties, but I find myself in a desperate situation and you are my only hope. I am unmarried, and my parents don't know that I had a baby. I left him in the foundling home because I have to work, but I miss him terribly and cry for him a lot ..."

Evita listened with a benevolent smile. The secretary was leaning in toward her, waiting for instructions.

"Well, that's easily fixed," she said, when the woman came to the end of her story. "Don't worry, *querida*. We'll find your child and see that he is brought to you and we'll make sure your parents will forgive you. Surely your mother will want to look after her grandson while you are at work."

She reached under the blotter on her desk and took out two fifty-peso notes.

"Here you are, that will tide you over." Then she motioned her to come closer. The woman shuffled forward shyly.

"Come here, *querida*," Evita said. "I want to hug you." She got up and embraced the woman, kissing the top of her head, unafraid of the lice that I suspect nested in her tousled hair, embracing her the same way she had embraced me. I reddened with embarrassment for Evita. Her gestures and her voice sounded sincere – was she a superb actress, or did she really feel a sympathy that made her neglect everything else, even the disgust she must surely feel when she touched that filthy young woman. It was painful to watch, and I felt an unreasonable jealousy. I didn't want to share Evita with her or anyone else.

The next petitioner was an old man with a tubercular hacking cough, but Evita embraced and kissed him too. I believe she would have kissed a leper.

"I am looking after a boy who has been abandoned by his parents," the man told her. He spoke humbly but with greater confidence than the woman before him. He seemed to be very sure of the justice of his cause and trusting in Evita's willingness to help. "I applied to have him placed in a welfare school," he said, "but that's a long time ago, and I haven't heard back from them. I would like to see the boy trained so he can find work when he grows up. I am old and poor and can't support him forever."

Evita nodded as she scribbled instructions on a slip of paper, signing it "E.P." with a rapid scratch.

"We'll look after that for you, *abuelito*," she said, and he departed with trembling gratitude after receiving another filial kiss from her.

Evita gave me a triumphal look. "You see," she said, "there is a great deal of work to be done." But all I saw was the great waste of Evita giving herself to people who were unworthy of her. She wanted me to congratulate her on her performance, and I was bursting with jealousy. I wanted to say: Why don't you leave that work to your ugly secretary? He could perfectly well take care of those people. But I swallowed the words and looked at her with longing. In any case, there was no time to talk.

A parish priest came in next, and the atmosphere in the room changed. His voice was commanding, as if he wasn't asking for a favour at all, but simply reminding Evita of her duty. "It's about children who are left alone during the day while their parents are working. They live on the street," he said. "They misbehave and get into trouble as children do if nobody looks after them. They need a caregiver to teach them discipline. So I'm asking you, Señora, pay someone to look after them and keep them out of mischief."

She didn't offer him an embrace. Her face remained hard, her bearing royally stiff.

"You should take care of your parishioners yourself," she said.

He looked back at her steadily. "We don't have that kind of money," he said.

Evita pursed her lips, but she scribbled the necessary instructions on a slip. "Here you are," she said handing the paper to him. "That should take care of the children." But she refused to smile. She turned away and asked the secretary to call in the next petitioner before the priest had even left the room.

The woman who came in had a care-worn face and filled the room with the pungency of unwashed sheets or worse, the stench of an incurable disease.

"I have four kids," she said uneasily, keeping her eyes on the ground. "Three of them are school-aged, but I can't send them to school because they have no shoes and their clothes are practically rags and they don't have the strength to do the schoolwork because we have nothing to eat, not even bits of bread to fool their hunger. I can't work because I'm sick. The doctor says I need an operation. But who will pay for that? And who will take care of the children when I'm in hospital?"

She paused, exhausted. Evita turned to the secretary. "Bring the señora a chair," she said. "Rest up," she said to the woman, "and take your time telling me everything that's on your mind."

The woman slumped down on the chair and breathed hard. Evita kept an attentive silence.

"I am ashamed to tell you, Señora," the woman said after staring on the floor for a while. "For the last seven years I have been with a man of property who allowed me to live in a cabin on his estancia without charging rent but now he doesn't want me anymore. Señora, I beg you to help me out with some money."

She spoke in a low voice, but with the courage of desperation. I could see that Evita was angry. A steep crease had appeared between her brows. "And why does the man of property not help you?" she said sharply. "I will send someone to make him pay. Not just for your children. For all the children in his village. I will teach him a lesson in humanity!"

Then her smile returned and she put the woman at ease, asking a few more questions about her health before dismissing her with the ready cash she kept under her blotter and with a fond embrace. She was the only one I wasn't jealous of. She was too wretched to arouse anything but pity.

Midway through the morning, a servant came in with a pot of hot water and a tray with mate gourds. She put a little pile of leaves into each gourd, topped them with sugar and poured on the water. On Evita's invitation she sat with us and we all sipped our mate through metal straws. It was the first time I tasted the herb. It left a muddy aftertaste on my tongue, but it was a relief to sit like that, in peace after all the misery. No one spoke. We looked at each other with love, and I felt included at last, although I would have preferred it to be just Evita and me.

After the break, the interviews continued. Evita listened to the requests of the petitioners, put her fingers on festering wounds and kissed disgusting lips eaten away by syphilis. She signed slips for housing, clothes, beds, food. The petitioners shuffled in and out of the office. She was inexhaustible, keeping the momentum of the show running. The only interruption in the endless shamble of ragged people and their wretched stories was a delegation of businessmen who presented a cheque for a charitable foundation Evita was planning to set up.

The secretary called in a photographer. The group posed for the camera, Evita holding on to the cheque with her white hand as the leader of the delegation presented it with a deferential bow. This wasn't an exercise in love. She showed them who was in charge.

"Alright, guys," she said briskly when the photo session was over, calling them *muchachos*, as if they were cowboys rather than the members of a board. "*Bueno, muchachos, hay que aflojar* – you need to bleed a bit more of the stuff." She was no longer the mother figure. She had turned into a union steward, her voice hard and her gestures peremptory. The men kept straight faces, but it was clear that they resented her tone.

As the morning session drew to a close and the last petitioner left the room, Evita turned to me with a radiant smile, but the morning was spoiled for me. She had made me suffer too much. I didn't hide my discontent.

"Why are you putting yourself through these ugly scenes?" I said.

She patted my hand as if she wanted to make up for neglecting me. "You are right, *querida*," she said. "The ritual is not necessary. An organization could deliver the same benefits, but human contact is important for these poor people. They need to see and believe that I care for them, that I love them."

You are spreading your love too thin, I thought, and showed her a sulky face.

She put her hands on my mouth as if she wanted to flatten out my crimped lips.

"Why are you so discontented, Mona?" she said.

"Because I feel left out," I said.

A light came into her eyes. "My poor child," she said. "I forgot. You need love too. I'm so sorry, but I'll make it up to you." She put her arms around me, and we stayed for a moment in an embrace that was very sweet.

Then she let me go. "Liliana will take you to lunch," she said. "I have a meeting with Juan."

So she had no time for me after all, and I had to go with Liliana, who was waiting for me downstairs.

"How was it?" she said when we sat down on the patio of an elegant café around the corner from the Ministry. I could tell that she was looking forward to hearing my complaints. I was full of complaints, but it seemed disloyal to Evita to vent them.

"She is doing a lot of good," I said.

"She is killing herself with all this do-gooding," Liliana said. "I told her: you are too fanatical, Evita. And you know what she said? Fanatism is good. It puts me in the company of martyrs and heroes."

I thought of the bronze bust of José Martí, the liberator, who died young. Was he Evita's model, the martyr and hero whose company she hoped to join?

"She has a tendency to lecture people," Liliana was saying. "She annoys me no end with her slogans. 'Life has no real value when lived in the spirit of egoism!' 'Surrender yourself to an ideal!' Stuff like that. She wants to make socialists of us all. Meanwhile she is dripping with diamonds. Ridiculous!"

"It looks like she has made some converts," I said and told Liliana about the businessmen delivering a check for Evita's charitable foundation.

Liliana sneered.

"You don't think they are giving away money voluntarily? She puts the thumbscrews on them. If they don't deliver, she sends her goons to sabotage their businesses. I heard that Mu-Mu – that's a caramel factory – sent her a bill for delivering 100,000 packages of bonbons she wanted to give to poor children. She was furious because she had expected to get them free of charge. So she sent her inspectors to the factory. They said they found rat hair in the chocolate and closed it down. The owners had to make a large donation to get the place recertified."

Liliana kept talking, and I pretended to listen, but I had closed my mind against her. I didn't want to believe what she said, and I wasn't going to allow her to blacken Evita. I had already placed her on a pedestal, beside José Martí.

When it was time for Liliana's afternoon stint at the office, she told the chauffeur to take me home. I guess she wanted to keep me marooned at the house so I couldn't run up another bill on her account. I stuck around the house for a bit, lounging on the terrace, wishing I hadn't left Evita's book in Juancito's car. It's not that I was desperate to read it. Lord Chesterfield's advice to his son was outdated stuff, good enough for teaching Evita

85

English, I suppose. I just wanted to look at the title page and reread her dedication to me. I wanted to lose myself in the loops of Evita's handwriting and conjure up her smile and the feel of her smooth arms around me. Of course the book wouldn't do the trick, it was just a poor substitute, something to tide me over until I saw her again. I badly wanted to be near her, but I was still puzzled by my desire. I couldn't figure it out. It was something between love and hero worship and a frisson of sexual attraction.

After an hour on the terrace, I was thoroughly bored and went for a walk. As expected, the streets were dead except for a car sharking around, maybe security, waiting for a crime to happen. I wish.

I thought the afternoon would never end, but when I got back to the house, a surprise was waiting for me.

First off, Rosa, who let me in, showed a new deference.

"There's been a delivery for you, Señorita," she said. "We put it into your room. It came with this letter." She handed me an envelope with the presidential seal.

I ripped open the letter as I was running up to my room. It contained a creamy sheet of paper, embossed with the Argentine flag, blue and white stripes with a golden sun in the middle. It was from Evita.

"*Querida*," she wrote. "You will need this-". That's as far as I got by the time I reached my room and opened the door. A portable wardrobe on wheels stood by the bed, a rack loaded with dresses, suits, and a couple of coats. On the floor beside it was a stack of hat boxes and a pile of small parcels.

I didn't have time to take it all in, let alone read the rest of Evita's letter, before there was a knock on the door, and Nancy poked her head in.

"I'm dying to find out what's going on," she said. "Mind if I come in? I saw them deliver the rack. Rosa said it was for you, from Evita Peron."

I waved her in, although not in a welcoming way. I wanted to read Evita's letter. "You will need this," the first line said. Need it for what?

"Just a moment," I said and left Nancy standing there while I went into the bathroom, shutting the door on her curious face.

"*Querida*, you will need this. You said you wished you could come with me to Europe. I have decided to take you along. I have ordered everything from Drecoll's. Phone them and tell them your shoe size. They will get the matching shoes for you. We'll talk about everything tonight. I kiss and embrace you. Evita."

I kiss and embrace you too, I thought with a melting sort of happiness. I had lost the book with her name and dedication, but this was even better. Now I had a whole page written in her hand. I wished Nancy wasn't in my bedroom, so I could lie down on the bed with Evita's letter and indulge in fantasies involving her naked body, which I pictured to be hard and skinny.

When I returned to the bedroom, Nancy was already going through the dresses, holding them up against herself.

"Are you going to try them on?" she said. "They look fabulous." She talked fast because, she said, she didn't have much time. The baby was napping. "He's due to wake up any minute now, and I want to see everything you got. Aren't you the lucky one!"

"I'm lucky alright. Evita has decided to take me along to Europe."

"No! That's why she is getting you these amazing dresses and coats? I already thought: where the hell are you going to wear these clothes? But if you go to state dinners and the like over there, you'll need them of course. Can I watch while you are trying them on?"

She settled down on my bed, ready for the fashion show. I slipped into the first gown with drop sleeves and a narrow skirt widening to a bell-shape below the knee. I took a few steps and admired the skirt undulating around my ankles. Looking up I saw admiration reflected in Nancy's eyes. It seemed to include both the gown and me. I hadn't thought of myself as admirable before. I had to get used even to the idea of being visible all of a sudden, of people paying attention to me: Liliana and Nancy, Juancito and Pierre. Even Rosa. It was the effect of Evita's eyes shining their miraculous light on me. They had brought me out of the shadows and made me visible.

I took a few more things off the rack and put them on one after the other — a soft black jacket with satin lapels, a narrow skirt with a hem of ocelot fur, a silky peach-coloured cape. I paraded them before Nancy's appreciative eyes.

"I wonder how Liliana is going to take the news that you are going to Europe with Evita," she said. "She thought *she*'d be invited to come along and that's why she had to stick around Evita every day, to be trained as her assistant. But I know why Evita is tying her up. To keep her from seeing Juancito. He used to come in the afternoon, you know, and they did it in the library. The maid walked in on them one day, or so I heard."

"In that case, Liliana should be pleased. If Evita doesn't invite her to come along, she can get together with Juancito on the old schedule."

"No such luck," Nancy said. "As far as I know, he is going with Evita."

The moment she said that, it all came into focus. That's why she was taking me along: not because she wanted my company but to throw me together with her brother, to distract him. It was all part of the favour she had asked me, and I had said yes because I loved her.

"Liliana thought she and Juancito were going to have a marvelous time in Spain, while Evita was busy with state affairs. At least that's my guess when I gave her notice last week and she was practically on her knees begging me to stay on. She absolutely needed me, at least for the duration of the trip."

We didn't get any further with the confidences or with my private fashion show, because we heard the baby cry.

"Here we go," Nancy said and heaved off the bed reluctantly. "Got to run. Talk to you later. Why don't you come along when I pick up the kids?"

I hesitated. I wanted to be alone with Evita's letter, but then I said yes because I realized: I also wanted to go on talking about her magnificent presents to me and about the trip to Europe — to someone receptive like Nancy. I couldn't very well gloat to Liliana or expect her to congratulate me. She would be furious. Also I wanted to hear more about Nancy threatening to quit her job.

"You gave her notice?" I said to her later when we were on our way to the school.

"I've had it with her and the kids. They treat me like dirt. I was going to leave at the end of the month, but she said she'd double my pay if I stayed on. She didn't say why, but I had already heard on the grapevine that she expected to go to Europe. When you arrived, I thought she'd rope you into the job, to take over from me."

"No way!"

"Right you are. I wouldn't recommend working for her. She is a shitty employer."

"Does she have anyone else lined up?"

She shrugged. "I don't know and I don't care. At first, she was trying to put pressure on me, like I owe her more notice, but I gave her a hint of what I knew about her and Juancito, and that was that. She became as mild as a lamb and offered to up my pay. But I don't want to work for her anymore."

"So where are you going next?"

"I've saved up enough to float until I find another job, and I can always ask a friend to let me stay at his place."

His place? A man? I didn't think Nancy was capable of roping in a man, let alone moving in with him. But maybe I was up against a cultural divide here. Argentine men might find Nancy attractive, and as Liliana said, they all had mistresses.

"A boyfriend?" I said.

"I don't know about 'boyfriend'. I've only known him for a few months. He works long hours, and so do I, so we don't get a lot of time together."

"What's he like?" I was curious to hear what kind of man would date Nancy.

90

"He's a decent fellow, just not very exciting, as a man, I mean."

Neither are you, as a woman, I thought.

"I mean he is kind of reserved. Doesn't talk much. Maybe that's a Belgian thing."

Belgian thing? I immediately thought of Pierre Adams. Was he the decent man who didn't talk much?

"But I like him," Nancy was saying. "He has been around. He lived in the Congo for some years, and in Spain before he came here. He wrote books, but he says he can't write in Spanish, or doesn't want to. It takes a long time to switch languages, he says. I know what he means. I've been switching back and forth between English and French all my life. That's how it is in Montreal. But I think he has an ear for languages. We speak French when we are together, since that's his native language, but his Spanish is perfect as well. And he speaks English beautifully."

"So what's he doing now?"

"He is working in security, for the Perons. That's how I met him. Every time they came for dinner here, he came along and waited in the hall downstairs. So we got talking."

"What does he look like?" I said, not so much to confirm my hunch – I was sure it was Pierre she was talking about – but to confirm my own impression of him.

"Nice, but bloodless. You'd expect someone in security to be beefy. He is more the intellectual type. Doesn't pack much punch."

"Maybe he is good with a gun."

Nancy looked at me thoughtfully. "Could be. Mainly he is good with his eyes. Nothing escapes that man. But there is something I can't figure out about him. He is holding back on me. He won't say exactly what he was doing in the Congo, or in Spain. Or, for that matter, what he did during the war. A lot of people don't want to talk about that time, maybe because it was traumatic for them, or because they were on the wrong side."

I was a little hazy about the war, but I thought all of western Europe was on the side of the Allies.

"Belgium was on the right side, no?"

"I'm not sure. Belgium was occupied by Hitler, and then freed by the Allies. I can't tell on whose side Pierre was."

I let that go by because I wasn't into history.

"So were you doing a little security work for Pierre, when you were out on the balcony the other night?" I asked.

Nancy laughed. "Naw, he doesn't need my help. On the contrary, he has told me some things I didn't know."

"Like what?"

"That Juancito took you to a tango bar and left you stranded, and he had to drive you home."

"I could have told you that."

"But you didn't. Sometimes I have the feeling I'm just wallpaper to you."

"Don't be silly," I said. "We are talking all the time. Like friends."

I shouldn't have added that last bit. I wasn't good at making friends and worse at pretending to be friends. It was such a patent lie that Nancy spotted it immediately. I could see from her sideways look that she wasn't buying it. She didn't say anything. She just kind of snickered, as if to say. Sure, suddenly we are "friends" and you are willing to talk, because I know something you don't.

She was right. I hadn't paid much attention to her until now. I was doing to her what I resented in others: looking through instead of at her. I lowered my head in case I was blushing. For a moment I couldn't think of anything to say, but the embarrassment passed. It wasn't really my fault. Nancy had a talent for making herself inconspicuous. I should have known, though: quiet people are keen observers. She and Pierre were a good match in that respect. Two observers. Still, I was surprised they hit it off. Pierre wasn't bad looking, and there was a calm assurance about him, an aura of competence. He was someone you could trust, who would take care of you if were in trouble. I didn't think Nancy would get lucky with a guy like him. I almost envied her.

9

That evening Evita received me without a smile, or with a very tight smile at any rate. No pajamas this time. She was still wearing the outfit she'd worn in the morning — a marine business suit and white blouse, almost like a man's tailored shirt.

I wanted to thank her for the clothes and talk about her letter and what it meant to me, but she cut me short.

"We'll talk about that later, *querida*," she said. "Let's get the work done first. I need to practice these speeches."

Someone at the English embassy had composed a couple of speeches for her, to be delivered at a press conference in London or at a banquet. "I'm not sure about the details yet," she said. "We may have to adjust the text. But for now, I will read them to you sentence by sentence, and you correct me and improve my pronunciation."

We went through the texts. She made notes in the margin. When we were through, she finally relaxed, took off her jacket and skirt, lay down on the bed, and patted the place beside her. I snuggled into her. She wore white garters to hold up her silk stockings. I thought they would be black. There was a run in one of her stockings, I noticed, but the flesh between the edge of her panties and the top of her stockings was perfect, smooth, the colour of milk-chocolate.

"Now about the clothes I had Drecoll's deliver to you," she said. "They had your measurements, they said. Do they fit? Do you like them?"

That tight smile, that matter-of-fact question diluted the love in me and thinned the pink clouds in my head. I didn't answer her question. Instead I said: "You just assumed that I would go on the trip to Europe with you, didn't you? You never even asked me."

"But you told me that you would like to come along," she said. "And you won't say no now, when I need you." Needed me for what? To entertain Juancito?

She cupped my face in both of her hands and looked into my eyes earnestly.

My resentment melted away. "I won't say no," I said. "Because I love you."

"I know," she said simply and allowed me to kiss her, as a reward, I suppose. I felt dazed by her touch, my hand sneaked up the side of her body to her breast, sheathed now in a crisp shirt. I wished I had used the opportunity the night before when there was so much skin to touch. She gently took away my hand, turned it over and kissed the inside. Her kiss made my veins pulse. I was more confused than ever, in a swirl of mixed feelings, most of them rising from the limbic underworld which couldn't be controlled.

"And Juancito will come along too," she said. "—
How are you two getting along?" She asked softly, as if she
was afraid of touching a sore spot.

So I'd guessed right. She was taking me along for his
sake. She wanted us to "get along". I shrugged off her
question. I wondered whether I should tell her that he
sneaked out on me the night before.

"You don't think he is handsome?" she said.

"He is good-looking alright, but I don't like the way
he acts. As if he was God's gift to women."

"He is an egoist, I admit, but he can be nice when he
wants to be. Make an effort to like him," she said. "Please.
For my sake."

I held out a little longer. "About the trip," I said.
"How long will you be in Europe? I need to be back home
in two weeks, to finish my school year."

"Don't worry. I'll make sure you will be back in time."

At ten, Juancito picked me up. I was surprised he
hadn't balked at the duty call. He must be under his
sister's thumb in spite of playing macho man. Maybe he
was just toeing the line in her presence, I thought. Maybe
he'll announce a change of plans once we are out of the
floodlight of her brown eyes. I half expected, maybe even
hoped, to see Pierre Adams waiting downstairs to take
over from him. I would have preferred Pierre's company.
But Juancito kept a straight face, playing the role assigned
to him, and handed me into the car like a regular escort.

Once we were on the road, he dropped the act and
said:

"We need to talk, you and I. Evita got it into her head
that you are the woman for me. No offense, *chiquita*. You
are a looker, but you aren't old enough for me. Or bad

97

enough." He looked over at me and grinned. "Maybe I should link you up with Juan. He likes them young."

"You know what?" I said. "I'm not interested in linking up with Juan, or with you. You aren't my kind of date. You are too full of yourself."

Now he laughed outright. A relieved laugh.

"Okay. I see we'll get along just fine. And now that we have that bit of business out of the way, let me take you to a nice place for dinner. Afterwards we'll go to a night club: Rendez-Vous. They have the Cuban Boys shaking their maracas there. Or The Embassy, if you prefer yanqui jazz. Those are the two hot spots right now. Packed every night, people lining up to get a table, but they always have one reserved for me."

"I don't want nice. Nice is boring. Why don't you take me to a dive?"

"A *dive*?"

"A low-class joint, like the tango bar we went to last night. Or something worse."

He gave me an amused look.

"I am starting to like you, *chiquita*. You want worse — as in drugs, gambling, whores?"

"Whores, I think."

"Have you been screwing around?"

"Not much. They keep an eye on me at home."

"Well, okay," he said. "But don't complain afterwards."

"I won't. I'll keep my mouth shut."

He made a U-turn in the direction of the harbour. I came back to what he'd said about Juan, that "he likes them young". Did Evita allow her husband to go off on that kind of thing?

"She has tried to put the brakes on him, but he is one guy she can't control. Juan is stubborn, you know, even though he doesn't show it. Very subtle, that boy, ready with the smile and the jokes. She fell for him heart and soul. It's understandable. Small town girl with big ambitions meets Mr. Personality who can make those ambitions come true. But he can't put one over on me. I don't care if he skied the Alps, speaks four languages, and has written books on mass psychology and military strategy. He's got a cock in his pants like every man, and he likes visiting schools and giving the girls rides on his motor scooter and feeling them up. I understand. He works hard, he has to have some fun. Evita knows it too."

"And she lets him get away with it?"

"Looks like it. But he is the only one who can pull it off. The rest of us have to do as she says."

"Even you?"

"Most of the time."

"By the way," I said. "I left a bag in your car yesterday, with my clothes and the string of pearls and a book Evita gave me."

"Oh, yeah," he said. "The bag. You wanted it back?"

"Of course I want it back."

I turned to see if it was still on the backseat, but it wasn't.

"I think the girl got it."

"What girl?"

"The girl I picked up last night at the tango bar. Adams took you home, I gather."

"He did. No thanks to you. But what do you mean 'The girl got it'? You gave it to her, or what?"

99

"Look, don't get sore at me. Just tell me what I owe you for the stuff."

"Nothing," I said. It wasn't a matter of money. I cared only about the book with Evita's name in it, but I didn't tell him about the magical draw of her name in ink and the imprint of her fingers on the pages. I was afraid he would mock me. I knew his type from school. He was a bully. You never show a bully what you care for, or he'll destroy it. In any case, I now had a whole letter written in Evita's hand, so I put up with the loss of the book.

We were passing through the narrow streets of the Boca now. Juancito slowed down and stopped at the back of a two-story house painted mustard yellow. The lower part of the wall was solid like a bunker. The second floor had a row of tall windows. Two of them had balconies with old-fashioned ornamental railings, the one in the middle had a Juliet balcony. All of the windows were dark. The house had a look of decay and abandonment about it. The iron railings were rusty, and the wooden shutters on some of the windows had come off and were stacked against the balcony railings. We walked around to the front of the building. The entrance was lit up by a garish sign with a palm tree and a hula dancer and the word "Bar" flicking on and off. Inside, the place was dimly lit and quiet. It smelled of old carpet. There was a band playing Latino music and a small dance floor, but no one was dancing. The little tables surrounding the empty oval were occupied by single girls or girls in pairs sipping drinks and playing cards, waiting – for customers, I assume. The scene didn't look very exciting to me, or very bad, which is what I had asked for.

We sat down at the bar, next to a large birdcage with a green parrot inside. He sidled along the perch and made discreet squawking noises at us. We were the only ones at the bar. Juancito ordered a bottle of champagne. They brought us two flutes with champagne that looked like it had been waiting around for us. There were hardly any bubbles rising to the surface.

Juancito surveyed the tables. One of the girls was eyeing him. She was not particularly pretty — wiry and hard-faced, with thin arched eyebrows, and jet black hair that had a blue sheen in the sad light blinking down from the ceiling. He nodded, she nodded back almost imperceptibly, got up, and passed through a door next to the bar.

Juancito got up too.

"Want to join us upstairs?" he said to me.

"Sure," I said, although I didn't like the braying laugh he gave me in reply.

We went through the same door as the girl and climbed the worn treads of a staircase to the upper floor. There were several doors off the dimly lit corridor. Juancito knew his way. He stopped at the second door on the right and went in without bothering to knock. It was a tiny room, almost entirely taken up by a bed covered with a rumpled sheet. A small sink with a cold-water tap was mounted on the wall. A limp towel hung on a hook beside it. The only other piece of furniture in the room was a plain wooden chair on which the girl had piled her clothes. She was lying on the bed, naked and spread-eagled, as if that was the most comfortable position she could think of. She wasn't trying to look inviting.

She lifted her head a little and pointed at me.

"If I have to do her too, it will cost extra," she said.

"Don't worry," Juancito said.

"That's okay," I said. "I'll just watch." The whore and the sheet on the bed didn't look very clean.

Juancito didn't bother to get undressed. He just opened his fly, moved in between the girl's open legs and started pumping. I heard a moan and realized it was me. I had to sit down on the floor because I was suddenly weak with desire, just watching their moves. It was over fast. Juancito didn't even give the whore time to wipe up before sliding his butt up to her face, but before they could give me another show, we heard the rumbling of a truck pulling into the yard. Doors slammed, a rough voice barked a command. There were rapid footsteps.

The girl slid from under Juancito and was at the window in a flash. "A raid," she said.

"Get her out," Juancito said pointing to me. "I'll talk to them."

He zipped up and moved out into the corridor. The whore slipped into her dress and shoes and took me by the hand like a little girl, leading me down the hallway. There was a window at the end of it, overlooking the parking lot. It was the window with the Juliet balcony I'd seen earlier. Juancito's car was below. The girl pushed up the sash of the window, wangled a leg over the sill, and dropped down to the ledge outside. She did it so smoothly that I suspected it was a practiced routine.

"Come on," she said in a hard, impatient voice, and I climbed up and let myself down on the other side, standing next to her. She took stock of the situation. We were only a little distance from the nearest window, which had a regular, wide balcony. She climbed up on the railing, steadied herself against the wall, and jumped across to the larger balcony with the agility of a trapeze artist. She stood still for a moment, then took one of the shutters that had come off the French doors and were leaning against the wall. She shoved it across to the Juliette balcony where I was standing, making a narrow bridge between the railings.

She whispered another "Come on", and I tried not to think, not to be afraid of falling, as I climbed up on the plank spanning the two balconies. I didn't look down, I shimmied across on my hands and knees. I could feel my nylons snagging on the slats and ripping. The girl reached for me and pulled, making me land hard on the other side and scraping my knee. We could hear another commando shout and the voices of people coming out of the bar, but we couldn't see anything. It was all happening around the corner, on the front side of the building.

The whore forced open the balcony door, and we passed through a shadowy room that looked like the one we had been in earlier, with the same arrangement of bed, chair, and sink, but a little larger. We crossed the room, stepped into the corridor, and sneaked down the stairs to a backdoor opening up into an alley. I breathed relief until I saw that the alley dead-ended on one side, barred by a chain-link fence. We could have climbed it, but it was lit up by a streetlight. Too risky, the whore said. They'll spot us. We couldn't sneak out on the side that wasn't gated because that's where the cops were. We'd run directly into their arms. So we sat on the ground with our backs pressed against the wall, knees drawn up tight to stay in the shadow of the eaves as much as possible. The alley was strewn with broken crates, rags, bottles, and the rotting remains of food. Directly under the streetlamp, in the cone of light on the ground was a seething mass of flying and crawling insects, the largest beetles I had ever seen. We heard more shouting and commotion around the corner. A cop appeared at the mouth of the alley and shone a flashlight our way. The jig was up. He pointed his gun at us.

"What have we got here?" he said, closing in and looming over us.

The girl pulled a few crumpled bills from under her dress (did it have secret pockets?). "That's all I have," she said to him, "but I'll do you for free."

"I'll take her instead," he said, pointing to me. "She looks cleaner."

He moved in front of me, toe to toe, his legs touching my drawn-up knees, as he was bending forward. "Go to it," he said and reached for his fly. After that, everything happened too fast for my understanding. I saw the flash of a knife, I heard him scream. A slit opened up along his thigh. He staggered back and dropped to his knees, cursing, as we scrambled up, ran to the other end of the alley and clambered over the fence. This time the whore didn't help me. I was on my own. I clawed my way up, dropped down on the other side and ran out to the parking lot, following her lead. We could see Juancito's car close by and, on the far side, at the corner of the building, the truck the cops had come in.

The whore tried the door of Juancito's car, but of course it was locked.

"Get down," she said, and we slid under the car on our bellies and stayed there, lying very still. The guy she slashed had probably gone for reinforcement. We heard the cops coming out of the bar, rough voices, boots hitting the pavement. From our vantage point we couldn't see the men. We heard someone approach the car. He stopped right beside it, and I recognized Juancito's polished wide-toed shoes. He has fat toes, I thought.

"Stay put," he said under his breath. He must have spotted us lying under the car when he came across the lot.

A few moments later, a pair of scuffed boots appeared beside Juancito's shoes.

"I don't carry much cash," Juancito said to the man in boots. "I'll get something to you tomorrow morning."

"I don't take bribes," the man said.

"Of course you don't take bribes, *che*, I know that," Juanito said pleasantly. I didn't know he could sound that way, as if he was really nice and considerate. "But one of your men has been stabbed, and the rest have worked hard. They deserve to be paid overtime. I'll get the money to you, and you'll see to it that it's distributed among them."

A charged silence hung in the air. Nothing further was said, but there was no need for words. They understood each other.

"So what's your name, *che*?" Juancito said.

"Jaime Solara." I could hear a faint smile in Solara's reply.

"Okay," Juancito said. "Tomorrow, look for an envelope with your name on it."

The heels of Solara's boots clicked together in a salute, and he moved off to join his men. When we heard the truck drive off, we wiggled out from under the car. My dress was filthy and my nylons ruined.

The whore thanked Juancito profusely.

"You shouldn't have knifed him, Soledad," he said mildly. "You are too impulsive."

"Yeah, I guess I'll have to find myself another place to work," she said. "The guy is going to come after me."

"Here is a little extra. Moving costs," Juancito said, stuck a few bills between her breasts and bussed her goodbye like an old uncle. Then he opened the car door for me and waved me in.

"You asked for bad," he said. "You got it, right?"

"I guess so. You expect me to say thank you?"

He laughed.

"You done good, *chiquita*," he said. "Maybe I'll change my mind about you."

"I'm not changing my mind about you," I said.

"Okay, I get it," he said and drove me home in silence. We had run out of things to say.

When we got to the Gutierrez' house, he turned off the engine. I wanted to get out, but he held me back.

"Your dress is a write-off," he said, "but don't throw it out. One of the maids will find it in the garbage and tell on you. Put it into a bag, and I have my chauffeur pick it up tomorrow."

"The butler will tell on me. He can see what state I'm in when he lets me into the house."

"No need to get him out of bed," he said. "I have a key. Let's hope you make it to your room without waking anyone."

"I'll manage," I said, although I wasn't sure that I could escape Nancy's all-seeing eyes.

We got out of the car and walked up to the house. Juancito unlocked the gate. We stood for a moment in its shadow. The house remained still and dark. We walked silently up to the front door and Juancito let me in and nodded good-bye.

I didn't turn on the lights in the corridor when I made my way upstairs, keeping a hand on the railing to guide my steps and listening for any doors opening or closing. The silence of the house was oppressive. The air seemed condensed with foreboding, but it was only the fear of being caught and questioned. It was a relief when I reached my room without rousing anyone. At least that's what I thought.

10

Next day, I put on slacks. Skirts and nylons were out for the time being. That adventure last night had left my knees scraped. My shins were lightly bruised in a few places. Nylons wouldn't have concealed the damage. I wasn't surprised when Nancy came to my room as soon as she had put down the baby for his mid-morning nap. I realized by then that her life was so dull, she had to live vicariously and was determined to sponge off my adventures and Liliana's adulterous affair. She didn't exactly question me about my night out. She talked casually, but her words were like secret signals. She had heard me come home early in the morning, she said. She was a light sleeper. I bet she had been at her post, lurking on the balcony, ready for the next instalment of the sex show. Liliana, I assumed, had been waiting up as well, for Juancito. I wondered whether he had any love left to give her last night. I had the feeling that even he had exhausted his sexual energies.

I managed to fend off Nancy's cleverly casual inquiries and I didn't see Liliana all day, so there was no need to make anything up for her.

When I met with Evita in the evening, she eyed my slacks.

"I thought you'd wear one of the new dresses," she said when I arrived, but she sounded distracted.

"I felt nostalgic for my slacks," I told her. "I'm used to wearing them at home."

"Nostalgic for slacks?" she said. It was the first time I felt we were out of sync. Until then I always felt understood, no, revealed under the light of her eyes. I found out things about me that I hadn't known before, but now I saw that there were limits to Evita's clairvoyance. I sensed the gap between us, in years and experience. For the first time and unwillingly, I noticed imperfections in Evita, a greyness under the surface of her perfect skin, a haggardness almost. It was as if she had lost weight since I met her at Liliana's house, a week ago, but perhaps it was only a trick of light and shadows.

"I like slacks," I said and took another critical look at her. She *has* lost weight, I thought.

"It doesn't matter if you are not dressed up for dinner," she said. "Juancito can't take you out tonight. He is at work. He and Juan have a lot to prepare in advance of my trip. Juancito is coming along with me to make sure everything goes okay. He'll be busy, but I expect he'll make time for you as well."

I didn't want him to make time for me, but I said nothing, letting the naked silence hang between us. I knew Evita expected me to like her brother, and I didn't want to hurt her feelings by saying that I was relieved he wouldn't pick me up tonight. I was glad I didn't have to go out with him. I didn't care if I never saw him again.

"So how do I get home tonight?" I asked.

"When we are through here, they will serve you dinner downstairs," she said. Her chauffeur was on standby to take me home afterwards.

"And when exactly are we leaving for Europe?" I asked.

"In four days."

"So soon? Why didn't you tell me earlier?"

"I told you the diplomats were still working on the arrangements," she said. "We only decided on the date yesterday."

The remaining evening was all work and no fun. Like Juancito, I was on duty, and Evita did not as much as sit down on her bed, although she looked especially enticing. She was wearing silver grey satin pants, a sky-blue blouse, and white shoes with cork heels. We sat at opposite sides of the writing desk in her private sitting room and prepped for the foreign press and the speeches she was expected to make. At ten she went to bed, dismissing me with a peck on the cheek, and I went downstairs to eat what they had prepared for me in the kitchen: a mixed asado. I ate alone, in a nook of what they called the breakfast room. I guess the table in the dining room (or rooms — there must be more than one in this vast palace) were too ridiculously big for one person. I was tempted to ask if I could eat in the kitchen, but I didn't. I had learned this much: keep your distance from the servants, don't let them enter your personal space, or they won't respect you. After dinner, Evita's chauffeur took me home. Upstairs, the corridor was empty, the door to the loggia shut tight.

It looked like Nancy had taken the night off and was resting from her spy work.

I didn't see Liliana over the next two days. We were like ships passing in the night – she was off to her assistant job before I came downstairs. When she got home, she skipped the usual wine and tapas in the library. For all I know, she was enjoying Happy Hour upstairs, in the privacy of her suite. I had the distinct feeling that she was avoiding me. Perhaps she was afraid that she couldn't keep a straight face and hide her annoyance at my rapid progress from unwanted visitor to competitor for Evita's favour and now the undisputed winner of the race. I was going to Europe. She was not.

I didn't see anything of Nancy either. She was stranded on the third floor. Rosa told me that the children were down with the flu and the little one had the sniffles. Nancy had to play nurse full-time. I woke up at night, hearing the baby cry. The bawling went on for a long time. I pitied Nancy.

The next evening, my tutoring session with Evita was a hurried affair, overlaid with other plans. We were scheduled to attend a performance of *La Bohème* at the Colon. Evita knew her speeches by heart now, and her pronunciation was respectable. We practiced while her hairdresser worked on finishing her sweeping updo. Both of us were dressed for the occasion. I didn't need to worry about my shins because I was told to wear a long dress, the one that belled out at the bottom, and a white mink stole, which was draped over my shoulders and made me look like a fairytale princess. I wasn't sure I liked my new image. What I saw in the mirror reminded me of my mother when she was on the prowl, all dressed up and hiding under a decorative foil, her real bitchy self invisible, tucked away inside. What I saw in the mirror wasn't me. My eyes were blank because I didn't know how to look the belle of the ball. I felt unmoored.

The Colon was putting on a gala performance as a kind of farewell to Evita before she embarked on her trip to Europe. They had brought in a celebrated baritone, Norman Cordon, all the way from the Metropolitan in New York. I rode in a car with an escort Evita had assigned to me, a young architect. Apparently Juancito wasn't up to that job or had other things to do. The architect gave me a running commentary on the opera house. The Colon was built in the Renaissance Italian style, well, neo-classical imitation of the Renaissance. He pointed to the triangular pediment as we drove up. "Look at the façade..." Blah, blah. I wasn't into architecture, but the foyer was impressive, with a stain-glass skylight high above. It looked like a giant ornamental spider web. The journalists were waiting in the foyer and flashed their cameras at the Perons and their entourage. At the top of the staircase, they were whisked away. The architect and the rest of us lesser beings were shown to our seats as well.

I saw Juan Peron holding court in a red-and -gold curtained loge, where he had been joined by a number of bemedaled men — members of his Cabinet, the architect told me. Evita and the ladies were seated in a separate box, in the centre of the horseshoe shaped auditorium, in full view of the audience. Everyone's opera glasses were trained on the Perons. I guess they had come to see them. The opera was just a distraction. The lights of the giant chandelier hanging from the cupola dimmed. There was polite applause for the conductor. The overture began, the curtains parted, and the first act opened with a scene in a Paris garret. – I can't say I enjoyed the opera. Not my kind of music.

During the intermission, the Perons were surrounded by the crème de la crème of Buenos Aires. It was the coming-out of someone's daughter, I was told. Someone important. She was making her first official appearance in public and was being introduced to Juan and Evita. My escort took me on a tour through the public rooms of the opera house and the pillared Salon Dorado, where people stood in little groups sipping champagne. He pointed out the gold-leaf paint, the marble from Italy, the brocaded panels. I checked out the women promenading the corridors in mink and ermine, their necks and ears glittering with diamonds. I wondered if it would be like that in Europe, if it was going to be a kind of guided sightseeing tour through the lives of the wealthy, but not in a fun way. Formals instead of parties, culture instead of dates. I was almost glad that Juancito was coming along on the trip. He wasn't my type, but I could count on him to relieve the boredom of the official acts I saw coming my way. I could always sneak off with him, take a walk on the wild side into the seedier parts of Madrid.

When I got home, I checked my legs – the black and blue of my shins was no longer as prominent. It was beginning to fade to a greenish yellow. Just in time because the next day I would have to wear a short dress again. It was our last day, and we were scheduled to go to a polo match in San Isidro. The cream of the "oligarchy" was there. The gentlemen were wearing striped trousers and gray top hats and had carnations in their buttonholes.

I checked out the ladies' dresses, then the satiny coats of the Polo ponies. Evita had assigned me another escort, this one a sportsman, an expert on the game. I was amazed when he told me what those ponies are worth. Before the official start, the Perons were driven round the course in an open carriage, like royalty. They were welcomed by the Chair of the Club and escorted up the steps of the grandstand to the Presidential gallery. People had their field glasses trained on them, and there was a storm of clapping. The game began, and my escort explained the rules to me, although what was there to explain? The teams hit a wooden ball with their mallets and drove it toward the goals at either end of the field. That was pretty well it. What was amazing was the way they leaned out of the saddle without falling off, and the way they sidled up to the opponent to head him off, or actually bump him and hook his stick, all the while keeping their balance. I got caught up in the general excitement even though I had no favourite team to cheer.

Between the chukkas, as the games were called, people strolled around, greeting their friends. I ran into Liliana and her husband. She was openly sulking. We had kept out of each other's way the last few days, which was easy enough. I had a busy schedule, and so did she. I assume Evita held her captive at the office, or else Liliana avoided me on purpose. But now that we were within a few steps of each other, she couldn't very well ignore me. Besides, Carlo did not want to ignore me. He greeted me cordially. It was the first time that he truly paid attention to me, I mean not just to my breasts. He looked me in the face. It was the effect of my new position. I had moved up a notch or two in his estimation now that Evita had given me companion status.

He beamed a smile at me. "So you are off to Europe tomorrow," he said.

"The chauffeur will pick me up after breakfast," I said. "In case I don't see you, I want to thank you both for your hospitality. It was very nice of you to have me."

"Our pleasure," he said. "Come again. You are welcome any time."

Liliana managed to squeeze out a few polite phrases as well, but she wasn't too friendly. She had learned her lesson. She had been burned once, when she politely offered to make me a present of the dress I got at Drecoll's, and I accepted it without qualm. And now I was going to Europe, while she was stuck in Buenos Aires. She was careful not to repeat her husband's invitation for fear I'd take them up on it.

11

The next morning, the European adventure began. We started for the military airport. A crowd of thousands was waiting for Evita there, just to wave good-bye. How did they even know at what hour she was leaving, when nobody had bothered to give me the schedule until the last minute. How did they get out to the airport? Did someone bus them here? Was it a pilgrimage on foot? They were pressing against the fence. From where I was, at the terminal waiting to board, they looked like a mass of bodies thrown up against the wire fence, multi-coloured, in constant move, a seething stew of people. I could see their waving arms and open mouths, although their shouts were only faintly audible, carried on the wind.

Three airplanes were waiting on the tarmac, one reserved just for our luggage. Mine had metamorphosed from one small bag on arrival in Buenos Aires into two large crate-sized portmanteaus on wheels and half a dozen pale blue leather suitcases, sitting beside them arranged in ascending order of size. Evita was bringing a room-size container full of clothes, as well as a photographer, her hairdresser Julio, her father confessor Benitez, who was supposed to go ahead to Rome and prepare for the papal audience, and of course her personal maid. The personnel travelled with the luggage. Father Benitez and two Spanish diplomats, the Marquis of Chinchilla and Count Foxa, travelled in the second plane with Juancito. I also had a glimpse of Pierre Adams and another security guard, but I couldn't make out whether they went with the luggage or the entourage. Perhaps Pierre was detailed to keep an eye on Juancito even up in the air.

The people at the fence were still shouting Evita! Evita! and throwing roses on the tarmac, but uniformed men had appeared now as well, forming a cordon and trying to disperse them as Evita and I got into a white convertible and rolled up to the third plane, which had the logo of the Iberian Airlines on it. I told Evita that it was my first plane ride. She said not to worry, I wouldn't even notice that we were up in the air or have any sense of the speed of travel. It was all very smooth and comfortable and air-conditioned, she said. The purring of the engine would put me to sleep at night. The seventeen hours would go by in a flash.

The pilot welcomed us on board together with the steward who would do chef duties, and a stewardess who'd be our maid. From the pictures I had seen of planes, I expected rows of seats, but the interior had been customized. There was a lounge with curved upholstered benches arranged in a round and a coffee table at the centre. Further down was a kind of booth with seats facing each other over a table, and behind the booth was the sleeping compartment with two washrooms separated by a dressing room, and two beds (berths, the stewardess said) screened with privacy curtains. The plane was a DC 4, the stewardess explained. She talked up the features like a real estate agent trying to rent us an apartment, although it was a non-place really and devoid of homey features.

We took our seats in the "booth". The pilot started the engines and lifted off. It wasn't as smooth a ride as Evita had promised. My stomach lurched as soon as we got off the ground. When the plane steadied, I made the mistake of looking out the round window at the city and the harbour below. Bile rose up and filled my mouth. I rushed to the bathroom and bent over the toilet, but all I could do was dry-retch. I had nothing to bring up because I had been too nervous to eat breakfast. When the retching stopped, I sat down on the toilet seat with my head spinning even though the plane was perfectly stable, and I could feel no movement at all. We had reached cruising altitude and everything was as steady as being on the ground, except for my nerves playing me tricks. My guts were in turmoil. I wasn't sure I could survive seventeen hours of this.

I thought Evita might come looking for me, ask how I was and comfort me, but she didn't. That put a chink in the platinum coating I had put on her in my mind, making her into some kind of idol. She wasn't a saint after all. Okay, perhaps she couldn't work miracles, but I had expected attention at least. I wanted to be redeemed from my friendless state. I wanted to be warmed by the sun of Evita's eyes. It is amazing how quickly I had become addicted to being noticed after all these years of neglect, how I craved her love and attention.

I must have sat on the toilet for half an hour, staring at the metal shelf with the soap and the mouthwash and a bottle of eau de cologne, each item with a little Argentine flag logo in blue and gold. Eventually my stomach steadied. I was left with only a slight headache. When I returned to the cabin, Evita was still sitting at the table in the booth, bent over stationary, writing. Her pen had the same Argentine flag logo I had seen on the toiletries in the washroom. When she looked up, I saw panic in her eyes. I couldn't believe it. Was she afraid of flying too? Perhaps she had only put on a brave face for me. But in her position, she must be used to flying! I sat down on the seat across from her. She looked up and said "No, come over here and sit beside me, *querida*." The usual force had gone out of her voice. When I slipped into the seat beside her, she held on to my arm with her left hand, while she kept writing. I saw that it was a letter to Juan.

"Don't believe a word those slanderers say about me," I read before she reached the end of the page and turned it over. She squeezed my hand, gave me a terrified look and continued writing. That anxious grip was unexpected. It was almost as if we had reversed roles, and I was supposed to look out for her and protect her. I couldn't see myself helping anyone in that way. I didn't have it in me. I didn't feel protective. That was her role.

I kept watching Evita, hoping for a pivot, for our relationship going back to normal.

She didn't seem concerned about hiding what she wrote, and I didn't have the strength to look away. I was alarmed. What was she afraid of?

"I adore you, Juan, my love," she wrote. "You are everything to me. I fought so hard to fulfil my dreams and suffered a great deal, until you came and made me happy. It was like a dream. I have never ceased to adore you for a single hour or to thank heaven and the goodness of God in giving me the gift of your love and I have always tried to be worthy of it by making you happy." It was soppy, saccharine stuff, but perhaps it was the Spanish language that made it sound so breathlessly romantic and old-fashioned.

"Juan, my darling, my beloved," she went on, "you have purified me of all my faults, because I live in you, feel for you and think through you..." I finally lowered my eyes. I couldn't stand another word of this treacle. I thought of what Juancito had told me about Evita's husband, his penchant for young girls, giving them rides and feeling them up. And Evita was writing this man a love letter, although this was more than a love letter. She was spilling her guts. She reached for a second sheet and filled that too with her large untidy handwriting, loops all over the place. The elation I had always felt in her presence was gone. I was so disappointed I could have cried. I couldn't stand the thought that she had fallen so far from her perfect state, that she too was needy and not loved enough by Juan.

I focused on the lines of her writing again, hoping it was just an aberration, a temporary weakness, that she might say something that showed her former strength, but it was just more of the same embarrassing stuff. Then she rounded off the letter:

"I didn't tell you any of this when I left because I was sad enough as it was and I didn't want to add to all of that."

Tell him what? I wondered.

"But you can be proud of your wife," she went on, "because I looked after your good name and adore you. Many kisses, but many kisses."

She sighed, let go of my hand and looked at me, as if she was coming out of a dream and surprised to see that I was there. Then she folded the two sheets into one of those white envelopes with the presidential seal and closed the flap.

"That's for Juan, in case I don't make it," she said. Her face was calm now, as if she had written the panic out of her mind.

"Why wouldn't you 'make it'? What's that supposed to mean?"

"You never know what will happen next," she said. "You can't change destiny."

"Are you afraid the plane is going to crash or what?"

"No, no, it's not that," she said. "I'm afraid for Juan. He is strong, but he thinks he is invulnerable, and that is dangerous. I'm afraid for my brother, too. He has no principles, doesn't take anything seriously, just wants to have fun. I wish you'd take care of him, *querida*. Won't you take care of him for me?"

"I can't promise that," I said, pushing back. "I don't really like him."

She nodded. "Thank you for being honest with me. Few people are." She kissed me on the top of my head. The look in her eyes was ineffably sad and broke down all my reservations. I hugged her, awkwardly, because we were sitting side by side, but she held me off.

"It's time for me to sleep," she said. I thought it was only afternoon, but of course the time on a plane is different, and I felt tired myself because I had hardly slept last night. Anticipation kept me awake.

The stewardess had made up our beds earlier and was keeping out of sight. I guess she bunked somewhere up front, in the pilot's cabin.

Evita went to her berth, kicked off her shoes and lay down, dressed as she was, turning her face to the wall. I followed her and stood in front of the cot, looking down on her. I didn't know what made her so afraid and sad or how to comfort her. I took off my shoes and squeezed in behind her, putting my arm around her waist and holding her tight. She didn't fend me off. Perhaps she no longer had the strength. Her body seemed frail. I felt the knobs of her spine pressing against my chest, her rib cage rising and falling against my arms. I was afraid of cracking her ribs if I embraced her too hard. I could hear her heart pulsing and, for the first time, I felt pity for Evita – not awe, not love, just pity. I nuzzled into her neck, breathing in the faint perfumy scent of her hair. She lay quietly in my arms, asleep perhaps, or just frozen with a fear I couldn't understand.

When I woke – it must have been hours later – with my legs twisted uncomfortably, she was still lying in the same position, on her side, her face turned to the wall. If she had not been warm to the touch, I would have thought she was dead. I moved quietly to my berth on the other side of the aisle. The droning of the plane put me to sleep almost immediately.

In the morning, or whatever time it was high up in the atmosphere, I woke to the smell of coffee. Across the aisle, Evita's berth was empty, the blanket only slightly rumpled. The curtain separating the sleeping area from the lounge had been pulled across. I couldn't see what was going on there, but I heard the clatter of china. The door to the dressing room opened, and Evita appeared, looking her old self, my idol, except that I had lost the pure faith I had in her now that I knew she was vulnerable. But yesterday's sadness and exhaustion were gone, as if wiped away or at any rate covered up, because I could see she had applied makeup and put on fresh clothes. Her hair was gathered in a knot at the back of her neck.

"*Querida*," she said, "now that you are awake, could you help me with the hair net?"

I crawled out of bed and helped her put a fine golden net over the bun and adjusted the combs that held it in place.

"Did you sleep well?" she asked, while I tidied her hair. We did a little polite dialogue of how are you but stayed away from explanations of what happened last night, the terror that had swept her and the letter she had written to Juan. She said something vague like "I am feeling much better this morning" but she didn't say what had bothered her.

"I have to be strong for the welcome reception in Madrid," she said, as if her will sufficed to make it so. She parted the privacy curtain and went through to the lounge, where the stewardess had already laid out breakfast and wished us a good morning. The letter Evita had written the night before was still lying on the table, by the side of the breakfast dishes.

"We will be landing in two hours," the stewardess said. She gave us the local time in Madrid. I slipped into the washroom and tidied up and changed into a fresh outfit before joining Evita in the lounge. We sat at the table across from each other, silently. Evita looked down on her plate as if praying, then she reached for her *cafecito*, drank it in one long sip, and started toying with the food. Finally she looked up and across at me. When our eyes met, I could see that she had her official face on, a commanding friendliness. She got up, reached for the letter to Juan, and put it into the folder in which she kept her speeches. We had planned to rehearse them one more time last night, but we never got around to it.

"*Querida*," she said, "I must ask you not to tell anyone about what I said to you last night. Will you promise me?"

"Tell what?" I said.

"How afraid I was for Juan and for my brother. It was silly of me to be afraid."

I studied her silently. I could see that she hadn't managed to get rid of her fear entirely. It was still sitting there, behind her confident brown eyes, casting a shadow on the glamorous smile spreading over her lips.

"Okay," I said, "I won't tell anyone, but I don't see what's wrong with you being afraid and worrying about your family."

"If you are in charge of a country, you cannot allow yourself to be afraid," she said. "You can't be a leader when you have fear in your heart. Remember that."

"I have no ambitions of being a leader," I said.

"You should," she said. "You have the strength, you have the intuition, and you have a feel for people."

I looked at her surprised. I had never thought of myself that way. I certainly wouldn't have described myself as "having a feel for people". I was in the habit of gauging people, but I was so often wrong about them or surprised or confused. I didn't think I had a talent that way.

"What do you want out of life?" Evita said. "Have you thought about it?"

Her demanding voice irritated me. I had no answer to her question. She had no idea how loaded that question was for me, all the circumstances that needed to be considered, none of them under my control.

"Graduate from high school and get into university?" I said. And even that meant fighting my mother. She wanted me to start working as soon as possible and get me off her budget. "We'll see what comes after that," I said.

"That's not good enough. You need to have a long-range plan."

Her voice was steely, but looking into her eyes, I saw that she was hectoring me to cover up the fear crawling there. Something was eating her, and she was taking it out on me.

"What's the use of long-range plans?" I said. "You can't predict the future. You said it yourself yesterday. And, from what I know, you planned on becoming an actress, and then you changed course."

"It all served a purpose. I learned to act, even if I didn't know my role then."

"So what — you want me to take acting lessons?"

She looked at me thoughtfully. "No, that's not for you. You don't like to act out your feelings."

She was right. I had bad experience with that. Every time I showed my feelings, I got punished for it. The only time I was rewarded was when I faked it. It was on my fourteenth birthday. I was upset because I had asked for a pet and my mother wouldn't consider it. Not even a gerbil or a turtle, never mind a dog which is what I had been begging for. Instead she gave me a cheap locket. When you opened it, there was a small photo of her on one side and the word "Love" in curlicue writing on the other. I looked from the bland smiling face in the photo to the bland smiling face of my mother expecting to be thanked and spun into furious blackness.

"Happy birthday, Mona," she said and made to hug me. Her words felt like a punch to my ears. I ducked her arms and howled open-mouthed. I lobbed the locket into a corner and ripped up the box in which it had come, tore it into little pieces and tossed them at my mother. We had a screaming match. She demanded an apology for hurting her feelings. I wanted to hurt more than her feelings. I wanted to pummel her. Instead I struck the coffee table, so hard that I cracked the skin on my knuckles and drew blood. At the sight of the blood seeping through the broken skin, I woke up from my anger. My mother looked stunned. It wasn't the first time I defied her, but until then I'd done it behind her back. This was the first time I stood up to her.

"I'll get you a Band-Aid," she said weakly. "Don't smear blood on the sofa. It's hard to get out."

I did apologize to my mother, but only after I thought of a use for the locket and a delicious revenge for my suffering. I replaced her photo with the picture of a dog and the curlicue inscription "love" with a bit of fluff I plucked out of a sofa cushion. At school, I told them a sob story. I said my dog had died. I opened the locket for everyone to see the bit of "fur" inside. I said it was to remind me of "Randy" and I was going to wear that locket forever. They were all over me, hugging me and making comforting sounds. Suddenly everybody was my friend. A couple of girls even shed tears for "Randy". I enjoyed the attention as long as it lasted – a couple of days. The experience confirmed what I already knew. It was best to fake sentiment and keep the real feeling inside.

"So what do you advise me to do?" I said to Evita. It was an ironic question. I was surprised myself. I didn't even know I could be ironic with her, but something had changed between us overnight in a subtle but essential way, after I had seen her weakness. We hadn't exactly switched positions, but she was no longer a goddess to me. Perhaps she had noticed it too.

"I may not be the right person to advise you," she said quietly, giving me a long steady look. "You have a talent for languages. Maybe you will be a writer?" Then she broke into a sparkling smile. "Or a companion for Juancito?"

I didn't smile back. "Definitely not," I said. "I told you I don't like him. And pushing me will only make me dislike him more."

"Then I'll bite my tongue. Is that how they say it in English?"

Our conversation was almost entirely in English now. She was a fast learner.

"In any case," I said, "don't worry about yesterday, about telling me that you are afraid. You don't have to put on an act for me."

She gave me another radiant smile, this one possibly sincere.

"Thank you," she said, and squeezed my hand. Sincere or not, her smile put me back into the love bubble and filled me with milky devotion. I didn't let go of her hand, until she pulled it away.

12

In Madrid, we were welcomed by a sea of spectators waving flags and bouquets of flowers. Guns boomed a salute, and Evita went into her luminous smiling and gracious waving act. But I was getting tired of that tableau, the breathless enthusiasm of the spectators, the dignified diplomats in their monkey suits, the painted smiles, the whole pomp and ceremony, repeated over and over, like a movie reeling off, like a play on its hundredth performance, with every step rehearsed and every line memorized. Watching Evita riding in an open car and waving at an adoring crowd had been exciting the first time around, but the show was wearing thin, perhaps because I was watching from the sidelines, because it wasn't my show. The ride through the streets of Madrid wasn't the worst part of the political theatre, at least there was excitement in the air. The official reception in the Palacio Real was worse: dodgy, dragging on, mind-numbingly boring. I was in back of the pack, the retinue trailing Evita as she nodded her way through a row of diplomats and their wives, shook gloved hands and made small talk. She herself was incandescent, wearing a white suit and a mink cape even though the weather was summery. I don't know how she managed to look so cool, how she managed to keep smiling and pretending to care. The ceremony finally came to an end with Franco pinning the Grand Cross of Isabella the Catholic to the lapel of Evita's suit. The cameras flashed. Then she was whisked out onto the balcony to show herself to the roaring crowd below. After that, the festivities moved outdoors. Dancers in regional costume were next on the programme. I couldn't take one more minute of it. I spotted Pierre in Evita's slipstream and sidled up to him.

"I'm tired," I said, keeping my voice low. "I'm not really needed here, am I? Do you think I could go back to the hotel?"

He kept his eyes up front. "Sure," he said without looking at me. "You can go back to the hotel if you want. I'll let Evita know."

"How do I get back to the hotel?" I asked.

"Walk," he said. "It's only fifteen minutes away. I can't talk to you right now, I'm on duty. I need to concentrate on what's going on, but anyone can give you directions to the Ritz."

I backed off and slipped away. No one cared what I did or didn't do, I realized. I could have left earlier. It occurred to me that I hadn't seen Juancito since our arrival in Madrid. He had skipped the whole boring routine. Smart guy. I wondered if he'd show up in the evening, if Evita had made plans for us. I wasn't keen on Juancito's company, but I was bored and you could count on him to liven things up. I wished Pierre would ask me out, but I guess he was Nancy's boyfriend now.

I walked out into the street and asked for directions from a passerby. The sidewalk was still crammed with people, but the crowd was thinning out now that the balcony scene was over. I walked along, hoping for something touristy to see on the way to the hotel, also a place where I could buy a postcard. I had written home only once since I left Toronto and not at all to Marco, as I had promised, mainly because the life I led and the people I'd met were hard to explain on the back of a postcard. The changes were so monumental they didn't fit even into my head. I stowed them all in the back of my mind for examination later. The stuff kept piling on top of the heap already there, crowding my thoughts. But there would be lots of time to sort it all out when I was back home.

I'm not sure what I expected to see on my way to the Ritz. As it turned out, that part of the city had nothing to offer me, only wide boulevards lined with old buildings and plazas with columned courts. All the shops were closed — on the occasion of Evita's visit, I was told. When I got back to the hotel, I asked for a map and tourist brochures at the reception desk and sat down in the lobby to look for what I had missed. Nothing. The buildings and the plazas were the main attractions. The avenue I had just walked, Paseo del Prado, was apparently tops. The brochure also listed the Fountain of Apollo and Neptune, which didn't raise my pulse rate, and the Prado, but I wasn't into museums.

The lobby at the Ritz was discreetly lit. The high ceiling and the semi-darkness gave it a cool, other-worldly look. It was as quiet as the nave of a church. There were a few people lounging on the blue velvet sofas and high-backed chairs arranged around glass tables. Although there was all that space, an old gentleman sat down right across from me and struck up a conversation. I guess he was as bored as I. He was wearing a tidy, old-fashioned gray suit and striped tie, but his face showed the untidiness of age, low-slung cheeks, droopy eyes with the lower lid sagging and exposing a red rim.

"I used to come here every spring," he said, "to get away from the London fog, but then the war came and put an end to all travelling."

I ask him a few polite questions about London.

"You are American?" he said. The pencil-thin mustache, which formed a black line above his fretted mouth, crimped a little.

I didn't bother to correct him. People forever confused Canadians with Americans, and I wasn't in the mood for chatting. Not with an old fogie. But he carried on.

"You Americans are lucky," he said. "You didn't have to go through what we did over here. The bombing, the shortage of goods, the constant threat of annihilation. And now that it's over and I thought I could pick up my life again and enjoy a peaceful holiday in Madrid, there is all this hullaballoo about the Argentinian first lady."

I only shrugged. I was done with the conversation, but he went into a rant about Argentina giving shelter to Nazis. "A rat line from Madrid to Buenos Aires," he said, "for those who can afford to pay the middleman. And America welcomes them too. They invited that man, Werner von Braun," he said, pointing a bony finger at me, as if it was my fault.

Really, I had no idea what he was talking about. I said nothing, I followed the complex pattern of the carpet, its grids and swirls. I let him go on.

"The market rules everything," he said. "It's all about money. Or strategy. Von Braun has the goods on the atomic bomb, so he is welcome. Argentina has wheat and oil, so Mrs. Peron is welcome, and they close the stores and offices to give the people time to gape at her and celebrate. Celebrate what? Corruption?"

He finally realized my total lack of interest and stopped.

"Of course none of this means anything to young people," he said bitterly. "How old are you, if I may ask?"

"And how old are you?" I asked back pointedly.

"Oh, I beg your pardon," he said, momentarily chastened. "I shouldn't ask personal questions." He gathered himself up with a grumpy decisiveness. "My apologies," he said, "and enjoy the rest of your stay here, young lady."

I too got up, swiped a few of the magazines laid out on the tables, and went upstairs. Evita's maid was there, tidying up, putting away the white suit and mink stole. Evita was back, then.

"She *was* here earlier, but she is gone again," the maid said. "She just freshened up and changed into evening clothes for the state dinner."

"How did I miss her?" I said. "I've been sitting in the lobby. I didn't see her coming through."

"They have a private entrance at the back for important guests, don't you know?" she said, shaking her head at my ignorance. "Those journalists would have crowded her to death otherwise."

"Did she leave a message for me?"

No, there was no message. Apparently I had the evening to myself. When the maid was gone, I called reception and asked them to connect me with Juancito. He was out. So no chance of having some fun. I didn't leave a message. Instead I called room service and ordered dinner. I was hungry and, when the waiter came with the cart, I was impatient with the fuss he made over serving it, unfolding a starched white tablecloth, laying out the plates and cutlery as if he was measuring out the exact distance between them, then lifting the silver lids from steaming plates like a magician revealing an astonishing trick.

I ate fast, swallowing the food without tasting much. It was odd how much I had enjoyed the bowing and scraping of the waiters at first and how quickly I got tired of it because it was just another routine. I was tired even of the royally decked out suite I shared with Evita. Why was she sharing a suite with me anyway – was she afraid of being alone? I missed having my own space. I missed being in a messy room without maids spooking around. I missed going to the movies with Marco, eating popcorn and making out with him in the back of the car, I even missed the catty talk of the girls in my class. I just wanted to be with people my own age even if they weren't my friends. My God, I thought, it can't be. I'm homesick! How soppy can you get? I wanted to push those feelings to the back of my mind with the rest of the freight I had accumulated in my head over the last few weeks. There was no more storage room, no space for added information. My head was stuffed, I couldn't take another thing, and it was better not to have homesickness inside me.

I finished dinner and sat down on the sofa. There was nothing to do. The stillness was giving me a pressure headache, the flawless order of the room was disheartening. I got up and turned on the radio, but the Spanish cadence of words and the Spanish music did nothing for me. I was hungry for the inflections and rhythms of North American music, the music that came out of the radio in our living room at home: Perry Como and Frank Sinatra. I hadn't missed any of that earlier because Evita's presence had kept my memories in check and so much was happening to me that I never had time to think of home until now.

I went into Evita's dressing room and looked through her clothes to revive her vibe. I tried on one or two things, unsure what I was looking for – the ghost of her fingerprint, a scent, but of course the clothes hadn't touched her body since they had last been dry-cleaned and ironed. In any case, none of her things fit me. I couldn't console myself with playing Evita, slipping into her persona. She was taller and slimmer than me. I made do with trying on her hats, but they only irritated me. I wasn't into hats.

I went back into the living room and leafed through the magazines I had taken from the lobby. I was still reading listlessly when Evita returned from the state dinner. I heard her warm voice saying good night to someone in the corridor, and I was instantly healed of boredom, of my longing for home, or whatever upset me earlier. I could hear the smile in her voice, but when she stepped into the room, she had no smile for me. She looked drained. She took off her ermine jacket and dropped it on a chair.

"Don't talk to me," she said when I got up to say hello. "I have to rest a bit first."

I slumped in disappointment. She wasn't treating me right. My mouth felt dry with discontent, and I swore I'd never wait for her smile again. But I immediately weakened, when I saw her lost in thought or just distracted by tiredness. She lay back on the sofa and closed her eyes. I sat down beside her and looked her over. Her face was beautiful in repose, but the symmetry was too solemn. She had dyed her hair a shade darker for the trip and put in red highlights. It seemed too vivid, too much of a contrast with the still, white face resting on the sofa cushions, although it did go nicely with her cream-coloured evening dress. It was a daring choice, off one shoulder and showing a lot of skin. There was a dark hollow under her collar bone, casting a gray shadow. It marred her beauty. The full skirt of the dress was trailing on the floor. She had slipped off her shoes, and I could see her naked feet. The straps had left marks on her ankles, as if she had been fettered. I lowered my eyes, or I would have cried for her.

For a while I sat staring at the floor, following the pattern of the carpet. Then there was a knock on the door. Evita's eyes fluttered open. She sat up.

"See who it is," she said to me, trying to compose herself.

It was Pierre, carrying what looked like a heavy suitcase.

"Oh yes," she said, "come in, Pierre."

He nodded to us and went through to her bedroom. Through the open door I could see him open the closet. There was a safe in back of it, big enough to hold a child – I had spotted it when I had gone through Evita's clothes earlier.

Pierre opened the suitcase, took out two steel boxes, and heaved them into the closet. From where I was sitting, I could see only his bent back as he was busying himself in there, putting the boxes away in the safe, I guess. When he came out of the bedroom, the suitcase looked light. It was swinging a little under his grip.

"All done, Señora," he said. "Jorge is on guard out in the corridor, and I'll be in my room if you need me."

After he had left, Evita said: "I didn't get to rest very long, did I?"

"Five minutes, maybe."

"Still, I'm feeling better," she said. "Come, let's talk. I need you to do something for me."

Not another favour! She had already asked me to make friendly with Juancito and to practice her English speeches with her, and the whole boring trip – trailing in her wake, sitting around waiting for her — was shaping up as just another big favour.

"What?" I said flatly. I did not soften my voice.

"Don't worry," she said, but I'd heard that phrase too many times, when there was plenty to worry about. "It's a small thing," she said. "I need you to go to Zurich tomorrow with Pierre and my brother and deposit two boxes at the bank there. Then Juancito will put you on the plane to go back to Canada."

"I thought you needed me in England."

"We had to cancel that part of the trip."

"Why? What's going on?"

"The diplomats were supposed to arrange an audience with King George for me, but he is not available on the dates I had in mind, and I'm not interested in meeting his underlings."

"But then this is our last evening together!"

She nodded and took my hand.

The ennui and the resentment I had felt earlier fell away from me. Suddenly there were so many things I wanted to say to Evita. I hadn't looked at her nearly enough or touched her enough to feel her essence, so that I could grow into someone like her. Her interior life was still hidden from me. I hadn't asked nearly enough questions. I didn't even have a chance to wear all the clothes she had given me. Not the fox stole, not the silver sandals, none of the coats because it had been too warm during the day.

In my confusion I could think of only one question. It had nothing to do with how I felt. I was just stalling, filling in the time until I could think of something more important.

"What's in those steel boxes?" I asked.

"My jewelry and some gold bars."

"Why do you need to deposit them in a bank in Zurich and why do I have to go with Pierre and Juancito? Can't I stay with you a little longer?"

She didn't answer my questions. She just said: "I want you to be there when they deliver the boxes to the bank. You will each get a key to the safe deposit box. To retrieve the boxes, all three keys are needed."

I could guess then why she wanted me to go along with the men. "The idea is to put a check on Juancito, right?

140

So he can't take off with the boxes or get at them later without you knowing. – But isn't Pierre enough guarantee?"

She sighed and reached for my hand again, pulling me close this time. I snuggled into her.

"I will try to explain it to you," she said. "The jewels and the gold are for an emergency. The two men in my life — my two Juans — don't know how to hold on to money. They love life too much. They want everything *now*. It is up to me to think about the future. What if there is a war, a revolution, illness, death? They don't think about that. I wish I could go to Switzerland myself but that is impossible. All eyes are on me, and this must remain a secret."

"And you think your secret is safe with the three of us?"

"It is sad to think that Pierre is the most trustworthy man I can think of at the moment – an employee who has been with me for less than two years. But he is a good man — the best at hand at any rate — I will ask him to deposit the key with my lawyer when we are back in Buenos Aires."

"Would it not be safter to keep one of the keys yourself?"

"No, it would not be safe with me. If Juan ever found out that I sent the jewels out of the country, he would try to talk me into giving the key up to him. He will say: If you love me, you must trust me. It is better if he knows nothing about this. And Juancito – he would find a way to take the key from me."

"You mean, steal it?" Or more likely take it by force, I thought. He was the type to use force if necessary.

"He would find a way," Evita said vaguely.

141

"What about my key? What do you want me to do with it?"

"Put it into a safe deposit box in a bank in Toronto until you hear from Luis Rinaldo, my lawyer. He will give you instructions."

"And Juancito won't find a way to get hold of my key?"

She sighed. "He will need all three keys to get at the boxes. You at any rate will be out of his immediate reach—"

"And you trust me?" The idea astonished me. I thought you had to be solid to be trusted, of an age when your mind had settled but before it started rotting. Nothing was settled in my mind. I was keeping my options open.

"Yes, I trust you," she said, "because I see love in your eyes, and because I see myself when I was your age, just as stubborn and needy of — I don't know what — money, men, love, everything."

It didn't sound like a very good reason to trust me. True I loved her more than anyone else. But was that enough?

"Keep the key in a safe place and give it up only to my lawyer. Luis Rinaldo would have been the right man to make the deposit for me. I have known him for a long time, when I was child in Los Toldos and he helped my mother after she was left a widow. I trust him completely."

"So why didn't you ask him to go to Switzerland?"

"I did. He said he was too old to undertake a strenuous journey like that. I didn't want to press him because I could see that he was not just making excuses. He is an old man, but he is loyal and he will write to you what is the best way to handle this. Or—" She hesitated and took my hand more firmly into hers. "-if after all you fall in love with Juancito and he with you, you can share the keys."

So that was the real reason why she wanted me to go along. To tie me to Juancito.

"You know I don't like him," I said and extricated my hand. "Why are you pushing him on me?"

"Because I am a romantic," she said, but it sounded like a question, and the romantic mood was over. She got up. Her voice was brisk all of a sudden. "I'll put in a wake-up call for you at 8. But maybe you should pack tonight. Wear a suit for the trip to Switzerland. I want you to look the part."

What part was that? I wondered. The part where I'm suddenly five years older, because that's how I felt, as if I had been replaced by an older and possibly wiser self, although I hadn't had time to digest everything I had seen and heard. Her words and my words were still all sitting in a heap waiting to be sorted out. Was my old self buried underneath, waiting to surface once I was back in my old surrounding, or had something permanently changed? I felt kind of make-shift.

"But let's not talk about practical things now, *querida*," she said. "Let's have some fun. We'll try on my favourite pieces of jewelry — one last time before they are put away. In any case, I should check that they are all there. I trust Pierre, or let's say I trust his intelligence. He knows he can't get away with stealing from me, but no one is entirely immune to temptation."

"Don't you need some of those jewels now, during your state visit?"

"Oh, I had duplicates made of them," she said. "They are such exact copies, nobody can tell the difference." She

143

disentangled a slim diadem from her hair and held it out to me. "It looks real, doesn't it? Everything I need, all the duplicates are in the small cask I brought with me. Everyone does it. It's too risky to wear millions worth of jewelry in public."

She stuck the diadem into my hair. "Have a look in the mirror," she said. "It suits you. You could have worn it tonight at dinner if you had come with me, but Pierre told me that you were tired of all the ceremony."

"I was tired, but not of being with you. Just of all that pomp and all the old men with their medals and their old fat wives."

She looked at me silently. I could tell I was disappointing her.

"We won't spoil our last evening talking about the importance of ceremony," she said. "I think you and I disagree about that. Instead, let's look at the jewelry."

I followed her into the bedroom. She asked me to open the zipper in back of her dress, slipped out of it, dropping it carelessly on the floor. Her slim body looked gorgeous in the silky, lacy white camisole. My love for her flamed up again and scorched my insides.

She opened the safe and took out one of the steel boxes. Inside were tiers of trays, each holding a necklace, some with matching bracelets and earrings. There were also two tiaras, one of them a duplicate of the coronet Evita had worn that night. Maybe she had dyed her hair a shade darker with glints of red because the simple spray of diamonds would hardly show against platinum blonde. In the bottom of the box was a tray with loose gems, some of them uncut.

She took the trays out, one by one, and spread the content on the bed, picked out her favourite pieces and put them on herself and on me. We moved the tilt-mirror from the dressing room and sat on the bed, admiring our jeweled ears and necks. As our two faces appeared side by side in the mirror, Evita changed into the teenager I had seen the first night I visited her, when her hair was in braids and she wore men's pajamas. Our hands were all over each other, as we hung more necklaces like leis, rearranged them, touching each other's shoulders and necks and arms and stroking back strands of hair to fasten and unfasten earrings. I was giddy with love, although I was in a panic because we were saying goodbye, and the more panicky I felt, the more I laughed, especially over the gaudy piece on the first tray, set with diamonds, pearls, and rubies. It was the same necklace we had looked at on our first evening together, when Evita promised to leave me a piece of jewelry in her will.

"The Bolivians gave it to me," she said. "It's worth a fortune, but the design is a little clumsy, isn't it?"

"So did they give you anything here in Spain?"

"A bottle of perfume by Dior — worth 4000 Dollars, one of the diplomat wives told me. She was probably advised to let me know. I'm not sure where it is right now, or we could try it out."

"And what's in the second box Pierre brought?

"Gold bullions. Want to see?"

I nodded. I wanted to handle the gold bullions. When would I ever have another chance to do that? They were not as shiny as I expected them to be, but very smooth, begging to be stroked. After we put back the boxes, Evita suddenly slackened. She had that on/off quality, like a mechanical toy, and now she had flicked the power switch.

"I'm completely exhausted," she said.

As she closed the door of the safe, the phone on her bedside table started ringing.

She answered it and started in on a long conversation. It was Juancito. She waved me off, and I retreated to my bedroom to give her privacy. After a while I heard her hang up and go into the bathroom. A little later she called me into her bedroom. She had changed into a sober linen nightgown and was sitting on the bed.

"Kiss me goodnight," she said, lying down and pulling the covers up to her neck.

"You want me to stay with you?" I asked. I was full of longing for her.

She opened the coverlet to me, and for a moment I had the velvety sensation of being fed love. I glided in beside her. I thought we would talk all night, but she fell asleep almost immediately, and I was left thinking long and despondent thoughts. I would never see her again, or not for a long time. Yesterday I had felt only pity for her, tonight I felt love again, and now I was sad for her and me. Better not let it linger, I thought, and slipped out of the bed.

As I reached to turn off the lamp on her bedside table, I saw the safe through the open door of the dressing room and idly wondered about the combination on the lock. Evita's birthdate? The equivalent of the letters in her and Juan's name, counting A as 1 and Z as 26? I was tempted to give the dial a spin. Then it hit me. I didn't need the combination. I replayed the scene in my mind: Evita putting back the two boxes and closing the safe. She was about to spin the dial when the phone rang. Perhaps she went back after the phone call and locked the safe. Or she was too tired to remember and it was still in the unlocked position.

I stepped across to the dressing room, careful not to make a noise. Evita didn't move. I reached out and tried the handle of the safe. It opened like Sesame. I flipped up the lid of the box containing the jewelry and looked at the Bolivian monstrosity in the top tray. She was going to leave me something like that, I thought. She meant me to have one of those pieces. I took out the necklace, switched the empty tray with one further down, closed the lid of the box, then the safe, spun the dial, and crossed over to my bedroom with the necklace weighing heavily in my hand.

The whole thing took no longer than a minute, but now I had second thoughts. *He knows he wouldn't get away stealing from me*, Evita said about Pierre. Maybe I wouldn't get away either. It was a stupid thing to do, but I couldn't put the necklace back. I had spun the dial on the safe and locked myself out. I was stuck with my loot, or as I thought of it at first, my souvenir. And where was I going to hide it? I tried a few places. I put it into one of my socks. No, that was so cliché and so obvious. How secure was my luggage anyway? What were the chances of anyone rifling through it? I had only a vague idea of what would happen to my luggage on the flight back to Canada. Were the people loading and unloading it unsupervised, did they have time to fiddle with the locks and steal something out of a suitcase? Maybe not. I wedged the necklace into one of my shoes, but it was too bulky and showed. Then I opened the hatbox and looked at the wide-brimmed hat nestled inside. I'd never unpacked it. I had refused

147

wearing it because I don't like hats. It sat on a wooden bowl which kept the shape of the crown intact. I lifted out the hat and loosened the stiff band surrounding the brim on the inside. I arranged the necklace in a circle, stuffed it behind the band and pushed the wooden form back in place. It was a tight fit — a near perfect hiding place. I replaced the hat in the box, closed it and finished packing up the rest of my luggage.

Then I lay down and thought about tomorrow, and beyond that about my mother, newly married, as I found out a week ago, when she splurged on a long-distance call to the Gutierrez house. John had come on the phone as well and said he was looking forward to welcoming me back as his daughter.

"Stepdaughter," I said.

"That's a long word," he said, which wasn't a bad answer, I had to admit. He was one of the more likeable boyfriends my mother had introduced me to over the years.

She will be gushing over all the goodies in my luggage, I thought. She will appropriate the dresses, no doubt. But I will hang on to the hat box with the necklace. It will be my own, I thought, my security against the curve balls she keeps throwing me. It will be my ticket to move out and do my own thing. It wasn't theft. It was an advance on the piece of jewelry Evita was going to leave me and a souvenir of the first evening I spent with Evita alone, when we looked at the necklace. And a replacement for the string of pearls she gave me to wear, which I lost almost instantly when I left the bag with my clothes in Juancito's car and somebody took it. Or maybe he gave it away carelessly, together with the book with Evita's name in it. No, this wasn't theft. It was compensation for what I had lost. It would be a charm, an amulet to protect me against being hurt by unseeing eyes.

In the morning I woke up to Evita's voice talking rapid fire to someone on the phone. There was nothing endearing in her tone. It was cold and imperious, and yet I felt a lurching pain in my heart, a dull throbbing beat between my temples. This was the last morning, maybe even the last time I would hear her voice. I thought about the necklace I had stolen and was consumed with guilt all of a sudden. Now that I looked at it in the light of the morning, I knew it had been wrong to take it. I'll confess to her, I thought. I'll give it back, and she'll forgive me.

I got out of bed, stepped into the shower and stayed under its hot stream for a long time, rehearsing my confession, putting it off a little longer, afraid to face Evita or even myself in the mirror. I needed time to think. I wasn't sure what to say to her, how to explain what I had done. "I took it because I needed something to hang on to when you aren't there to love me and hold my hand?" Perhaps, she would smile and say: "Keep it, *querida*." When I toweled off and looked in the mirror, the remorse showed: I looked like a sick animal. Anxiety was written all over my face.

Evita was no longer on the phone. The place had gone quiet. Now was the time to confess to her, but when I stepped into the living room, I saw that she was gone. A sheet of notepaper was lying on the table.

"*Querida*, it is too painful for me to look into your dear face and say good-bye. I embrace you in my thoughts. Evita." At the bottom of the sheet was another line, written in a hurry, an afterthought perhaps: "I send you my hairdresser."

I read her note, sitting down in the chair in which she had sat not half an hour ago. I'd missed my chance. Tears rose to my eyes, which had stayed dry through a lot of shit, the tirades of my mother when she was drunk, the put-downs of her rich friends, the schoolyard teasing. I had managed to stay dry-eyed through it all, and now I wept over lost love. But why think of Evita as lost to me? I will see her again, I thought. I am determined to see her again, and in the meantime, she "embraces me in her thoughts."

I was reading those lines over again, when the telephone rang in my bedroom. It was the official wakeup call. Maybe it was symbolic. It was at any rate a clarifying moment in which I summed up the situation in my head: my loss and my consolation prize, the necklace. That and the letter in Evita's hand and the note she had written me — things she had touched, which held the magic of her presence. They were more than souvenirs to jog my memory. They were charms that perpetuated her presence in a mysterious way. I was no longer sorry I missed the opportunity to confess to her that I had taken the necklace. I no longer felt guilty. Is a starving man guilty who steals a piece of bread? I needed those tokens of Evita's presence in the same desperate way.

I went to the bathroom, washed off the tears and straightened out the thoughts in my head. I looked into the mirror and saw the answer to the questions staring at me: No need to confess. You aren't guilty. And if you are, consider yourself forgiven. You can't be blamed for what you had to do.

In any case, I thought, why confess if you aren't caught?

Pierre

13

It is early morning. There is no one in the garage of the hotel, no one in plain sight at any rate as Duarte stows the boxes in the car.

It was a mistake to decline the bellboy's help.

"Let him do his job," I said to Duarte. "If you want to stay under the wire, it's best to stick to the routine. Anything out of the ordinary will attract attention."

But Duarte doesn't listen to advice.

"No way," he said. "I don't want anyone else handling the boxes."

Chances are the bellboy will remember our departure because he lost out on a tip, and the doorman will wonder why we didn't use a valet to bring the car around. Franco's security men also know that something is up. They have been asked to supply a bullet-proof car and discreetly cover us on the route to the French border. Too many eyes on us.

"So, how exactly will this work?" I asked Duarte after I was assigned to the job.

"We drive to Martigny," he said. "We transfer to a private plane, which takes us to the vault. We deposit the stuff. The pilot flies us to the Zurich airport. Done. We put Mona on the plane to Toronto. That's her taken care of. We take the plane to Rome and rejoin Evita there. Simple, no?"

"Simple, in theory," I said. "And why do we have to take the girl along?"

He shrugged. "Yeah. I don't like it either. But you can't argue with Evita."

So now we are wrangling the boxes into the car. Duarte gets into the driver's seat and takes the car around to the entrance of the hotel, where Mona is waiting for us. The bellboy puts her luggage into the car. Three large suitcases and a hat box. She has done well. Evita is generous when it comes to rewarding service. I don't know what service Mona was providing. I suspect it has to do with Duarte.

Evita's team has given Mona a makeover for the occasion, I see. She is wearing a beige suit and white blouse. Her hair is swept up and held in place with combs and enough lacquer to give it a sculpted look. The mascara and the makeup are impeccable, stage-ready.

Duarte is holding the door for her with mock courtesy.

"You look all grown up, *chiquita*," he says, leering at her.

She smirks and says with exaggerated courtesy: "Thanks, Juancito!"

Juancito. I'm glad I'm not on a first-name basis with the man. I couldn't get my tongue around the diminutive. There is nothing diminutive about that ape.

"So do I look the part?" Mona says to me, using her pouty teenage voice. It's a voice that roils me. It loosens a memory that is better left buried.

"Whatever part it is you are playing," I say.

"Being old like you guys," she says, looking at Duarte to see how he's taking it, but he is already getting into the car and pays no more attention to her.

I have been watching Mona with longing. It's a dangerous attraction, something that could be fatal, a fire I need to quench before it melts the core. I've come dangerously close before, when I got up on stage in the tango bar and sang to her, or perhaps I should say, to the memory of someone like her: Colette, irrepressible, full of wants and expectations that cannot be dampened by disappointment. *Cuando yo te vuelvo ver, ni habra penas ni olvidos.* When I see you again, there will be no tears and no forgetting.

I picture Colette the way she looked when I saw her last, in a hotel room in Brussels, drunk on champagne and the hope of getting away. When she threw back her head and opened her legs, she was no longer thinking of me. Her ecstasy was for the future, for the Latin lovers awaiting her in Buenos Aires. That was three years ago, and when I made it to Buenos Aires, I didn't look her up. I didn't think I had a chance. I belonged to the past. She was on to her next adventure. I'm not sure Colette got what she wanted, but I am sure that nothing will flatten the thrill of life for her. She is one of the fortunate who have no conscience and no regrets, who leave the

157

shipwreck of the past behind and head for the far shore. They turn their faces to the sun and are reborn. Duarte is one of them too - irrepressible, unwilling to take the past as an omen for the future. But in his case, it's stupidity, the inability to learn from experience. An enviable stupidity. I wish I could switch off my mind occasionally and get away from analyzing every detail, every nuance, from the relentless need to make inferences without ever coming closer to certainty, the terrible urge to draw conclusions – and that's what I'm doing now, talking to myself in my head: This girl isn't for you, Pierre. Just like the other one she reminds you of. Not that they look alike. Mona is slight, brown-eyed, dark-haired. Colette was blonde, her eyes light, almost colorless, her body too curvy, too fleshy to be graceful - a woman, not a girl like Mona beside me. But it isn't Mona's youth that attracts me, it's her voice - that questioning, disturbing hitch in her throat, the breath at the end, which keeps me listening for more. It vibrates excitement and makes everything else seem insipid.

We are off on the first leg of our journey to Martigny. Duarte is driving. Mona and I are in the backseat with the two steel boxes at our feet.

It's about 700 kilometers to the border, then another 800 to our destination in the Alps. Most people would prefer sitting back and be chauffeured, especially on a trip like this, with the road stretching ahead endlessly. Not Duarte. He likes to be at the wheel, in charge of where he is going and how fast he is going.

"No motorcade for us?" Mona says, leaning forward and putting her hand on Duarte's shoulder. An unmarked hand, childish like the gesture itself, half trusting, half asking for attention.

He ignores her.

"Hey, Juancito," she says, "are we no longer on speaking terms?" Her hand sneaks up to where his hair curls over his ears. He twitches her off.

"Shut up," he says.

He is all nervous energy. His head and shoulders keep moving in a jittery kind of way.

"The black car behind us?" he says to me, looking in the rearview mirror. "That's them?"

"Yes, Franco's men," I say.

"Are they supposed to protect us, or what?" Mona says. Her voice has switched into neutral.

"That's the plan," I say.

After that, the talk dries up.

Duarte is smoking non-stop. Usually he keeps up a patter, a bit of boasting, a bit of baiting. But he hasn't said much since we've left the city behind and hit the open road. After a while he starts fiddling with the radio. The local station plays folk music. He makes a guttural sound of disgust and turns it off again. I watch the distance markers by the side of the road.

We ride in silence, the watchful kind, waiting for something to happen. A lot can go wrong between start and finish: trouble at the border, a heist, bad weather grounding the pilot.

Beside me, Mona is fidgeting. I am keenly aware of her body next to me, the small movement that brings her hips closer to mine when the road curves and makes her slide away when it straightens again.

"This is going to be so boring," she says. "Talk to me, somebody."

"Why don't you go first?" I say. "Tell us your life story - go ahead." I'm smiling at her, making it sound like a joke, but I am serious. I want to know what made her the way she is, what makes her tick.

"My life? That would be really boring," she says. "Let's talk about yours."

"Yeah," Duarte says. "I bet he could tell us a few things, but he won't."

"Why not?" Mona says, turning to me, her dark eyes a bottomless shimmer.

"Because he is Security," Duarte says. "They get paid to keep their mouths shut."

Mona ignores him. "So what made you leave Belgium and go to Argentina?" she says to me.

"The war," I say. "The Germans occupied Belgium."

"And the Allies liberated it in 1944," Duarte says. "That's why he had to get out."

His spite is lost on Mona. She is too young to remember anything about the war. She doesn't understand the innuendo, what it means that I had to get out and couldn't go back.

"Do you miss Belgium? Do you ever think of going home now that the war is over?" she says.

What I miss is the old-world culture, the feeling of being surrounded by centuries of history. And the familiar sound of people speaking my language.

"I miss speaking my native language," I say.

"Come on," Duarte says. "You speak Spanish like a native."

160

"And English, too," Mona says. "You never make mistakes."

But language isn't made up of grammar. "Still," I say. "I'm a foreigner in Argentina."

"You mean because of your accent?" Mona says. "So what? Quebeckers have an accent when they speak English, and I don't think of them as 'foreigners.'"

No, that's not what I mean, but it's no use explaining. People don't understand what it means to let go of one's natural language. It is a kind of suicide, an erasure. I've lost the flavour of my memories because they are bound up with the words I knew first. I remember Colette in French, in a code that defies translation. She has become remote now, muted except when a sound, like Mona's voice, rings an alarm and shakes loose old memories resting at the bottom of my brain like dust on unused furniture. There are such moments, but the rest of the time I am an exile, banished to the loneliness of a foreign language. I miss the familiar idioms. *To drink like a hole. To cut the eyes from your head. To hit a rake.* I miss the poetry that accompanied the lyrical moments of my life, the intonation, the shape of words, the verses I learned by heart in school. They slip under your skin. You quote the first line, and someone nods in recognition and takes it from there, like a relay in which you hand a baton to the next runner. That race is over. I am on a new course. I tried to start over in Buenos Aires. I was determined to make myself at home in my new language. I read the Spanish classics. My God, I read the Spanish dictionary page for page, chewing each word like cud! I carefully listened to the rise and fall of Spanish voices in a room, in the street, in the bars. I listened to the tango lyrics for words that would match my feelings. I said them aloud, I sang them to myself at home, I tried them out on others at office parties. When people complimented me, I felt that I had made progress in making myself at home. I connected with them, at least while I was mouthing the lyrics, but I think it was the music that connected us. When the sound waves stopped, it was over. The words didn't do the trick, because there was no personal history to link us. Sometimes I wonder. Perhaps I am rationalizing and the problem is larger than finding the right words in a new language. Perhaps it is a congenital flaw of mine, an inability to be at home with other people wherever I am.

"Where did you learn Spanish?" Mona asks.

"I lived in Spain for two years before I emigrated to Argentina."

"And how did you end up in Spain?"

"It's a complicated story," I say. "So complicated that I haven't figured it out myself."

In the silence that follows, I think of the last time I was in Madrid.

14

1944.

Sitting in my hotel room in Madrid. The news coming over the radio: The Allies have reached Brussels, the Germans are retreating. I had no strategy to deal with that development, didn't know how to go forward. I certainly couldn't go back to Brussels now. Fear was clotting my brain. I was no longer a visitor in Spain. I was a refugee.

A year later, I had turned from a refugee into a fugitive from justice. But whose justice? What did I do wrong? There was a warrant out for me — Pierre Maye, collaborator. But I wasn't guilty of collaboration, I was guilty of naivete, thinking that culture was above politics, thinking that I didn't have to take sides. I'd been writing articles for the *Journal de Pays*. About my travels in Africa and South America. About history. About architecture. Should I have written articles about Hitler instead and denounced the German troops occupying Belgium? Lascelles, the owner of the *Journal,* wouldn't have published them. When the Germans occupied Belgium in 1940, he walked a fine line, maintaining a rightist slant just short of truckling to the new regime. He managed to keep the journal going, while others folded, shut down by the Germans. I began to write about music and sports, two areas in which one could still say good things about the Germans or, if you will, "collaborate" with them. By 1944, Lascelles could see the writing on the wall. The Germans were losing the war.

He called me into his office. On the wall behind his desk was a series of 16th century prints, woodcuts depicting bookbinders at work. Lascelles was a collector of print paraphernalia. On his desk was a business card holder made in the shape of an antique letter press. A tray of wooden type fonts was laid out on a side table.

"Have a seat," he said, stubbing out his cigarette in the overflowing ashtray.

I sat down, and he came around his desk to join me, as if I was a visitor rather than an employee. The gesture put me on guard. This is going to be personal, I thought. Maybe he's had a fight with Colette. Maybe she's told him about us. I wasn't sure what their relationship was — an open marriage? She didn't care about him, or not anymore. She told me as much. I suspected that she didn't care about me either. We didn't have that kind of relationship – loving or romantic. Mutual passion kept us tied up, but that could change any time. I knew Colette wasn't for keeps.

As it turned out, the interview wasn't about our affair.

"Colette keeps nagging me," Lascelles said. "That cousin of hers in Buenos Aires has written again — everything is better over there. No shortage of goods, no ration cards. And of course, no war. Life is fun: movie theatres, night clubs. So why are we staying here? Colette says. Let's sell up and go. Every night the same conversation: What are we waiting for? Let's move to Argentina. She is wearing me down."

He paused. I wasn't sure what he was getting at, what it had to do with me.

"So, you are thinking of moving to Argentina?" I said.

"Yeah," he said. "I'm giving it some thought at any rate. The problem is how to pay for the passage. It costs an arm and a leg. And then we need something to start over in Buenos Aires. I'm not sure how much cash I can raise even if I sell everything."

He wrinkled his forehead and looked at the bookcases in his office, full of valuable first editions, as if he was already toting up their cash value.

"And the journal?" I said. "You are going to sell that too?"

"No, not the journal. That's why I wanted to talk to you. If I leave, would you keep it going for me?"

The offer caught me by surprise. My first reaction was to say no. I didn't relish the role of a placeholder. I'd been a placeholder for Colette as well. She took me on as a lover while she was waiting for someone better to come along. Louis Lascelles was fifteen years older than she. Too old for her taste. She was on the look-out for someone virile, entertaining, generous. Someone worthy of her gifts. In the meantime she made do with me. But if they moved to Argentina, it was the end for us. I couldn't think for thinking of Colette.

Lascelles took my silence as hesitation and started flattering me. "If anyone can pull it off, it's you, Pierre. You've got what it takes."

"I'm not so sure," I said. "I'm a writer. Running a journal requires administrative work."

"I realize it means putting in a lot of extra hours. I meant to offer you a raise of course – if you are willing to take on the responsibility."

I pushed Colette out of my head to deal with the situation at hand.

"Be honest, Louis," I said. "You want to get out while you can. Things are tough. It's a bad time for running a journal, and it's going to get worse, a lot worse."

"Until it gets better. I'm old enough to remember how it was after the last war. 1918 was a black hole, but the economy recovered eventually. Things went back to normal. If that maniac hadn't lit the world on fire in 1939..." He sighed. "But that's neither here nor there. The war will come to an end, and things will improve, I'm sure of it, but I'm too old to sit it out. You are what? Twenty-six? You've got your whole life ahead of you. You can afford to wait."

When I was still holding out, he sweetened the pot: "I would even consider co-ownership."

That proposition got me thinking. I had money in the bank, which was worth less now than it had been a year ago. It was losing buying power by the day. A devaluation was looming. Why not put it to use and invest in the *Journal*?

"Now you got me interested," I said to Lascelles.

My mind was still hammering away at the one message: Colette is leaving. But something else was kicking in: ambition. I should have declined Lascelles' risky proposition. The war had gone badly for the Germans in the last year. It was anybody's guess what would happen if the Allies pushed them back. But I couldn't resist Lascelles' offer: the power that came with part-ownership and the position of editor-in-chief, to decide who and what gets published. He was offering me a chance to put my stamp on the journal. Lascelles had been educated in a Jesuit boarding school, and there had always been the smell of incense about his publication and his deference to tradition. I wanted to transform the journal into something more edgy, more avantgarde.

After that, things moved fast. Over the next few days, we hammered out an agreement and signed a contract. He sold up his belongings. Colette gave me the gift of a last, passionate night in a hotel, leaving me with the faint hope that she would refuse, at the last moment, to go with Lascelles. But they left for Morocco together. From there they sailed to Buenos Aires. The next issue of the *Journal de Pays* came out with my name on the masthead. Half a year later, the Allies liberated Belgium, and suddenly every editor who had not worked for the Resistance was on trial for "collaborating" with the Germans.

In a way I was lucky. When the Allies took Brussels, I was in Madrid, on an assignment I had given myself to get away from the daily grind: an article on bullfighting. My euphoria at the news of the defeat and ouster of the Germans was short-lived. It looked like the victorious Allies were setting up as arbiters in turn and I would have to answer in *their* court of justice. I had bent my views to German dictates and compressed my sphere of work to fit the rules of their censorship. I had done everything to avoid being closed down by their regime and nothing to protect myself. I knew there was going to be trouble. I didn't go back to Brussels. I thought I'd wait and see, stick it out in Madrid while the war lurched to its chaotic end. Half a year later, the Nürnberg trials opened in Germany. Belgium conducted its own investigation into wartime activities. As expected, I was on their radar. When the official summons reached me to appear before the court in Brussels, I refused to return. They tried me in absentia and handed down the sentence: guilty of collaboration. Six months' prison to punish me for the six months in which I had a say about the contents of the magazine, in which I had wrestled with the contributors, haggled with the censors, and got nowhere with my literary ambitions. The *Journal* was shut down. My investment was lost. I was penniless. The only thing I had left was the parental home in Brussels which I had inherited jointly with my stepbrother. The solution was to sell my half to Maurice. It was a good deal for him. I was in no position to bargain. He deposited the money into a bank account in Madrid and offered to ship my furniture, paintings, and books once I found a permanent home in Spain, but we both knew that was unlikely.

At the time I did what I had to do. I went through the motions mechanically, my feelings, my attachment to the house cauterized. I had reached the point where all sentiment dried up in me except for the desperate will to escape the judgment and keep out of prison. I felt no pain at letting go of the house where I had grown up. Perhaps I had already entered that phase of my exiled life, when speaking a new language suppressed the memories couched in the old or one's consciousness always lags behind what is going on. It was not until much later that I began to feel the loss. One day I woke up in my hotel room in Madrid, missing the view from my window in Brussels. My parents' house looked out on the Avenue de Tervueren, a broad thoroughfare lined with trees and a tram running down the middle, which fascinated me as a child. When I sold my half of the house to Maurice, I had no mental picture of it. I thought only of practicalities, of my father's foresight in buying a prime lot and building a house when it was still affordable. I thought only of what it represented to me as a refugee in Spain: a means of survival. The memories of Brussels came back when the heat of the transaction was over, when my immediate problems of survival were solved, and I was safe for the time being. It was then, lying in my bed in a shabby hotel room that I remembered with longing the façade of our house, which the architect designed on my father's request, the elegant simplicity which distinguished it from the traditional mansions on either side. At that moment, lying on the bed and looking up at the cracked ceiling, I missed the Avenue de Tervueren.

For the first few weeks in Madrid, before reality sank in, I had stayed at the Palace Hotel, one of the best in the city. In my mind, and sometimes even on paper, I kept writing reports, acting like one of the foreign correspondents I met in the hotel bar every night: Paul Kennedy of the New York Times, and little Robertson of the Evening Standard. I pretended to myself that I was one of them.

In the early evening, I sat in the lobby, which resembled the foyer of a Court house more than a hotel with its colonnaded passages in faux Regency style.

Choosing a seat with an unobstructed sightline, I watched the people coming out of the bar or stepping off the elevator – an international who's who. Ministers emerged, flanked by journalists crowding them, asking questions and being waved off. Businessmen spread their dossiers on coffee tables, taking thoughtful sips from a *cafecito* or a glass of manzanillo, while going through their files and making calculations. I saw gamblers who had been expelled from Monte Carlo, prostitutes eyeing the quarry of wealthy men staying at the hotel, and black-robed Jesuits – they seemed to be everywhere in Spain. South American diplomats greeted each other with gravity, shook hands, then stood close and tapped each other on the chest in a gesture that might seem pugnacious elsewhere but was, in Madrid, a sign of cordiality. They had a desire to touch the man to whom they talked. I watched military personnel, officers in khaki, with polished boots, purple sashes and medals from the war in Morocco, and one corpulent gentleman wearing dark-blue glasses, who resembled a Mexican Colonel but was a Parisian, or so I was told, negotiating business interests in French Africa. He was on the way up the ladder of success. Whereas, another fat little man with slicked-back hair was on his way out, after a coup in his homeland. Someone told me his name. He was the ex-president of a central American republic, but I had never heard of him before. We all recognized the true celebrities: the daredevil pilot Michel Detroyat, Mussolini's mistress who arrived with sixty suitcases, and the torero Manolete, ugly, skinny, dried out and brown like a cigar.

Manolete was the hero of the day. The local papers called him the most talented torero in two generations. He had granted me an interview, grateful for the international exposure, he said. I didn't correct him. I knew the *Journal de Pays* had folded, but I relished talking to Manolete and dutifully jotted down what he said – about the thrill of facing the bull, the rhythm of the *faena* which was like a dance, the roar of the crowd. He spoke of bullfighting with religious fervor, a devotee to an ancient rite that had the aura of a sacrifice. I would have liked to interview another man as well whom I had met in the hotel, who led a life more dangerous than Manolete's battle with the bulls: Michel Skolnikoff, a Russian crook in the service of the Nazis when they held sway in Paris. He was rumoured to have amassed a fortune in gold and jewels worth millions. I would have loved to hear his story but I was too late. The French resistance fighters, the *maquisards*, caught up with him. His charred corpse was found on a road in the suburbs. The assassins had poured gasoline over him and set him on fire.

For a while I clung to the pretense that I was a journalist gathering material for an article, but the dream dissolved as time dragged on and I was obliged to move into the small, modestly furnished room of a cheap hotel in an effort to preserve what money I had. Then came the notice from the Spanish authorities. They had received a request for extradition from the Belgians and were about to cancel my residence permit. I had thirty days to leave voluntarily, or be deported. For a tiny moment I allowed myself to think that it was an error. The notice was addressed to "Pierre Maye Adams" but I quickly realized that they had merely added Adams, my mother's name, according to Spanish custom. If I didn't act fast, they'd hand me over to the Belgian court. The scramble was on to find another country to take me in.

I had stayed in touch with Lascelles. At first we just carried on the necessary business correspondence, but after a while it turned into something more personal. I was curious how the adventure of emigration was working out for him and Colette. I still regretted losing her, but I had resigned myself to the inevitable. I admit I felt an ugly kind of satisfaction when he told me that she left him soon after they had landed in Buenos Aires. She wasn't a woman anyone could mark as his own by putting a ring on her finger. Custom and tradition meant nothing to Colette, ordinary life was insignificant in her eyes. The present bored her, I know. She lived in her longings. She was a shape-shifter, always in between what she had been so far and would be in future. When she left for Argentina, she wasn't looking for a new life, she was looking for a new self.

Apart from his private misery, Lascelles had managed well. He found his niche in the book trade. While looking for buyers for his first editions because he needed cash, he latched on to a network of collectors, and now he made regular trips to the US on behalf of a dealer. He also had plans of getting up an international journal with articles in English and French, he told me. He had already lined up backers. Buenos Aires was full of immigrants eager for news of back home, he wrote. They were keen on discussing the political ramifications of the peace treaties and to tell their own story.

"I need contributors," he wrote after I told him of my newest difficulties. "You could work for me, freelance at first, but eventually I'll hire people full-time. I'm trying to get in with the powers that be. I even managed to get an interview with Peron, a solid man, very sympathetic to my project."

My feelings about Lascelles were mixed. When I got stuck in Madrid in 1944, I thought of him with some bitterness. I wavered between blaming him for my situation and cursing myself for having been too ambitious. Sometimes I felt he had tricked me into investing my money in a sinking ship, at other times I exonerated him. Nobody could predict the future, a lot of people were eager to invest their money at that time, afraid that the currency would collapse. Lascelles didn't need me. He could have found other buyers. He hadn't put undue pressure on me to buy. I myself had been eager to direct the *Journal* and remake it into a first-rate literary magazine. And in the time of my need, when I was marooned in Madrid and under the threat of extradition, Lascelles offered me help. His good will was almost embarrassing, considering that I had screwed his wife. I wasn't a religious man. I had no moral scruples, but I liked Lascelles and felt, let's say, uncomfortable about the affair. So, who had wronged whom? I found it difficult to settle that question in my mind.

Lascelles urged me to join him in Buenos Aires. "What have you got to lose?" he wrote. "You are a hunted man over there. Sooner or later they'll catch up with you. Go to the Red Cross, tell them you lost your papers, and get a new passport under an alias. Then go to the Argentinian embassy and apply for an immigration permit. You need two guarantors to support your application. I'll be one, and I'll get you another. They are looking for immigrants here – engineers and scientists mostly, but they'll take you if I can get someone on Peron's staff to write you a letter of reference. I know a couple of guys there."

My back was up against the wall. I took his advice and went to the Spanish Red Cross. The queue of applicants for ID papers snaked around the block. My companion – a man I had paid to confirm that I was who I claimed to be – lit a cigarette and took a long drag, eyeing the crowd through a haze of exhaled smoke.

"This is going to take hours," he said. "I have a few errands to run. You mind? I'll be back in an hour."

His name was Daniel. I didn't know him very well. He was an acquaintance of an acquaintance, an out-of-work actor. He looked presentable and talked well. We had a deal: half his fee up front and the rest when he had testified on my behalf. We rehearsed my life, trying to anticipate the questions the people at the Red Cross would ask us. He took notes. He seemed intelligent enough to recall the details if needed. He was an actor after all. He should be able to memorize lines, I thought.

I watched Daniel walk away, feeling helpless. I didn't dare make a fuss and disgruntle him. I depended on his good will. When he didn't return after an hour, I wasn't surprised. I couldn't expect him to be an honest man. After all I paid him to lie. He had probably decided that the rest of the fee wasn't worth the trouble. I would have to go it alone.

When there were only three people in front of me, Daniel returned.

"Gave you a fright?" he said with a pale smile. "It took a little longer than I thought."

Then we were let into the building, an old warehouse. The caged lightbulbs mounted on the cross beams cast a harsh light. The rusting shelves, at one time stocked with merchandise, were filled with cartons bulging with papers. Stacks of files were piled on the wooden floor as well. The air felt short of oxygen and smelled of fear and unwashed bodies. A vein in my neck began to throb.

Half a dozen desks had been set up with signs indicating the language the clerk spoke: Spanish, English, French, Italian, Russian. There were lineups at each desk. We joined the one at the Spanish table because it was the shortest and the clerk looked too tired and harried to give us trouble. He was an older man with grey, thinning hair, a retiree from middle management perhaps. Daniel had warned me. Let's avoid the women clerks, he said. They search your soul, and they are better at spotting lies than men.

There was no privacy. We could hear the questions being asked of the couple ahead of us and of the people interviewed at the next table. Their dialogue served us as a kind of rehearsal. I looked at Daniel and saw with relief that he, too, was registering the questions and answers. The actor in him had come to life. He was learning his lines on the go.

When it was our turn, I told the old man that I had lost my papers. My briefcase was stolen. I told him that I'd been a freelance writer in Belgium and fled to Paris when Brussels was bombed in May 1940. From Paris I had made my way to Spain. I told him a version of the stories I had heard of people coming through the Pyrenees on foot, without papers, without money, starving. The clerk had probably heard it all before as well.

He inserted an application form into his typewriter and tapped out the information I gave him. He asked a few probing questions, for which I was prepared. Where had I lived in Paris? When did I cross into Spain? Daniel testified that my name was Pierre Adams and that I'd been renting a room from him for the past two years.

I explained that my residence permit was about to run out and handed over the deportation notice. "Maye" was my middle name, I said. Luckily the letter didn't specify the reason for not renewing my permit.

The clerk held up the notice. "Where is the envelope in which this came?" he said. He wanted to verify my address, but I had anticipated that. The address on the envelope was of course that of the hotel where I was staying.

"I threw it out," I said. "I didn't think I'd need it."

He nodded. The swivel chair in which he was sitting creaked faintly as he looked past me at the line of applicants.

"Come back in three days," he said. "If your application is approved, we'll have your papers ready."

Daniel and I went to the nearest bar. I stood him a beer and paid out the rest of his fee.

"You know," he said, "I actually enjoyed that. I always liked ad-libbing." He downed the rest of his beer. "I miss being on stage," he said. "Hell, I miss the audience and the applause more than the pay."

When I returned to the Red Cross office three days later, my new ID papers were waiting for me. I had a feeling of solidifying, growing into my reinvented self. The Argentinian embassy was the next stop in my transformation. I felt quite comfortable with the roleplaying by then. I said I was glad I had made it to safety and didn't want to go back to Brussels. I had nothing to go back to. My house had been destroyed in a bombing raid. I had lost all my possessions. I had no close relatives back home and wanted to move on, start a new life. Friends in Buenos Aires were willing to act as guarantors and take me in. I gave them Lascelles' address. He would provide them with the necessary references, I said.

Lascelles came through, and I started life in Buenos Aires as Pierre M. Adams.

Duarte is right. It's not a story you want to tell anyone, least of all Mona who hadn't lived through those times of upheaval in Europe and had no idea of the complexities of my situation. I have learned to keep my mouth shut, but that has nothing to do with being in Security. Life taught me that lesson.

15

In the late afternoon, we reach the French border. We show the border guards our papers. Duarte has a diplomatic passport. The men salute and wave us through. A few minutes later, Duarte pulls over to let me take the wheel. He decides to sit up front with me. I thought he'd prefer Mona's company, but this afternoon he is all business and no play.

"You should have arranged for a French car at the border," I say. "The Spanish licence plates are conspicuous."

"French licence plates may be less conspicuous but moving the boxes from one car to another would have been risky," he says.

A little later we approach a village. It's early evening. The setting sun leaves a copper sheen on the roofs, the fields are turning russet.

"What's with that guy?" Duarte says, pointing to a man standing by the side of the road ahead of us. His toes are practically on the asphalt. He is facing us with a fierce determination as if he wanted to step into our path and commit suicide.

Duarte reaches inside his jacket, pulls out a .45 and holds it on his lap. The steel of the barrel gives off a bluish sheen under the strobe of the streetlights. "Don't slow down," he says and rolls down the window.

As we come up, the man turns around. With a quick movement he pulls down his pants and moons us.

Duarte starts laughing, but before he can develop his laugh full scale, something splats against the windshield, like a giant bug. It's a rotten tomato. I flinch and the car veers slightly. Duarte ducks down into his seat as well, as if the missile could reach us through the glass. He swears under his breath.

He cocks the pistol and sticks the barrel out the window, pointing it at the man.

"Take it easy," I say, but he ignores me. I hear the crack of a shot and look into the rear window. The man is standing by the road, looking after us. The bullet has missed him.

Duarte gives me a look of black anger because I have seen him miss.

"You can't aim accurately from a moving vehicle," I say.

He rolls up the window and puts the gun away.

"What was that all about?" Mona says from the backseat.

"The Spanish license plates," I say. "Some people here don't like Franco."

"When are we going to stop for the night?" she says. "I need to get out of here."

"We aren't stopping except for gas," Duarte says.

We keep driving into the night. There are fewer towns now that we are nearing the Alps, and next to no traffic. We pass tiny villages, the black silhouette of a church tower showing against the night sky, a lonely farmhouse still and self-contained, giving the illusion of a simple life. Points of light float in the distance. Every so often the headlights of the car strafe a sign or a distance marker which throws back a metallic glow.

When we stop for gas, Mona gets out to stretch, sighing with the pleasure of unknotting her legs. While she asks for the key to the washroom, Duarte goes into the store and buys a bottle of the local hooch, pear schnapps. Back in the car, he uncorks the bottle and takes large gulps between drags from his cigarette. At that rate he'll be drunk in half an hour. I hope he doesn't turn violent, but from what I've seen, he is more likely to turn stupid. After a while he puts the bottle away, stubs out his cigarette and tilts back his seat. In a few minutes, he is asleep. I can hear him breathing – a rasping sound just short of snoring.

Looking in the rear mirror, I see that Mona has fallen asleep as well, slumped against the window.

Two or three hours go past. My attention flags. I wake up Duarte.

"I'm getting tired," I say.

He sits up and yawns, expelling an alcoholic breath. "Where are we?" he says.

"Getting close to the turnoff," I tell him.

We are both watching the road now.

"Here we are," Duarte says as the sign comes in sight. Mona wakes up when we change drivers.

"I feel sore all over," she says, rubbing her shoulder. She cracks open a window and lets in fresh air, a breeze carrying the scent of vegetation. "Look at that sky," she says. "There are a million stars."

The Milky Way is floating above us like a luminous cloud.

"Cut out the crap," Duarte says.

We are crossing the mountains now. He is in a hurry to get where we are going and takes the turns at a suicidal speed.

Half an hour later, we reach a dead-end. I can make out an airfield and the shape of planes. I check my watch. It's past midnight. We stop in front of a hangar, a steely hulk lit up with blinding arc lamps.

"It looks like something from outer space," Mona says. "Where are we anyway?"

Nobody answers. What is there to say? We are out in nowhere.

A man in a mechanic's overall comes out of the hangar and opens the gate for us. We park.

"Go inside," he says, pointing to a kind of shed attached to the hangar. "There are a couple of vending machines in back if you want something to eat or drink. The cafeteria opens up for breakfast at 6 in the morning."

"Go ahead," Duarte says to me. "I'll stay in the car and watch the stuff."

Mona and I go into the low-slung building. It's one long room. I see a cafeteria counter at the end of it, but no one is in attendance. There are vending machines, tables and chairs, and benches lined up against the wall.

"I'll have a coke," Mona says. "I don't want anything to eat. I'm just tired." – "Tired from doing nothing," she adds as an afterthought.

"Okay, make yourself comfortable," I say.

Mona drinks the coke, beds down on one of the benches with the curled-up looseness of a child and falls asleep again almost immediately. I pick up a couple of sandwiches and two bottles of beer and join Duarte in the car.

The sandwiches are stale.

"A few days old, I bet."

"So who cares?" Duarte says. He waves off the beer I've brought and takes a swig from his booze bottle instead. Then we lean back in our seats. I doze for a while, then fall asleep. When I open my eyes, the sky has turned a sluggish grey. Duarte is awake too. We take turns going into the hangar for breakfast. I go first. Mona is already up and sitting at a table with a tin mug of coffee in front of her and a Bakelite plate with slices of fruit cake. Her "Good Morning" sounds surprisingly cheerful. She is starting to enjoy her little adventure.

"This cake is revolting," she says. "Mushy. Sticking to the roof of your mouth. But I'm hungry."

The lacquered helmet of her hair has held its shape, but the makeup is pretty well gone, soaked into her skin. She excuses herself and goes to the washroom. When she comes back, her cheeks have a scrubbed look. She has combed out her hair and is a teenager again.

I get myself breakfast. Mona is right. The cake is awful. I go to the washroom, clean up and gurgle to get rid of the sticky sweet taste in my mouth.

"So what happens next?" Mona asks when I get back.

"We deposit the boxes in a bank vault. The pilot will fly us to location."

"Oh no," she says. "I'm not good at flying. Why did I even have to come along? Evita doesn't trust you guys, or what?"

"You said it."

"And I'm going to keep you two from taking off with the jewels?"

"Let's be a little more discreet," I say lowering my own voice. I look past Mona at the cook in the cafeteria, but she isn't listening in. She is busy at the sink and in any case she wouldn't be able to hear our conversation over the running tap.

"Oh, okay," Mona says and gets up from the table. "I'm going for a walk along the road, catch some fresh air."

I go out with her and take my turn watching the boxes. Duarte is standing beside the car and gives Mona an appreciative look.

"Hanging in?" he says to her in English – wherever he has picked up that phrase.

"Hanging in there," she says, giving him a sober look back.

The sun has come up over the horizon. A small aircraft is waiting for us on the field. When Duarte is ready, I call Mona. We hand the two boxes to the pilot, who stows them inside the craft. We board. It's a four-seater, Juan sits up front with the pilot, I take my seat beside Mona. We taxi down the field and lift off. As the plane climbs and goes into a wide curve, Mona starts retching. She claps her hands to her mouth. I hand her my handkerchief, and she bends forward and heaves into it, presumably bringing up the breakfast cake. Her eyes are tearing. She breathes hard and looks at me helplessly.

"What do I do with this?" she says, holding up the handkerchief, which she has folded over to conceal the mess.

I shrug.

She puts it down on the floor, digs into her purse, comes up with a paper napkin, and wipes her face, leaving faint beige and black traces on the tissue. I guess the makeup didn't come off completely when she washed up.

Duarte looks back once and says "Jesus!" under his breath.

"Sorry," Mona says, crumpling up the napkin. "I shouldn't have looked down."

She leans back and closes her eyes.

It looks like we are flying right into a granite wall, but at the last moment a way through opens up. We go over a pass in sparkling sunlight, dip, bank to the right, and glide along a shadowy valley. Then the plane levels off. We land and roll to the end of a narrow, bumpy airstrip.

Mona looks shaky as the pilot helps her down.

"How's it going?" I ask her.

"Not good," she says. "I'm feeling queasy." But she regains her balance as we walk across the field to the metal shed at the far end. A car is waiting for us there, a military-style jeep. The driver takes us along a winding gravel road.

"Could be a scenic drive if I felt better," Mona says, "and if you stopped smoking, Juancito."

"Shut up," he says.

She cranks down the window on her side and leans into the rushing air.

The road ends at a metal-studded entrance carved right into the mountainside, looking like the adit to a mine. The wind feels barbed when we get out of the car, as if the season had changed overnight, and we had skipped the spring and summer.

We walk through the door, which has opened at our approach - some technical alert and response. Inside the mountain, there is a reception area with another steel door at the far side, flanked by a pair of guards. They are armed with machine guns. A gentleman in a pinstriped gray suit receives us with a deferential bow. He seems out of place in this mafioso setting, a banker gone astray. He should be sitting behind a large, polished desk in an office in Zurich. His cheeks are the kind of rosy that doesn't tan. His neck bulges a little above the immaculate white shirt collar. He isn't fat, but substantial, a man with a good digestion and easy conscience.

He introduces himself: Reinhard Behrle. We shake hands. He asks us to sign our names in what looks like a guestbook, except that we also have to ink our thumbs and provide a fingerprint beside our names. Then Behrle looks at our passports and wrinkles his brow.

"I didn't realize that one of the parties is underage," he says to no one in particular. He avoids looking at Mona directly.

"Is that a problem?" Duarte asks.

"Not for the bank," Behrle says. "There is nothing specific in our regulations, although perhaps we should address that point in future." He speaks excellent English in a kind of sing-song that seems to be a feature of Swiss-German.

"So?" Duarte says impatiently.

"I mean if there is need in future for a court intervention, a juvenile may not have standing – depending on the jurisdiction of course."

"Don't worry," Duarte says, using the practiced phrase of evasion. "There will be no court intervention." There is a threatening tone to his voice. I notice his hands are fisted as if to say that any problem would be solved by him personally, without resorting to the law.

Behrle smiles amiably.

"Then let us proceed," he says.

He leads on past the guards, through a narrow door and a passage carved into the rock. The air is stale. Wall sconce with caged bulbs cast a yellow light on the concrete floor. A pipe runs along the wall. I can hear water trickling through it – that and our footsteps are the only sound. Duarte and I each carry one of the steel boxes. His breath is a little labored. We pass through another door guarded by men with machine guns and come to a round steel portal looking like the door of a giant washing machine. Behrle spins the wheel mounted on the portal, using the bulk of his body to shield his exact movements from our eyes. The guards step forward and help him pull open the door. Behrle waves us through. The room inside looks like what you would expect to find in the back of a bank. It is brightly lit, has a tiled floor, white walls, and a row of safe deposit boxes of all sizes sunk into the wall. Duarte and I place our boxes on a long counter in the middle of the room. All four of us stand close, watching Duarte open up the box containing the jewelry. The guards with the machine guns have taken up position at each end of the counter. Duarte takes out a fresh pack of cigarettes, but there is no ashtray, and Behrle says apologetically: "May I ask you not to smoke, Mr. Duarte. The air circulation here is limited."

Duarte puts the cigarettes back into his pocket. His mouth is crimped shut because he is not used to taking orders.

"Perhaps you could lift out the trays," Behrle says, "and I will check off each item." He has placed a list on the counter and taken out an elegant black and gold pen.

Duarte opens the box and hesitates. "The trays are out of order," he says and looks at each of us in turn. "Number 2 is on top."

Mona cranes her neck and says: "They are numbered?"

"Yes," Behrle says and points his pen at a small number stenciled in the corner of the top tray. "We will begin with Tray 2 then," he says and starts reading from his list: "One amethyst and diamond necklace set in gold, matching bracelet and earrings."

He looks at the items and checks them off. Duarte lifts out the next tray. When he comes to the fourth tray, we see that it is empty. It's the tray numbered "1".

Behrle, who has started reading the description, comes to a stop.

"The necklace is missing," Duarte says, as if we couldn't see it for ourselves and needed an interpreter.

No one says anything.

"Perhaps Evita decided to keep it back?" Duarte says slowly and gives Mona a questioning look.

"Don't look at me," she says. "How would I know?"

"She did say something about giving jewelry to the shrine of the Virgen del Pilar in Saragossa," Duarte says. He keeps looking at Mona and me.

It's a good thing I have an alibi. I was never alone with the boxes. Jorge and I picked up the suitcase at Airport Security and took it to the hotel. He stood on guard in the corridor while I was in Evita's room, putting the boxes into the safe, and he saw me coming out of the room with the empty suitcase. In fact, he opened it and checked that it was empty. He wasn't a man to neglect due diligence. The next morning, Duarte picked up the boxes from Evita's room and brought them downstairs to the car. He was the only one who had an opportunity to take anything, unobserved.

"You were with Evita last night," I say to Mona. "Did she take the boxes out of the safe and check the contents?"

She shrugs. "I went to bed right after you left. I don't know what she did later on."

"I'll talk to Evita when we get back," Duarte says. "We don't have time to deal with this now. We need to get back to the airport. So let's just strike that one from the list."

Behrle draws a thick line through the item on the list. We all initial the erasure and continue with the count.

"Everything else seems to be in order," Behrle says after we have inspected the last tray and counted the loose stones at the bottom. The second box contains no surprises. The gold bullions are all there and accounted for. Behrle signs the list to acknowledge receipt of the two boxes. We countersign. A clause at the bottom of the page says that this is merely to certify the quantity, not the quality of the items. Then Behrle opens one of the safe deposit boxes in the wall. He carries the key around his waist, secured to a metal belt by a long chain. He reaches for it as if for a concealed weapon.

Duarte places the two boxes in the safe. Behrle locks up with his key, then hands us each a tiny key, and directs us to take turns applying them to the lock.

Duarte looks up in surprise.

"Three keys?" he says. "My sister put me in charge of the boxes."

"These are my instructions," Behrle says. "I have the letter in the file here, if you would like to check."

Duarte wrinkles his brow. "Let's get it over with, then," he says.

We put our keys to the lock, first Duarte, then Mona, then I.

"The safe will have to be unlocked in the same sequence," Behrle explains.

Back at the car, Juan lights a cigarette, cupping the flame against the brisk wind. He exhales and says to Mona:

"Hang on tight to your key, *chiquita*." There is an ugly sneer on his face.

"I'll guard it with my life," Mona says and sneers right back at him. She is growing up by the minute. She undoes the top button of her blouse and pulls out a thin chain with a locket, a cheap, brassy thing.

"I'll keep it with Randy's fur," she says.

"What fur?" Duarte says.

"My dog's. We had to put him down last year. I still miss him."

If she is looking for sympathy, she's looking at the wrong man. He shakes his head and laughs.

Mona opens the locket. It takes some fiddling, but she manages to fit the key in with the piece of fluff that's there and to click it shut. She slides the chain back inside her blouse.

"Safe enough?" She gives Duarte a look that says, "I dare you to come back with snark."

"Okay," he says, momentarily cowed.

It's a good thing she is flying back to Canada because he will go after those keys, I'm sure of it. I may be first in line, though, and I won't be safe until I have handed the key over to Evita in Rome. I will do it at the first opportunity, but he will watch his chance to get at me, I'm sure of that.

We deliver the car to the airport in Zurich. One of Franco's men is supposed to pick it up and drive it back. Mona will fly on to Toronto. It's a long flight, with a pit stop in Iceland and refuelling in Gander — a long flight for a girl with a queasy stomach.

"Wait," Mona says to the porter, as we make our way to the counter to check in her luggage. "I want to get my sweater." Right there in the hall, she opens one of the suitcases. She shrugs out of her jacket, folds it into the suitcase, takes out a nubby sweater, slips it over her head, and pulls it down over her budding breasts. She gets curious looks from passengers and porters who have to make their way around Mona, crouching beside her suitcase.

"Come on," Duarte says impatiently. She ignores him. She digs deeper into the suitcase, fishes out a pair of socks and white sneakers and exchanges them for the high heels she is wearing. Then she straightens up, runs her fingers through her hair and tousles it, completing the transformation from Evita's helper to the girl from Canada.

"Are you done?" Duarte says. "Let's go and check in your luggage."

We see her to the gate. She turns to say good-bye. There is something flirtatious about the way she looks at us, circling, approaching as if to kiss Duarte, retreating in a feinting motion and putting out her hand.

"I didn't get to say good-bye to Evita," she says to Duarte. "She sneaked out on me yesterday, you know. When I woke up, she was already gone. Tell her from me: I love her, I really do."

"I know," he says, stubbing out his cigarette and grinding it into the terrazzo floor of the departure hall.

"And tell her: I hope I'll see her again soon."

"Not likely," he says, clamping another cigarette between his lips and flicking his lighter.

"Why not?" Mona says.

He gives her a blank look. The macho drains from his eyes and leaves them dull.

"Because she is dying," he says.

16

On the flight to Rome, Duarte is restless. Although we no longer have to dodge potential heists, his nerves are on edge. Although it's hard to tell with Duarte. He always has an air of contained anger, of barely controlling his impulses. He opens and closes his hands. He twists in his seat. Is he thinking about Evita or, more likely, mulling over how to get at the key in my wallet?

When the stewardess serves us drinks, he finally settles down.

"You know," he says, "that girl has ruined my day."

"Mona, you mean?"

"The way she looked at me when I told her Evita is dying. As if *she* was on her deathbed. I swear she's in love with my sister."

"She, and a million other people." They all idolized Evita. Mona was no exception. But there had been no need for Duarte to tell her that Evita was dying, not in that blunt way.

"Of course she was shocked," I say. "What did you expect? Why tell her at all?"

"Because it's a fact."

Because he is a brute.

"She would have found out soon enough," I say.

Yes, Evita is dying and she won't be able to keep the news out of the papers much longer. The rumours are flying already. The signs are there for all to see. She has lost weight. She is starting to look gaunt. Her energy is flagging. You can't camouflage cancer in the long run. Death is written in her eyes, at least for those who can read the message, who have seen death before. Mona probably hasn't. She was shaken when Duarte told her.

"She has a crush on Evita," he says. "You think she is a lesbian?"

"No idea."

"You know what I think? She isn't sure herself. She doesn't know which way she wants to be fucked."

I say nothing. I don't want to talk trash about Mona. I want to safeguard my memory of her. Maybe it's the association with Colette that makes me shy away from talking about her at all, as if saying her name gave away something private, something precious in my past that I do not want to surrender. Or maybe it isn't about Colette, and I like Mona for herself even though her youth makes her unknowable, fluid, unpredictable. Evita at any rate saw something special in Mona. She recognized it at once. It took me longer. She made no impression on me at first except by association, because I heard Colette's voice in hers. Mona isn't beautiful in the conventional sense and she makes no effort to be agreeable. Moody, stubborn, defiant without manners – that's how she comes across.

Nevertheless, there is something about her: a raw intelligence, a liveliness, an irrepressible will to get what she wants. Like Colette. And the thought of her body beside mine, the hours of proximity in the car, raised a desire, a longing to know how we fit. Like Colette.

"I don't know why Evita wanted her to come along," Duarte says. "And now she has taken the bank key with her to Canada. I wonder what her instructions are, what Evita told her to do with the key."

"No idea."

"What about your key?"

I have been waiting for him to ask that question. He wants to keep track of those keys.

"I have instructions to give it to Evita on arrival in Rome."

I can tell he is annoyed that she left him out of the loop, that he has to ask these questions and show his ignorance to me.

"I expect she will give it to Juan, so that he and I have one each," he says. He expects to be Juan's co-heir, to get half of the loot after Evita's death. His voice sharpens. "But why leave the third key with that little minx?"

I don't have an answer – in fact I have been asking myself the same question.

I don't think Duarte expects an answer from me. He is just talking to himself and doesn't know how to keep his mouth shut.

"I wonder if Evita thinks I'll get together with Mona. She's been trying to hex her on me, you know. Sometimes she has totally unrealistic ideas. Ideas you think will never come off, but then, somehow, she makes them happen. She manages to make a go of it. Not this one, let me tell you. I want no part of that girl. She is going to grow up and turn into a great bitch. Good luck to the guy who takes her on. He'll be in for surprises, some of them ugly, I suspect. I don't know why Evita thought she was the one for me."

So that's what this was all about? Evita saw potential in Mona and put her to use, as she always does when she recognizes talent. She tried to hook her up with Duarte. Did she think a 16-year old, even an extraordinary girl like Mona, could handle a bully like him? More likely she thought that Mona could sidetrack him with her mix of pouting, coquettish circling, and naivete, that she'd get him to drop Liliana Gutierrez, but still it surprises me that she was willing to sacrifice the girl to him. Or did she really believe that Mona could "save" her brother?

And who will save Peron when Evita is dead? He is going to go down with her. Peron is a good front man for Evita's ambitions. He knows how to posture, but he is too full of himself, thinks he is Napoleon and Julius Caesar combined, soaks up flattery, can't resist the good things in life. Meanwhile, the generals and the oligarchs have their knives out for him. Without Evita to rally the masses, he won't be able to hold out against his enemies. There will be a palace revolt. They'll topple him. But Duarte will go down first. He is a mindless thug. His blustering and his brutality have made him a lot of enemies. Without Evita to back him up, he won't be able to hold on to power for long. She did the right thing when she put him in charge of the movie industry last month. It's more in his line of business than playing Peron's "aide". Pimping starlets comes natural to him. It was also a smart move to get the gold and jewelry out of the country, stow it in a bank vault and triple-lock it, except that I think Duarte is prepared to kill for the loot. Once Evita is dead, he'll try to get hold of the other two keys to the safe. Mona is out of harm's way for now, but not out of Duarte's reach entirely. They have hired guns in Canada, too. The whole thing would make for an entertaining crime novel, if I wasn't a character in it.

"How ill is Evita really?" I ask Duarte.

"Who knows." He shoots me an ironic look. "Trying to figure out when it's time to bail?"

"Should I?"

"That's for you to decide."

I will be a man without a job in the near future. Would it be better not to return to Argentina, to quit now and start writing again? In French – Spanish won't do. My brain and my imagination are wired into French, but I can't go back to Belgium. I could try my luck in Paris. Is there an extradition treaty between the two countries, I wonder? Or I could go to the French part of Canada. Quebec. Nancy might sponsor me — if I committed to her. And there is the financial aspect of moving to another country. The money I have is tied up in Argentina, in my flat in the Calle Guemes. I own it, my *propriedad horizontal*, as they call it. Lascelles is my guarantor for the mortgage.

I don't relish the idea of letting the apartment go. It's small, but I'm chez moi. I have imposed my order on it. My books are there, a few paintings, the bits and pieces I've collected over the past two years. The idea of packing up once again and moving to Canada or anywhere else is not particularly appealing. And the real question is: if I need Nancy to sponsor me, am I willing to pay the price for yet another passport of convenience? Or inconvenience. Getting my papers in Madrid was a matter of paying an out-of-work actor and waiting for three days. Getting Canadian citizenship means coming to some arrangement with Nancy. I think of her body: clean, spare, hard. And her mind. She is so rational, so calm. She barely parts her lips when she talks. No, I don't think I can do it.

My relationship with Nancy was incidental at first, but a mutual need kept it going. When Evita put me on Duarte's tail, I made it my business to know who was who in Liliana's household. It was good to have an inside contact. I was thinking of the housekeeper, but she was a fortress of loyalty. I didn't consider Nancy at all. As a foreigner, she was as much an outsider as I. Besides, her sphere of activity was limited to the children. And she looked dull and inattentive to her surroundings. I was wrong on every count, as I discovered one night, when I was parked on the street waiting for Duarte to leave or be thrown out if Liliana's husband caught the pair in the act. They were playing a high-stakes game, the two of them, meeting at the house. Unless, of course, Carlos Gutierrez was turning a blind eye to his wife's affair.

That night, as I was parked in back of the house, Nancy came up to my car and knocked on the window. It was past midnight, and the street was deserted. I had spotted her coming toward me, ambling casually along the sidewalk like someone out for a walk. I wondered what she was up to — meeting with a lover, was my guess, but she wasn't dressed for a date. She wore solid walking shoes, the sensible kind, and a dress that didn't flatter her.

I watched Nancy approach — unseen by her, or so I thought. I had turned off the headlights and parked in the shade of a tree, out of the circle of light cast by the streetlamps. She caught me by surprise when she stopped beside my car and knocked on the window, peering in. There was no excitement in her face, no light of inquisitiveness. I couldn't second-guess her purpose.

I got out of the car and asked what I could do for her.

"I've seen you waiting for Mr. Duarte before," she said. "Are you his bodyguard?"

"In a way," I said.

"Then tell him that he should go about his business a little more discreetly," she said. "The whole household knows that he is having an affair with Liliana."

"Even her husband?" I said.

"That's what I'd like to know," she said. "Either he is blind, or it's in the interest of his career not to see anything."

I had underestimated Nancy's potential as an informer. I changed tack.

"I've been asking myself the same question," I said. "We should get together one evening and compare notes."

She laughed. "Get together? Are you asking me for a date? Next you'll tell me that you find me really attractive."

She wasn't as insipid as I thought. It was probably worth making a play for her.

"You mean I can't possibly find you attractive?" I said. "Why are you putting yourself down?"

She looked at me thoughtfully. "Okay," she said. "Let's get together."

We started seeing each other casually, when our free days coincided. She turned out to be a good contact. She had the right level of idle curiosity, and the inconspicuousness of the plain-looking. To my surprise

199

she was rather good company. She was never at a loss for words and sometime witty, but she had no charm for me. There was no spark between us.

"You've got an accent," she said to me on our first date. "Where are you from?"

"Belgium."

"And why did you leave?"

I gave her the official story, that I had lost everything in the bombardment of Brussels, fled to Spain and got a visa for Argentina because I had friends in Buenos Aires who promised to get me a job.

"You don't look like a bodyguard. But maybe I'm wrong. I mean there could be a good body under that bulky suit jacket."

She said it as if she was secretly amused. It almost sounded like a come-on, but the emphasis was on "bulky". She wasn't hinting that she was interested in my body.

"Are you carrying a gun?" she said.

"Comes with the job," I said.

We were sitting at a table in a sidewalk café. The drone of the city was all around us, so that we had to lean toward each other in a confidential way. Nancy had dressed up for the occasion, I noticed. She was wearing a blouse with a floral pattern and bouffant sleeves, a skirt that hugged her rather broad hips, and open-toed shoes. She had painted her toenails red. I wondered whether I was getting myself in too deep here. But she was agreeable company, and a change from the routine. I hadn't made many friends in Buenos Aires. I was vulnerable to friendly talk, dissatisfied with my life which had become so pale, so devoid of words, so scaled down to a physical routine. Nancy was a change at any rate, but I wanted to keep it at the game level, a game of questions and answers, a clever matching of minds, who could find out the most without giving away too much.

"What did you do before you became a bodyguard?" she asked me.

"I was a writer."

"You wrote books?"

"I did publish a couple of books, but mostly I worked as a journalist."

"What are the books about?"

"My travels in Africa."

"I'd like to read them."

Her interest caught me by surprise.

"They are written in French," I said.

"That's okay. I grew up in Montreal. We spoke English at home, but I went to a French school. Can I borrow one of your books?"

"I didn't bring them with me. I told you, I fled Brussels during the war. I barely escaped with my life. Taking along books was the last thing on my mind."

Nancy was getting too inquisitive, too personal. Turn down the volume, I thought. This isn't what I want in a woman. She is hip-heavy and flat-chested. She doesn't know how to make things exciting. I can't warm up to her. It's time to stop seeing each other. I thought I'd cut back gradually, let the relationship fade out. Then things got complicated.

Nancy lost her job.

"Liliana paid me the absolute minimum," she told me. We had met at our usual rendezvous spot, a café on the Avenida Cabildo. She moved her cup of coffee a little to the right, deliberately, as if she was making a chess move.

"I said I'd quit at the end of the month if I didn't get a raise. I thought it was the right time to put pressure on her. She needed me desperately because she was going to Europe with Evita. I thought it wouldn't harm to hint that I knew about her affair with Duarte. But that didn't go anywhere. I guess her husband knows already and doesn't care. And when it comes to money, Liliana is hardnosed. She said she'd think about it."

We looked at each other across the little table on the sidewalk, the canopy over the storefront cast a shadow over her face. I couldn't make out her expression. Was she just telling me the facts or was she working up something else, asking for my help perhaps? Although I didn't see how I could help her find another job.

Then Liliana found out she wasn't going to Europe after all, Nancy said. Evita had no more use for her. Mona had replaced her. She was Evita's newest protégée.

Nancy paused. I still couldn't tell whether she just wanted my sympathy or something more tangible. Then she veered away from the question of her employment.

"What do *you* think of Mona?" she asked.

"I don't know her well enough to have an opinion."

"You drove her home one night. I saw you drop her off at the gate."

"I drove Mona home because Duarte was otherwise engaged," I said, keeping my voice level. I didn't know where this was going. "We exchanged maybe ten words. It wasn't exactly a social occasion."

Nancy didn't let go. "So, on the basis of those ten words, what's your impression?"

"You know Mona better than I. What's yours?"

"She's sly, *viva*, as they say." She told me that Mona bought a dress in an haute couture salon downtown and put it on Liliana's account. There was an argument over the bill later when Liliana told her husband that she had made Mona a present of it because she couldn't very well ask her to pay. He shouted at her, loud enough for everyone to hear.

"Anyway," Nancy said, "when Liliana found out she wasn't going to Europe, she accepted my resignation. So now I'm out on my ass."

Nancy was plain-spoken when she was bitter or angry. Using crude language was her way of venting. Liliana had let her go, and I would have liked to do the same thing, but I had missed my opportunity. The situation had turned awkward.

"Pierre," she said, finally coming to the point. "Can I ask you a favour? Can you put me up for a bit?"

"For how long?" I said.

"Two weeks, until I've found something else. Or maybe I'll go back to Canada."

I hesitated. I didn't want to prolong our relationship, but I didn't want to be a brute and kick her when she was down.

She pleaded with me. "I'll make it up to you, Pierre, any way I can."

"I only have one bedroom. You'd have to sleep on the sofa in the living room."

"Maybe I'll have a look at your apartment first," she said, taking my answer as an agreement to let her stay with me.

She came and walked around the apartment, inspecting it as if it was up for rent and the final decision was up to her. She looked into the kitchen drawers, opened the closet doors, checked the bathroom. She lingered in front of the bookcase and read the titles on the spines of the books. I had taken the precaution of hiding the books I had written under my old name. They were tucked in behind the front row.

She bounced her hand on the sofa in the living room and said it was okay to sleep on.

"Thanks, Pierre," she said and kissed me on the mouth. I didn't resist when she pressed into me. I ran my hands down her spine, cupping her buttocks. She owes me, I thought. Her body was not unpleasant, her hair smelled nice. I could see she was willing to sleep with me as a way of making good on her promise to *make it up to me, any way I can.*

As we undressed, she said: "Do you have a condom? Because I don't want to get pregnant."

I did, but for a moment I was wondering whether I could go ahead, whether I could get it up with her. It was all so prosaic, so businesslike. She had no bedside manners.

"Don't put it on yet," she said. "I want to make you hard."

She was willing to service me, and to my surprise I got it up easily. I don't know why I had doubts about my ability to perform with her. You don't need to be in love to have sex, but afterwards, when she said, "Maybe I don't have to sleep on the sofa after all," I felt a dark pit of remorse opening up inside. I shouldn't have taken her to bed. Forfeiting my solitude in exchange for sex was a mistake, I thought with belated lucidity.

A few days later I found out from Jorge, my boss, that I had been detailed to join Evita on the trip to Europe as her personal bodyguard. Nancy would have the apartment to herself. It was a relief. I didn't have to share space with her after all, but I needed to take some precautions. She was nosy. She would go through everything in the apartment. I packed up what I didn't want her to see – my financial papers, the books I had written under my old name, anything revealing my past — and took the suitcase to Lascelles' office. I explained the situation to him and asked him to store the stuff for me because I had a house guest.

"How do you know *I* won't look at whatever you have in there?" he said, swiveling back and forth in his chair.

"You already know all my secrets," I said.

He grinned. "But you want to keep them from your 'house guest'?"

"She needed a place to stay for a couple of weeks, that's all. I couldn't say no, but she is the type to root around, and I don't want her to dig into my past."

I looked at the photo of Colette on the wall behind Lascelles' desk, her smooth plumpness, the predatory dark lipstick – another piece of evidence, a reminder of who I was once — less calculating, more passionate. I was on the point of asking Lascelles about Colette. How was she doing? But I didn't ask. It made no sense to have the past intrude on the present — not in my own mind, not in conversation with Lascelles or with Nancy. That's why I wanted to store the suitcase with him, my locked-up past.

On the day I left for Europe, I said to Nancy:

"If you move out before I'm back, drop the key off with a friend of mine." I gave her the address of Lascelles' office.

"*Radiolandia*?" she said. "That's a racy publication. You have a friend there?"

I was sorry I'd mentioned the connection and given her one more piece of information about me. I should have thought of a different arrangement for dropping off the key.

Duarte beside me is fumbling and bringing me back into the presence, the last leg of the Evita's European tour: Rome.

"I'm out of cigarettes," Duarte says and calls the stewardess. He scowls when she tells him they do not have Lucky Strike. You don't get those in Europe except in luxury hotels, he should know that by now. They were 20 pesetas a pack at the Ritz in Madrid.

"I guess I'll have to wait until we are in Rome," he says to me and settles for a pack of Philip Morris.

"Is someone from the embassy picking us up?" I ask. The Argentine embassy was hosting Evita during her Rome visit.

"Yeah, there'll be a limousine," Duarte says. "But I'm staying at the Excelsior. They'll drop me off there first."

"No room for you at the embassy?"

"Not enough room for my taste," he says. "I like to keep my distance from Evita. She's too controlling, you know what I mean?"

I know what he means.

"They put a shitload of money into smartening up the embassy for her visit," he says. "I saw the itemized list. They repaved the driveway, bought potted palms for the courtyard, reupholstered the furniture. And they billed us for fifteen pictures of Peron, gold-framed. They must have hung one in every room. Including the toilets. You take a shit, and there is Peron looking down on you! And get this – there was a public urinal at the corner down the street from the embassy. They ripped it out. Can't have ordinary Romans piss within a mile of Her Majesty, right?"

He laughs and looks across at me, checking my reaction. I manage a grin. There is something comical about all the fuss over Evita, a woman who ten years ago was a nobody, too poor to travel outside the country except maybe taking the ferry across the river to the Uruguayan beach. Now every step she takes turns into a triumphal procession. In Madrid they took her to a bull fight. They dyed the sand in the arena blue and white in her honour — the national colours of Argentina. There were more cheers for Evita than for the toreros. The people adored her. Of course she was up to her old tricks, carrying handfuls of pesetas to distribute to the children crowding around her car. One little boy said he didn't want her pesetas, he wanted the insignia on the hood of the official car. Evita had the chauffeur unscrew the little figure, "The Spirit of Ecstasy", and gave it to him. The spirit of ecstasy. What a name for a hood ornament. I suppose Rolls Royce will provide Franco with a replacement. She demanded to be driven to the slums and talk to the poor. She kissed babies, leaving scarlet lipstick smear on their cheeks. I don't know why she does it. There is no need to capture Spanish hearts. It isn't a popularity contest. Argentina is popular in Spain and will be as long as the wheat and the oil imports keep coming. I don't know what any of this means or what purpose is served by these state visits of hers unless it is to camouflage the deposit of her gold and jewels in Switzerland. Or perhaps it's the panic of seeing her life ebb away and wanting to live it to the fullest to the very end. Evita has always been imperious but I have never seen her so capricious, so insistent that every whim of hers be fulfilled. More flowers, more flags, more honours, more ovations. The illness blurs her judgment, I think. She makes mistakes. On the balcony of the Palacio Real she announced grandly: "I come as a rainbow between our two countries."

Nicely put, but when the masses gave her the fascist salute, she returned it. Well, perhaps, it was just a stiff wave of the hand, but that's how the papers interpreted it: a fascist salute. Not a good idea when Peron is trying to cozy up to the Americans.

The plane begins its descent into Rome. The city appears below us, the famous seven hills, the classic and the imitation neoclassic monuments, Mussolini's city until a few years ago, a republic now- for how long, I wonder. Will there be another strongman?

17

After landing, we are whisked through customs on the strength of Duarte's diplomatic passport. A limousine is waiting for us. Duarte tells the chauffeur to take us to the Excelsior, Via Vittorio Veneto. When we pull up, the bell boy springs into action, taking Duarte's luggage out of the trunk. The doorman, glorious in his maroon uniform and golden epaulettes, holds open the door for him. I have a glimpse of the lobby, marble, gold, crystal, a figure rising from a settee, a flash only, a movement dissolving at the edge of my vision, but it ripples through my brain and congeals into certainty: Liliana Gutierrez.

"See you, or not," Duarte says to me and heads through the door.

"The embassy?" the chauffeur asks me. I nod, but after he has driven a block, I tell him to pull over.

"Wait here for me," I say. "I'll be back in a few minutes."

I return to the hotel. In the lobby I stop for a moment to take in the coolness of the enclosed air, the quiet hum of voices. I survey the scene, just in case Duarte or Liliana are lingering. I watch the little unthinking movements of people in conversation, listen to the scraping of chairs by the window where a couple is getting up to leave. Then I cross to the reception.

"I would like to leave a message for Mr. Duarte."

The receptionist moves with the dignity of a butler. He opens a ledger, runs his finger down the list of guests. Their names have been entered in calligraphic writing, easy to read upside down. His finger stops at Mr. and Mrs. Duarte, Suite 601. He hands me a pad with the Excelsior crest.

"On second thought," I say, "I'll talk to him on the phone."

"Very well, sir," he says, and points me to the house phones.

The operator dials the room for me. No answer. "Mr. and Mrs. Duarte" are busy, I assume. It doesn't matter. I just wanted to double-check.

On the way out, I stop by the desk of the concierge.

"Would you remember the party in 601?" I ask him, putting my hand on the counter with a tip discreetly showing under my palm. "What does Mrs. Duarte look like?"

"Blonde. In her thirties," he says without hesitation. "South American. Her husband just arrived. He got a loving welcome. I hope he is more generous with the tips than she."

I walk back to the waiting limousine and tell the driver to go on to the embassy. Evita's ploy isn't working.

Mona hasn't sidetracked Duarte – no surprise there. But I didn't think Liliana Gutierrez would run that kind of risk. She must be crazy for him.

Near the embassy, we run into a roadblock, manned by police. Down the street in front of the embassy I see a crowd of protesters waving placards. They are chanting "Evita go home!" and "Peron Fascist!" The flowerbeds outside the embassy are trampled. The police keep a wary eye on the demonstrators. Then two men start throwing stones, and they intervene. There is a scuffle, but they want no witnesses and direct the chauffeur to turn around and take me to a back entrance.

"What's going on?" I ask him.

"The usual," he says. "Every day somebody protests something: the low wages, the high prices, the Communists, the Christian Democrats, what do I know. Under Mussolini they'd all be in jail. He didn't put up with that kind of nonsense."

Half an hour later I report to duty and am briefed on the schedule. The first day didn't go smoothly, Jorge tells me. Evita complained that the welcoming committee at the airport wasn't high-level enough. There were no adoring masses. There were also problems with the luggage. The black flowered silk dress and the white fox cape she had planned on wearing to the evening gala wasn't unpacked in time. She was half an hour late for the performance of *Aida* which had been put on for her at the ancient Baths of Caracalla. In the end everything was fine. The audience waited patiently and gave her a rousing welcome when she arrived.

"Let's hope today goes without a hitch," Jorge says to me. He always sounds hoarse, as if under a perpetual strain to make himself heard. "We are on schedule for the papal audience this afternoon. And *you* are scheduled for an audience with Evita right now. Don't keep her waiting. We want her in good mood for the press conference." He gives me a mirthless laugh. "Maybe you should do a Gardel song for her, you know the one, *Borra la tristeza, calma la amargura.* You are pretty good at tangos."

Erase the sadness, calm the bitterness. I wish I could work that miracle.

When I am shown into Evita's suite, she is getting ready for the show. Her assistant, a chunky woman with a motherly air, is putting the last touches to her hairdo.

"Thank you, Anita," she says. "I won't need you until the evening when I have to get ready for the banquet. You can do a little sightseeing in the meantime."

I wait for the assistant to leave the room before I report on the successful completion of our mission. The boxes have been deposited in the vault, I tell Evita, and Mona is on her way to Toronto.

"Good," she says, turning toward the mirror for a last check to make sure she looks perfect for the papal audience.

"There was a surprise, though," I say. "When we opened the boxes to check the contents against the bank's list, we found that Tray 1 was empty. It was supposed to contain a necklace. Señor Duarte thought you might have donated it to a monastery."

The muscles on Evita's neck tense, but she has her back to me and I can't see the expression on her face. When she turns back, her eyes are opaque.

"That's alright," she says. She doesn't confirm that she gave the necklace away. I suspect that Duarte took it and she is covering up for him in my presence, keeping the show-down for later.

"Anything else?" she says.

"The key to the bank safe," I say and reach for my wallet, but she holds up her hand.

"Keep it until we are back in Buenos Aires. It wouldn't be safe here in my suite or on my person. I intend to have my lawyer take care of it. I will ask Rinaldo to collect the key from you and make the necessary arrangements. In the meantime, don't let anyone know that you still have it—" She hesitates. "Not even Juancito."

"As you wish," I say. She has good reason not to trust him, especially if my hunch is correct, and he stole the necklace.

"And as we discussed earlier," she says. "Not a word about the mission to anyone."

She speaks quietly. She does not threaten and say, "or else you are a dead man," but her voice is hard-edged.

I nod. It is understood that I will keep my mouth shut. That comes with the job. I just wonder what promises Evita made to Mona to keep her silent. And if she has the reach to enforce her silence.

I don't like the idea of being saddled with the key until we get back to Buenos Aires, but there is nothing I can do about that. I will certainly not mention it to Duarte. He would try to get it off me one way or another. Of course, my key by itself won't do him any good. It's only a first step in the process.

"Did Juancito come here with you?" Evita asks.

"I dropped him off at the Excelsior," I say. I'm not sure how that announcement will go over, but it seems she already knows.

213

"Good," she says. "He took Father Benitez' advice."

That explains it. Benitez who made the arrangements with the Vatican wanted to keep Duarte out of the way, and it happened to suit him as well. He could meet up with Liliana there without a need for explanations. Rumour had it that Duarte was persona non grata at the Vatican. His scandals almost ruined Evita's chances of an audience with the Holy Father. Whatever the difficulties, she has prevailed. They are granting her a twenty-minute audience – only royalty is allotted that much time.

Her outfit is demure, fitting the occasion: a long-sleeved dress of heavy black silk, topped with a black lace mantilla. Franco's medal, the cross of Isabella, is pinned to the front of Evita's dress. It is the only piece of jewelry she is wearing.

She turns again to the full-length mirror, sighs, and reaches for a pair of black lace gloves. For a moment she looks haggard. Death is dulling her eyes, then she pulls herself together.

"Ready," she says.

I hesitate. Should I tell her of Liliana's presence at the Excelsior? I decide to let it go. She has more pressing concerns. Besides, she may know already that Mona wasn't up to the job of sidetracking Duarte and condone Liliana's presence in Rome to keep him occupied and out of trouble.

Downstairs, I join Jorge and the Italian security contingent. At the Vatican, Evita is welcomed by an entourage of Italian dignitaries dressed in their historic garb — gaiters, cloaks and ruffs. They conduct Evita through the apostolic palace, followed around by five Swiss guards with halberds and helmets. In the presence of the Holy Father, Evita kneels to kiss his ring, as is the custom. Then, uncharacteristically, she falters. Her face takes on a devout cast. She talks to the pope in a low and distant voice I have never heard her use before. Has she found religion, as people do on the brink of death? Ever since Duarte said it out loud — "she is dying"—images of grieving run through my head. I have heard that low voice before, in women who lost their husbands in the war and among penniless exiles in Spain. Despair weakens the vocal chords.

At the gala dinner in the evening, Evita is back in form. She is wearing her most sumptuous dress yet, a gown of cloth of gold, clinging to her body like a skin and matched by golden sandals with gem-studded heels. Her neck and hair are glittering with diamonds. Her honey-coloured hair is shaped into a pompadour and covered with a gold lamé veil trailing down to the floor.

I am stationed at the door to the entrance hall, keeping my eyes on her, watching the movement in the room. Her face is very pale against the dark lipstick. It is a face of suffering in spite of the smile she never relaxes until it too turns into a grimace of suffering.

The shadow of death is becoming more visible. It makes me lose my concentration. Instead of watching the room, I think of my own situation. I wish I could go back to writing. Maybe this is the right time to put together a memoir, "My Travels with Evita." But I would have to write it in French. I feel illiterate in any other language. In Spanish, the words do not function the way I want them to, I can't shift the intention of my words from one language to another. In ordinary conversation – sure, but not in a book that has to get across the right nuance without the help of body language. Perhaps if I regarded writing simply as a job and hired on with Lascelles?

I try to turn off the thoughts and focus on the room again. This is my job now. I am paid to watch Evita. I owe that job to Lascelles. He introduced me to his contact in Peron's office, the Head of Security. Jorge hired me. As a favour to Lascelles, and against his better judgment, he told me later. I didn't look like a guy who could do security. To his surprise I worked out well. He had been looking for someone more solid, someone burly, he said, but my brains made up for my lack of muscle. He looked embarrassed when he said it. Jorge isn't into compliments, even lopsided ones. In any case, I don't know why people equate a thick neck and bulging muscles with strength. My body has always served me well. I took up Greek wrestling and Judo when I was in high school. It isn't bulk, it's skill and training that make the difference. A sense of tempo and measure, and the ability to react fast.

The waiters are removing the dessert dishes. The evening is coming to an end. The hum of conversation is turning mellow, and my thoughts wander back to my writing career, or my failure to make a career of it. I'll talk to Lascelles when I get back to Buenos Aires, but I'm not sure I can work for him again.

Lascelles never got that international news magazine off the ground. He ended up publishing a tabloid, *Cinelandia,* a weekly magazine about movie stars. There are a few articles, but mostly it consists of photo spreads: starlets in bathing suits, baring their long legs and parting their red lips in a swoon of ecstasy. Their clothes are as skimpy and their poses as risqué as he can get away with. His office is decorated with out-takes from the magazine, glossy black-and-white photos, including one of Colette, reclining on a chaise longue.

"She is in the movies now?" I asked on my first visit, shortly after my arrival in Buenos Aires.

"Radio," he said. "When they need someone with a French accent. They produced a few episodes on Napoleon and hired her to read Josephine. She has a good voice, actually."

"So you are still in touch?" I asked.

"Oh sure," he said. "We are still friends. I give her a plug when I can."

Lascelles would hire me as a reporter for *Cinelandia*, but I don't have what it takes for that kind of job — the lack of discretion, the disregard for truth and accuracy. I wonder, could I acquire those skills? I am a natural observer. I segued into the job of bodyguard, because I'm always on guard, even without pay, looking but not joining, moving through the panorama, taking notes, keeping a journal. I like describing *choses vues,* "things seen," as Victor Hugo called them. There is a certain romance in distant watching and living in the slipstream of famous people. But there is no subtlety to the lives lived in tabloids, no texture, no hues or shadows. They are flat, monotonous, tailored to a formula. I want to write about my own life, as it was and as it is now, and what the war did to it, the world shaping itself around me and the years coming on like a changing sky, with drifting clouds at first, then great rolling billows, with a foretaste of rain and a semblance of fate. Those years have left me with a sense of dislocation, especially the events of the last two years — Peron's rise to power, the marches of the workers, women obtaining the vote —my God who would have thought that possible in Argentina! I realize of course that no one would be interested in *my* life. I'm no celebrity, I've never played the lead on the world stage. It will have to be about me *and* someone famous like Evita. I could sell a memoir with a title like "My Travels with Evita" or something a little snappier: "Evita and Me". I bet there would be multiple publishing offers for that kind of memoir. Evita is a subject that sells, her personality, her glamour, a presence that turns every event into a grand scene. The gala tonight was no exception- another of her miracles. Her eyes settle on the smallest detail and magnify it, suddenly making it seem important. She smiles her winning smile now as she rises from the table. The dinner has been a rousing success for her.

By the time I get back to the embassy, it is midnight. My room doesn't match the splendor of the public rooms downstairs. It is small and simply furnished, but at least I don't have to share, as I did at the Ritz in Madrid, where they put me together with Evita's photographer, a smoker of cheap cigarettes and a snorer. It's been a long day. I am about to go to bed when the phone rings. My watch shows ten to one. When I answer, the caller identifies himself as *policia*.

"Is this security?" he asks.

"Yes," I say. "What is this about?"

He is holding a couple in custody, he tells me. Mr. Duarte claims they are residents of the Argentine embassy. Could I confirm that he is the brother of Mrs. Peron?"

I wonder what kind of trouble Duarte is in this time. Illegal gambling? Public drunkenness? Brawling?

"Yes," I say, "that's correct. He is Mrs. Peron's brother."

"I'll let you talk to him."

Duarte comes on the phone. "Listen, Adams, I lost my key. Could you come downstairs and let us in? Luckily Liliana speaks Italian." His voice sounds entirely natural. He is a better actor than I would have thought. He pauses only slightly after mentioning Liliana's name, no more than it takes to draw a breath. I realize he has thrown in her name to prepare me for what I am going to see and already know: that he is together with her.

"We are at a police station a few blocks from the embassy. I asked the officer to phone you," he says. "We don't want to wake up the ambassador or Evita."

"You want me to come to the station? What's the address?"

"No, they insist on driving us to the embassy and verifying that we are residents there. Just meet me outside."

I get dressed and go downstairs. The night clerk is dozing at his desk. He sits up when I come through the lobby and gives me a curious look when I pass him to go outside.

A patrol car is parked at the curb. The officer is leaning against the car. Duarte and Liliana are standing beside him. He looks disheveled. The skin above his cheekbone is split open and smeared with blood. Someone has punched him hard. There will be damage, a black eye at any rate. Liliana's makeup is smudged with tears. Anxiety makes her look old and bloated.

"You know Mrs. Duarte?" the officer asks me.

"I do."

"But that's not the name on her ID," he says.

"I told you it's my maiden name," Liliana says.

"You happen to know the lady's maiden name?" the officer asks me.

"Gutierrez," I say. I assume that's the name on the ID, whatever she showed him.

He nods.

"*Bene.* I'll see you tomorrow at the station," he says to Duarte, and to me: "You make sure he understands."

Duarte understands that much. Italian is close enough to Spanish.

"Tell the officer," he says to Liliana, "if there is a fine, I will pay it now." He pulls out his wallet.

She translates. The officer exchanges looks with his colleague who sits in the car with the window rolled down.

"Tell him: I apologize for having only limited funds on me," Duarte says, counting out the bills.

Liliana translates. The officer in the car nods.

His colleague takes the money offered. "Next time, keep out of trouble, my friend," he says to Duarte. "Especially when you are in the company of a lady."

Liliana is smart enough not to translate that, and I hope Duarte doesn't understand it all. He isn't good at taking advice. I'm afraid he'll blow up and ruin the deal.

The officer gets into the car beside his colleague and sits there. They don't move off. I guess they are waiting for confirmation that Duarte and company are in fact staying at the embassy.

"Let's go inside," I say.

When I come in with the pair of them in tow, the night guard blocks our way.

"Excuse me," he says. "Who are these people?"

Neither of them looks very presentable – Duarte with his bloody cheek and Liliana with her makeup dissolving.

220

"Just friends of mine," I say.

"They'll have to check in," he says.

Duarte scowls. He is starting to say something, but Liliana puts a hand on his arm and I flash him a warning look. He closes his mouth again and drops the bravado. He realizes that he is out of his depth.

"I'm not taking them upstairs," I say to the guard. "We'll just be a minute."

"I'll have to report that," he says doggedly.

"Look," I say, "you know I'm security myself. And this is Mr. Duarte, Evita Peron's brother. I am sure she will show her appreciation if you are discreet."

He taps his pen on the desk. "I'll see what I can do," he says finally. "Write down their names for me and where we can reach them."

I write down the information on a scrap of paper and hope he will keep it to himself.

"They are staying at the Excelsior," I say. "Could you call them a taxi?"

"I guess I can do that," he says gruffly. "The whole thing is highly irregular, though. I'm putting my job on the line here."

He is flexing his muscle, but he makes the phone call. He knows he'll get his reward one way or another.

"You have enough money left to pay for the taxi?" I ask as we move to the door.

"I do," Liliana says.

The police car is gone. I walk them to the gate.

"I owe you, *che*," Duarte says, as we wait for the taxi to show up. "Anything I can do for you, tell me."

"I might be out of a job soon," I remind him.

"I'll get you a job," he says, clapping me on the shoulder. "You can do security for me."

There is a little pause, then he laughs. He knows that I am detailed to keep a watch on him. "What does Evita pay you?" he says. "I'll up the ante."

18

Back in Buenos Aires after Evita's grand tour, I found Nancy still occupying my apartment, still without a job.

"I bought a few things for your kitchen," she said. "A cutting board, a colander, oven mitts. I don't think you ever did any cooking in that kitchen."

"Not much," I said. "I usually eat out."

"And your books."

"What about them?"

"You said you didn't bring any books along when you left Belgium. But there are quite a few here." She looked at me with those calm eyes of hers that gave no hint of curiosity, and yet she wanted an accounting for everything until all the details came together and made sense to her, as if my life was a crossword puzzle she had to solve.

"I had to leave my books behind, as I told you, but I missed them. So I trolled the second-hand bookshops here and bought whatever classics I could find."

"I tried to read Proust," she said. "He is incredibly boring. Can you explain to me why that man is so famous? He goes on and on. Nothing ever happens."

"Except words," I said.

"I grant you he has a way with words, if that's all you are looking for. And then those volumes of Dostoyevsky. I read *Crime and Punishment*. Really depressing. I don't understand why the guy had to confess when he could have gotten away with the murder."

"Because he felt remorse?"

"His sister got to him, if you ask me, with her religious mania."

We left it at that. I was used to people being unsympathetic to my choice of books. I didn't expect any understanding from Nancy.

She said nothing more about finding another place to live, but I no longer resented her presence. After the smell of death surrounding Evita, after seeing death imprinted on her face every day, I was glad to put my arms around Nancy's sturdy body and settle into the permanence she radiated. She was solid, her upper arms were sculpted as if she had trained to hold on to me. I embraced her common sense and made love to her gratefully, enjoying the brief release from the besetting presence of my thoughts and from the compacted pressure of my job — observing others. Sex with Nancy was good, even if I thought afterwards that the bed wasn't wide enough for our two bodies.

We slipped into a routine. The passage of time cemented our mutual accommodation into something like permanence. I no longer questioned the arrangement. I came to realize that Nancy and I had interests in common.

We could be useful to each other. I had offered her a place to live because she asked me, and I did not see how I could refuse without looking like a cad. But now I needed her help in turn. The idea of moving to French Canada was still on my mind. Nancy was my channel to a residence permit and, if it worked out, to a passport. Of course there was a price to pay for that favour. I broached the subject casually. We were sitting on the sofa in the living room, in companionable closeness. She was reading a magazine. I slid my arm along the back of the sofa.

"Are you still planning to go back to Canada?" I said.

She looked up from the magazine and wrinkled her brow.

"Why don't you just say it, Pierre: I've overstayed my welcome." She looked straight ahead at the coffee table. "I'm sorry," she said without turning her head to look at me. "I didn't think it would be so difficult to get another job. It's because Liliana is badmouthing me. She won't give me a reference. I may *have* to move back to Canada. - Are you desperate to get rid of me?"

"That's not why I asked," I said.

"So why did you ask?"

"Because I was thinking of going to Canada myself. I want to live in a place where French is spoken."

She raised her eyebrows.

"Why is that so important to you?" she said.

I had a sense of déjà vu. Mona had asked me the same question. Was it really necessary to justify nostalgia for one's native language? I must be an outlier. No one else seemed to be obsessed with idioms, with the way a word rises, a sentence holds, a rhythm opens. I explained it to Nancy without much hope that she would understand. I

225

didn't bother to talk of the more esoteric elements in my longing to speak French again, the joy of playing with words, the importance of the way in which they are formed in the mouth, the sensation on my tongue.

Nancy inclined her head in a show of sympathy if not understanding.

"In that case," she said, "why don't you go back to Belgium?"

"I have nothing to go back to," I said. "I was thinking Paris maybe, but from what I've seen on the trip with Evita, Europe is in a post-war slump. There are no jobs. I'd better stay on this continent. Quebec is a possibility."

"I could sponsor you," she said. She was making it easier for me than I had expected.

"Thanks for the offer, Nancy. That would be great. I'll look into what's involved."

"I tell you what's involved," she said. "We'd have to get married. You can only sponsor family members."

As she said it, she moved away a little, toward the far side of the sofa, as if she wanted to give me space to consider my options or just to get a good, head-on look at my reaction.

So that was the price to pay for her sponsorship: marriage.

"*Would* you marry me?" I said, as if to tease her, but she seized on my words immediately.

"Is that a question or a proposal?" she said.

I looked at her steadily. I understood. It was an ultimatum. Either or. Her words pierced the comfortable setup we had. As we looked at each other, the veneer gave way and showed what was below — a tally of advantages and disadvantages. I did not want to look at our relationship in the harsh light of Nancy's expectant eyes. New contours had appeared in her face, a steeliness which I had never noticed before. I felt cornered. But I had no choice. I had to give her an answer and pay up if I wanted to go to Quebec, if I wanted to take up writing again.

"It's a proposal," I said.

She put her arms around me and gave me a chaste kiss. "But you haven't even said that you love me."

I was prepared to say that I liked her. But love? I couldn't go that far. I couldn't say the words.

"I'm not the demonstrative type," I said. "You should know that by now, but *I'll make it up to you in any way I can,* as you once said to me."

"Did I say that?" She looked at me thoughtfully.

"Besides, *you* haven't mentioned love either," I said.

"That's because I'm not sure."

It was relief to hear her say that, but why raise the question of love in the first place if she was unsure herself? She shrugged. "What does that word mean anyway?" she said. "You are a good fuck, Pierre, and we get along. That's more than most couples can say about their marriage. That's why I'm offering to sponsor you."

If she hadn't used the word "fuck" I wouldn't have known that she was upset. Her eyes were calm, but her crudeness was a giveaway. It bothered her that I wasn't in love with her. She understood the situation perfectly well. There was no need to spell it out: She wanted love. I wanted a passport.

For a few days after my forced proposal, nothing further was said about moving to Canada. I didn't want to appear too eager. Why show Nancy my hand? I knew that revealing the existence of a desirable object had already

227

put me at a disadvantage and invited her to manipulate me. Worse, disclosing things about yourself is intrinsically sensual, and I was not entirely proof against Nancy. Intermittently she seemed desirable, calming in the light of day, exciting in the darkness of the bedroom. I was also in sympathy with her investigative mind as long as she did not apply it to me. I discovered, for example, that she knew about the Swiss safe deposit. A rumour had been circulating in the Gutierrez household even before Evita's departure for Europe. Duarte must have blabbed to Liliana. She may have told her husband. The circle of those in the know widened. Liliana's chauffeur was in the know as well. Nancy heard him say something about the rats leaving the ship, the Perons depositing their money in Switzerland, and that was the real purpose of Evita going to Europe.

But the tabloids were saying that Evita had gone to Europe because she was seriously ill and wanted to consult medical experts there. "How much of that is true?" Nancy wanted to know from me.

I saw no point in denying what she already suspected. Both rumours are true, I said. Evita has terminal cancer, and she has deposited a substantial part of her assets in a Swiss bank. I no longer held out against Nancy now that our Canadian plans were firming up. I began to think in terms of "the two of us". But when the day came, when I put my signature on the marriage certificate and signed off on my application for a residence permit in Canada, I felt pangs of conscience again. The wedding vows were an aural smear. The visit with Evita afterwards was worse. Jorge was one of our witnesses. He had mentioned our forthcoming marriage to Evita. We had to appeal to her because I needed a birth certificate to get married. It was lost, I said – the church in Brussels where I was baptized had burned to the ground in 1944, the registry no longer existed. On a word from Evita, I was issued a "duplicate". She asked us to come to her office after the ceremony. She wanted to congratulate us in person.

The waiting room was crowded with wretched people marked by sickness and poverty. There was a long line of supplicants snaking up the stairs. We were conspicuous in our wedding outfits, I in a dark suit, Nancy in a virginal white dress and high heels. Jorge took us to the head of the line. We were admitted into Evita's private office almost immediately.

I was struck by the rapid deterioration in her appearance since I had seen her last coming back from Europe. She was skeletal, her face was drawn, her cheekbones sharply outlined. It was a warm spring day, but she had a cape with a fur collar draped over her shoulders. An aide standing beside her stepped up and helped her to her feet.

She stood with her shoulders sagging and slowly put out a hand to shake mine. I introduced Nancy to her. She made an effort to smile at us and say a few pleasantries. I had never seen her like this before. She had always been so voluble and so ready with a radiant smile. She kissed Nancy on both cheeks, but I saw her arms slide off Nancy's shoulders and her fingers tremble helplessly. The aide stepped up quickly and helped Evita back to her chair. She looked at him wordlessly and pointed at an envelope lying on the desk. He handed it to me.

"My wedding present to you," she said. Her voice was shaky.

I thanked her, but there was one more piece of business I had to settle: the handover of the key. It was not a good time, but there would be no other opportunity.

"Excuse me for taking up more of your time, señora," I said, "but there is a matter that should be taken care of before we leave for Canada. – You will remember our conversation in Rome. Rinaldo never got in touch with me."

I was not sure if the hint was enough. I did not want to be more explicit in the presence of her aide, but she nodded.

"Luis Rinaldo is not well," she said with an effort. "And I-"

She did not need to finish the sentence. And she herself was no longer capable of dealing with the situation. She looked as if she was going to faint. Her aide was alarmed. He stepped across to us.

"I believe we have to move on," he said in a low voice and ushered us out. The next petitioner got up, but the aide held up his hand. "There will be a ten-minute break," he said. "I'll call you when we are ready."

"What was that about?" Nancy said as we were going downstairs. "And what's in the envelope she gave you?"

I sidestepped the first question and opened the envelope instead. It contained the discharge of the mortgage on my apartment.

Nancy was impressed.

"Do I get half of that?" she said.

"You get *me*," I said. "Isn't that enough?"

She laughed pleasantly. "I'm not complaining," she said in her bloodless way.

So, the question of the key to the bank safe remained unresolved. I would have preferred to be rid of it. Things weren't going the way I wanted. For one thing, I was disgusted with myself, for accepting Evita's gift and good wishes on the farce of my marriage, but I blamed Nancy for making me perform and keep to the lines she wanted to hear. She made it taboo to say that this was a marriage of convenience. She did not believe in confessing inconvenient truths. As she said of Dostoyevsky's Raskolnikov: Why confess if you don't have to? I felt I was changing under her direction, that my outward actions led to an interior transformation. I didn't like this warped version of myself, but living with Nancy had established a structure that was hard to break out.

A month later, I sold my apartment and moved to Canada with her.

Mona

19

March and April are the meanest months in Toronto. Spring is supposed to happen and doesn't. Winter hovers, the temperatures take surprising leaps, leaving you with hope one day and dashing it the next. Yesterday I pushed back the sleeves of my sweater and thought about taking my winter coat to the cleaner's. I stood at the window and watched the kids next door playing street hockey. They were in their T-shirts, passing a puck between them. It smacked into the curb, sending up a spray of salt water and crumbling ice.

No, it's too early to celebrate spring, but I have a special date coming up: April 12. Generally, I don't care about anniversaries and the like. I hate family gatherings, with everybody putting on a greased smile, or birthday parties with the ritual exchange of presents no one needs or wants. Or let's just say, my mother has never given me anything I didn't immediately want to return or exchange. She probably feels the same way about my presents. Not to mention that I'm expected to come up with presents for John, who has stuck it out with her for five years now. As far as I can see, he doesn't want anything he can't buy for himself, although he does deserve a medal for hanging in, and perhaps that's something to celebrate. But for me there is only one day that counts: April 12, 1947, when I met Evita. That date invariably makes me run hot with unfulfilled love and cold with the thought of unfulfilled promises to myself.

I have failed to live up to my model. Six years later, I have not become a second Evita. Not even remotely. I haven't stuck with my imperfect husband the way she stuck with Juan. I am certainly not glamorous. I haven't made anything of myself so far and have serious doubts about my future. I don't know that doing an MA in English literature will take me any place I want to be. So far, my studies have had only one effect – lit crit is interfering with my memories. Instead of taking them as they come, I make them the subject of close readings, the text of my life. I go over every line, every minute of my time with Evita, checking the story arc and improving it by cutting out the festering parts. When I remember my trip to Argentina now, it is as a series of diary entries that need reshaping into a good story. My pre-English, unstructured memories were awkward, even painful. Once I got into the rewrite, I immediately realized: the scene at the Zurich airport had to go. I couldn't bear the aural devastation of Juancito's words "She is dying." He said it so casually. He didn't change the tone of his voice or soften his look even when I howled and dug my nails into his arm and Pierre pulled me off and held me tight like a lover and stroked my hair and steadied me with his own body until I calmed down and saw the uselessness of questioning death. I understood that much immediately. I knew I must cut out all thought of Evita's illness and shape the story of my time with her into something more useable. Each flashback should come with a new significance, a new perspective. That was the point, wasn't it? You relive your life ever so often to make it fit into the continuing narrative.

That's what my academic training has done to me. It interferes with common sense. I see all my thoughts and actions in the light of literary criticism. I have to ask myself: Is that why I moved out on Phil, because I thought his character no longer fit the story line? And why was I sure that my marriage could never have a happy ending — because happy endings are considered cheesy by critics? But no, I started on that kind of analysis before I ever took a course in English literature. I started years ago to rearrange the story of my life. It began on the plane flying back to Toronto. No, the irreversible shift in the arrangement of my brain cells began even earlier, in New York when Anne took me to the harbour, when I decided never to be humiliated again, and it gelled into determination when I entered the circle of Evita's light.

There was plenty of time to think about my life on the long flight home from Zurich six years ago and during the first stop in Iceland, where the northern lights made for a never-ending day, and the next morning when we sighted land again over Labrador and I saw the milky, turquoise sea and patches of rock and soil through the torn clouds. I was afraid I'd be fighting nausea the whole time, as I did on my first flight with Evita and again on the short flight to the vault in the Swiss Alps, but I felt alright. It had probably been a case of nerves, or the novelty of the experience that made me sick the first couple of times. And when I puked into Pierre's handkerchief, I had reason to be unnerved. Besides, it was a small plane and a choppy flight on account of the weather. By the third time I had gotten the hang of it.

My stomach didn't rebel even though I was off balance when I boarded in Zurich. When the plane rose into the air, I looked at the clouds and let their gray softness expand into my breast and the monotonous noise of the engines blur my bodily sensations and put me into a kind of trance. I watched the shadows of the night rising gradually from the ocean. The distancing from time and space felt like an escape, an out-of-body experience.

I concentrated my thoughts and right then, looking out on the bank of clouds, I began to alter the story of my life. I made Juancito's words at the airport fade to black and instead thought of the bits I could rehash without regret, meeting Pierre, for example — "Evita's spy," as Juancito called him. But those memories proved intractable as well because they ended up with Juancito saying "she is dying" and Pierre hugging me, his hand rubbing my back, his reassuring voice. Of course, the calm steadiness of his voice didn't change the facts. I couldn't quite pull off the trick of altering the story of my life. The words and gestures went into an endless loop. I fell into a kind of narrative addiction, caught up in that scene, with the same words and gestures over and over again, until the plane crossed Lake Ontario and landed at Malton Airport in Toronto.

John picked me up and eyed the three suitcases and the hatbox on the luggage cart. "Whoa," he said, "that's a lot of luggage." But he didn't ask any questions.

My mother hadn't come with him. I guess she had to stay home and fortify herself against my return with a couple of drinks. I could smell it on her breath when we got to the house and she gave me a welcome peck on the cheek.

"What's with all the luggage?" she said.

"Presents from Evita Peron," I said.

"What happened to that little suitcase I lent you with the decals from all the places I had been to?"

"I threw it out," I said. "It was garbage."

"Oh sure," she said. "You can afford throwing stuff out, especially my stuff. You heard that, John?"

John said nothing, either because he wanted to keep out of the argument or because he needed his breath to wrestle the suitcases upstairs and into my room. My mother followed us and stood in the door, watching me unpack. When she saw the fancy dresses, coats, and shoes Evita (or more likely, the ladies at Drecoll's) had chosen for me, she stepped into the room and started gushing.

"Oh my God," she kept saying as she picked up the dresses and jackets and skirts one by one. "Did Liliana give you these things?"

"No, they are presents from Evita to make me fit in when I went with her to Europe."

"Lucky you! Look at this, oh my God, I love that pea green jacket. And that cocktail dress – to die for!"

"You can have them all," I said. "Where would I wear this stuff anyway? It's not as if I am going to a prom every week."

"You mean it?" my mother said. She was all smiles now, looking at me with warm, alcoholic enthusiasm. "But of course you're right. These dresses aren't suitable for a girl your age. Not at all." She lifted the pieces up and admired them again. "But they'll be okay for me," she said. "—if you really don't want them." She lowered her eyes to conceal her excitement. She was embarrassed by her own greediness and trying hard to curb her enthusiasm.

"I'll have to have them altered, of course," she said as if she was reluctant and as if letting out the seams was against her principles. She was just covering up her eagerness. Or maybe she did feel uneasy because she stopped midway through the sentence and looked at me thoughtfully. "And Evita Peron really gave you all that stuff? You didn't"– she paused – "*borrow* those suitcases?"

"What are you talking about?" I said. "She gave them to me!" I raised my voice a little, but I didn't protest too much because there had been a few incidents in the past when I "borrowed" things. I didn't want to kick up a fuss and have her bring up the antecedents. And then there was the necklace, which Evita had *not* given me. I just wanted my mother out of the room, so I could open the hatbox and make sure it still was where I put it.

"So you don't have to worry about wearing the dresses," I said to my mother. "You can have them all. I'll keep only the hat." I pointed to the box in which I had hidden the necklace.

"A hat?" she said. "Since when are you into hats?"

"Just as a souvenir," I said. "Plus, I can wear it at the next Halloween party. For laughs."

"Let me see it," she said.

I opened the lid of the box, but I didn't lift out the hat. I was afraid the necklace might slip and show. I allowed her only a peek at the crown of the hat before closing the box again:

"So, can I have some privacy now?" I said urgently. "I need a rest, mom. It's been a long trip. Just take away the dresses, if you want them."

"There is no need to use that snarky tone with me," she said. "I'm going already." She started gathering the dresses. I watched her impatiently. Finally she left with the clothes bundled in her arms. I shut the door on her and snatched up the box. I was afraid she might come back for some reason and catch me out, so I moved halfway into the closet. If she came back, the open door would provide cover as I pulled Evita's necklace from behind the hatband. Yes, it was there, looking as gaudy as ever. The memory of Juancito's words "She is dying" was still in my ear, still raw, and touching the gems felt like touching a dead body. They felt clammy. I turned off the memories and instead started looking around for a new hiding place for the necklace. I decided to put it in with my own cheap costume jewelry, which I kept in a purple felt bag – we had an abundance of those bags in our household. They came with the Royal Crown Whiskey bottles.

No one, least of all my mother, had an interest in looking at my hoop earrings, friendship pins and charm bracelets, the stuff I kept in the Royal Crown bag. I shoved in the necklace and buried it under a pile of sweaters.

April 12 is coming around again and I can't get past it without going into a kind of religious funk, an irrational desire to confess what I did and what I failed to do, as they

241

say in church. Not that I'm religious. I haven't been in a church in years, but the rhythm of the biblical language I heard as a kid has stayed in my ear. Here is what I have failed to do: Instead of making concrete plans to follow in Evita's footsteps, I indulged in fantasies and made a fetish of the necklace I stole from her. I fell into the sick habit of taking it from its hiding place every few weeks. I stared at it and thought maudlin thoughts and fingered the gems like prayer beads. Sometimes I put on the necklace to feel it on my skin, as if it was possible to wear Evita's personality like a piece of jewelry. It didn't work, but it felt good. When I fastened the necklace around my neck, an electric sizzle started up in my blood, sending a thrill of memory from skin to spine, and I was happy in Evita's atavistic presence.

The necklace moved with me: from my mother's house to Phil's apartment when we got married, and from there to the Wilsons' house, where I am staying now. Leaving him was a step in the right direction. It was all very well for Evita to stick with Juan. She loved him. I was unhappy with Phil for two out of the three years we were married. It was my fault, I know. It wasn't Phil's idea to get involved with me. I made a play for him. It was part of my resolve not to be overlooked or dismissed or counted as zero. The desire to be noticed started with my trip to Argentina — Cousin Anne giving me the cold shoulder in New York and Liliana trying to keep me on the sidelines in Buenos Aires. They pushed me over the top, but it was Evita who set the course. Once I had experienced the power of her eyes, the life-giving beam of light infusing me with a feeling of completeness and belonging, I started craving it. That's when I began to make a play for people's attention. I discovered that it helped to say something outrageous from time to time like "God doesn't exist" or use forbidden words like "clitoris" or wear my skirt a little shorter than everyone else or wiggle my body a certain way. It made people take notice. By the time I entered university, I was no longer as desperate for attention. I had made my mark, but Phil's cultivated disdain for his undergraduate class got to me and revived my desire to be noticed.

I wasn't going to let him get away with disregarding us, or at any rate, me. I *made* him look, and I savoured my triumph when I saw his eyes stray from my face to my tight sweater while he struggled to maintain a blasé lecturing tone. I cornered him after class and asked him questions about the assigned texts. I had worked so hard to make them intelligent questions that it turned into a fun thing to ask them, like a quiz show.

"But what is the implication of the author talking about tropical heat – is it just descriptive? Is it a metaphor?"

It definitely turned into a metaphor as Phil and I picked the text apart and talked about body heat, the shimmering air, the breathless atmosphere, the hothouse jungle.

After a couple of weeks of metaphorical flirting, Phil took it a step further and became literal.

We were talking after his lecture, in the empty classroom, he leaning against the lectern, me sitting on a desk in the first row, slowly swinging my legs back and forth. The movement seemed to cast a spell on him. He ran out of words. To cover his speechlessness, he straightened up and coughed.

"Why don't we discuss this over coffee in the cafeteria?" he said in a laboured voice, as if something was stuck in his throat.

"I hate the coffee in the cafeteria," I said. "It's just brown water with a burned taste."

He swallowed hard and averted his eyes from the hypnotic swing of my legs.

"We could go to Gino's," he said.

I gave him a bright smile. "Okay," I said and hopped off the desk. "I do have a few other questions I meant to ask you." I wasn't just pretending. I wanted to go on talking. I thought I was falling in love with him as he was falling in love with me.

Gino's was a small deli off campus. Maybe the owner's name really was Gino. In any case, he went for the Italian look. There were Chianti bottles in straw baskets hanging on the wall and the little tables in the back were covered with red-and-white checkered tablecloths. Phil steered me to a table tucked away in a corner. He wanted privacy.

"So, tell me," he said after an awkward pause of opening sugar packets and stirring his coffee. "What made you take my course in the first place?"

He was looking for a compliment, of course, something along the lines "I heard you are a great teacher" but I treated it like a real question and told him about my interest in literature. The words came easy because it was true. I liked getting away from reality and dive into fiction.

"I noticed that," he said. "I love it when students are enthusiastic about the assigned readings, but those are just the basic texts. If you want to go beyond that, I can give you supplementary readings, and we can discuss them during office hours."

I was playing around with my spoon, moving it back and forth over the tablecloth. When I stopped, he sneaked his hand closer to mine and patted it in a fake-fatherly gesture. I looked hard into his eyes until his patting changed to a sort of rubbing motion. Then he looked past me at the woman behind the counter as if he was doing something naughty and was afraid of getting caught.

"That would be great," I said, and his hand stilled.

After that, we met in his office twice a week. The consultations were getting longer and more personal. We moved from interpreting the text to interpreting our feelings. When the cleaner looked in on us one evening and said "Sorry, I'll come back later" Phil said: "I guess we'd better find another place to talk."

We ended up at his apartment, on his bed, to be exact, where bodily action replaced talk and moans of pleasure stood in for words.

I took it from there and moved in for the kill. Three months later we were married. I thought I had won first prize. So did my mother. There was a touch of admiration in her voice when she congratulated me, and she stayed miraculously sober at the reception. Or maybe I should chalk that up to John policing her.

My attraction to Phil wasn't all make-believe. For a while I was convinced that I could be happy with him. I was under the influence of Evita's enduring love affair with her husband. I tried to adore Phil, so he too would be everything to me. I wanted to make a god of him, to love everything he loved. He accepted my adoration as his birthright, and I have to admit, our marriage had its moments of passion that first year, the satisfaction of being fucked frequently, the endless talks in the aftermath of love-making. We talked in bed, or at the kitchen table among the breakfast dishes, or in the street walking along oblivious to the weather, or late at night drinking and sodden. I wasn't just imitating Evita. I *was* in love with Phil then, but it didn't last. The first anniversary was black-dog depressing. By then, reality had set in. I should have known. Marriage, the actual thing shorn of its corny metaphors, wasn't acceptable, even though I made an enormous effort to think my way out of that reality, to live it Evita-style and imitate her loyalty to Juan. I remembered the words of the letter she wrote to him on the plane to Madrid. "I adore you, Juan, my love," she wrote. "You are everything to me." That's how I wanted it to be between me and Phil. It didn't work out that way.

I discovered within a few months that we disagreed on almost everything, but I also realized that quarreling with him was pointless unless I was prepared to act, to split up. At that point I couldn't do it. Quite apart from violating Evita's code, I didn't want to be a twenty-year-old divorcee, duplicating my mother's life. She had run away from her first husband after six months, stayed with the second only until I was out of my diapers and she could deposit me in a childcare centre. She was now in a third marriage kept together, I suspect, by financial need and the torpidity brought on by alcoholism. So, warned by my mother's example and guided by Evita's, I stayed with Philip even though I understood by then: He was terribly ordinary. He was too predictable. I could feel my insides gel, my brain waves flatten and turn sluggish. My whole life went into slow motion.

It took an enormous effort to keep going, to overlook the irritation I felt with Phil. I told myself that it was petty to chafe at trivial things — certain involuntary movements, like the dusting motion Philip made with his hands when he was impatient, or the way he pursed his lips while reading as if he wanted to whistle a tune, or even things he couldn't help — that his cheeks were easily flushed, that one of his front teeth was slightly crooked, forming a jagged line. The irritations piled up until it took an almost tantric endurance to put up with him. He had a grimace for every occasion, a tired repertory: a tight smile when he was embarrassed, a serene smile when he felt superior, slack-mouthed and looking at me mildly inattentive when I asked a question that he thought wasn't worth answering. That was the worst: he had fallen back into inattention. I was not prepared to put up with that and go back to the neglected life I had led pre-Evita. I wanted to be looked at and listened to with total understanding. I expected Phil to be that source of light for me, and during the first year of our marriage he was. He looked at me closely, with love, but then he developed a kind of myopia. His look always fell slightly short of me. I moved to the periphery of his vision and became a blur. He lost passion, even for sex. It turned into another of his routines, an organic process as regular as his food intake. In the morning, before I was fully awake, his hand sneaked across along the familiar path, from my shoulder to my left breast for a slight rub and squeeze, across my belly, touching my thigh as if to verify that it was there, and down between my legs, carefully exploring my wetness. And I colluded. I shut off the reality of his shambling body and his wandering hands and moved into Wonderland, making up my own scenario.

247

For a long time, the scene in the Boca with Juancito straddling the whore did it for me, his commanding whiskey voice, the energy and tension rolling off his shoulders, his large hands kneading her body, or in my fantasy, my body. Sometimes I pictured Pierre, soft-spoken, touching me with his elegant piano man hands, fingering me. I had never seen Pierre naked, but my imagination supplied the contours of his body. I pictured his skin stretched taut over his bones, smooth and unblemished like a child's – I was giving his muscles a mental upgrade perhaps, but it was expedient. It made me come. Lesbian scenes worked too, spun off the early sex games with Katie. Those fantasies broke me loose and made me convulse and peak, sometimes even before Philip had finished with his mouth-breathing rhythms. But I craved sex in the sunlit now of our bedroom rather than in my amber-coloured imagination. I wanted the touch and smell and rub of a real body carrying me to ecstasy, or else why bother? I could satisfy myself better than Philip did, or at least than he had done for a long time. Those sessions of morning sex left me deep in the muck of regret. But it was Philip's reaction to Evita's death last year that brought on the liberating eruption of anger. His words struck at the core of a long and deeply buried memory. "Are you crying for a little whore who made good?" he asked, breaking the spell that had kept me tied to our routine. I woke up to the memory of Evita's tireless passion, shed my inertia and felt a new lust to live. It was the catalyst that made me realize that I must make a move if I ever wanted to make good on my ambition to be like her. Taking the first step and leaving Phil was easier than I thought.

I looked around our apartment and saw nothing I cared for. Not Phil. Not the living room furniture dating from the time before I moved in with him, not the prints on the wall, not the random plates and cutlery we had accumulated, certainly not the bed on which we had sex with diminishing returns. The few things I needed or wanted – some books, my typewriter, clothes, and my fetish necklace –fit into a couple of suitcases.

"Phil," I said to him, talking fast, rushing on before he could make that sweeping gesture with his hands and dismiss my words. "Phil, I can't take it any longer, I mean the way we live. I need to get out. We don't love each other anymore, I'm angry all the time, and everything about you irritates me." I went on talking, mixing clichés of the Miss Lonely Hearts kind with real anger and regret. I was afraid to stop and give Phil a chance to make a disparaging motion. I was afraid he would say "You can't leave" and "I love you" in that threatening way which demanded reciprocity, but he surprised me.

"I saw it coming," he said.

I had been prepared to argue my case, and now the words just piled up in my head, unused. He agreed with everything I said. He was feeling the same disappointment, the same regrets, the same anger mixed with helplessness.

"I've been feeling frustrated for a long time," he said, "but I was ashamed because I'd made a promise. Till death do us part, and all that, you know."

I was surprised when he said that. He was a more decent man than I had given him credit for, or should I say, a more conventional man. He was prepared to suffer me and live up to the promise we made to each other, the words imposed on us by a tradition no longer relevant to me.

"Oh, that," I said, moving away from the core, our failed relationship. There was something to argue about after all, peripheral but nevertheless a point allowing discussion, the fact that Phil still vaguely believed in the powers above.

"Those words are meaningless. The whole Bible needs to be rewritten," I said. "Take the Ten Commandments. Why should you not make an image of your God — imagination being the saving grace of religion." And why honour my alcoholic mother, I thought, and what's wrong with fornicating?

But Philip was not prepared to go off topic.

"This isn't about the historicity of the Bible," he said and gave me the distant look reserved for ludicrous questions. "This is about you and me." He started in on his own list of grievances. I didn't mind. It felt almost soothing to go through the litany of our mutual disappointments. When he was done, we moved on to practicalities.

"So, is there someone else?" he said. "Is that why you want to leave? I'm asking because I'm prepared to move out if you want me to."

"No, no," I said, embarrassed now by his good will. "I'll move out. I couldn't afford this place on my own. I'll rent a room for the rest of the year. Or move into a dorm."

We drifted to the question of telling our friends. He wanted to make sure they understood that this was a mutual decision.

"Whatever," I said. "You tell them." I could see that he was worried about his image. He didn't want his friends to think that he had been unable to hold on to me.

"And how will you manage?" he said. "You can't live on your scholarship money."

"I'll borrow money from my mother," I said, although I knew it was hopeless to get anything out of her. "And next year, we'll see. I'll find work. Teaching in a private school, maybe."

"Don't. You won't survive it. You don't have the patience to teach little girls. You should go on with graduate studies."

It was the friendliest conversation we'd had in a long time. The prospect of freedom made us both generous. It was like early days. It almost made me believe that our marriage was salvageable, but then I remembered the irritations, the bad sex, and his obtuseness when he said I "was crying over a little whore who made good" and knew it was the right thing to do. I needed to start a new life.

20

Moving out on Phil was easy in the end. Finding the money to support myself was more difficult. As expected, I couldn't get a loan from my mother, but a colleague of Phil's was going on sabbatical and needed a house sitter, so the question of accommodation was settled for the time being and I could start on my MA without worrying about rent.

So I'm in the Wilsons' house now. It's too large for one person and too dark for my taste, but it's a cheap solution to my financial problems. The living room is haphazardly furnished with inherited pieces. The sofa and the two armchairs are well-worn, the veneer of the coffee table blistering a little at the edges, but the shabbiness is redeemed by three walls of bookcases reaching to the ceiling, packed with solid knowledge and poetic beauty. Tucked into the corner is a round footstool on casters, one of those they have in libraries so you can reach the top shelves. The Wilsons have taken the trouble of sorting their books. There are separate shelves for non-fiction and fiction. The novels are arranged in alphabetical order and, I suspect, by date of publication. The 19th century is well-represented with Dickens, Trollope, Austen, and Bronte. They obviously appreciate the Russians. Dostoevsky, Tolstoy, and Chekhov fill a couple of rows, but I notice a tapering off in the 20th century after Henry James. There is a dearth of contemporary authors, I'm not sure why – because they are outside their professional expertise or because the every-day language found in contemporary books pollutes the Queen's English, or the protagonists think indelicate thoughts and act out their animal desires? I can't be bothered to figure it out. My curiosity in the literary taste of the Wilsons is limited by the temporary nature of our arrangement. I can see that they are plant lovers, but in that department they are disorganized. There is a jungle of plants on every floor, lining the windowsills, blocking the daylight and requiring frequent watering.

The Wilsons left me with a sheet of instructions together with a diagram showing the location of fuse boxes and furnace switches, and a list of emergency phone numbers I haven't used so far and hope I won't have to use. I need to pay only for the electricity and for the heating. Even so, my scholarship money doesn't cover all the expenses and won't last me all the way. I will have to come up with more money soon.

The summer of Evita's death was followed by a gorgeous fall and the duty (according to the Wilsons' list) of raking up the leaves and bagging them for disposal. Winter came. I located the snow shovel in the basement, although it was not in the corner indicated on the Wilkins' diagram. I did what the duty list commanded: shovel the walkway and the twenty feet of sidewalk in front of the house. That's over now. We are into hopes of spring.

When I moved into the Wilsons' house last September, I put my belongings into the closet of their guest bedroom. Evita's necklace went into a new resting place, the drawer of my bedside table. Before I put it away, I laid it on the bedspread and waited for the voodoo magic to happen, but it didn't quite come off. And it hasn't worked since. The secrecy that surrounded my ritual when I lived with others, the fear of being caught in the act is missing. I think that's why the ceremony has lost some of its effect, the aura of a quasi-religious experience, a resurrection. I took out Evita's necklace and became a believer, like Thomas when he put his finger on Christ's stigmata. Now that I am living on my own, there is no need for furtiveness, no worries about getting caught. The mysterious aura and the warm holy feeling are missing when I look at the necklace out in the open. I still think of Evita with a visceral intensity. I still take satisfaction in knowing that her hands have touched the necklace. Fingering the stones still produces a vivid memory, but the necklace has lost its miraculous power.

I let a couple of weeks go by and tried again. Still no magic, and I thought, perhaps just as well. Enough with the fantasies. I have to wean myself from this superstitious practice, from the need for a prompt to dissolve into a maelstrom of Evita memories. I need to make a fresh start.

I still look at the necklace from time to time, but I no longer have the same desire to make it a spiritual exercise and immerse myself in a vision of Evita. It has become more of a pilgrimage into my past — no, more like an archeological dig, the discovery of my historical self, the schoolgirl I was six years ago, in the process of becoming who I am now, a twenty-two year old woman on the way to finalizing her divorce. Whatever it is, pilgrimage or archeology, it's no longer the same as the earlier, ceremonial handling of the necklace. It has lost its atavistic radiance. It has lost its relic status.

When I take it out today, I see it the way I saw it the first time, when Evita showed it to me and we laughed about its ostentatiousness. I have laid it out on the bed, but this time there is no ritual purpose. I have a practical reason for scooping it up in my hand. I need money. The Wilsons will return in two months. I need to find another place to live and the rent money to go with it. The solution is to sell some of the precious stones in Evita's necklace. The glitter will finance the rest of the year.

I take a last look at the necklace before undertaking the necessary mutilation and wish I had chosen a better stand-in for Evita, a better prompt for my memories. Also that I had received the necklace from her as a gift. But then again, if she had given it to me as a token of her love, I might not have the heart to mutilate it. It's better to look at the ugly truth: I stole it.

I take the necklace to the Wilsons' kitchen and put it on the counter for the operation. It turns out to be hard work to pry loose two of the diamonds. The Wilsons' butcher knife doesn't do the trick. I'm afraid I'll break its point. I have to go out and buy a pair of plyers, clamp down on the setting and bend the claws that hold the stones before I can finally ream them out. By themselves, removed from the garish setting, the two stones are beautiful. I fight the temptation to keep them after all, or at least one of them. Enough of the fetishizing, I tell myself. Face reality. I need the money those gems will bring in.

I have already checked the Classifieds in the paper. There is a pawnbroker on Church Street who advertises regularly for estate jewelry. Perhaps they'll take loose stones as well. But I decide to try a local jeweler first, to see if the stones are saleable and also to rehearse the sales talk. I pass the store with its artless display of rings and watches every day, on my way to campus, and I have seen the owner sitting at a brightly lit workbench in the back, a grandfatherly type in shirt sleeves.

But then remorse sets in. I suddenly feel sad about the business of selling or pawning Evita's diamonds, as if I was giving away something more than her property, a piece of her radiant smile or my memories of it. For a long time I had kept alive the fantasy of confessing the theft to Evita one day, returning the necklace to her and asking her to forgive me. I told myself that I had that option even if the chance of doing so became more remote with every year that passed, and now that Evita is dead the chance to confess and be absolved is gone forever. It is irrational to hesitate or have second thoughts about selling the stones now that I absolutely need the money.

Still, I put off the visit to the jewelry shop from one day to the next, not just out of nostalgia, but also for practical considerations. I know I am no good at bargaining. Besides what if questions arise about the provenance of the diamonds. Was there some sort of registry for stolen jewelry? A list of heists with detailed descriptions of the goods taken, the setting and the gems?

Could one even identify stolen gems? Did they have some sort of pedigree like purebred dogs?

Finally I work up enough courage to do it and walk to the jeweler's shop. The bright morning sky has turned cloudy, and the dullness of the day seems to follow me into the store, which is ill-lit except for the neon light above the old man's desk. He gets up from the work bench where he has been examining a watch and puts down his loupe. He flicks a switch on the wall. A bank of lights above the counter comes on, suddenly illuminating the store.

The rim of the loupe has left an impression on the soft folds of skin under the old man's eye and makes him look wounded. I can see the shadow of disappointment on his face when I explain my errand, when he realizes that I have come in to sell rather than to buy. The customer-friendly smile fades.

"Let's see," he says, spreading a felt pad on the counter and once again pressing the loupe to his eye. He picks up the stones one by one. His fingers look too pudgy for the job, but they are surprisingly nimble at handling the gems.

I watch him with an irrational dread of being caught red-handed and delivered up to the police. Fear has me by the throat. I swallow hard and focus on the bald spot that shows at the crown of the old man's head now that he is bending over to inspect the stones.

"Where did you get these?" he asks, looking up. His eyes droop at the corners, giving him a melancholy cast.

I have my answer ready.

"From my Scottish grandmother," I say. "She didn't like the setting and broke the stones loose. She meant to have them reset..." I trail off. "Why are you asking? Do I need some sort of paper to sell them?"

"No," he says. "I'm just curious. I don't need a paper to tell me what they are worth. It depends on clarity, colour, and cut." He gives me a probing look. My stomach knots.

There is a silence in which I can hear the noise of the traffic in the street, the tires hissing over the wet pavement.

"I can give you fifteen hundred for the both of them," he says at last, and I recover my cool.

This is just a trial run. I'm not going to accept the first offer I get. I'm doing this only to give me an idea of how much the stones are worth.

"Thanks," I say, scooping them up and putting them back into the little box I brought along, the box my wedding ring had come in. "I thought they'd be worth more. I'll get another estimate."

I am pleased with myself for playing it cool.

He shrugs. "Good luck," he says.

When I am at the door, he calls me back.

"I'll make it 1700, but that's all I can offer you. At that price there isn't much in it for me. Maybe with a nice setting..."

I turn back to him and say: "2000." My nervousness has settled down into a stony heaviness. My voice is firm.

He shakes his head, as if he was sad to see me so hardened. "Look, Miss," he says. "I run a business here, not a charity. 1800, and that's my last offer."

Now I am in two minds. Should I take the stones to a larger store or to the pawnbroker running the ads in the paper? Was it worth going through the agony of bargaining a second time? No, I am not up to it.

"Alright," I say and put the box back on the counter.

He brings out a book of receipts, carefully places the carbon paper between the pages, makes out the bill, hands me the bluish duplicate, and writes me a cheque. When I give him my name and address, I am jittery again, afraid there might be a last-minute snag, a trick, a mechanism to trace stolen goods after all. He seems to hold something back. I am nervous when he comes around the counter and walks me to the door. Close up, he no longer has the benevolent grandfather look. His eyes are shrewd and his skin is leathery in the daylight, as if it had been baked too long in the neon light above his worktable.

"These are exceptionally fine stones," he says before letting me out. "I'm curious. Where did your grandmother get them? If you find out anything more about their provenance, let me know."

I give him a weak smile. The fear of discovery has exhausted me. "I can ask my mother, but I don't think she has any more information."

I go home, determined never to look at the mangled necklace again. I need to put distance between it and me, find a place, where it can be interred, a final resting place. The obvious solution is to take out a safe deposit box at my bank. Even that transaction roils me because everything about it reminds me of the trip to the Alpine vault – the business-suited banker there, Mr. Behrle, the backroom he led us to, and the wall lined with rows of little steel doors. But it needs to be done. I pull myself together and take the mauve bag with the necklace to my bank.

It turns out to be simple after all and not nearly as painful as I thought. The clerk takes me to the room with the safe deposit boxes, unlocks one of the numbered doors for me and pulls out a metal drawer. He carries it to a walnut-paneled cubicle that looks like a telephone booth and stands back discreetly to give me privacy. I fit the felt bag with the necklace into the narrow drawer and tamp it down to fit. I keep thinking of the Swiss vault. My hand goes up to the locket holding the key to the safe, and I know what I have to do to slay the dragon. I pull the locket up from inside my blouse, take out the Swiss key, and put it into the safety box with Evita's necklace. It's a reunion of sorts, the stolen necklace and the key to the rest of her jewelry. It's almost as good as restoring it to the owner. When I am done, the clerk steps forward, and together we lock up the box.

I think of the fake dog hair flattened against the back panel of my locket – all that is left in it now — and wonder why I'm hanging on to that bit of fluff. I guess I'm preserving the memory of my first social triumph. Besides, I have been feeling the warm brass oval against my skin for so long. I sleep with the locket, I keep it on even in the shower. I put my palm against it now and feel it lying against the V where the collar bones meet. If I discarded it, the empty spot on my chest would feel cold and exposed somehow. Then I realize that I can put the locket to a new use. It's the perfect place for the new safe deposit key. It's smaller than the old one and a better fit. Done. I slide the locket back inside my blouse, pleased with the exchange of the legit for the illicit. Really, there was nothing illicit about taking Evita's jewels to the Swiss bank vault. I just think of it that way because of the secretiveness surrounding the trip and the secluded location and the heavily armed guards there, which gave the operation an aspect of organized crime. And because of the stolen necklace that should have been deposited there with the rest of the jewels.

The trip itself was perfectly legitimate. I didn't question the procedure at the time. It was later, on the flight home, that I began to wonder why Evita needed to send the boxes out of the country. Was there no place in Buenos Aires safe enough for them? Still later, when I read up on the history of Argentina and realized the unstable nature of military governments, the frequent revolutions in South American countries, and the rapid turnaround of power, I realized that Evita had been wise and thinking ahead. She was at the height of her popularity then, but she was fatally ill. I finally understood the panic I had seen in her eyes on the flight to Madrid, the letter she wrote to Peron. It wasn't a love letter. She was saying farewell to him. Looking death in the eye, she feared for her husband. Peron was nothing without her. His position was precarious. He might be forced into exile. In that case, Evita's stash would come in handy.

But the obituary mentioned that "the bulk of her jewels were missing." I know that Evita didn't want Peron to know about the deposit to keep him from spending what she had earmarked for an emergency. She meant to deposit the keys with her lawyer – the one who never followed up on his letter to me, Luis Rinaldo. But I did expect to hear from him after Evita's death. Does proofing a will take that long? Perhaps the legal situation is complex. Who is the legitimate heir to those jewels and gold bars anyway – Evita's brother or her husband, or both? One way or another, I'll hear from the executors. Will they merely ask for the key, or will my presence be required to join in the ceremony of unlocking the treasure? I have no desire to see Juancito again and to put up with his macho acts, although the idea of meeting with Pierre is beginning to take on a piquant interest in my mind. I wonder whether I am over-thinking him and he is of interest to me only in the Argentine context, our mutual history. But he is making frequent appearances in my sex life, which consists entirely of imaginary scenes now. That is the problem of course – the fact that I need a fantasy man. My real life in the aftermath of separating from Philip is lonely. I have to fall back on the imaginary Pierre, who opens his arms to me and speaks in a caressing voice. His dream body makes me come in my now solitary sex acts, but once the orgasm is over, the memories turn fluid. I can no longer tell how much I remember of him and how much I have made up. All I know is that I find memories of Pierre comforting, the way he put his arms around me at the airport in Zurich to shield me from Juancito's words "She is dying." I picture Pierre's slender body, the body of a long-distance runner conditioned to perform, the hands of a piano player –no, violin he said — but his face remains featureless. I can't remember it, perhaps because it was so regular, the colour of his eyes so vague, grey perhaps, the colour of his hair vague as well, sandy perhaps. Only the mouth I remember. It was too soft for a man, too indulgent.

21

Almost a year has gone by since Evita's death, and still no one has asked me about the key to the Swiss safe. Then, finally, I hear from Argentina, but not from the lawyer. Juancito contacts me. How he got my, or rather the Wilsons' phone number, I don't know. I guess he has international reach.

"How would you like to join me for another trip to the Swiss Alps?" he says, skipping the small talk.

"No thanks," I say. "I didn't enjoy it the first time." If he can't be bothered with small talk, I will come to the point as well. "Do you even have a right to those boxes in the safe?"

"What's it to you?" he says. "You don't want to come along, fine. I just need the key. How much do you want for it?"

I wonder, has he asked Pierre the same question? And has he agreed to sell? Maybe Juancito is asking me first because he thinks I am an easy mark.

"It's not for sale," I say.

"Evita meant those boxes to be mine, you know," he says. His voice darkens and takes on a menacing tone.

"Then why don't you do things up front though a lawyer?"

"It's not that simple," he says, retreating from his earlier bravado.

No, I guess it's not simple to commit theft on that scale. I am convinced he has no right to the boxes. He is bluffing.

The phone has gone quiet. Juancito is waiting for some come-back from me, maybe a question: How much exactly was he willing to pay? But I am in no mood to play his game. It has landed me in dangerous territory before. I'll give up the key to Juan Peron's lawyer—assuming that Peron is Evita's heir – but not to Juancito.

I am about to hang up on him, when he starts in again.

"Why are you so stubborn, *chiquita*? If it's a matter of price-"

"It isn't. It's a matter of legitimacy," I say, laughing silently, because I have a taste for the illegitimate myself, provided that I can get away with it. But I have no taste for his bully tactics. I don't like Juancito, except as a sexual fantasy, when his macho and his domineering voice work for me.

"Alright," he says, "have it your way, *chiquita*."

I am surprised he is giving up so easily. Perhaps he realizes that he has hit a wall, but even so I would have expected him to explode in anger and treat me to a volley of expletives before hanging up.

My mind goes back to our joint ventures, my narrow escape from the whore house, his escape from the tango bar leaving me stranded with Pierre, and my secret view of him shagging Liliana in the Gutierrez backyard. I wonder, is he still seeing her? I haven't given much thought to Liliana since the time when she was my reluctant hostess. During my ritual reminiscing on my anniversary date with Evita, I kept to the European triad of Evita, Juancito, and Pierre. I never thought of Liliana because there was nothing thrilling about her, no mystery, no trait to ponder and turn over in my mind. She was one of the brainless rich, her taste questionable, her character weak. Not that I require more honesty from others than I have myself, but her lies of convenience were boring, too bare to hold any interest. I passed Nancy over as well. She seemed insignificant at the time, although my interest was piqued when, a year after my return to Toronto, I got a letter from her, or rather a wedding announcement with a Canadian stamp. She and Pierre were getting married in Ottawa! What? Unbelievable. It was only then that I reexamined my memory of Nancy and fixed on her inquisitiveness, her spying on Liliana without any fear of being caught, a risk-taking which didn't go together with her phlegmatic movements and her dowdy appearance. I should have known that there was more to her than met the eye the day she told me that she was going to quit her job and stay with Pierre. Is he your boyfriend, I asked her. I don't remember her answer or anything else about Nancy very distinctly. I only know that I underestimated her. She deserves second thoughts. Reviving memories of Nancy has an odd effect on me. Now that Juancito's phone call has triggered those memories, I start seeing Nancy's face everywhere.

I am sitting in the Wilsons' study on the second floor, which I have made my working place. I am hunched over my typewriter, working on my research piece about the psychological torment of women in Shakespeare. I take a break to straighten my back and flex my fingers. I wander to the window and look out on the street and the strip of lawn on the other side. The neighbourhood uses it as a dog park. But there is no one out that morning. It's one of those in-between days, with reminders of winter and harbingers of spring. It has rained overnight. The layer of dead leaves which has accumulated under the trees bordering the parkland is covered with crusty, melting snow. The ground is still frozen and the lawn soggy with water that has nowhere to go. A woman comes into view. The hood of her jacket is up and drawn forward, shielding her face. She walks along the street to a parked car. Before getting in, she pulls off her hood. A crisp wind comes up and blows strains of hair across her face, and at that moment I think with surprise: It's Nancy! Something about the colour of her hair and the angular movement of her hand when she opens the car door made me think of her. I crane my neck to get a better look at the woman, but she has already ducked into the car and is driving off.

The next day, I am in the university library. The stone crest above the entrance shows an oak tree with that quintessential Canadian animal, the beaver, crouching below, and the motto *Ut arbor in aevo*, "Like a tree through the ages." I find the crest amusing. The tree won't last through the ages. It doesn't stand a chance against the beaver's innate desire to gnaw it to death.

268

The campus is a cluster of Victorian buildings in fake Tudor style with quads and imperfect lawns damaged by punishing winters and guys playing pickup football in the summer. I go to the library every day to do research although at this point it amounts to no more than rummaging in the stacks and changing a phrase here and there in my project paper, which is due shortly. I take the elevator up to the periodical section. Someone gets off on the second floor, and as the elevator doors swish open, I have a glimpse of a woman in the stacks, who looks like Nancy. She is wearing a non-descript white blouse and slacks. Her face is turned the other way, her hand reaching for a book. I don't know what makes me think of Nancy. There is nothing distinct about the woman's clothes or her bearing, and yet Nancy's name has popped into my head. The elevator doors close, but I am so obsessed with the coincidence, this second sighting of "Nancy", that I run downstairs and look around. No one resembling her is in the stacks or sitting at any of the study tables. But now that I have turned my thoughts to Nancy, I remember what she said in answer to my question —Is Pierre your boyfriend? Not really, she said, just a friend. She went on to tell me that he was Belgian and had been a travel writer before he started working for Evita. He spent years in Africa, she said. On impulse, I go to the reference department and checked the card catalogue. But, as I more or less expected, there is no Pierre Adams in the authors' list. I look in the subject catalogue under "Travelogues, African" and find a book entitled *Mes Voyages Africains* by one Pierre Maye, published in Brussels. I get it from the stacks. Facing the title page is an illustration showing a man in a safari outfit wearing a pit helmet and sunglasses. Beside him stands an Arab in a flowing djellah, holding the reins of a camel. The caption says: The Author at Luxor. I peer at the white man in the photo. It could be Pierre. Or not. It's hard to tell. The sunglasses are obscuring his face. I scan the introduction. The author talks about the difficulty of understanding a foreign culture, especially if one doesn't speak the language. Something is lost in translation, he says. Even if you know Arabic, there is more to a language than grammar and inflection, there are centuries of cultural heritage behind every word that a stranger cannot fathom. It sounds eerily like Pierre. In fact, it reminds me of a conversation we had on our road trip to Switzerland, about the difficulty of switching languages. It is a day of strange coincidences: seeing "Nancy", then finding a travelogue by a Belgian writer named Pierre Maye who sounds like a mouthpiece of Pierre Adams.

When I leave the library in the early afternoon, it's balmy, for Toronto at any rate – it's above freezing. Some guy is punting a ball across the muddy lawn. Everyone is going crazy sniffing the first warm breeze of air. Me too. I take off my jacket and turn my face to the pale sun. I decide to take a short-cut, a gravel path winding between two colleges, nicknamed "Philosopher's Walk". A cyclist is coming toward me, another spring-crazy guy. This isn't exactly biking weather. The snow is gone, but there is a dirty crust of ice along the edge of the path, melting into puddles. The cyclist is coming toward me, no, straight at me. He looks young, a teenager misjudging the distance perhaps. I move to step out of his way, but he picks up speed and veers to the right where I'm standing. As he passes me, he shoots out his arm and knocks me to the ground. In a moment he is gone. A young couple coming out of the Music faculty breaks into a run and shouts after him, but he has already merged into the street traffic. I scramble up. My elbow is chafed, and my ribs feel bruised where the handlebars of the bike have grazed my side.

The young couple has come back to check on me.

"That guy is nuts!" the woman says. "I couldn't believe my eyes. Are you okay? Do you need help?"

"I am fine," I say, picking up my jacket, which has dropped on the ground. I brush off bits of grass and ice.

"There is a spot of blood on your neck," the woman says.

I reach up, rubbing my neck, and realize that my locket is missing.

"Oh," I say. "I've lost my locket. The chain must have broken."

We search the ground, but it's gone.

"You know what?" the man says. "The guy ripped it off you. Was it valuable?"

"No, it was a piece of costume jewelry," I say.

"He probably thought it was real," he says. "In any case, you should let the administration know. They need to put out an alert."

It is possible but unlikely that the fellow on the bike mistook the locket for a genuine piece of jewelry. It is so obviously a kid's plaything, a tinny imitation of an heirloom pendant. In any case the chain was barely visible above the collar of my sweater, unless you were looking for it. As I replay the scene in my mind, I become certain that I have been targeted. I can't come up with a continuous story for what happened, an explanation without gaps, but I am sure it was no coincidence.

271

Someone was after the locket, someone who knew, or thought he knew, that it contained the key to the safe deposit box in the Alpine vault. Juancito. He must be behind this. Was he in town? The thought creeps me out. But it would explain why he took my refusal to sell him the key so meekly. He already had a plan B. He wasn't meek when the Swiss banker doled out the keys. I remember his clenched-teeth response, his angry reaction when he found out that he wasn't the exclusive keeper of Evita's treasure, that there were three keys. "Guard the key with your life, *chiquita*," he said to me in a voice disguised to sound jocular, but I understood. He meant to threaten me. I stared him down and put the key into my locket. It was a stupid attempt at bravado. I shouldn't have shown him where I kept the key. And I should have deposited it in the bank right away rather than waiting six years to do it. I should have known better. If Juancito wasn't the legitimate heir to Evita's treasure, he would try to get his hands on it another way. He was a thug, but did he have enough reach to organize a robbery here in Toronto? And in this haphazard, amateurish fashion, in public, before witnesses? The idea seems far-fetched, but I can't come up with another explanation.

I go back to my bank, tell them that I have lost the key to my deposit box, get a duplicate, and put the incident out of my mind — until Phil phones me a week later and says that a friend of mine from Argentina was trying to get in touch with me.

"I gave him your number at the Wilsons' house," he says.

So that's how Juancito found out where I lived.

272

"You gave him my number?" I say to Phil. "Without asking me first?"

"But he already had it — the old one at any rate. And he said his wife was in correspondence with you, or something like that."

"His wife? What wife?"

"How am I supposed to know?"

"Wait," I say. "Are we talking about Juan Duarte?"

"Duarte? No, he said his name was Adams. – Look, I'm sorry if this is a problem. You didn't want him to get in touch?"

"Never mind," I say. "It's done now. Just don't give out my phone number to people without asking me first. I mean that's basic courtesy. Do I have to tell you that?"

I wasn't annoyed with Phil, I was annoyed with myself, for the way I reacted to Pierre's name, a man whom I had last encountered in an imaginary sex scene. Like an idiot, I felt a jolt of sexual desire. But it takes me all of ten seconds to shift gears when I consider the sequence of phone calls. First Juancito wants to talk to me, and now Pierre. Are the two of them ganging up on me? Whoever was behind the robbery would know by now that the locket contained the wrong key.

I waste the rest of the morning going over possible scenarios, rehashing memories, mostly of Pierre, his strangely touching tango performance, his rescue acts, driving me home from the bar, handing me his handkerchief when I was sick on the plane, stroking my back in the airport in Zurich, and most of all, his stellar performance in my imaginary sex acts. I am in two minds whether I want to talk to him or not. If the phone rings, should I pick up?

The phone rings in the afternoon, and I do pick up. It's Pierre. He is in town, he says, and wants to get together for drinks. I feel that prick of desire again. I also know it's dangerous to bring fantasies to life. The real man is bound to be a disappointment, but I'm inclined to run the risk. Then there is the other risk: that Pierre isn't interested in me personally, that he is collaborating with Juancito, that both men are after my key.

"Is this about the key to the Swiss safe?" I ask him point blank after he suggests getting together.

"What?" he says. "The key? No, I just thought it would be nice to catch up."

Why do I even bother to ask? If Pierre is after the key, he won't admit it.

"How long are you here for?" I ask, trying to sound distant.

"Just for the day."

"On business?"

"I'll tell you when I see you," he says.

His cageyness makes me apprehensive. My thoughts switch from the vague hope of pleasure back to the unpleasant memory of the bike incident and the possibility that I was wrong suspecting Juancito, that Pierre was behind it. I immediately discard the idea again. Using violence was at odds with the mellow voice on the phone and everything else I remember about Pierre. After all, he was the first man to give me a loving embrace, at the airport in Zurich, at a time when I needed it most. And you always remember the first time. No, Pierre was not a violent man and what good was the key to him? Well, it was good for money. Juancito was prepared to pay for it. I hesitate and waver. Juancito gave up too easily when I declined to sell the key to him. He didn't even curse. He probably had Pierre lined up already. Pierre was his Plan B.

"Are you still there?" he says. "Is this an awkward time? Should I call back later?"

"No, no," I say. "It's okay. So what time do you want to get together, and where?" In spite of my misgivings, I still want to see him again.

Pierre is staying at the Windsor Arms, a small hotel downtown where the university sometimes puts up visiting academics. We agree to meet at the bar. How risky can it be to see him in a public place?

The hotel dates back to the 1920s. It has an impressive stone portico and stain glass windows, but the brick façade, darkened by age, looks rather shabby. I am surprised to see the elegant interior, the starched white tablecloths in the dining room, the black-suited waiters, the chandeliers, the burgundy carpet with a heraldic pattern. The bar is made to look old English, with hunter-green stools and a brass railing along the bottom to put up your feet. Pierre is already there. When he sees me, he gets up, his movements doubled in the mirror behind the bar. He looks formal in a suit and tie. I feel underdressed and vulnerable to the scent of his aftershave when he kisses me on the cheek.

"You look just as I remember you, Mona," he says. "Flammable, if that's the right word. Alive, I mean."

I am in the spotlight of his eyes. I feel the heat rising to my cheeks and am angry with myself for blushing at this odd compliment, a come-on really.

"And how is Nancy?" I say pointedly, thinking of my "sightings" of her in the dog park and at the library. They seem prescient now, harbingers of Pierre's appearance on the scene.

He ignores my question. "What would you like to drink?" he says and signals the barman. When the man has taken my order, I ask Pierre what he is doing in town.

"I'm on my way to Buenos Aires," he says. His face has a focused expression, as if he had to assess the situation before going on. "Nancy went there for a holiday last week. I just found out she was involved in a car accident."

"That's unfortunate," I say politely. "Was she hurt?"

"I don't know the details. That's why I'm going to Argentina, to find out what exactly happened."

Pierre's voice is so calm that his words come across like white noise. They register only on my brain. They loosen no emotional response. I know a few sympathetic words are wanted from me, but Nancy and Buenos Aires seem very far away. Her accident remains just a word, and I don't know how to slot the mysterious sightings into the news of her accident. I don't know how to react, and Pierre's face gives me no clue. He seems unmoved himself.

"I'm so sorry," I finally say. "It must have been a shock." The words come out stiff and insincere. I find it hard to concentrate. I'm thinking of my earlier suspicions connecting Juancito's phone call with Pierre's. Now it looks more like coincidence.

"The news of Nancy's accident certainly came as a shock," he says. "I haven't been in touch with her for quite a while. We separated two years ago. I don't relish the idea of having to deal with the authorities in Buenos Aires, but we didn't get a legal divorce, and so I show up as next-ofkin. I am legally obliged to give consent on her behalf if she can't."

"It must be pretty bad if she can't give consent to whatever treatment is necessary."

"It is serious," he says. "Perhaps all of this could have been done through lawyers, but you know the system down there, the red tape. Nothing ever happens if you aren't there to push it along in person. I wonder if anything has changed since I left in '48. In a way, it will be a memory trip for me."

Would these memories include me? He is separated from Nancy. He is available. I search Pierre's face for clues to guide me but see only an inscrutable frown.

"Phil and I separated as well," I blurt out, and am instantly sorry for telling him. What a stupid thing to say, and totally irrelevant.

I tense at the look he gives me in response, halfway between interest and surprise.

"I see," he says.

To correct my faux pas, I steer back to Nancy's accident, but he cuts me off.

"I really don't know any details at this point. Let's not go on about it. Tell me about yourself, Mona. — I know you once said you did *not* want to talk about your life because it was boring. Have things improved?"

"Not a great deal," I say, glad to get away from Nancy and the need to show a concern I do not feel. "And you didn't want to talk about *your* life either because you hadn't sorted it out, you said."

"You remember that?" He smiles. I notice that his teeth are straight, unlike Philip's. And that he has his hand movements under control, unlike Philip. I still can't make out the colour of his eyes in the muted light of the bar, or the colour of his hair which is indefinite, shades of sand and ash.

"Have you sorted your life out by now?" I ask him.

"As much as I ever will."

We go on in this cautious, cagey way, giving out bits of information with loopy boundaries between spilling and guarding our privacy. Pierre lives in Ottawa, on the Quebec side of the river, he says. He is working for the government, translating documents into French. I tell him that I have finished my undergraduate studies and am doing an MA in English lit, but I am unsure whether to go on and work toward a PhD or look for employment.

It is desultory talk. I feel I'm not getting at the core, that he is hiding out on me, holding back a great deal, and all the time I am conscious that I want to touch him and find out whether he matches the imaginary body, wearing the same skin I have given him in my sex scenes.

When I say I have to go, he asks if he should call me a taxi.

"I was going to walk home," I say. "I live only a short distance away."

"Then I'll walk you home," he says.

Neither of us talks much on the way. It is as if we were imitating the quiet of the streets. Toronto doesn't have much of a nightlife, and once we have turned off into the residential part, we are on our own. The silence between us is charged. We are watching each other. It strikes me that Pierre is holding his arms very close to his body, as if he was trying not to take up space or wanted to pass undetected. I noticed earlier how still his face was, except for his eyes, which are alert, observant. Even on the way home, when I talk only about trivial things to fill the void, he seems to listen carefully as if every word was important and contained something that was crucial to understanding me. Then we run out of things to say. The silence between us spreads. Casting around for another topic, I remember that I looked up his name in the library catalogue.

"Nancy once told me you wrote a book about your travels in Africa," I say, "and I came across a travelogue in the library, *Mes Voyages Africains* by one Pierre Maye. In the introduction he talks about the difficulty of understanding the cultural dimension of foreign languages. You said something very similar to me once."

He stops and gives me a surprised look. "That is in fact one of my books," he says.

"But the author's name was Maye."

"That's my pen name."

"Is that why you moved to Canada, to get back to a French-speaking environment?" I say. My real question is: Did you marry Nancy for her passport?

"It was on my mind," he says, "but as it turns out, speaking French wasn't the bridge I thought it would be. Quebec is still a foreign culture to me."

When we arrive at the house, we stand in the driveway. I am reluctant to say good-bye.

"You are flying out tomorrow?" I ask him.

"In the afternoon," he says. "I have a layover in Miami."

I wonder why he didn't fly out of Montreal.

"You didn't come to Toronto just to see me?" I say lightly. I avoid looking into his face. My eyes latch on to the porch light of the house across the street.

"Yes, just to see you," he says.

"But why?"

"Because I fell in love with you on that road trip to Switzerland, or maybe even earlier," he says. "I fell in love with your joie de vivre or your energy, or whatever you want to call it. That's why I wanted to see you again, to find out if you are still like that or if you have become bored with life like most people."

"And what's the answer?"

"You are still like that: fearless," he says and takes my hand, his long fingers settling between mine. It is only natural then that he should lean in and kiss me and that I should push into him and bite his lips, which are too full and tender for a man.

"Do you want to come in?" I ask, when our mouths separate, and he says "Yes".

Surprisingly, his naked body matches my imagination very closely. His skin does stretch taut over his slender body, although I did not picture the fine blond hair curling on his arms and chest. I fold into him easily. He touches my face before he puts his hands on my body. We kindle to each other right away and I open my thighs wide to his thrusts. When I sense that he is on the verge but holding back, I stroke his buttocks, and he comes fast. So do I. With ease. No need to come up with a fantastic scenario.

"I'm sorry," he says into my neck, holding on to me. "I came too fast."

I am lost in a fog of pleasure and satisfaction. I am speechless. I can only sigh.

He nuzzles my sweaty cheek and says: "I see. It was okay then."

He moves away from me, sliding to the other side of the bed and lies there looking up to the ceiling. I can tell that he has moved away in his mind as well, is already on his way, back to the hotel perhaps, or thinking of the trip tomorrow. I no longer have a presence in his thoughts. In my imaginary scenes, he held me close and told me that he had never had such good sex before and that he loved me madly. That part doesn't happen. But then I haven't said anything to Pierre either, although I am on the way to loving him madly.

After a while he gets up and goes to the bathroom. I listen to the patter of the shower, doze, wake up again when Pierre returns to the room and begins to dress. His voice comes to me out of the darkness:

"I noticed you no longer wear that locket."

I freeze. I am fully awake now. My suspicions were right. He wants the key. He just pretended that he was interested in me.

"My locket?" I echo.

"The one you always wore. You put the safe deposit key into it – right in front of Duarte, as if to say, 'Come and get it'. I hope you are keeping it in a safe place now."

"What's it to you, Pierre?"

He reaches for the lamp on the bedside table and turns it on. The expression on his face is unreadable.

"You sound angry all of a sudden," he says. "Did I say anything to upset you?"

I tell him the story of the robbery, slowly and in unnecessary detail because I am unsure what ending to give it. Then I make up my mind.

"So I lost both my dog souvenir and the key," I say. I cut the story short there. I do not tell him that the Swiss key is safe, that it is in my deposit box now.

"Perhaps you should let Duarte know that it's gone," he says.

"I don't want to have anything to do with him."

"You may have no choice. In fact, I'm surprised he hasn't made his move yet. I myself expected to hear from him immediately after Evita's death, but I can see why he is sitting it out. Because he has no legal right to the keys."

"Then who does?"

"Juan Peron, presumably."

"Then why didn't his lawyers contact us?"

"They may not know about the boxes. Evita had a personal lawyer, Luis Rinaldo. She wanted me to deposit the key with him, but he never contacted me or made any arrangements, and he died last year. I heard from Duarte then. He wanted to know if I still had my key."

"And you said?"

"I lied. I said I'd given it to Rinaldo."

"Evita would have mentioned the keys in her will, don't you think? In any case Peron realizes that her jewels are missing."

"I don't know what's in her will. It's clear that Juan does not know about the deposit we made at the bank or the keys. I have no idea why she didn't tell him, but her behaviour in Spain and Italy became erratic, you know. I think the disease or perhaps the medication she was taking muddled her brain. Or she was in two minds whether to leave her jewels to her husband or her brother or to both and never made a decision. It's all guess work. But one thing is sure: Duarte will try to get his fingers on

282

the keys to that safe deposit box. He'll come after you. And after me as well, if he finds out or suspects that I lied about giving it to Rinaldo. I'm sure he had his goons ransack Rinaldo's office."

"You may be right."

"That's why you should let Duarte know. For your own safety. If you no longer have the key, he won't bother you."

I'm not entirely convinced that Pierre is on my side, that we are in this together.

"And what will you do about your key?" I ask.

"Go to Juan Peron directly," he says.

"And sell him the key?"

"I don't know that the key is worth anything to him. The information about the deposit certainly is. Once he knows where the boxes are, his lawyers can apply to the bank. If he is Evita's heir, they will give him access with or without the keys. Juancito has a chance to get at the boxes only as long as Peron doesn't know where they are. The people at the bank are obliged to open the safe to anyone who has the three keys, but so far he doesn't have them. And once I am in Buenos Aires and inform Peron where the boxes are, the game is over."

"And you don't think Juancito will come after you for spoiling his game?"

Pierre shrugs. "He may. I'll watch my steps."

He gets up to go. I walk downstairs with him, naked as I am. At the door we embrace. I am a believer again. I badly want him to stay. I can feel him hardening and cling.

"Pierre," I say, "will I see you again? Are you going to stop over on your way back from Buenos Aires?"

"Do you want me to?"

Maybe it isn't wise to say so. Don't let on to your feelings, I think. Fake it. But I break my rule and admit: "I do. It has to be mutual, though."

"It is mutual," he says, but he is no longer holding on to me. He lets go and turns to the door.

I realize I've been too pressing. I have asked too many questions, but I can't help asking another.

"So when will you come back?"

"That depends."

"On what?"

"On what I find out about the accident."

I feel abandoned after Pierre has left. Back upstairs, I can't sleep for thinking. I want that man. I reason with myself. This is what they call "being on the rebound." I am lonely on my own, after splitting with Philip. I'm vulnerable. Or, the past is spilling over into the present and I am fascinated with Pierre because he is a character in my past. I associate him with Evita, the woman I want to be. Looking back into that corridor of my life, I see her clearly for a moment. I am back in her room in the presidential palace, in the halo of her presence. In the darkness of my bedroom, I try on her brilliant smile, hear her persuasive voice, feel her comforting arms around me, but the fatigue of love-making is taking over and I close my eyes. Evita fades and Pierre surfaces again and stays with me as I fall asleep.

In the morning, when I wake up and my jumbled thoughts start to take on an orderly shape, reason kicks in. The doubts are back. I can't make up my mind what role Pierre was playing, lover or con-man, but I come back to the crucial question: What good is my key to him? It's good for money, a lot of money, I suspect. He could sell it to Juancito. Is that why he is going to Buenos Aires? He may already be working for him. If Pierre organized the bike incident, he will know by now that the locket contained the wrong key. It is smaller than the Swiss key, and of a different shape. When he asked about my pendant yesterday, was he fishing for information, to find out where I kept the real key?

There is a way to settle that question conclusively. I go to the bank as soon as it opens and retrieve the Swiss key. I put it in an envelope with an explanatory note addressed to Pierre and leave it with the receptionist at the Windsor Arms. There is no reason for me to hold on to the key. In fact, it seems dangerous to do so. If Pierre has been playing games and looked me up only because he was after the key, I will never hear from him again.

Pierre

22

When I check out of the Windsor Arms at noon, the receptionist hands me a letter.

"This came for you in the morning," she says.

It's from Mona. While I wait for the taxi, I open the envelope. It contains a small key I recognize at once. The key to the Swiss deposit box. She has enclosed a note, a few lines in round handwriting, closely spaced so that the loops touch. She doesn't explain why she told me that bizarre story about being attacked by a bicyclist and losing the locket. She must have made it up on the run, but why? Did she think I was after the key, or, more likely, that I was working for Duarte? I could see that my question threw her off balance, but that story of hers wouldn't have deterred a hired thug from putting a gun to her head or searching the house. And why is she giving the key to me now?

I assume you'll be seeing Juancito in Buenos Aires, the note says. *Give the key to him. Or give it to Peron. I*

don't want anything more to do with this crazy affair. As
you said: If I don't have the key, no one will bother me.

The note says nothing about last night or meeting
again. I feel a lurch of regret. I shouldn't have mentioned
the locket, but I thought she needed a warning, perhaps
because I still remember that air of naivete about her. She
has grown out of that. Perhaps some of her liveliness and
spontaneity have gone too, or have been given a veneer of
sophistication. Except for the dark timbre of her voice, she
no longer reminds me of Colette. It's hard to say now what
I thought the two women had in common. Passion, yes,
but Colette was passionate with the abandon of an animal,
Mona's cravings are tempered by thought. I'm prone to
the same fault, if thinking is a fault. It puts the brakes on
a relationship, but this isn't the right time for me to start
anything new. I'm not done with the old. I haven't told
Mona that Nancy died in the accident. I didn't want death
to intrude on our time together. I didn't want to say
"Nancy is dead" because I am not even sure I believe it
myself. Maybe the accident never happened. Maybe she is
alive, and this is a trap, a ploy to make me go to Argentina.
Duarte wants to collect the keys to the Swiss deposit box
now that Evita is dead. He knows I won't make it easy for
him, but it might be easier to put the thumbscrews on me
in Argentina, where he has clout. I wouldn't put it beyond
him to arrange for a kidnapping and demand the key as
ransom.

On the way to the Toronto airport, the taxi passes
through the suburbs of the city I didn't bother to look at
yesterday. I saw the streets like a sleepwalker. I went past
buildings, shops, and people, lost in thought. I live in my
head too much. I justify my preoccupation, calling it

planning, but that doesn't change the fact that I am absent from my lived life. I wasted my time with Mona yesterday, weighing her words and hedging my answers to her questions. Sex was a brief release from the tyranny of thinking, the endless attempts to work the trick and piece the strains of my life together. I should have savoured the short time when I was skin to skin with Mona, when my brain cut back to basic instincts, but once my cock had shot its load, like a fool I just wanted to sleep -

The taxi stops at the curb of the terminal and yanks me back to the present. I pay the fare and check in at the airline counter, but when I sit down in the passenger lounge, the thoughts are back, crowding my mind. Airports are conducive to rumination. So many empty hours, such featureless, utilitarian structures, and a dystopic view of runways and planes. It takes an effort to remember where I am. There is nothing to hold my attention in these generic surroundings. I turn inwards again to the familiar landscape of my mind, and the thought that I am about to fall into a trap.

I am almost certain that Duarte has no legitimate claim to those jewels and gold bars. Evita meant them as a hedge for Peron in case he was ousted and forced into exile. She knew he wouldn't be able to hold on to power after her death, not for long. If she had designated Duarte as the heir or joint heir, I would have heard from his lawyers by now. Giving up the key was the safe thing to do for Mona. I'll do the same with mine, but I won't hand them to Duarte. Giving the keys to Peron is the better option. Less lucrative but satisfying a long-standing desire to frustrate Duarte. I relish the thought of getting back at him for all the times he treated me like dirt. But it's also the more dangerous option. You don't cross Duarte without getting punished. Alright, let him try to punish me. I am ready for a fight. I am tired of the safe, steady, boring life I've lived over the last few years. I miss the pressure of the moment, the dense feel of a calculated risk, the thrill travelling my spine, and I want revenge for the slights, the dismissiveness, the baiting I had to take from Duarte. It's an archaic desire, I realize, like slapping a glove across a man's face and challenging him to a duel. Delivering the keys to Peron is like that — a slap to Duarte's face.

I sit in the passenger lounge watching the customers at the Duty-free, people buying liquor or perfume or silk scarves. A cleaner comes by and I watch him emptying the ashtrays and replacing them with clean ones, observing him out of habit, while observing myself. I am looking for inner confirmation that my hunch is right, that Duarte is playing games with me, that he has an agenda for me in Argentina. But I can't get a clear answer in my own head. A shadow of doubt remains that my suspicions are unfounded and everything is exactly as it looks – a formality, a legal requirement. I'll go to the morgue, identify Nancy's body, and make the necessary arrangements with a funeral home. I collect the death certificate and fly back to Canada. The end. A more definite end than a divorce or the stopgap of separation.

After Nancy and I moved to Canada, I found a job as a translator. She started work in a childcare centre. Nothing much changed in our relationship once we settled in Ottawa, except that our characteristics became more pronounced over time, her inquisitiveness, my reticence. We both avoided arguments. We both worked hard to maintain a counterfeit relationship with flickers of friendliness and tactile comfort, and we managed to stay within the realm of good-enough. I resigned myself to going on in this way. It takes five years to obtain Canadian citizenship, and for that I was prepared to suffer an arrangement ripe with decay. In the end, it was Nancy who made the move to independence. She decided to go back to university and get a degree in social work. She'd move to Montreal, she said. She had been accepted into a programme that alternated study with paid internships.

"Is that the end of our marriage?" I asked her.

"Don't worry," she said. "You are safe. This won't affect your application for citizenship. I'm just moving out. I'm not asking you for a divorce."

Instead, she asked me for money. I paid for my freedom. After all, the arrangement suited us both.

Because we weren't divorced, the notification of Nancy's death came to me, on official letterhead with all the necessary stamps and signatures, but was it genuine? Duarte could easily bribe someone to draw up a notice like that. Nancy may be alive, on a holiday for all I know, enjoying the sights of Buenos Aires. Or held in some windowless room by Duarte's goons until I hand over the key.

It isn't paranoia to think that he is setting a trap for me. I have reason to be suspicious — the things I found when I went to clear out Nancy's apartment. I had never visited her in Montreal, even though our separation was amiable. So I was curious what kind of space she had created for herself. Utilitarian, I was sure. Every decorative piece in the apartment we had shared in Ottawa was mine: the books on the shelves, the pictures, the Argentine souvenirs. Her only contribution was a clock she had inherited from her grandparents. Otherwise, she made no effort to put her personal stamp on our place.

The super let me into Nancy's apartment when I showed him the death notice. He took down my name and telephone number and asked about the rent payments. I said I was going to cancel the lease formally once I had all the papers in place. There were no esthetic surprises when I looked around Nancy's apartment. It was sparsely furnished and so neat it looked uninhabited. There were no dirty dishes in the sink or perishables in the fridge, no clutter in the bathroom, no plants on the windowsills. The bed was made, the pillows on the sofa in the living room were plumped up. She had taken the grandfather clock with her when we separated. It was mounted on the wall behind the sofa, in splendid isolation. The rest of the wall was an empty expanse of white. Over against the opposite wall was a plain desk and a small bookcase, which held a dozen paperback novels — romances and whodunnits. There were no sentimental relics, no family or boyfriend photos, no knickknacks. I remembered Nancy commenting on the books in my apartment in Buenos Aires. Proust bored her. Dostoyevsky disgusted her. She shrugged her shoulders at the rest of the classics. Dumas, maybe, but she preferred love and adventure in an easy style, with a happy ending and all loose ends tied up neatly.

The wastepaper basket beside her desk was empty, the desk itself swept clean. It was as if Nancy had not planned on coming back and readied the apartment for the next occupant, but then she had always been a tidy person. The drawers and closets in her bedroom were half-empty, but then she had never been into fashion. I started dumping the contents into garbage bags — dresses, underwear, jackets, coats, bedding, bathroom supplies – and stopped halfway through. What if the notice of her death was fake? It was better to wait with clearing the apartment until my return from Argentina. There were two bills left to pay, I saw, from the electricity company and from Bell Telephone. I noticed a cluster of calls to and from Argentina a few weeks ago and was curious enough to check the numbers. One was unlisted. The second belonged to the head office of the Argentine Film and Radio Corporation. In other words, Nancy had been in touch with Duarte before she left for Argentina.

I made a more systematic search, rifling through everything in case there was some indication of what the two of them were up to. I checked Nancy's coat pockets and turned her purses upside down. I went through her address book. The unlisted number was Duarte's, as I had suspected. She hadn't spelled out his name. He appeared as "JD". Mine was under "PA". Liliana's and Mona's numbers were listed under their full names. I found nothing else of significance, but I held on to the address book just in case. I looked at the thin blue copies in Nancy's checkbook. She had paid for a bus ticket to Toronto and a plane ticket to Buenos Aires. It didn't add up to anything definite. I still didn't know why Nancy went to Argentina. I had told Mona that she had gone on a holiday. Perhaps she did. Perhaps Duarte invited her or offered her a job. It was all speculation, and maybe I was paranoid after all and there was no reason for suspecting that the notice of her death was a fake.

What did I really know about Nancy? Even after living together with her for three years, I didn't feel that I had

295

come near the core. She had always played her cards close to her chest.

I stop rehashing my relationship with Nancy when the plane breaks through the cloud cover and the stewardess collects the trays and tells us to fold up the tables and put our seats into the upright position. We will be landing in twenty minutes.

23

At the airport in Miami, I get away from thinking by doing the practical things required of me, retrieving my luggage, checking into a hotel for the night, eating dinner, and then I'm too tired to think, to build backward and outward from my memories, piling up a rat's nest of "what ifs".

I fall asleep. I don't wake until daylight creeps into the room and it's time to get going on the final leg of my journey. But as soon as I have boarded the flight to Buenos Aires, my brain is at it again, an endless line of questions coming around in circles. Am I falling into a trap? What role is Nancy playing in all of this? Is she alive or dead? How much do I really know about her? Perhaps I didn't make enough of an effort to understand her, but our knowledge of others is so fragmentary, limited to the hints they give us, the vibration of their words in the air.

She liked me enough to sponsor me, but not enough to stay. Did she come to resent the absence of love in our marriage? Did she feel used? I admit there was a moral ambiguity about accepting her offer to sponsor me and marrying her for that purpose, but after teasing the question apart, I decided that strict morality was reserved for philosophy books or literature. In real life it was a luxury I couldn't afford. Most of the time I compromised and maneuvered between what was good for me and what I could square with my conscience without totally disgusting myself. Besides, Nancy knew what she was getting. I made no pretenses. I never said I loved her. We had no pet names for each other. We did not hug or cuddle. Except for sex, when we both needed it, we lived like roommates. Esthetics kept us apart as well. Nancy provided no esthetic pleasure. Her clothing seemed the wrong cut, her jackets lugubrious, her shoes of a functional ugliness. I tried to make my eyes glide over her without seeing, I allowed her voice to fall through me. Occasionally we clicked and had a good time, and for a couple of days we felt the afterglow, the warmth of companionship. But it never lasted, and soon we were back to the usual – a convenient arrangement even if it was constraining. Let's say, a bearable arrangement.

When Nancy was ready to move on, she made me pay for my freedom. I didn't argue. It was a fair price for slipping out of the straitjacket which tightened my heart. After Nancy left for Montreal, I came alive again, hospitable to chances and opportunities, sensitive to the promises of life. I had a heightened sense of possibilities. I was willing to indulge in romance once more and fill the cracks in my soul. I tried at any rate — first with Julia, whom I met in a bar, an old-fashioned kind of lounge, with dark wood-panelled walls and a star-burst patterned carpet which didn't show spills. The counter was a cheerful laminated red with the bar stools upholstered in matching red vinyl, and the lights were on low to flatter appearances. Julia was there with a group of friends. Their joshing and bantering attracted me because of the absence of such a setting in my own life. A thick layer of familiarity surrounded them, as if they had known each other for ever. Maybe Julia felt watched. She turned, caught me looking at her and returned my look with a darting sexiness in her eyes. The bar counter curved in a shallow u-shape making it easy for her to lean across and extend the conversation to me, drawing me into her circle. She had the athletic body of a swimmer or a runner, I noticed. Her blonde hair was straight, touching her shoulders. Her cheeks dimpled when she laughed, and she laughed not only with her eyes and lips, but twisted her head back, and wiggled her shoulders, and moved her hands in sync with her laughter. She looked lively. We left the bar together that night. We both wanted the evening to go on. We had a need and a use for each other – shouldn't that make things easy? Maybe not, because I wanted more of a challenge, more of a push-back. I needed unpredictability to get to the point of pure desire, but mainly I needed conversation, and we didn't seem to have much to say to each other once the afterglow of the sex act had faded. Joshing and kidding and running a few good lines was Julia's forte – we never got beyond that. The feeling that we weren't a good fit was mutual, and the relationship petered out by consent.

After that, I started dating one of my colleagues. Cathy was a lover of language. It was easy to talk to her, but she turned out to be entirely into mind games and content with a celibate life. I was not. After a few weeks, we returned to being just colleagues.

Then I met Marie in the elevator of my building. She had recently moved in, she said. The first date was promising. We had things in common, an easy give and take of words and ideas. It made me feel that I wasn't in a walled-off place after all. Our lives were sharable. She cut an elegant figure in clothes and was beautiful without. She had a delicate face, clear gray eyes, and soft skin that made her look vulnerable. She kindled my fire. There were warning lights, mind you —Marie needed to be reassured, endlessly.

Every date started with her angling for compliments.

"You haven't said anything about my new dress."

"Sorry. Was I supposed to say something?"

"You don't like it, right?"

"It looks fine."

"Be honest. It makes me look fat."

"It doesn't. It suits you."

I was willing to humour Marie and pay her compliments, if that's what she needed, but she wanted unconditional love, and I wasn't up to that. It didn't matter whether we talked about politics, food, books, movies, or the weather. There were preliminaries to get through first: pats and strokes, endearments, assurances of love. Sex was good, once we got there, but working up to it was strenuous, and there was the question of birth control. Marie was Catholic. She was willing to commit the sin of sleeping with me, but she had qualms about methods of birth control.

"Let's just use the natural method," she said. "My periods are pretty regular."

"But condoms are safer."

"Ugh, condoms," she said. "Gross."

I couldn't tell whether she meant my use of the word or the thing itself. In any case, I didn't want to run the risk of getting her pregnant. We went on seeing each other but it was clear that this was a sticking point we couldn't get past. The breakup was bitter and "my fault". I wasn't sure how to get back to friendliness with Marie. Luckily we didn't run into each other very often. If we did, in the parking lot or on the elevator, we kept to comments on the weather, but I could tell she hadn't forgiven me.

It wasn't just sex that stymied my relationship with women. I simply couldn't connect in the intimate, effortless way that brings you home and bonds you. Not with Marie, not with the others. Whether we talked or made out, nothing entered the deep part of my cortex. Everything seemed to involve a lot of maneuvering and smiling on cue. I was afraid that marriage to Nancy had ruined me for any more profound relationship. I suspected that I had been rational too long and lost my ability to feel passion. It had been so easy with Colette — kindling a desire, achieving an absolute state of flesh, losing myself in the moment. Perhaps it was the thrill of adultery, or the vertiginous power of being young. No, I fought the idea that I had somehow crossed a threshold and couldn't go back. It was just a matter of finding the right woman. After all, when I saw Mona in Toronto, I immediately felt the erotic charge, the thrill I had been waiting for, the surge of happiness. And that night could have been perfect if I hadn't ruined it with my question about the key to the safe. Mona's note, the letter the receptionist handed me when I checked out of the hotel in

Toronto, told me that it was over. Or was it? I parsed Mona's words, going on another round of dissecting, probing, second-guessing myself, slipping into the condition I want to avoid. I swear, once I'm done with Argentina, I'll stop watching myself instead of the outside world. I will go back to living in the moment.

24

Lascelles picks me up at the airport in Buenos Aires. The rainy season has started. It's a relief, he says. It's been a long dusty summer.

The road glistens with wetness, the air is moist and pleasantly cool. I always liked the fall season. Each day goes through the seasons, crisp mornings, a spring-like awakening at noon, a drenching shower or two, and now as we step out of the terminal, the warmth of the afternoon sun.

"Sorry to hear about Nancy," he says. I had told him about her death in a car accident, but not about my doubts. He spares me the condolences and the need to act solemn. He knows that we separated two years ago and that it was a marriage of convenience in the first place. "What exactly happened?" he asks.

"I don't know. I guess I'll find out."

"Or not. You know how it is with government agencies. If it involves looking up a file, they'll give you the runaround."

When I phoned Lascelles and said I was coming, he invited me to stay with him, but I declined. I said I was getting too old to bunk with friends.

"So why didn't you stay with me – have you turned into a loner?" he says as we move along the perimeter road and merge into heavy traffic.

"Maybe I've always had a tendency that way. I never liked to share quarters."

"Is that why you held out so long, while the rest of us got married young?"

"No, that wasn't it," I say. "I was in love with your wife. – Now it can be told, I guess."

"I've known that for a long time," he says. "You had an affair with Colette."

"How did you find out?"

"Colette was spiteful. When we broke up, she counted off the men she had slept with, all of them better in bed than I, she said. – You were one of them."

There is no resentment in his voice. Or embarrassment in mine, when I say: "I see." It seems too long ago to matter to him.

When we arrive at the hotel, he says: "I have to go back to the office, but let's have a *cafecito* and catch up on everything."

We go to the café next door and sit across from each other at a small glass table. Lascelles' hair is thinning, I notice. His glasses have slipped down and reveal two raw dents at the side of his nose. He pushes them back up.

"How's business?" I ask.

"Okay as far as the numbers go."

I hear the hesitation in his voice. "But?"

"But I'm not in charge. It's no longer my magazine. You know that Duarte is the head of the National Radio and Film Corporation now?"

I can guess what's coming: Duarte is working the system.

"And he collects 'donations' from you?" I say.

"I could live with that, but he has turned into a silent partner. He decides what I can publish and what I can't publish."

"What's it to him?"

"He wants publicity for his favourites — agents who pay him or women who sleep with him — and he wants to cut out others who have gotten on his wrong side, who aren't toeing the line. I've had it with the hassle. I want to retire, but on what? At least I changed my savings into American dollars some time ago. Thank God for that, because the peso is sinking like a stone. You were lucky you sold your apartment when you did. The whole country is going to the dogs."

"I take it there was a run on the banks after Evita's death."

He nods. "The people who kept their heads went to the bank, cashed in their savings and converted them to foreign currency. The rest went crazy. Instead of looking after their interests, they lined up to view the coffin. Two million people. You should have seen the flower tributes piled up against the wall of the Ministry, a meter high. It was mass hysteria. Everything came to a standstill. The shops closed. Hotel guests had to make their own beds. You couldn't get a taxi for days. And the nastiness if you didn't fall in with the general mood, if you didn't wear black or, God forbid, dared to laugh! Then it was decided to build a crypt for her, modelled after Napoleon's tomb, with a giant marble statue of a *descaminado*. But the mood has changed, and Peron is up against the military and the oligarchs."

"I didn't expect him - or Duarte- to hold out even this long."

"Especially not the way Peron is carrying on. He is going senile. He has turned his estate at Olivos into a recreation centre for high school girls. He watches them play basketball for hours, I am told, drooling over them. And he gives them rides on his scooter, feeling them up. Rumour has it, he is keeping a 13-year old as his mistress, one Nelly Rivas. It would be great fodder for the magazine, but of course Duarte won't let me print that. It's in his interest to protect Peron."

Lascelles lets that information sink in. "But he can't go on like that forever. There will be a revolution. Soon." He pushes away his empty coffee cup and makes ready to get up.

"Are you still in touch with Colette?" I say.

He is standing now. "I haven't seen her in a year."

"You have her address? I might look her up."

"I wouldn't if I were you. She is a mess. Drugs, alcohol. She'll pump you for money. Don't give her any. It goes straight up her veins." He makes a motion like stabbing his arm with a needle. "She got in with the wrong crowd. Duarte's crowd. He got her hooked on drugs. She pimps for him, I think. It's an ugly story. — Duarte wants to talk to you, by the way. And that's an order, as you know. Did you tell him that you were coming to Argentina?"

"Why would I?"

"He didn't get it from me either."

My suspicions are back. Duarte is up to some trick.

"Did he say why he wanted to talk to me?

"Not a word. All I can say is *ojo!*" He pulls at his eyelid, giving me the familiar Argentinian warning. "He's a dangerous man."

Lascelles needs to get back to work. We hug local style, with our hands clasped and patting each other's shoulders.

"Look me up before you go back to Canada," he says. "Let me know how it all panned out."

25

The next morning I go to the morgue. An attendant in scrubs takes me to a bare windowless room with a tiled floor. The air is stale. Maybe this is the smell of decomposing flesh. As he wheels out the steel gurney with Nancy's body, I have a glimpse of the room beyond, a warehouse of corpses stored on long shelves.

"Brace yourself," he says. "She was in the water for two days. It's an ugly sight."

In the water? I thought it was a road accident. But perhaps it happened on a bridge or in the harbour. Did the car go off the road?

He folds back the sheet wrapped around the body and uncovers her face. It looks beaten up, disfigured with gashes and lacerations. The eyes are closed, the skin is pulpy and discoloured, the mouth grotesquely swollen. There is no humanity left in this face. It is bereft of every expression, even the terror she must have felt as she was drowning. It has as much in common with the Nancy I know as a piece of squashed and rotten vegetable in a garbage bin. She is dead alright. No tricks being played here. I look at the attendant, unsure what I am expected to say.

"It's a shock, I know," the attendant says sympathetically. "They don't look like themselves when they've been through something like this."

"That's just it. She doesn't look like the woman I remember." I am aware of the irony of my words. What do I remember of Nancy? I'd often thought of her features as non-descript. Now she was truly faceless.

"Would you like me to uncover the rest of the body? Is there an identifying mark you are looking for?"

"A mole on her right arm."

He folds back the sheet to expose the arm, but it is mangled and the skin has sloughed off.

"Not helpful?"

I shrug.

He covers up the body again. "Just one more step," he says soothingly. "Signing the papers. Then you can collect the death certificate."

I sign the sheet he puts in front of me.

"How did it happen?" I say. "Is there a report on the accident?"

"You have to go to the police for that," he says and gives me the address of police headquarters.

I take a taxi there and inquire at the front desk. I give them Nancy's name and the date of death and ask to see the report on the accident. I am shown into the office of the sergeant in charge.

"What report?" he says. "There is no report."

He stares me down, but after I offer him a *coima*, he relaxes.

"I can't give you the file," he says. "It's classified. Someone was involved who can't be named."

"I see."

I wait in case he has more to tell me.

"You are from Canada?" he says. "Your Spanish is pretty good."

"I lived here for three years," I say. "I worked for Security."

He leans back in his chair and laughs. "Well, then, what are you doing here, *che*? Ask *them*. They hold the strings." He moves his hands up and down like maneuvering marionettes. "Nothing happens here without their approval."

I thank him. There is nothing more he can do for me. I look up my old boss next. Perhaps Jorge can tell me what happened. He still occupies the same grubby office in the Ministry of Labour, with two steel desks painted industrial grey, one for his use, the other permanently vacant, a place to deposit files, coats, overflowing ashtrays — the litter of Jorge's office life. A faded map of the city is tacked to one of the walls. The others are pockmarked with nail holes and show faint, discoloured outlines where other maps or pictures hung at another time.

Jorge offers me a chair.

"Back for a holiday?" he says, beaming at me. "How's the wife?"

I come right to the point. "Nancy is dead. That's why I'm back. She died here, in an accident."

Something comes on in his eyes, a light or an alarm.

311

"I'm sorry to hear it, *che*. My condolences," he says. His voice is formal all of a sudden. "Anything I can do for you?"

"I was wondering, is there's a way to find out how the accident happened."

"You should ask the police."

"I did. They sent me here."

He sighed. "You've been out of the country too long, my friend. And you've forgotten everything I taught you. If they tell you to ask Security, you don't need to ask, okay? You have your answer."

"I thought you might be able to do me a favour," I say.

"I would do you a favour any time, *che*, but not in this case. I can't." He looks at the map on the wall as if he was getting his instructions from there.

"No way to get at the information?"

He shakes his head. "I report to CIDE, and there are people you don't want to cross."

CIDE? State Intelligence? My suspicions revive. Was Duarte the driver of the car? Was he drunk?

Jorge gets up and takes my arm.

"Where are you staying, Pierre? I'll give you a ride."

In the car we make desultory conversation.

"So how's it going in Canada? What are you doing?"

"Working as a translator. From English to French."

"They speak French in Canada?"

"In one of the provinces. Quebec. —And how's it going with you?"

"Not as good as before."

"You mean, now that Evita is dead."

"Yeah. With her you knew where you stood."

"Not with Peron?"

"Not with him, no. And he might not be president much longer."

"They'll always need security," I say.

"Right. But will they need *me*? My son has an estancia in the south, near Rivadavia. He tells me to come and live with him and his family. But my wife doesn't want to leave Buenos Aires. What's there in Patagonia, she says. Only sheep. I can't talk to the sheep. On the other hand, they don't harm you, I say. She knows I'm right. She'll come around."

At the hotel we shake hands and wish each other good luck.

There is no use going through official channels, that much has become clear to me. I try another tack and phone Liliana. She owes me a favour. I got her and Duarte out of a tight spot in Rome. She might be able to connect me with Peron.

"How nice to hear from you, Pierre," she says, and immediately asks about Nancy.

I tell her that we separated two years ago. I don't say anything about the accident.

"She had a deft hand with children," Liliana says, "but I had to let her go." It sounds as if she is still holding a grudge against Nancy.

"Did she ever tell you why I let her go?" she says.

"I thought she quit."

"She tried to blackmail me. Either I'd give her a raise or she'd quit. So I let her go. Actually, I think she just tried it on. She wanted to go back to Canada anyway."

There is a pause. Liliana doesn't make it easy for me. She doesn't say: What's going on in your life? Or, why don't you drop by?

313

"I need to ask you a favour," I say.

"What favour?" she says. She doesn't sound too friendly.

"Could you put me in touch with Juan Peron? I need to talk to him privately."

She hesitates. "Is this about the safe in Switzerland?"

"Among other things," I say.

Nancy was right. Duarte had blabbed to Liliana.

"The papers have gotten hold of that," she says, trying to cover up her source. "A rumour is circulating that Evita deposited a casket of jewels in a Swiss bank," she says. "Peron is after the jewels of course, but nobody knows exactly where they are. The newspapers at least are making a big mystery of it. Carlos says it's not that easy anyway. According to the law, Peron has to divide everything with Evita's mother. – So, you want to talk to him? I suppose I could set up something for you. He usually takes his lunch at the Claridge." She makes apologetic noises. "I would have the two of you over for dinner, but Carlos doesn't want to associate with Peron anymore. It's politically risky, but mainly: Peron is going gaga."

"Going gaga – in what sense?"

"Well, to give you an example. When our daughter had her *quinceañera* at the Jockey Club, we couldn't very well *not* invite him. He came and ogled all the girls and said inappropriate thing to them. So Carlos said: That's it. We won't have him over anymore. But the poor man! He is so lonely now. I'll call him and set up lunch for the three of us. He'll jump at a chance to talk."

"Thanks," I say. She still hasn't said a word about the last time we saw each other, her nighttime visit with me at the embassy in Rome, the fact that she owes me a favour.

"Are you still seeing Duarte?" I ask.

"Oh no," she says, "that's over. I haven't seen him in years."

I'm not sure she will arrange anything for me, but she does. That same afternoon, she calls and says the three of us are on for lunch at the Claridge the following day.

I would have preferred to see Peron on my own. I can't talk about Nancy's accident or about the keys to the Swiss safe with Liliana there, but at least the lunch date will give me a chance to ask him for a private meeting later.

The taxi pulls up in front of the hotel entrance flanked by Ionic columns. I walk through the atrium into the wood-paneled dining room. I am early, but Peron is already there. He looks as buff and handsome as ever, although there is more gray in his hair now. He sits by himself at a table for six in the centre of the room, watching the scene with a patronizing smile, as if it had been arranged for his personal amusement. I wonder who else will join us.

He greets me cordially, as if we had known each other for a long time, but I recognize his amiable smile for what it is. A politician's non-committal friendliness. Peron has a talent for condescension and measures out the quantity of affability just so.

The headwaiter takes our order with a deferential bow. Another man comes over with a message from Liliana. She is delayed, unfortunately. No need to wait for her though.

"Liliana always has something on the go," Peron says with a salacious grin. "She's a nice enough woman, but not my type. She's always been a bit overweight, and now she's gone to lard. Carlos should have gotten rid of her long ago and found someone younger."

I am not sure what he expects me say, but he doesn't wait for my comment. He goes on talking.

"I like them young," he says. "I have a thirteen-year old living with me. She is hot. People are shocked when I tell them, and you know what I say? She's thirteen, yes. But I'm not superstitious, you know."

He laughs at his own joke, a chain smoker's rumbling laugh.

The tables around us are filling up. I see now why he has commandeered the centre table. People have to pass by us on the way to their table. Peron is looking for acquaintances and waylaying them. He doesn't even pretend to be interested in me. I am only a prop for his public performance. He leers at the women. He puts out his hand to the men as they pass. He is working the field.

Liliana never shows up.

I try to make conversation but Peron barely listens. A flicker of interest appears in his eyes when I mention that I accompanied Evita on the trip to Europe in '47.

"You did?" he says. "I'll tell my lawyers to contact you. They have a few questions for the people who were with Evita at that time. It's about a bank account she supposedly opened in Madrid or in Zurich. Do you know anything about that?"

"No," I say, "I know nothing about that." I've changed my mind. I don't think Peron is the right man to tell about the Swiss vault or, let's say, there won't be anything in it for me if I do. I'll have to rethink my plan.

He starts in on another question but is sidetracked by the arrival of a couple at a near-by table. "Do you know that fellow over there?" he says, staring at the man with hatred and making no effort to lower his voice. "He's the head of the Socialist party, a troublemaker. I said to my people: I want that man clubbed and hanged!" Then he turns his eyes back to me and comes to his senses. He takes up his napkin and puts it to his lips as if to seal them off. "What were we talking about?" he says vaguely.

"Your late wife," I say.

"Oh yes, Evita, the love of my life," he says.

There is absolutely no use in telling him about the keys to the Swiss safe or asking for his help in finding out more about Nancy's mysterious accident. Liliana is right. Peron has gone soft in the head and is losing his grip. He still has the presidential bearing. He looks sharp, but perhaps that's just the cunning of an idiot. I am not sure that he is capable of going beyond the immediate present. You don't want to deal with a man like that.

I tell him that I am expected at a meeting and excuse myself. He raises his hand in a kind of farewell blessing and mumbles "Good to talk to you". I make my escape.

There is one more thing I have to do before going back to Canada: look up Colette. I don't think of it as a social call. I think of it as a task, a closing out of my memories. It will be painful. Lascelles has warned me off, but she is part of the past which needs to be settled and sealed off before I can move on. There is too much cross traffic in my head, too much interference. I want to go back to Toronto, to Mona, with a clean slate. Past experience is useless because nothing is ever the same. I want to put it away in a book and leave it there, between the covers.

26

Colette lives next to the elevated beltway. When they put that road in ten years ago, they cut a swath through the city, demolishing anything directly in the way of construction and leaving the buildings on each side, with their balconies almost touching the guard rails. Only people who have no alternative live with the inferno of noise that penetrates the walls, the ceaseless rumble of cars and trucks and the exhaust fumes settling in every crevice and turning the air a hazy blue.

The taxi drops me off at the entrance to the building.

"You want me to wait?" the driver says. He means well. The neighbourhood isn't safe, and it may not be easy to find another taxi. A chain link fence with a razor wire on top borders the sidewalk. It goes all the way to a factory building in the distance. Trucks rumble by, turning in at the gate. On the other side of the street, a shirtless man lies on the ground in the shadow of the highway, strung out in a drugged sleep. A couple of young men linger in front of a kiosk selling drinks. Music is blaring from inside the hut. The men are punching each other, sparring, laughing.

I tell the taxi driver to wait for me. "I'll be half an hour or so," I say.

At the entrance to the building, I hesitate. There is a charred desolation about the place, but I will myself to go on. The inside of the building matches the raw concrete of the road. The corridors are unswept. Discarded food wrappers, broken glass, and dust have accumulated in the corners. Colette' flat is on the third floor, level with the traffic lanes. Through the window at the end of the corridor, I can see a blur of metal in motion. The walls echo the dull boom of the traffic.

When I knock on Colette's door, it gives way. It is unlatched and swings open at the touch of my hand. In the half-light coming through the lone window I see a room that is living- and bedroom and kitchen all in one. On the coffee table in front of the couch is a spoon with burn marks and a length of pipe. A half-smoked cigarette, balanced on the edge of a saucer, is streaming a thin, acrid wave of smoke.

I hear a toilet flush, then a woman's voice:

"Be there in a sec."

She comes out of the bathroom, a stick figure of a woman. Colette, or a dystopic vision of her, wearing faded red shorts and a halter top.

"Who the fuck are you?" she says, holding on to the bathroom door, ready to retreat behind it. Then a light of recognition comes into her eyes. "No," she says. "Not possible! Pierre? Is that you? What the hell are you doing here?"

"I thought I'd look you up. Not a convenient time? You are expecting someone?"

"Yeah, I'm expecting someone. Doesn't mean he'll actually show up. So, sit down." She points to a chair and lowers herself on to the couch, which serves as her bed. She untangles a bottle of vodka from the sheets. "Want some?" she says holding it out to me."

"I just want to talk."

She shakes a fresh cigarette from a pack, lights it, takes a long drag and leans back, pulling up her skinny legs and showing me her meager knees. "You are in luck. I'm almost sober."

This is the woman for whom I felt passion once. I remember the feeling in a cerebral way, as if I was telling myself a story, but I can't recapture it or even recall Colette's face as it was then. I see familiar traces in the lines around her mouth, in the shape of her chin, but it is a faint resemblance, and there is something too nocturnal about the woman on the dishevelled bed. Colette's hair which used to be abundant looks brittle now, her soft hands have turned bony. It isn't just the passage of time, it is something more ruinous that has taken hold of her. I find it a laborious climb back to the past I remember. But then she switches to French, and the timbre of her voice is intimately familiar, although it too has coarsened.

"I thought you married and moved to Canada," she says. "That's what Louis told me. You've decided to come back?"

"Nancy –my wife– was back here for a holiday and died in a car accident. That's why I came. To identify the body and sign off on the papers."

"Nancy?" she says, giving the name a French inflection. There is a glimmer of sudden insight in her eyes.

It is jolting to hear Nancy's name spoken by Colette — two women I have never linked in my mind until now when I make the connection. *She got in with the wrong crowd,* Louis said. *Duarte's crowd.* Did Nancy get in with his crowd as well?

"You heard about the accident?" I say.

"All I heard is that she had it coming. She tried to put one over on Juancito. Selling him a fake. Big mistake. You don't play games with him. But you probably know more about it than I."

I have asked for information in all the wrong places, and now I've found the answer here in Colette's apartment, together with my past.

"So he killed her," I say.

"Or took her on a scare tour."

"What does that mean?"

"Oh, I don't know. Shove a broken bottle into her cunt. Beat her up. Show her who's boss. Kill her slowly."

There is no mobility in Colette's face. It's an ordinary story to her. You live dangerously. You die. She is dying too. Duarte is merciless. He makes no exception for anyone.

"You are not afraid of him?"

"Afraid of Juancito? Nah, more like: I hate his guts."

She is talking with nervous animation now, with a sudden alertness in her eyes, a light I recognize from long ago, although it is charged with a different kind of energy now, the potency of hatred.

"If anything, *he* should be afraid. He has a lot of enemies, you know, because he can't stop himself from ruining people. Everyone he touches turns to rot. He keeps a .45 in his bathroom. It's no good keeping it there, I tell him. You won't have time to get it when you need it. But he only laughs. I know who has it in for me, he says, and who I can trust." She shrugs. "Last time I looked, the gun was still there, behind the mirror, together with a wad of dollars. I was tempted to take the money, but..."

She trails off, takes a last drag on her cigarette. When she leans forward and butts it out on the saucer, I can see the track marks and bruises on her arms.

"And he trusts you?" I say.

"Yeah," she says. "Especially when he is drunk. Which happens a lot lately. He's a lost boy now that Evita is dead."

She leans back. The light in her eyes has gone out. She looks at me dully and picks at the scabs that pockmark her arms. Duarte is killing her slowly.

"Does he do drugs with you?" I ask.

"Nah, he doesn't do drugs," she says. Her speech and all her movements have slowed down. "He just drinks himself stupid." She stares past me at the door. The steady throb of the traffic noise fills the silence that has fallen between us.

"I guess the guy isn't coming," she says, pulling at her earlobe absentmindedly. Her face is washed clean of expression. "Listen, can you lend me some money?"

"I don't think so. You'll spend it on drugs."

"And you are going to be my saviour, or what?"

She is right. I can't save her. She is too far gone.

"How much do you need?" I say.

323

"You have dollars? A hundred would be nice."

I give her two twenties.

"Gate-keeping, are we? Well, thanks anyway."

She tucks the bills into the folds of the tangled sheets. I get up to go. She follows me. At the door, she hesitates.

"Where is-?" she says thoughtfully.

"What?"

"My keys. Oh, never mind. I'll just bolt the door. Safer anyway."

She holds the door open for me. I'm relieved she doesn't lean in to kiss me. We just look at each other silently, for a final measuring up.

The taxi driver has turned around the car and is waiting for me on the other side of the street. I hear the click as he unlocks the car door.

"Got what you wanted?" he asks.

I nod, although I'm not sure I did. I wanted to close a chapter in my life, so I could move on, go back to Toronto, be with Mona. But that chapter of my past is still open-ended. One more move, one more action is required to shut it down for good.

27

When Lascelles said that Duarte wanted to see me, I thought: Let him find me. I have nothing to say to him. Later when it became clear that Peron was losing it, that there was no use talking to him, I played with the idea of negotiating a price for the keys with Duarte after all. But there wasn't enough satisfaction in that for me. Making him pay wasn't going to hurt him enough. Besides, there was always a risk of being double-crossed. *Ojo*, as Lascelles said. Why run a risk? But that was yesterday's thinking. Now that I've seen Nancy's bloated body and Colette's dead eyes, Duarte is on my list of unfinished business. It's no longer a question of getting back at him for petty stuff like sneering at me and treating me with contempt. He has ruined lives and managed to get away with it. I'm not sure that I am the man to make him pay for his crimes, but a vague plan is taking shape in my head and then, determination.

Looking up Colette was supposed to close a chapter. Instead it opened up a new one. When I went to her apartment, the photo above Lascelles' desk was in my mind's eye. It had been taken years ago and I had made the necessary adjustments. I expected her to be thicker in the waist, more into middle age and mellowed. I expected her to look at me with a tolerant smile, remembering the folly and the pleasure of an affair with a young man in Brussels. She taught me some of life's pleasures — not the mechanics of sex, I mean, although she was good at that too, but living life with intensity. I cut out what Lascelles told me about her drug habit. I thought that seeing her again would revive something in me that I had lost during the age of reason – my partnership with Nancy. I thought I could bring something away from this visit and carry it forward. It needed only a spark for me to live again – I did not dare couple that thought with Mona's name. I suppressed it, so as not to disturb the natural progression of things and jinx the revival of passion. Close one chapter first, I thought, then go on. That's what I wanted from my visit with Colette, even though Lascelles had warned me.

He was right. Seeing Colette the way she is now, didn't provide the transition I'd hoped for. It only extended the story and forced me to tack on a different ending: revenge, which burns hotter than passion. But I didn't understand any of that when I left Colette's place. In the taxi, during the ride back to the hotel, I was still sorting out what I had seen, the ruin of a woman, and what I had heard, that Duarte was involved in Nancy's ruin as well. Colette was cryptic about what exactly happened. The name "Nancy" seemed to awaken something in her, but I couldn't be sure that she knew anything or just made it up. She was too far gone to trust.

Now, in my hotel room, looking up Duarte's number in Nancy's address book, the reasons are coming together in my mind, in a vague and unsatisfactory way at first. I want to do business with Duarte, I am thinking, but what kind of business? There is a discordance, a discrepancy between today's truth and yesterday's expectations. It is only when I dial his number that I begin to understand what I am feeling: wrath. Only the biblical word will do. A rage is broiling inside me against the man who ruins lives to satisfy his need for money, for power, for the sheer pleasure of watching them suffer. It feels like a new sensation, but it stirs something that is old and has been in me for a long time: the desire to get even. I can taste revenge in my mouth now. It has a tinny flavour.

The moment of clarity seems to bring everything into focus, even the room I'm in. I see the bed anew, the black telephone on the nightstand, the picture on the wall — a reproduction of an impressionist painting of a Paris street in the rain. I hear the faint rattle of the window sash, which isn't closed all the way and makes the curtain undulate in the draft. I see the hurrying clouds and the dark sky outside and note that it matches the one in the painting. I hear the first rain drops drumming against the window and go to shut it. Then I dial Duarte's number.

He answers on the second ring.

Digame, he says in a voice edging on a snarl.

I say my name. "Lascelles tells me you want to talk to me."

"Yeah," he says. "I have a job for you, Adams. Come by tomorrow." His voice has evened out, but a vague atmospheric hostility remains.

"It'll have to be tonight," I say. "I'm flying out tomorrow morning."

There is a pause. I can hear him ask a question of someone before he comes back on the line. "I'm busy this evening," he says, "but you can drop by later, at - let's see - eleven. No, better make it midnight."

He gives me the address: the office of the Radio and Film Corporation. It's in walking distance from my hotel.

I check the time. It's seven o'clock. I wish I did not have five hours to think about what I will say to Duarte and what I might do. I am afraid that my wrath will diminish and my will erode.

I take a shower and get changed. I go out and wander aimlessly through the streets, rehearsing my thoughts, etching them into my brain to make them permanent. It is raining steadily now. The doorman at the hotel has supplied me with an umbrella, but water is starting to soak through the seams of my shoes. I look into a bookstore and scan the titles on the shelves. Nothing appeals. Fiction is too trite, history meaningless, travel guides no help. I buy a newspaper and sit down in the café next door to read it, but I turn the pages without concentration, every headline blurs into Duarte's name. I walk back to the hotel, turning the list of his crimes over in my mind. They are well known, too common among members of the government and administration to raise eyebrows. Duarte isn't the only one who skims off money, extorts payments, procures women for himself and his friends. But the others camouflage their crimes out of fear of punishment or a residue of shame. Duarte glories in them. People tell stories of the weekend orgies on his island retreat in the Tigre, of the men and women he has ruined. They tell stories of personal humiliations with a false grin to cover up their embarrassment and the helpless fury they felt when Duarte made them crawl. They don't have the courage to show their resentment openly, not yet. Liliana's husband is a bellwether. Gutierrez no longer wants to associate with Peron and his hangers-on. The Peronists are marked men, smelling of doom. The revolution is coming, but not fast enough for me.

I eat dinner in the dining room of the hotel, distracting myself by watching the other patrons — mostly businessmen, a few tourists, men engaged in deal-making, old couples eating in silence. It is a relief to contemplate the ordinariness of the scene. If this was a film, I think, ominous strains of music would well up right now, foreshadowing dramatic action. I wipe the scene from my mind. I am falling into the old mistake of watching myself act instead of taking action.

I sign the waiter's chit and walk out into the street. It's only 11:30. I will be early for my appointment with Duarte, but I'm too impatient to wait any longer. The rain has turned to drizzle. I still don't know for sure that Duarte wanted to lure me to Buenos Aires and was setting a trap for me. I am still not sure what Colette knows and what she was making up, what is the truth and what merely a drugged fantasy of hers. Nancy's death was real, although the secrecy surrounding it makes me think that the accident was the fault of some big-shot, whose reckless driving was being covered up. Maybe Duarte himself, maybe one of his associates. He kept an eye on the aftermath. That's how he found out that I am here to sign the papers. I know what "job" he has in mind for me: selling him the key. Or, failing that, robbing me. He may have put his goons on my tail, but I doubt he will go further until he finds out whether or not I am willing to make a deal with him. Still, it pays to play it safe and keep my eyes open. I might be walking into something fatal.

This is the hour when the city's night life moves into full swing. There is safety in numbers. I relied on bar-hopping men, romantic couples, and passing cars to stay in the public eye, but in this damp weather, there is little foot traffic. I pass a restaurant. The revolving door pushes bits of laughter and conversation out into the street. At the corner, the lit sign above a bar casts a reassuring light across the pavement. Then I'm on my own for a stretch. In my mind I am back on the security beat, keeping my eyes out for sudden movements, shadows, dark recesses. A muscle memory of the holstered gun I used to carry makes me reach up and pat my chest to make the phantom weight go away.

A guard patrols the sidewalk in front of the Film and Radio Corporation. He stops when he sees me crossing the street and takes up station in front of the entrance. He has probably been told to be on the lookout for me.

"I'm here to see Señor Duarte," I tell the guard.

He doesn't ask my name. He opens the door for me and follows me into the hall.

"Just a moment," he says. "Okay if I check you?"

I nod, and he pads me down. After he has satisfied himself that I don't carry a gun, he turns to a phone on the wall. He lifts up the receiver. A moist film of drizzle glistens on his sleeve.

"Visitor for you, Señor Duarte," he says, hangs up and gives me the go-ahead, pointing to a door at the top of a flight of stairs.

I walk upstairs and knock on the door. A voice calls "Come in" and I enter a small lobby. It opens into an opulent living room that affects the atmosphere of a British gentlemen's club. It is furnished with squat leather sofas and chairs. Persian carpets cover the parquet floor. On the far wall is a screened fireplace with the grate set for a log fire. A large painting of a hunting scene hangs above the mantle. Duarte lives here, above the offices of the Radio and Film Corporation? Convenient for interviewing hopeful applicants, I suppose. Only a few steps from his office to his bedroom.

Duarte is sprawled on a couch in front of the unlit fireplace. He turns around but doesn't bother to get up. He is well into the drink. There is an almost empty bottle of whiskey on the coffee table. He motions me to sit down on the couch and leans over to get another glass from a bar cart stocked with bottles, carafes, and mixing paraphernalia. His movements are slightly off balance.

He hasn't changed much since I've seen him last. Same equine forelock, same dark seriousness in his eyebrows, same broodiness. He is still leading-man handsome, large-chested, with a commanding voice – a little raspier maybe. There are other barely visible changes I notice now that I look at him more closely. The skin around his jaw has lost tension. And the drink has stalled the kinetic energy in his broad shoulders.

"Sit," he says, as if talking to a dog.

331

I take the drink he offers me. "So, you have a job for me?"

"I need the keys to the Swiss safe," he says. "Have you brought yours by any chance? I'll buy it off you."

"I didn't bring it along. I thought it would be safer at home."

He scowls.

"You saw Peron before you phoned me."

"Did Liliana tell you?"

"I don't need Liliana to tell me anything. I have my own people. You offered him the key and he didn't go for it? Wasn't prepared to pay your price?"

"I didn't offer him the key, and he doesn't have to pay me. He has a right to it, no?"

Duarte doesn't answer. He rubs his eyes, as if my question had irritated them. "I'll buy it off you," he says. "Tell me what you want for it. That wife of yours, Nancy – or is she your ex-wife? –she did a botch job. I should have gone to you in the first place, but she phoned me a couple of months ago and offered to get the key from Mona. I thought the two of them were friends or something. I didn't ask any questions. I had nothing to lose. I paid her a bit of money up front, the rest to be paid on delivery of the goods. So then she tells me she's got the key and wants to collect the money. She comes here and tries to pawn off a fake on me. I don't know what the hell she was thinking. Nobody fucks with me like that."

"I know," I say. "I've got the death certificate."

"So maybe *you* can do the job for me," he says. "We'll make a deal for both keys – yours and Mona's." His voice is sluggish.

I look at him steadily. "Okay," I say. "I think I can do the job for you."

"Yeah," he says, "I remember you were making nice with the girl. You still in touch with her?"

"Not really."

"Well, get in touch and work the magic. I'll make it worth your while. You can name your price."

"How do I know you'll pay up?"

"I pay for what I get. Ask anybody. They'll tell you: I pay up." The words come out slurred.

"Alright," I say. "I'll think about it. We'll talk about the price when I have both keys."

We sip our drinks and make desultory conversation, saying nothing much. The dialogue is going better than I expected. Duarte supplies the cue. I answer. It's as if we had rehearsed the scene a hundred times before. He asks what I'm doing in Canada without listening to my answer. I ask him about the Argentine film industry. He gives me what sounds like a well-rehearsed clip for the press, but his voice is thickening and his tongue gets in the way.

"You flying out tomorrow?" he says, emptying his glass. He pushes out the words with an effort now. "When?"

"I have to be at the airport at eight."

I check my watch. "It's late. I'd better be going. Can I use your washroom?"

He doesn't answer, just gives me a sodden look and points toward the hallway. The effort of speaking is becoming too much for him. His eyes are glassy.

The washroom is all white tiles. It has the sanitary look of a hospital ward. No cozy Britishness here. I check the mirror. It is built up, two inches off the wall, to allow for a shallow closet behind. You have to be in the know to see that it can be opened at the side. If Colette hadn't mentioned that Duarte was hiding a gun behind the mirror, I might not have noticed it. I open the side panel and peer into the narrow shaft. I see the gun and recognize the grooved wooden grip. It's an army-issue Ballester-Molina, the same I trained on when I was in Security. I pull it out. It is loaded and lies in my hand heavy and solid, beautifully made by a company that builds trucks. I tuck it into the inside pocket of my jacket, then change my mind. Too awkward to reach. Too obvious. I change it to my right outside pocket. What else is in the mirror closet? I reach into the cavity and touch something soft, a rolled-up wad of banknotes. As I retract my hand, my fingers pass over a piece of metal. I slide it toward me. A key. Duarte's key to the Swiss safe. I put it into my back pocket, next to my wallet.

I close up the cabinet and wipe off the fingerprints with a towel. Before I go back into the living room, I flush the toilet for audio effect and go through the motions of washing my hands in the sink. The gun forms a visible bulge but that can't be helped. I sink my hand deep into the pocket to camouflage it and step out.

Duarte is still sitting on the couch, but his feet are up on the coffee table now. His head is resting on the back of the sofa, his mouth open. I listen to his breath coming regularly, with a slight rasp in his throat. He looks peaceful. The drink has put him to sleep. I walk up to him and put the gun to his head, as close to his right temple as I can without touching it. I pull the trigger. The gun makes a sharp barking noise. The force of the impact kicks Duarte's head sideways. His eyes snap open and look at me for a moment with wonder, then close again, but a brilliant, angry eye opens up in the side of his head, welling with red hot fury. I wipe the grip of the gun with my jacket and put it into his right hand.

I wait a moment in case someone has heard the shot, but I know it's unlikely. The house is silent, except for the muted sound of a passing car coming through the windows. The guard will have resumed his patrol outside. I look around the room for traces of my presence. Only the glass from which I have been sipping. I wash it in the kitchen sink and put it back on the bar cart. On the way out I check my face in the hall mirror and run my fingers through my hair. I look calm. I feel nothing, not even satisfaction, although there is a pulsing in my temples.

I walk downstairs softly as if I could wake up Duarte. The guard is standing under the globe light illuminating the exit, smoking a cigarette. I pass him, raising my hand in salute. He grunts, balancing the cigarette on one side of his mouth.

Out of the corner of my eye, I see a car parked on the other side of the street. Someone is standing on the pavement beside it, smoking. I see only the glow of his cigarette. I walk on and hear the engine come to life. At the end of the street, as I turn into the broad avenue leading to the hotel, I look back discreetly. The car hasn't moved. It is still idling in front of the Film and Broadcast Corporation.

I am strangely calm considering that I have just killed a man. I imagine a soldier must feel like that after killing an enemy. He has done his duty. No need to feel guilty, no need to make excuses. I have done my duty. I owed it to Colette, to Nancy, to myself. With luck I'll be on the plane tomorrow before they discover the body — the body of a man who committed suicide, the gun still in his hand, fingers on the trigger stiffened by death. I don't look back, I look forward. If any suspicion falls on me because I was the last person to see Duarte alive, I have my story pat. He was drunk and despondent over the situation after Evita's death, I'll tell them under interrogation. He was afraid. "I have too many enemies," he said to me. "If Peron falls, they will have their knives out for me. I might as well kill myself." That's what he said to me, but of course I took that to be the maudlin words of a drunk. I didn't think he would actually do it.

It is past one o'clock when I arrive in the hotel lobby. I ring for the night clerk, pay my bill, and ask for a wake-up call at six and a taxi to take me to the airport.

Upstairs, I pack my suitcase. As I gather my belongings, I have a vague sense that someone has been in the room during my absence. Things are not quite as I left them. In the closet, the hangers are pushed to one side, as if someone had wanted to put my navy suit jacket on display. Did I do that when I took out the gray jacket this morning or did Duarte use my absence to have the room searched for the key to the Swiss safe? Did he think I'd be careless enough to leave it here? I impulsively check my wallet. Both keys – mine and Mona's — are still there. I reach into my back pocket and add Duarte's. The three keys distort the soft leather of the wallet. I will find another place for them when I get home. But that's a job for tomorrow. I go to bed and fall asleep almost instantly.

I wake up to the ringing of the phone. The front desk. My wakeup call. As I reach for the receiver, I cast a glance at my watch and see that it is only a little after 5. What the hell?

I answer the phone.

"Jorge here," a voice says. "Listen, *che*, I'll be at your door in a minute. Get dressed. We haven't got much time."

Then there is a click. He has hung up.

Have they found Duarte already? Is Jorge in charge of the investigation? Potential scenes race through my mind as I splash my face with cold water and get into my clothes. Jorge is at the door before I have put on my shoes.

"I see you are packed," he says. "Good. Let's go. I'll drive you to the airport."

"What's going on?" I say, searching his face for answers, but it is unreadable, the same benevolent mask he wears at all times, the same jolly smile.

"Later," he says.

I follow him down the corridor to the elevator.

He waves me past. "We'll take the freight elevator to the garage," he says.

On the way down, he looks at me and shakes his head. "When I hired you – when they *made me* hire you – I thought to myself: That guy isn't cut out for the job, but I was wrong." He nods sagely. "You are a man full of surprises, Pierre."

We walk past the garage attendant, asleep with his head down on the counter, out to Jorge's car parked at the curb. When we are on the highway, he opens up.

"So, I get a call at three in the morning," he says. "They tell me to go to the Film and Radio Corporation immediately. Duarte is dead. My first thought was: Peron's people got him. Duarte was a liability. They tell me that the guard at the Corporation made the rounds. He

337

checked Duarte's door. It was unlocked. He went in and found the body. And a suicide note. Then they tell me Duarte had a visitor who left around 1 am, a guy with an accent. They guard described him. I realized it was you, but I kept my mouth shut and thought I'll talk to you first. I'm not sure how this is going to pan out."

"What did the suicide note say?"

"I haven't seen it. Maybe it doesn't exist, maybe it's just an alternative explanation, if needed, in case Peron gets blamed."

He gives me a sidelong glance to see my reaction.

"It was suicide alright," I say. "I didn't think Duarte would actually do it. He was going on about the political situation and his private enemies. He did say something like 'I might as well kill myself,' but I didn't take him seriously. He was falling-down drunk when I left."

"You can tell that to the judge. Maybe he'll believe you, maybe not. Apparently, two friends of Duarte were sitting in a car downstairs, waiting for you to leave and for Duarte to give them instructions what to do next. It looks like he wanted you roughed up, and shot himself instead." He gives me an ironic look.

"I don't know what *they* will tell the judge. If I were you, I wouldn't wait to find out. That's my thinking at any rate, so I booked you on a flight to Miami at 7 am. Better get out. And sooner rather than later."

He lights a cigarette, waiting patiently for my response. He knows he has backed me into a corner.

"Thanks, Jorge," I say. "What do I owe you?"

"The fare. Plus interest. I've handed in my resignation, you know. I'm leaving at the end of the month. My wife has finally come around. We'll move to Patagonia.

I thought you wouldn't mind contributing to my pension fund."

"I'm not a rich man, Jorge."

"I know. You said you work as a translator. Don't worry. It will be a one-time payment. You'll buy a nice piece of property near Rivadavia. I'll arrange it all for you. The only problem: By mistake they put my name on the deed."

"I see."

We arrive at the airport. He parks at the curb, reaches into the glove compartment and brings out a file.

"It's a property my son recommended to me. I brought along the sales contract just in case. All you have to do is sign."

He points to the line below the purchase price. 3000 Dollars.

"Nobody wants pesos, but the properties are still very reasonably priced in Patagonia," he says and reaches me a pen.

I sign.

"Thanks, Pierre," he says. "I would have hated to run you in."

I get my suitcase out of the trunk, and we shake hands.

"Good luck in Patagonia," I say.

"And good luck to you, too," he says. "I will always remember you fondly – the man of surprises."

28

On the flight, I am strangely at peace. My mind has run out of thoughts. I seem to have lost myself. Jorge driving me to the airport, the suggestion of a cover-up, my signature on the sales contract all happened in a dream. I am a man without a past. Of course, that's why I went to Buenos Aires in the first place, to shut down the old and make room for the new. But I didn't expect such complete success, if you can call the loss of my past and the emptiness within "success".

In Miami I come out of my numbness long enough to buy copies of the New York Times and La Nación. Both carry articles about Duarte's death. La Nación quotes his suicide note. So they have decided to go with the "alternative", as Jorge put it. The note they fabricated is addressed to Peron. It explains nothing and ends "*Viva Peron! Viva la patria!*" You would think they'd come up with something that has a more genuine ring, with words Duarte might actually have used, like "Fuck you all!" The

New York Times speculates that he killed himself because he had a terminal case of syphilis.

On the connecting flight to Toronto, I doze, images flitting across the insides of my lids. Then the images stop and I sleep like one sedated. I wake up once when my neighbour in the window seat wants to get past, and again when the stewardess serves dinner. I keep waiting for shock to set in, for a tumult of fear or a blast of remorse to hit me, but the barrier to the past is still up. My mind only permits considerations of the future like meeting up with Mona in Toronto, but there is nothing to consider. Everything depends on her. I can't form any concrete thoughts about what will happen when we see each other again, I have only a loose assembly of hypotheses: She will put her arms around me, or she is too busy to see me, or we have nothing to say to each other, or we make passionate love. I give up on what might be and think instead of the three keys in my bulging wallet and the option they offer. That part of the future is entirely up to myself. I take the keys out of my wallet and weigh them in my hand. They differ slightly in their contours. I have memorized the shape of the protruding points on mine to distinguish it from Mona's. They have to be applied in the correct order, the banker explained. First Duarte's, then Mona's, then mine. Duarte etched a line into the flat part of his key. He was a man who left his mark on things. I line up the keys on the tray table in front of me. My neighbour looks up from the book he is reading and eyes my arrangement of keys for a moment before turning back to the page. I pass my fingers over the metal and think about my choices. Go for it – fly to Switzerland and take possession of the boxes in the vault. Risk it. They are worth millions. I would have to give the bank advance notice of course. It's not like going to a regular branch. I need to make an appointment with the dapper Mr. Behrle. No doubt he will look into the legitimacy of my request, and that will be the end of it. Even assuming that I can pull off the caper, I will have to live the rest of my life as a fugitive. I will have to stay in places that have no extradition treaties, Brazil, let's say, although there is no country that offers protection against assassins. I remember the charred corpse of Raskolnikov – no, that's Dostoyevsky's antihero, I mean the charred corpse of Michel Skolnikoff in Madrid. He paid with his life for the money he made off the Nazis. And suddenly, like Skolnikoff, I am doused with a flammable substance, remorse, and caught in the firestorm of conscience. It races through the past I thought I'd lost, all the questionable parts: screwing Lascelles' wife, dealing with the Germans, living under a false name, marrying Nancy for the sake of a passport, killing Duarte. I desperately look for a way out. I didn't ruin Lascelles' marriage, I tell myself. It was dead already. That much is certainly true. A lot of Belgians truckled to the Germans, and no one lost their life or ended up in a concentration camp on account of what *I* said or printed in my magazine. Also true, but less clear-cut. As for Nancy, she knew exactly what she was getting herself into. I never said I loved her. And Duarte deserved to die.

I wish I was still a Catholic believer and could kneel in the embracing stillness of a Gothic cathedral and beat my breast, mumbling *mea culpa*. I wish I could kneel in the confessional and ask the parish priest to absolve me from my sins, do penance, raise my eyes to the stain glass windows and be illumined. No, I wish I was an Old Testament Jew. An eye for an eye would justify killing Duarte. There would be no need to beat my breast. But that way out is barred. I no longer believe in a God in heaven.

The firestorm of remorse is abating, consuming itself, and collapsing into ashes. All that's left is the dull sense of an irredeemable past and a hard, secular present. I am reminded of another plane ride, from Madrid to Buenos Aires in 1946, and the sense of relief I felt then: I was no longer hunted. I was a new man with a new name. On that occasion, too, I lost myself and my past. The emptiness I felt earlier was of the same kind, I realize – the calm after the storm. I should be satisfied with that.

The three keys are still lying on the tray table before me. I've made up my mind. I won't challenge fate. I won't go to Switzerland. Better write that adventure out of my mind and make it a travelogue, the story of a clandestine trip to a vault in the Alps, make it a part of the memoir I contemplated a few years ago: "Evita and Me." There is one problem, though. Who will be the author of that book? Pierre Adams? That name has served me well but it won't stand up to scrutiny if the book draws attention. I can't afford publicity. I have to content myself with a quiet, anonymous life and go back to my translation work in Ottawa. It fills the day but not the mind or heart or whatever organ determines the level of satisfaction in a man's life. Mona could fill the void, I think, and with her I could leave the past behind and start another life in which there is no need to lie or cheat or pretend anything I do not feel. But perhaps the kind of satisfaction I am looking for — sex and romance — is reserved for the young.

I am thirty-two and tainted with death. It would be a bad deal for Mona. There is no future for us unless I can do away with the past.

It is late when the plane lands in Toronto, but I decide to look for a phone booth and call Mona before I even retrieve my luggage. I am hungry for my future, but unsure how much to tell her about my past. The phone rings half a dozen times, and in those seconds I confess everything to her, my whole misshapen life. Then she answers.

Mona

29

After delivering the key to Pierre's hotel, I go to Grand &
Toy and buy a diary. It is a sober affair, a black moleskin
notebook, nothing like the one I got on my twelfth
birthday, a padded powder blue thing with a clasp and key
to lock in secrets no one cared about or everyone could
guess— anguish over being friendless, belly-aching over
marks I thought unfair, anger because my mother
wouldn't let me have a pet. The black moleskin diary is for
sobering thoughts. Or else I'll go insane with longing for a
life that makes sense, for a story that isn't ramshackle,
that has a clear beginning and a solid end. Right now,
nothing make sense. I am paralyzed by the confusion in
my mind, unable to move on. I need to dispel the fog,
move my fingers and write it out of my head. Seeing the
letters take shape on the line will give me at least an
illusion of resolve and activity, taking stock of what I did,
giving up my key, and where I'll go from here:

April 15

After leaving the envelope at the reception of Pierre's hotel, I walk around feeling drained. The loss of the key has left me impoverished. My memories of Evita are the sum of many parts, a rich assemblage of anecdotal pieces, and one is missing now. I still have the necklace, but I have given up something else that connected us. Although I am confused about the "us" part. Perhaps the key connected me with Pierre, with our joint adventure in the Swiss Alps. Now that I have offered it up to him, it has turned into a touchstone. If I am unimportant to Pierre, and he looked me up only because he was after the key, he won't come back. I won't see him again.

On the way home from the hotel, my mind went on automatic repeat *If he was after the key, he won't come back. If he was after the key, he won't come back.* The words have a rhythm you can march to. The moment I put one foot in front of the other, the mantra starts up, falling in with my movements. It felt good to write those words out of my mind, to deposit them on the page of the diary, letter for letter, and be done with them. Except that I'm not done with them. They're on a loop, going round and round in my head.

Before Pierre, I had plans for the summer months. I had my days down to a static image, a controlled order. Each morning I was going to walk to the library and do research on the thesis topic I intend to propose to the committee. I want to write about women in Shakespeare.

But too much has been written about that already, I need to refine the topic. Mad, angry, assertive women in Shakespeare? Or settle on a less prominent author, someone obscure who has never attracted the attention of scholars because he is dull, like the man on whom Phil has been working for the past five years and intends to build his career on — Thomas Nashe, an obscure sixteenth-century English pamphleteer. That's probably the better way to go. Dullness is no drawback in academics, but I am not even sure that I should go on with graduate studies, that I am cut out to be an academic. Doing a daily stint of research might prove it one way or another. If I could spend the next few months sitting in the library reading earnest books and making earnest notes when I might spend the summer working on my tan in the backyard or taking the ferry across to the islands and lie on the beach — if I can let that go without regret, I am clearly destined for an academic career. That's what I was thinking about, before Pierre.

April 16
I didn't go to the library. Or even outside to enjoy the mild weather. The muddle in my mind is nailing me down. A drought of constructive thought keeps me from making any plans. I stayed in bed all morning, not exactly sleeping in, just doing the If he was after the key *loop. When I dragged myself out of the bedroom, I made it only as far as the living room couch and spent the next couple of hours there, trying to get off the loop and pick up the phone and return my mother's calls.*

351

After years of neglect she is suddenly taking an interest in me or rather in where I will live when the Wilsons return from their sabbatical. I will have to find another place. I suspect she is afraid I'll ask her for money, or worse, that I'll move back in with her and occupy my old room. Her worries are unnecessary. I have the money from the sale of the diamonds. I don't want to share space with anyone, least of all with her and John. I have gotten used to living alone. I shy away even from minor social interaction. I look away when the cashier at the grocery store asks "And how are you" which isn't exactly an intrusion on my privacy. She is asking the question a hundred times a day. She doesn't expect a real answer. It would only slow her down. Yesterday someone asked me for directions, and I almost went to pieces. I could barely answer, my voice had shrunk into my chest. Why are people asking me questions? I am anguished just listening to their words, no matter how trivial their remarks.

I did get up from the couch at any rate and watered the plants and went shopping for bird food. I am responsible for keeping the Wilsons' canary alive, and that's as much as I can manage right now – the basics of "live and let live." Even that is almost too much. I belatedly see the wisdom of my mother denying me a pet. I don't have what it takes to be a caretaker.

Not sure if the diary does for me what I thought it would. It seems to work while I'm writing, while the words still eddy with experience, but the moment I stop and look back on what I've written, it has already changed and turned into a stale memory. I try to get back into what I've felt a moment ago while writing the lines, but no, they can't be reanimated on demand. Still, putting my thoughts into words provides short-term relief, of which I should be more appreciative. When I do my next entry, I'll try to make the relief last longer. I'll mouth the words, I'll be alert to the movement of my hand as it passes over the page, and the tension in my fingers as I hold the pen. I'll deep-breathe.

April 17
Trying to deep-breathe as I put pen to paper. No relief.

Dragged myself to the library, but only to look through newspapers from last July and the issues of Time Magazine that carried articles about Evita. I thought it might cure my heaviness. I need Evita to re-energize me. I need to go back to the point where my life veered into a new lane and left me disoriented: July 26th, 1952, the day Evita died. Reading the articles didn't do me any good. The photos accompanying them invariably showed Evita triumphant, looking magnificent in svelte evening gowns and glittering jewels, or close-ups of her smiling Madonna face. I reread the tributes, the accounts of the people lining up to see her coffin, a petition to the Vatican to have her canonized. Saint Evita — maybe I should pray to her to deliver me from my depression. But calling on the intervention of saints seems too complex in my catatonic state. I need something simple and primitive like voodoo or the sympathetic magic of her necklace. But that doesn't work anymore.

April 18
Went to the hairdresser today. I picked a salon where they don't know me, because Dillon who usually does my hair is temperamental and imperious. He despises the word "hairdresser". He is an artiste who takes no orders from the client. He would have argued with me if I told him that I want my hair bleached platinum blonde, and I fear his disapproval. I don't have the strength to talk back to him and explain why I want my hair blonde, pulled back straight and gathered into a bun at the neck, and why I need to have my eyebrows plucked to form a perfect arch. The stylist at the dumpy neighbourhood salon, where I ended up, asked no questions. She doesn't care whose hair she ruins. I needed her total lack of personal attention, her complete indifference to my life. I find it hard to move my lips these days and make small talk, to play the word tricks that make nothing sound like something. I have only one sentence left in my mind: If he was only after the key, he won't come back.

354

I check if the hair magic is working, if like does produce like. Have I changed into Evita yet? Is there an analogous effect, a spurt of energy, a smile appearing on my lips? Is my skin starting to gleam? No, nothing. My feelings are just as bruised as before, There isn't the tiniest upbeat in my mood. My face is all wrong. My skin has turned to plastic. My eyes lack lustre. I practice Evita's radiant smile in front of the bathroom mirror without success. I don't have her heroic profile. I can't even recall her voice anymore. I do remember her arms around me, her breath warming my face, the jolt of happiness running through my body. Her caress is still imprinted on my skin, but the memory fails to comfort me, the retelling doesn't work. Giving away the Swiss key has flattened my senses, diluted them, all my memories are split now between Evita and Pierre.

Tomorrow I'll try a different tack to revive my memories of Evita: replacement therapy, the fabric of a dress as a stand-in for her body. I'll pay a visit to my mother – long overdue, according to her, but she doesn't mean it, she doesn't want to see me any more than I want to see her. But I need to check whether she still has any of the dresses I brought back from Argentina. She is a hoarder. She doesn't throw things out. Chances are they are still hanging in her closet or are bundled up in one of the labelled cardboard boxes she keeps in the basement, a kind of archive of my time with Evita. Those dresses might still have something of Evita's touch about them and release healing emanations. My mother had them altered to fit her fuller figure, and now that I have gained weight thanks to that final wretched year with Philip, I might even fit into one of them.

30

My mother still lives in the same place, in the east end of the city, on a street with tidy clapboard bungalows and modest brick houses with Dutch roofs and dormers. It's the one constant in my life of revolving dads — the neighbourhood where I went to school, the house I grew up in, except that John has made it his own over the last few years. His tools and his golf clubs are in the garage now. Every time I visit, I expect my mother to say that "it's over". The durability of their relationship surprises me. Maybe age promotes domesticity. Or maybe three husbands are a sort of natural limit and my mother has run out of options. The fact is that she and John are still together, still in the same house but with a new couch in the living room and a well-stocked liquor cabinet. My mother is forced to do her drinking in the open now. John has deprived her of the upstairs hideaway. He paid for major remodeling, knocking down a wall to create a master bedroom that accommodates a queen-size bed and clunky his and hers dressers.

As I turn into the street, the sun breaks through the clouds and casts shafts of light on the sidewalk as if to start Act I of an entirely new play. But right away I get the wrong cue. I see John pulling out of the driveway. He stops the car, rolls down the window, and says hello. He is off to visit a buddy of his, he says.

"Poor guy's in the hospital for a hernia operation," he says. His hair is bristly, fresh from a buzz cut. He has a character actor's face, craggy around the chin, pouches under the eyes.

"Sorry, I'm in a rush," he says. "See you another time."

That's too bad. I was hoping for his moderating influence. The conversations with my mother tend to be testy if it's just the two of us. When John is there, she puts on her amiable face and blathers hostess phrases. The incessant acting must be hard on her. That's why she uses John's absence to drop the pretense and relax into her cantankerous self. Or treat herself to a drink. He usually hangs around in the mornings to keep an eye on my mother and prevent her from starting before noon. He probably figured it was safe now to leave her in my hands and go visit his buddy.

"Why don't you answer your phone?" my mother says before I'm halfway in the door. "If there's an emergency, I know whom *not* to call. I can't depend on your help, that's for sure."

"Was there an emergency?" I say, staring her down. Who is she to complain? She was never there for me when I needed her.

"Not exactly an emergency," she says. "But we had a break-in last Wednesday." She makes air-quotation marks around break-in. "We come home, and the patio door is open. Someone forced it."

I want to say: You needed a break-in, mother. You are a pathological hoarder. The place is full of junk. Whatever the thieves took, good riddance. Instead I say: "So what did they take?"

"Nothing. They rooted around. The place was a mess. Must have been kids doing it for a lark."

"They didn't take your booze?"

She ignores the dig. "Nothing. They just went through everything. Those clothes, the ones you brought back from Argentina, were scattered all over the floor. I no longer wear them. I keep them only because they are beautiful, even if they are out of fashion now. That's why I packed them away. They are in the closet in your old bedroom. Although, you know what they say: if you haven't worn something for three years, throw it out. But I can't get myself to do it."

"Must be the season for break-ins," I say. "My neighbours told me that their dog started barking at three in the morning. They looked out the window and saw someone skulking around in the lane between our two houses. Looked like he was trying to get into the Wilsons' garage. They let out the dog and he took off."

"Did you report it to the police?"

"There was nothing to report."

"Well, we did report the break-in, but I don't expect them to find whoever did it. Obviously, it's not a high-priority case. John put a new lock on the patio door and wedged a stick into the groove, so you can't slide it back even if you jimmy the lock."

"So, those dresses I brought back from Argentina are still here? Can I have a look at them?"

"Don't tell me you want to wear them. Is this a retro-thing? I read there's a shop selling old haute-couture dresses. Maybe I should take them there."

"I just want to look at them — nostalgia, I guess."

I am trying to sound normal and give nothing away as we go upstairs, but somehow my mother picks up a vibe.

"Are you okay, Mona?" she says with a knowing tilt of her head. "You don't look good. You look like you've lost weight. Are you eating properly? Ever since that woman, Evita Peron, died last summer, you've been acting strange. In fact, I said to John, that trip to Argentina did something to you. You came back a different person, and I hold that woman responsible for it. It's insane to shower a teenager with expensive clothes and take her on a trip to Europe. John agrees. All that extravagance ruined your character. And then last summer after you read her obituary, you got mad at Philip and decided to leave him. At least that's what he told us. I had to ask him because you never bothered to explain it to me."

"What's that got to do with anything?" I say, although she was right to make the connection. Evita did have something to do with my decision to leave Philip.

I go into my old room, which has survived John's renovations, except that it is a junk room now, an extension of the basement storage, where stuff is piled that no one needs, yet is too good to throw out, at least in my mother's eyes.

"You tell me what's wrong with Phil," she says, following me into the room. "When I think what I had to put up with from your father – the drinking, the womanizing, the fights over money. He nickeled and dimed me. Philip never kept you short of money. He is a decent guy with regular habits. Why would you leave a man like that?"

"Because I couldn't stand him any longer."

"Couldn't stand him? What did he do that you couldn't stand? There has to be some give and take in a marriage, but you are totally inflexible. Everything has to be exactly the way you want it to be."

I don't bother to listen to the rest of her tirade. I open the closet and sort through the clothes hanging in there. She watches me silently, her eyes following each piece I pull out.

"Is it okay if take this one?" I say, holding up the suit I wore on the road trip to the Alps. Evita picked it out for me on the last day of our togetherness. It has the stamp of her approval.

My mother shrugs. "Sure, take it. It might come in handy for a job interview. Are you looking for a job?"

"Eventually," I say and shoulder past her.

She follows me downstairs. "You can tell me the truth now, after all those years. Did she really give you those dresses or did you swipe the suitcases?"

I turn around and face her. "Mother. Please. How can you swipe three suitcases and not get caught?"

She shrugs. "I don't know, but a couple of years ago or so, there was this letter from Argentina. From a lawyer. You had moved into the dormitory by then. I never told

361

you about it because I didn't want you to do anything rash. You were so impulsive then. Well, you still are-"

"A letter for me, you mean? What did you do with it?"

"I steamed it open-"

"You opened a letter that was addressed to me?" I couldn't help raising my voice.

"See what I mean about impulsive? Why are you screaming at me when I just wanted to protect you? So yes, I steamed it open, but of course it was in Spanish. So I tried to figure it out with the dictionary. It was something about a trip and a key they were going to get from you. So I closed the letter again and sent it back: Addressee unknown. I guess that did it, but that's why I'm asking: Did you steal the suitcases and the keys from Evita Peron?"

"I did not," I said. "And now, can we give it a rest?"

I mulled it over on the way home. The letter must have been from Evita's lawyer, Rinaldo. He first wrote to me a few months after my return to Toronto, telling me to hang on to the key for the time being. I had been on the lookout for that letter and snagged it before my mother came downstairs. He must have written again a year later or so, when I no longer lived at home, finally giving me directions about the key. Apparently there was no follow-up after my mother returned the letter "addressee unknown," most likely because Rinaldo died, as Pierre told me, and now that Evita was dead as well, the whole affair of the keys was in limbo.

April 18

I realize what's wrong, why I can't slip into Evita's skin. I'm still too fat. I can't change the fact that I am not as statuesque as Evita, but I can lose weight. That's one advantage of having no energy and just lying around. I eat less, I can't be bothered to go shopping for food. I've already lost a couple of pounds, as my mother noted. No dinner for me tonight. Although somebody said (Freud?) that self-denial is a delusion of grandeur disguising trauma. So what? As long as it makes me feel better.

April 19
Voluntary starvation. I will live on soup crackers and salad from now on. I squeezed into the skirt that goes with the suit I brought back from my mother's. I listened to myself: Does it make me feel better? I opened my mind wide to channel Evita's spirit, but she remains on the outside. I may have to fall back on my fetish, the necklace which has actually touched Evita's skin and hope it will transfer her persona to me on contact. I know the magic didn't work the last few times I tried it, but who knows, I might coax it back to life.

I go to the bank and ask for my safe deposit box. The clerk puts me through the same ritual as before. We go to the backroom, apply his/my key. He takes out the drawer, puts it on the narrow counter in the cubicle, and turns his back to me to give me privacy. I take the necklace out of its felt bag and pass my hand over the fancy enamel work between the hexagonal cut rubies. I finger the black-pearl pendants and the two empty and mangled braces where the diamonds were, but the touch fails to work miracles. No trumpets, no surging Wagnerian chorus in my head. The necklace is just sitting there, weighty, massive in its inertness, almost ugly. I shove it back into the bag and return it to the drawer.

On the way home, I realize that I was wrong thinking that the ritual did not help me. It did. Handling the necklace had a subliminal effect, despite its newly discovered ugliness. Something inside me has moved. I feel a small surge of energy, enough to do some sorely needed housework when I get home. While I wipe the sticky kitchen counter, I turn philosophical, trying to solve the question: Why did I think the necklace was ugly all of a sudden? What is beauty anyway? If I could understand the concept of beauty/ugliness, would it help? No, that doesn't make sense, but does anything make sense at this point?

April 20
The concept of beauty is elusive. Have been watching the men around me closely for markers of beauty, getting some surprised looks and one or two wacky comments. The workers at a construction site on the corner of Bloor and Sherbourne wolf-whistled as I walked by, but they might have done that even without me staring at them. In any case, I have eliminated the construction worker's physique from defining absolute beauty. Hairy chests, a scraggle of belly hair showing between sweatshirt and slacks, ultra-defined muscles – all that is out. So is the classical ideal. I checked

out the Royal Ontario Museum. The Greeks look like hairless construction workers. Next, I checked Look Magazine to study the American movie idol. Marlon Brando is too brutalist, faintly reminiscent of Juancito, although I am drawn to the factoid that Brando refused to learn his lines. I like spontaneity, but it has nothing to do with beauty. Errol Flynn's moustache is a definite turn-off. Rock Hudson has something sensuous that catches my attention, but his jet-black hair — I don't know. I'm more into blonde. And as far as I can remember from the movie in which he played the lead, his movements are a little too sinuous. I think of Pierre. I think of him a lot, the crisp shirt he wore when we met in the bar of the hotel, his poised off-handedness, why I prefer his lithe body to the muscled apes, why his voice is a turn-on, and how it was so easy to come when we had sex that one time, without any need to fantasize.

The memory makes me hot and sluices down my spine, and immediately I hate myself for heating up at the idea of Pierre. Sex isn't supposed to be about ideas. I want Pierre's hands on my body. The real thing.

It seems I always fall for the same type of man, the small-boned type like Philip, with his narrow wrists and pointed elbows, the cerebral type, but no, Pierre may be small boned but otherwise he has nothing in common with Philip at all. He is no academic, he doesn't have Phil's ironic detachment, his long-distance look as if he lived inches behind his eyes. On the contrary, it's Pierre's total focus on me, his attentiveness that turned me on when we were together. Is beauty really in the eye of the beholder, do I become more beautiful if Pierre turns his eyes on me, focuses on the middle of my face, and listens to me with a deeply serious expression? I look down on my body, which does in fact look shapelier but that may be because I've lost weight. Still, in my imagination I connect my body with Pierre. He has become part of my memory craze, the wish to be transformed into someone else, Evita-like, but still me, and shaped by Pierre's attentive eyes.

I suspect there is something more than his eyes that attracts me to him.

I add a coda to my last diary entry.

When I looked for a definition of beauty, I looked only at bodies. What about the mind? Evita had a beautiful mind. She was a generous giver of love and, if my theory of transformation holds, she had all these qualities in her from the beginning – the energy, the beauty, the love, and the saintliness. They just unfolded when she moved from Los Toldos into the presidential palace. And Pierre? He started out as a writer and became a bodyguard, a retrograde transformation, I would say. Did he tuck away his love of language when he hired on with Security, and then unfurled it again when he became a translator in Ottawa?

I am mulling the question over when Phil calls me up.

"Are you okay?" he says. "I phoned a couple of times yesterday. No answer."

"I was at the library," I say. "What is it?"

"I just wanted to tell you that another of your Argentine friends called, a woman by the name of Nancy. I didn't give her your phone number since you told me off last time. I just said you'd moved out."

"Did *she* leave a number?"

"No, she didn't."

So maybe I hadn't seen ghosts when I spotted Nancy in the library a couple of weeks ago, but wasn't she supposed to be in Argentina then, comatose from an accident?

Now, at any rate, she is here, her presence confirmed the very next day when I see her again wandering aimlessly in the library stacks. This time I catch up to her and put my hand on her shoulder to make sure she's real.

"Nancy!" I say, "finally we connect. My ex told me you called, but you didn't leave a number."

She steps back, as if my touch was out of order or painful to her. But she doesn't look surprised.

"No, I didn't leave a number," she says. "I'm only here for a couple of days. For a workshop. I'm staying at a dorm. They don't have phones in the rooms, just one out in the hall, serving the whole floor."

We go downstairs and sit in the cafeteria to catch up on our lives. Nancy looks pale, more haggard than I remember. She has a dusty parched look. Perhaps that's a consequence of the car accident Pierre told me about. She is badly dressed – no surprise there – in a tan jacket that matches her colourless cheeks, and pants that droop and sit on top of her boots in untidy folds. She is doing a degree in social work, she says. She tried to reach me, but Phil wouldn't give her my phone number.

"I know," I say, "I told him not to give my number to anyone."

"He said you moved out." She gives me a long look, letting her arms dangle. "Pierre and I have separated as well."

I pretend their break-up is news to me. This is not the time to tell her that I saw Pierre and slept with him. There is something in Nancy's face that warns me against confidences of any kind. She looks furtive, I would almost say, up to no good.

I expect her to talk of the accident in Buenos Aires, but she says nothing about that, and I can't ask without giving away that I've seen Pierre. After a bit of chit-chat, she comes out with the reason why she tried to get in touch with me.

"I might as well tell you," she says. "Juancito phoned me a few weeks ago and said he had a job for me. If I could pull it off, I'd be set for life — that's how he made it sound." She pauses to catch her breath, as if she had been running hard. "He told me that Evita gave him some jewelry to store in a vault in Switzerland. I had heard rumours about that when I was still working for Liliana. So then he said that three keys were needed to open the safe. He had one, and Pierre and you had the other two." She looked at me for confirmation.

"And he wants those keys?" I say.

"Exactly. I asked him why he didn't collect them directly from you and Pierre – that's assuming Evita had left the jewels to him. He maneuvered around that question, but obviously he has no right to the cache. That's why he is willing to pay for the keys."

"If you ask me, Evita meant those jewels to be an emergency stash for Peron."

"And Juancito has to get his hands on the keys before Peron finds out where they are. Of course Peron realizes that the jewels are missing, but apparently no one knows where they are now, except the three of you. Juancito thinks he can buy out Pierre, but you won't sell the key to him. I said: Did you ask? And he said: I don't need to ask, I know. That girl is stubborn as hell."

"He did ask, and I said no."

"I wonder if Pierre sold *his* key to him and how much he got. In any case, Juancito said he'd pay me to get the key off you. He told me that you kept it in a locket you wear at all times."

"He asked you to steal my locket?"

"He didn't ask me to do anything in particular. He just offered me a lot of money if I could get the locket. You already know what I came up with. I hired a little thug and paid him to rip it off you."

And the break-in at my mother's? And the burglar scared off by my neighbour's dog? Were those attempts part of Nancy's plan as well? But how does that fit in with what Pierre told me, that she was laid up in a hospital in Buenos Aires? Unless he made it up, and there was no accident. One of them is lying. And why is she even telling me this story?

"So you were behind that-" I can't make up my mind what to call it – robbery, theft, assault? "-that incident?" I say. "But the key in the locket wasn't the key to the Swiss safe."

369

"That's what I found out when I delivered it to Juancito. It was the wrong key. What was it for, if you don't mind me asking?"

"The key to the diary I kept as a teenager," I say on impulse and despise myself for coming up with a lie so readily. But I didn't mean to lie. "Diary" popped into my head because it has become code for shoving something into the memory box, something I no longer want to think about, something I want to write out of my mind. But I have no time to think that through because I have to deal with Nancy, here, now.

She laughs. "I don't know why I'm laughing," she says. "My life is on the line here."

"Oh, come on. Your pay-out is on the line, that's all."

"No!" she says with a howl like a wounded animal. Heads are turning. She falls silent and takes a sip of her coffee. Then she pulls up the sleeve of her blouse.

"See that?" she says. There are faint lines on her arms, like cuts that have recently healed. "The night before I was scheduled to fly home, Juancito phoned and said to come to his office. What for, I said. To talk strategy, he said. You haven't finished the job I asked you to do. You want me to try again? I said. Exactly, he said, so let's talk about it. I was afraid of saying no to him, so I went to his office. He wasn't there, but three of his goons were waiting for me. They forced me into the backseat of a waiting car, tied me up, gagged me, and took me out to the Boca. I sat wedged between two of them. One held a gun to my head. The other took out a knife and started cutting my arm as if he was fileting fish."

Nancy is speaking in a rapid whisper. I have to lean forward to catch the words.

370

"They pulled up to a car parked next to a pier," she says. "A woman was sitting behind the steering wheel. The place was deserted. They told me to get out and have a look at her."

There is a click in her throat, a dryness. Her mouth has turned ragged. She swallows before going on. "She was dead, strapped in with the seat belt. Her face was bruised. There was blood all over the front of her dress. That's what happens to cheats, they said to me. Then one of them pushed me up against the car and—"

She stops and looks at me. I am afraid of what she is going to say. Her mouth is hanging open as if she couldn't get enough air to push out the words. She licks her lips. Her breath is laboured when she goes on: "Then he did it to me, from behind, and all the time he kept my face pushed against the window so that I was still looking at the corpse."

"Stop," I say, horror creeping over me and chilling my breath. "Please, Nancy, don't go on. I believe you. I'm sorry I said it was only about the money. I'm sorry."

I say a whole lot more, but my placating words, the dowdy repeat of "sorry, sorry" doesn't stop the words pouring out of Nancy's twisting, gasping mouth.

"I shut my eyes but I could still see her," she rasps out.

I grab Nancy's arm, leaning across the table. I don't care that people are looking at us. She stops for a moment. Her arm feels limp, as if it had been stripped of muscle. I let go, and she continues as if releasing her arm had given her permission to go on.

"I thought they were going to kill me too," she says, "but they put me back into the car the way I was, tied up

371

and bleeding from the cuts on my arms. One of them stayed with me in the backseat, the other two pushed the car with the dead woman into the water and watched it sink. That's what's going to happen to you, they said, unless you come up with the right key."

My chest contracts painfully. I want to be back in the safe haven of a time before I heard Nancy's story. Is that the "accident" Pierre was talking about when I saw him a week ago? I am confused about the time frame. When did all this happen? Did Pierre pick her up? Have they come back from Buenos Aires together?

She reaches across the table and holds out her hand, palm up.

"So I'm asking you, please, Mona, save me. Give me that key. If they pay me, although I'm no longer sure they will — I'll split the money with you."

"I can't help you," I say. "I no longer have the key."

"What do you mean? What did you do with it?"

So, she didn't meet with Pierre in Buenos Aires, or she would know that he has the key. Or maybe he didn't tell her. I say the first thing that comes into my mind: "I threw it away."

I expect her to scream, but she lets out a quiet moan. Her shoulders collapse, she leans her elbows on the table and buries her head in her hands.

"You what?" she says quietly, hopelessly.

"I threw it away," I say more firmly now. "But they won't be able to get at you here, Nancy. You are safe."

I am not convinced, and neither is she.

"I doubt I'm safe," she says.

I shouldn't have lied. I should have told her that I saw Pierre and gave him the key, that it's on its way to Juancito, so not to worry. I should have handed on my mantra to her, sticking in Juancito's name: If he was only after the key, you won't hear from him again.

"Maybe I'll go back to Ottawa and make it up with Pierre," she says. "He always knows what to do."

Now I'm glad I didn't tell her. She gets up from the table and turns to leave. Neither of us says good-bye or good luck or any of the usual phrases. The usual won't do, and we have run out of words simultaneously.

April 21
Juancito is dead. I heard it on the news. He committed suicide. Nancy is safe from him now, but I'm stuck with her rape story. Did she think telling me the story would lessen her pain? Did seeing the horror in my face console her? She is traumatized. Of course she is, but what right do I have to spiral deeper into a depression?

I stop writing. It doesn't help. I can't find my way back to the life I led the day before. Nothing makes sense anymore. Doing research in the library seems inane, all literature is outdated and irrelevant, tomorrow is nebulous. All that matters now is getting rid of the images Nancy put into my head with her words: *She was dead, strapped in with a seatbelt. Her face was bruised.* It's unfortunate that I am so well trained in language, in understanding signifiers, so talented in translating words into pictures. Nancy's face remains pressed against the window of the car, staring at the dead woman inside. I can't shift the image. I wonder how long it took for the woman to die, the time between her blood beginning to spill out of her body and the last breath entering her lungs. Did she struggle with her killers? I try to break up my thoughts, to think of words to get around the image of the dead woman, to replace them with curative Evita stories, but all I come up with are the newspaper photos showing the coffin with the glass lid and the long line of mourners. My face remains pressed against the glass lid staring at the dead woman inside. The tissue of my brain is too soft, too easily stamped with words and images. They leave an inconvenient, lasting impression, strings of words on repeat, images that remain lit up.

When the phone rings, the image dissolves and I am flooded with relief. Whoever it is, even if it's my mother, I need a human voice to overpower the voices in my head. The dead woman fades, takes on the colour of the wall, turns into a blank.

The voice on the phone is Pierre's. He is back in Toronto, he says. He has come back. The old word loop that has been playing in my head over the last week blips up one last time and breaks into little pieces: *if he. key. come back.* Pierre is at the airport. He asks if he can come by, or is it too late?

"Sure, come by," I say, trying hard to sound normal, to give my voice a neutral tone. The relief from my nightmare thoughts has come so unexpected, I am jittery. "It will take you – what? Half an hour?"

"More like an hour. I'm at the airport, waiting for my luggage and I need to find a hotel. I didn't book anything because I wasn't sure when I'd return."

"You can stay overnight here," I say. I am desperate for company, for a solid body to block my thoughts. "You can have the guest bedroom."

"I'll take yours," he says.

Isn't that a little glib? I was hoping for more substance, a counterweight to my thoughts.

"Okay," I say, wondering how my voice sounds to his ears. I feel shaky, like having stepped into a void, or fallen off a cliff. I have no idea where I'm going to land, and whether it's going to be a soft landing.

31

I put on the porch light for Pierre. How will I make a whole hour go by until he comes? My newly bleached hair is a mess, so brittle it looks metallic. What am I going to wear? I pull out a few things, go through two or three changes of dress. Nothing looks right. I give up and go for comfort. My oldest t-shirt and a pair of shapeless slacks. The image of the dead woman lingers, but at least the *if he was only after the key* mantra is gone. I wait for Pierre in the new uncomfortable silence of my mind.

When I hear the taxi pull up, I stand at the window and watch Pierre walk up the driveway, one shoulder lopsided from carrying a suitcase. I open the door to him and stand back to let him in without even offering him a hug. It may be too soon for a show of affection. I am unsure about the timing. He has put down his suitcase and is looking at me. I can't read the expression on his face. It is too still to give anything away. I just stand there, at a loss for words. Then he puts his arms around me, and things fall into place naturally. As we go upstairs to my bedroom, we say forgettable words to each other, but I measure something in the air between us, a stirring hunger, catch it and hang on to it when he deep-kisses me. It feels good to be consumed like that. We take off our clothes hurriedly and heave into each other with airless freedom, ignited with desire. We feel each other up like testing the flesh. I want him to imprint his body on mine and travel under my skin. The pleasure comes with such strength that I almost faint. I lie back on the bed, weary with satisfaction.

"Why do you have sex with me?" he asks me later, as we are lying side by side.

He doesn't say "make love" or "sleep with me" or "fuck". It is a strange question, put in this clinical way, but now that he has asked me, I am looking for an answer. Why *do* I show my vulnerable self to this man at a moment when my brain stops and I am just an animal? I turn on my stomach and look into his watchful eyes.

"I know what you are fishing for," I say. "You want me to say that I love you."

"That wasn't the point. I just wanted to know why you are willing to take a risk on me, to get involved with me."

What risk? Of being disappointed?

"You are taking the same risk," I say, resisting to go in the direction of saying something romantic, like "I needed you". It would be a mistake to admit that. It's no good letting my feelings show. I will only get punished for it.

"It's just a physical need," I say in a careless way to put him off the scent.

"True," he says, "but I meant why *me*?"

My resistance weakens. I make a small concession: "I've been waiting for you to come back."

"That's something to hold on to," he says. "I know so little about you, nothing about your likes and dislikes, who are the people in your life, what matters to you – nothing at all."

We aren't doing well in this post-coital conversation, but he is right. We don't have much of a back story. Large parts are missing, gaps that will be hard to close.

"You just have to make it up," I say. "That's what I do. Nobody tells you who they are."

"So what have you made up about me so far?"

"You are a man of words. Well, I didn't make that up. You actually told me that language is important to you."

"You mean I am a man of words – not deeds?"

"I guess you do what you have to do. But you are better at watching. I like that about you, Pierre. You pay attention to me."

He tries to pay attention to my words, but I can see he is fading. We are both fading and fall asleep cheek to cheek, with vestiges of words playing in my head.

I wake up late in the morning. Daylight is slanting into the room, painting the ivy on the windowsill a lush green. I'm lying so close to the edge of the bed that I almost go over. But when I turn on my back, I see that I'm on my own. Pierre must have gotten up very quietly. I listen for sounds downstairs, steps, a clattering of dishes. Nothing. The house is silent. Has he left – just like that, without saying good-bye?

I get out of bed and go downstairs. Pierre is sitting in the Wilsons' reading chair, with a book open in his lap. I squeeze in beside him and kiss him behind the ear, mindful that I haven't brushed my teeth yet. He makes room for me and nuzzles my hair, but he doesn't close the book. He keeps one hand on the page, as if I was interrupting something that he can't put off.

"What are you reading?" I say.

"Dostoyevsky. *Crime and Punishment*."

"Wouldn't be my first choice," I say and lean in to read a few lines on the page.

What a brutal state I am in.

A poignant and rebellious doubt surged in his heart.

But he did not repent of his crime. He recognized his criminality only because he had confessed it.

"The moral argument is interesting," Pierre says.

"But not convincing," I say and read one line out loud. "*He recognized his criminality only because he had confessed it* – come on, that's nonsense. You know when you've committed a crime. You don't just realize it at the point of confession. That's an artificial construct. In that particular case there was no need for the man to confess at all. He could have gotten away with the murder."

I know I wouldn't confess to stealing Evita's necklace now that she is dead, unless I was caught out, and I don't need to make a confession to understand that it was theft. I am sorry I took it, even if I was under a strange compulsion and couldn't help it at the time. If I had a chance, I would have confessed it to *her* because I loved Evita and wanted to make things right between the two of us. But Dostoyevsky's protagonist – whom did he want to please? God?

"That ending makes no sense to me," I say.

"You don't believe in a natural need or a moral obligation to confess?"

"No," I say firmly, and he closes the book, finally looking me in the face.

"I'm not up for a literary debate before breakfast," I say apologetically.

I really don't want to talk about Dostoyevsky. I want to talk about Pierre and me. I want to put us together on the same canvas and see a picture emerge that's recognizable to me.

Over breakfast in the kitchen, Pierre says: "What's with the hair? Are you trying for an Evita look?"

I lower my eyes to the bowl of cereal in front of me. He's caught me out. I am not sure it's entirely safe to give away my obsession with Evita and talk to Pierre about my superstitions. I make a partial confession.

"I wanted to transfer some of her energy to myself," I say with a mock laugh. "So far it hasn't worked."

He doesn't comment on that. He only gives me a questioning look.

I stir my cereal flakes. "I was shocked when I saw Evita's obituary in the paper last summer," I say by way of explanation, "I was shocked even though I was expecting it ever since Juancito told me at the airport in Zurich."

"He wanted to hurt you because he thought you were in love with Evita. Were you?"

"You could call it love. I don't know. Not the way I'm in love with you – okay, now I said it. That's what you've been waiting for, right?"

I know I have made a tactical mistake. I should have waited for Pierre to say it, but I blinked first. It could also be a thinking mistake. Maybe I don't love him. If someone puts a plate of potatoes in front of me and I am hungry and wolf it down, does it mean I love potatoes? No, it just means I'm needy.

"What about you?" I say. "I want to hear you say it back to me."

"I am in love with you, Mona," he says gamely, and I feel stupid because it makes me happy like a puppy. I no longer need a diary to write the looping words out of my head. Or put on the suit Evita picked for me to feel her energy. Too late I realize there was no need to ruin my hair, bleaching it platinum blonde. I have no need for voodoo now that Pierre is sitting across from me and has said the magic words. I just have to get rid of Nancy's rape story. That's all that's left to do. I bravely wade into that murky water. I don't ask Pierre how he is feeling about Nancy. That's too large a topic. I narrow it down and ask him only about the "accident". I want to hear his version of the story, his reaction to the horror.

"Tell me about Nancy," I say. "What exactly happened?"

A shadow passes over his face. He looks closed off somehow, unreachable.

"I still don't know the details," he says, "and I don't need to know." The words come out flat. I don't know what to make of the expression on his face.

Now I do ask the question: "So are you going to get together with her again?"

He takes a sip of coffee and sets the cup down again. "No. That's over." He is holding the cup with both hands, squeezing as if he wanted it crush it. In the bright morning light coming through the window he looks weary, with a bruising stain of tiredness under his eyes.

"I didn't want to tell you," he says and pauses.

I can see it costs him to go on, whatever it is he didn't want to tell me.

"Nancy died in the accident," he says.

What? What? Is this supposed to be metaphorical?

"I went to Buenos Aires to identify the body," he says. "I kept it to myself because I didn't want death to intrude on my time with you. Like at the airport in Zurich, when we said good-bye and Duarte told you about Evita. I didn't want to spoil our first evening telling you about Nancy's death."

I think he means it literally. He wants me to believe that Nancy is dead.

"Why are you lying to me, Pierre?" I say.

"What do you mean?"

His confusion is pitch perfect. My God, the man is a good liar!

"I talked to Nancy two days ago," I say. "So, don't tell me she is dead."

The colour drains from his face, as if wiped by an invisible hand.

"If that's true, they played a trick on me," he says, his face as lifeless as a mask. "I was told she drowned. The car she was driving ended up in the river. They showed me her bloated, mangled corpse at the morgue."

The truth hits us both forcibly. Someone set him up and wanted to give him a graphic warning. I realize: He and Nancy were made to look at the same dead woman, the one in the car Juancito's goons pushed into the Rio de la Plata.

"It could have been anyone," Pierre says, "but the label on the gurney said 'Nancy Adams' and the official letter I had said she was dead. The death certificate had her name on it."

"Nancy is alive," I say and tell him the nightmare story. As I repeat her words, the horror slowly leaves me, but it doesn't dissipate. There isn't enough air in the room to thin it out. I am merely shifting the burden to Pierre. The expression on his face is frozen, his hands still clutch the coffee cup.

We look at each other silently, then he releases his grip and lays his hands flat on the table, the slim piano hands I love.

"So that's what happened," he says and draws a deep breath. He has taken it all in, taken it over from me, and is suffering the same way I did. We have finally come together, sharing the same space with our thought bubbles merging.

"And you gave Juancito my key?" I say, trying to help him get away from Nancy's story although I know it can't be done by sleight of hand, by shifting the conversation. He seizes on the new topic gratefully.

"I didn't," he says, "but that's immaterial now. Duarte is dead."

"I heard it on the news."

Pierre has pulled out of our common space. His mind is far away even though his mouth is making sounds here in this room. I was wrong when I thought I could dispense with magic. I need it after all.

"You still have my key then?"

"Do you want it back?"

"Here is what I want us to do," I say. "At the end of the street is a ravine with a creek at the bottom. I want to go down there, throw in the key and let the water carry it away. Want to come along?"

He gives me a pale smile. "A kind of exorcism?" he says. "You think it will help?"

"It might."

There is a pause as if he had to make a difficult decision. Then he says:

"Alright, let's do it. I need to exorcise a few ghosts myself."

He goes upstairs to fetch the key. Our fingers touch as he hands it to me, presses it into my palm and holds it there as if we were sealing a pact.

We leave the house, solemnly walk to the dead-end and skid downhill between the tangled branches of shrubs still bare and waiting for warmer days to bring out budding leaves. For most of the year the Don is no more than a creek, a sluggish stream bisecting the city, but at this time of the year it swells into a river carrying urban refuse into Lake Ontario.

On the path along the river, a narrow ribbon of gravel and dirt, I can see a man in a corduroy jacket and a long woolen scarf, walking his dog. The air is fraught with stillness, the man and his dog a mirage under the glittering sun. We wait until they are out of sight before we head for the wooden footbridge spanning the river. We stop to look down into the swirling, muddy water. I lean over the bridge railing, stretch out my arm and dangle the key for a moment before letting it go. It hits with a soft plopping sound and sinks out of sight.

We turn to face each other.

"So that's it?" he says. "Did it help?"

Hard to say. Maybe I'll get lucky.

I put my arms around Pierre to comfort him or find comfort myself — I can't tell.

End

Acknowledgements

I would like to thank all my friends who read the manuscript of this novel at various stages of development, especially Karin MacHardy, Karen Rushfield, Susan Ingram (a great fact checker), and Graham Lute who did the wonderful cover image. I also want to thank Daniel Willis for keeping the historical novel tradition alive.

About the Author

Erika Rummel has taught history at the University of Toronto and Wilfrid Laurier University, Waterloo. She divides her time between Toronto and Los Angeles and has lived in villages in Argentina, Romania, and Bulgaria. She is the author of more than a dozen books on social history, and has written five novels, *Playing Naomi, Head Games, The Inquisitor's Niece* (awarded the Evvy prize for best historical novel in 2018), *The Road to Gesualdo, The Painting on Auerperg's Wall,* and *The Effects of Isolation on the Brain,* an excerpt of which was awarded the Random House Creative Writing Award in 2011. She is the translator of the correspondence between Alfred Nobel and his Viennese mistress. *Three Women and Alfred Nobel,* a novel based on these letters, was released in September 2018.

Phillip Otts	A Storm Before the War
	The Soul of a Stranger
	The Price of Betrayal
Erika Rummel	The Inquisitor's Niece
	The Road to Gesualdo
Vanessa A. Ryan	The Trouble with Murder
J. M. Stephen	Nod
	Into the Fairy Forest
	Rise of the Hidden Prince
	Silence and Ruptured Waters
	The Rise of Runes and Shields (Jul 2022)
Larry F. Sommers	Price of Passage (Aug 2022)
Jessica Stilling	The Weary God of Ancient Travelers
	Between Before and After (Nov 2022)
Christopher Tuthill	The Osprey Man (Jul 2022)
Claryn Vaile	Ghost Tour
Felicia Watson	Where the Allegheny Meets the Monongahela
	We Have Met the Enemy
	Spooky Action at a Distance
	The Risks of Dead Reckoning

Daniel A. Willis   IMMORTAL BETRAYAL
              IMMORTAL DUPLICITY
              IMMORTAL REVELATION
              PROPHECY OF THE AWAKENING
              FARHI AND THE CRYSTAL DOME
              VICTORIA II
              THE CHILDREN OF VICTORIA II

Joyce Yarrow   SANDSTORM